NICHOLAS SPARKS

The Longest Ride

GRAND CENTRAL
PUBLISHING

NEW YORK   BOSTON

For Miles, Ryan, Landon, Lexie, and Savannah

Copyright © 2013 by Willow Holdings, Inc.
Author's Note copyright © 2014 by Willow Holdings, Inc.

Grand Central Publishing
Hachette Book Group
1290 Avenue of the Americas
New York, NY 10104

www.HachetteBookGroup.com

Printed in the United States of America

RRD-C

Originally published in hardcover by Hachette Book Group.

First trade edition: May 2014
First trade media tie-in edition: February 2015

10 9 8 7 6 5 4 3 2 1

Grand Central Publishing is a division of Hachette Book Group, Inc.
The Grand Central Publishing name and logo are trademarks of Hachette Book Group, Inc.

The Hachette Speakers Bureau provides a wide range of authors for speaking events. To find out more, go to www.hachettespeakersbureau.com or call (866) 376-6591.

The publisher is not responsible for websites (or their content) that are not owned by the publisher.

The Library of Congress has cataloged the hardcover edition as follows:
Sparks, Nicholas.
    The longest ride / Nicholas Sparks. — First edition.
        pages cm
    ISBN 978-1-61969-138-4 (audiobook) — ISBN 978-1-61969-185-8 (audio download)
    1. Unmarried couples—Fiction.   2. Man-woman relationships—Fiction.
    3. Life change events—Fiction.   4. Large type books.   I. Title.
    PS3569.P363L66 2013
    813'.54—dc23
                                                                    2013004653

ISBN 978-1-4555-9039-1 (Scholastic pbk.)
ISBN 978-1-4555-3480-7 (Walmart media tie-in pbk.)
ISBN 978-1-4555-3481-4 (Target media tie-in pbk.)

ISBN 978-1-4555-8472-7 (media tie-in pbk.)

PRAISE FOR THE NOVELS OF
#1 *NEW YORK TIMES* BESTSELLING AUTHOR
NICHOLAS SPARKS

THE LONGEST RIDE

"Sparks is a poet...a master." —*Philadelphia Inquirer*

"THE LONGEST RIDE is epic Sparks...[It] showcases the author's most accomplished work to date...There are moments of perfection." —*Mountain Times* (NC)

"Exactly the kind of feel-good we could all use at Christmastime. I was left smiling and wanting to hold my loves ones close." —*First for Women* magazine

"I read the entire book in one day. Nicholas Sparks writes with such magic that he's simply impossible to put down." —ReadingwithStyle.blogspot.com

THE BEST OF ME

"A creative genius...This book is great for any love story enthusiast." —HubPages.com

"Unforgettable...Makes you settle in for another romantic date with this well-respected and talented storyteller." —*Fredericksburg Free Lance-Star* (VA)

"I could not put it down...a classic Nicholas Sparks tragedy but with a twist of hope...If I can pick my favorites from him, *The Best of Me* will rank with *Message in a Bottle* and *The Notebook*— it was *that* good." —BookReporter.com

DEAR JOHN

"Beautifully moving... Has tremendous emotional depth, revealing the true meaning of unconditional love."

—*RT Book Reviews*

"For Sparks, weighty matters of the day remain set pieces, furniture upon which to hang timeless tales of chaste longing and harsh fate."

—*Washington Post Book World*

AT FIRST SIGHT

"An ending that surprises."　　　—*New York Times Book Review*

"Nicholas Sparks is one of the best-known writers in America and overseas for good reason: He has written stories that reveal the yearning for our most prized possession: love."

—*Mobile Register* (AL)

TRUE BELIEVER

"Time for a date with Sparks... The slow dance to the couple's first kiss is a two-chapter guilty pleasure."　　　—*People*

"Another winner... a page-turner... has all the things we have come to expect from him: sweet romance and a strong sense of place."　　　—*Charlotte Observer*

THE WEDDING

"Packs a punch... There is a twist that pulls everything together and makes you glad you read this."　　　—*Charlotte Observer*

"Sparks tells his sweet story...[with] a gasp-inducing twist at the very end. Satisfied female readers will close the covers with a sigh." —*Publishers Weekly*

THE GUARDIAN

"An involving love story...an edge-of-your-seat, unpredictable thriller." —*Booklist*

NIGHTS IN RODANTHE

"Bittersweet...romance blooms...You'll cry in spite of yourself." —*People*

"Extremely hard to put down...a love story, and a good love story at that." —*Boston Herald*

A BEND IN THE ROAD

"Sweet, accessible, uplifting." —*Publishers Weekly*

"A powerful tale of true love." —*Booklist*

THE RESCUE

"A romantic page-turner...Sparks's fans won't be disappointed." —*Glamour*

"All of Sparks's trademark elements—love, loss, and small-town life—are present in this terrific read." —*Booklist*

A WALK TO REMEMBER

"An extraordinary book...touching, at times riveting...a book you won't soon forget." —*New York Post*

"A sweet tale of young but everlasting love." —*Chicago Sun-Times*

MESSAGE IN A BOTTLE

"The novel's unabashed emotion—and an unexpected turn—will put tears in your eyes." —*People*

"Glows with moments of tenderness...delve[s] deeply into the mysteries of eternal love." —*Cleveland Plain Dealer*

THE NOTEBOOK

"Nicholas Sparks...will not let you go. His novel shines." —*Dallas Morning News*

"The lyrical beauty of this touching love story...will captivate the heart of every reader and establish Nicholas Sparks as a gifted novelist." —*Denver Rocky Mountain News*

ALSO BY NICHOLAS SPARKS

The Notebook

Message in a Bottle

A Walk to Remember

The Rescue

A Bend in the Road

Nights in Rodanthe

The Guardian

The Wedding

Three Weeks with My Brother
(with Micah Sparks)

True Believer

At First Sight

Dear John

The Choice

The Lucky One

The Last Song

Safe Haven

The Best of Me

Acknowledgments

The *Longest Ride*, my seventeenth novel, could not have been written without the support of many wonderful people. At the top of my list, as always, is my wife **Cathy**, who has remained after all these years the best friend I've ever had. My life has been enriched by her presence on a daily basis, and part of me knows that every female character I've ever created is in no small way inspired by her. It's been a joy to share with her the longest ride, this thing we call life.

I must also thank **Theresa Park**—my literary agent, manager, and now producing partner—yet another extraordinary blessing in my life. It's hard for me to believe that we've been working together for nineteen years now. Though I've told you many times before, it's time for me to put it in writing: I've always considered myself to be the fortunate one.

Jamie Raab, my editor, is priceless when it comes to making my novels as good as they can possibly be. She has been my editor since the very beginning, and working with her has made me one of the luckiest authors around. She deserves my thanks not only for all she does, but also because I consider her a cherished friend.

Howie Sanders and **Keya Khayatian**—my film agents at UTA—are quite simply the best in the business. More than that, they're creative geniuses in all aspects of business. Add in kindness, honesty, and enthusiasm, and the more time I spend with them, the more thrilled I am to consider them friends.

Scott Schwimer, my entertainment attorney, is yet another member of my team who has been with me since the very beginning, a man who has gifted my life with his wisdom and advice. Add in friendship and laughter, and my life has been enriched by his presence.

Elise Henderson and **Kosha Shah**, who run my television production company, are two amazing people, gifted with motivation, intelligence, and humor, and I'm fortunate to consider them part of my team. Also thanks to **Dave Park**, for his guidance and support in my early TV endeavors, and to **Larry Salz** and **Lucinda Moorehead** for their stellar efforts at UTA.

My thanks also go out to **Denise DiNovi**, who has produced—with style and quality—any number of films adapted from my work, including *Message in a Bottle*, *A Walk to Remember*, and *The Lucky One*. I very much enjoy working with you and look forward to seeing *The Best of Me* on the big screen. I'd be remiss, of course, if I didn't thank **Alison Greenspan** for all she does as well.

Marty Bowen is yet another producer with multiple films adapted from my work to his credit, and I'd like to thank him for the work he did on both *Dear John* and *Safe Haven*. Along with Theresa and me, he'll be producing *The Longest Ride*, and there's no doubt that it will be an amazing film. Thanks also to **Wyck Godfrey** who works with Marty on all their endeavors.

I also have to thank **Emily Sweet** and **Abby Koons** at the Park Literary Group. Emily not only works with my foundation and the website, but handles all those jobs that fall into the gray areas of my ventures with energy, enthusiasm, and efficiency. Abby, who is responsible for all things foreign, is fantastic at her job. I consider both of them my friends, and I don't know where I'd be without them.

Michael Nyman, Catherine Olim, Jill Fritzo, and **Michael**

Geiser at PMK-BNC, my publicists, are all terrific at what they do. I want to thank them for all the extraordinary work they do on my behalf.

Laquishe Wright—also known simply as Q—who runs my social media pages, and **Mollie Smith**, who handles my website, also deserve my gratitude. Both of them are incredible at what they do, and it's because of them that I'm able to let people know what's going on in my world.

For further helping to keep me up to speed on the latest in technology, I'd like to take a moment to thank **David Herrin** and **Eric Kuhn** at UTA, who are always there to answer my questions.

Thanks, also, to both **David Young** and **Michael Pietsch** at Hachette Book Group. I'll miss working with you, David, and I look forward to working with you, Michael.

I'd like to extend a special thanks to **Sean Gleason**, COO of Professional Bull Riders, Inc., for his painstaking review of the manuscript and all of his and the PBR's enthusiastic support for this book. Bull riding is a thrilling sport, and you run an amazing organization, Sean. Working with your tireless lieutenants, Ellen Newberg and Denise Abbott, has been a privilege.

Larry Vincent and **Sara Fernstrom** at UTA also deserve my thanks for the fantastic work they do in branding and corporate partnerships; it's been an amazing experience so far, and I look forward to all that will happen in the future.

My thanks also go to **Mitch Stoller** for all of his early contributions to the Nicholas Sparks Foundation, and to **Jenna Dueck**, the most recent addition to the foundation team, who I know will bring invaluable expertise and energy to our efforts in support of education.

I also want to thank **David Wang**, the acting Headmaster at The Epiphany School of Global Studies, a school that my wife and I founded in 2006 and that continues to inspire us to dream of a better world.

I'd be remiss if I didn't thank **Jason Richman** and **Pete Knapp,** neither of whom work directly for me but nonetheless find themselves working on my behalf anyway. Thank you both for all you do.

Rachel Bressler and **Alex Greene** also deserve my thanks for helping to keep the wheels turning smoothly when it comes to the Novel Learning Series and all things contract related, which can be a never-ending task.

Micah Sparks, my brother, also deserves my heartfelt thanks not only for being the best brother a guy can have, but for all the effort, hard work, and vision he has brought to the Novel Learning Series.

Emily Griffin, Sara Weiss, and **Sonya Cheuse** at Grand Central also deserve my thanks for all they do. Emily helps to guide a project near and dear to my heart, Sara handles an amazing workload at GCP on my behalf, while Sonya is a fantastic publicist in charge of my book tours.

Thanks also to **Tracey Lorentzen,** the Director of the New Bern office of my foundation, and to **Tia Scott** for all things assistant related. She keeps my life running smoothly, which is no easy matter. Finally, many thanks to **Jeannie Armentrout** for all she does at the house.

I must also thank **Andrew Sommers,** who does so much for me in yet another complex and critically important area of my life.

Pam Pope and **Oscara Stevick,** my accountants, are wonderful at what they do, and I'm thankful to consider them part of my team.

Courtenay Valenti and **Greg Silverman** at Warner Bros. feel like family to me after all these years, and I hope to work with both of you again.

Ryan Kavanaugh, Tucker Tooley, Robbie Brenner, and **Terry Curtin** at Relativity deserve my thanks for the terrific work they did on *Safe Haven*, and I'm looking forward to working with all of you very soon! We make a wonderful team.

Many thanks to **Elizabeth Gabler** and **Erin Siminoff** at Fox 2000 for agreeing to make the film version of *The Longest Ride*. I'm excited to be working with both of you.

David Buchalter, who helps to arrange all my speeches, also deserves my thanks. I appreciate all you do.

Todd and **Kari Wagner** also deserve my thanks for what they did—I trust they know what I'm talking about.

And finally, thanks to friends new and old who've added much joy and laughter to my life, including **Drew** and **Brittany Brees**, **Jennifer Romanello**, **Chelsea Kane**, **Gretchen Rossi**, **Slade Smiley**, **Josh Duhamel**, and **Julianne Hough**.

1

Early February 2011

Ira

I sometimes think to myself that I'm the last of my kind.

My name is Ira Levinson. I'm a southerner and a Jew, and equally proud to have been called both at one time or another. I'm also an old man. I was born in 1920, the year that alcohol was outlawed and women were given the right to vote, and I often wondered if that was the reason my life turned out the way it did. I've never been a drinker, after all, and the woman I married stood in line to cast a ballot for Roosevelt as soon as she reached the appropriate age, so it would be easy to imagine that the year of my birth somehow ordained it all.

My father would have scoffed at the notion. He was a man who believed in rules. "Ira," he would say to me when I was young and working with him in the haberdashery, "let me tell you something you should never do," and then he would tell me. His *Rules for Life*, he called them, and I grew up hearing my father's rules on just about everything. Some of what he told me was moral in nature, rooted in the teachings of the Talmud; and they were probably the same things most parents said to their children. I was told that I should never lie or cheat or steal, for instance, but my father—a sometimes Jew, he called himself back then—was far more likely to focus on the practical. Never go out in the rain without a hat, he would tell me. Never touch a stove burner, on the off chance it still might be hot. I was warned that I should never count the money in my wallet in public, or buy jewelry from a man on the street, no matter how good the deal might seem. On and on they went, these *nevers*, but despite their random nature, I found myself following almost every one, perhaps because I wanted never to disappoint my father. His voice, even now, follows me everywhere on this longest of rides, this thing called life.

Similarly, I was often told what I *should* do. He expected honesty and integrity in all aspects of life, but I was also told to hold doors for women and children, to shake hands with a firm grip, to remember people's names, and to always give the customer a little more than expected. His rules, I came to realize, not only were the basis of a philosophy that had served him well, but said everything about who he was. Because he believed in honesty and integrity, my father believed that others did as well. He believed in human decency and assumed others were just like him. He believed that most people, when given the choice, would do what was right, even when it was hard, and he believed that good almost always triumphed over evil. He wasn't naive, though. "Trust people," he would tell me, "until they give you a reason not to. And then never turn your back."

More than anyone, my father shaped me into the man I am today.

But the war changed him. Or rather, the Holocaust changed him. Not his intelligence—my father could finish the *New York Times* crossword puzzle in less than ten minutes—but his beliefs about people. The world he thought he knew no longer made sense to him, and he began to change. By then he was in his late fifties, and after making me a partner in the business, he spent little time in the shop. Instead, he became a full-time Jew. He began to attend synagogue regularly with my mother—I'll get to her later—and offered financial support to numerous Jewish causes. He refused to work on the Sabbath. He followed with interest the news regarding the founding of Israel—and the Arab-Israeli War in its aftermath—and he began to visit Jerusalem at least once a year, as if looking for something he'd never known he'd been missing. As he grew older, I began to worry more about those overseas trips, but he assured me that he could take care of himself, and for many years he did. Despite his advancing age, his mind remained as sharp as ever, but unfortunately his body wasn't quite so accommodating. He had a heart attack when he was ninety, and though he recovered, a stroke seven months later greatly weakened the right side of his body. Even then, he insisted on taking care of himself. He refused to move to a nursing home, even though he had to use a walker to get around, and he continued to drive despite my pleas that he forfeit his license. It's dangerous, I would tell him, to which he would shrug.

What can I do? he would answer. How else would I get to the store?

My father finally died a month before he turned 101, his license still in his wallet and a completed crossword puzzle on the bed-stand beside him. It had been a long life, an interesting life, and I've found myself thinking about him often of late. It makes sense, I suppose, because I've been following in his footsteps all along. I carried with me his *Rules for Life* every morning as I opened the shop and in the way I've dealt with people. I remembered names and gave more than was expected, and to this day I take my hat with me when I think there's a chance of rain. Like my father, I had a heart attack and now use a walker, and though I never liked crossword puzzles, my mind seems as sharp as ever. And, like my father, I was too stubborn to give up my license. In retrospect, this was probably a mistake. If I had, I wouldn't be in this predicament: my car off the highway and halfway down the steep embankment, the hood crumpled from impact with a tree. And I wouldn't be fantasizing about someone coming by with a thermos full of coffee and a blanket and one of those movable thrones that carried the pharaoh from one spot to the next.

Because as far as I can tell, that's just about the only way I'm ever going to make it out of here alive.

I'm in trouble. Beyond the cracked windshield, the snow continues to fall, blurry and disorienting. My head is bleeding, and dizziness comes in waves; I'm almost certain my right arm is broken. Collarbone, too. My shoulder throbs, and the slightest twitch is agonizing. Despite my jacket, I'm already so cold that I'm shivering.

I'd be lying if I told you I wasn't afraid. I don't want to die, and thanks to my parents—my mother lived to ninety-six—I long assumed that I was genetically capable of growing even older than I already am. Until a few months ago, I fully believed I had half a dozen good years left. Well, maybe not *good* years. That's not the way it works at my age. I've been disintegrating for a while now— heart, joints, kidneys, bits and pieces of my body beginning to give up the ghost—but recently something else has been added to the mix. Growths in my lungs, the doctor said. Tumors. *Cancer.* My time is measured in months now, not years . . . but even so, I'm not ready to die just yet. Not today. There is something I have to do, something I have done every year since 1956. A grand tradition is coming to an end, and more than anything, I wanted one last chance to say good-bye.

Still, it's funny what a man thinks about when he believes death to be imminent. One thing I know for sure is that if my time is up, I'd rather not go out this way—body trembling, dentures rattling, until finally, inevitably, my heart just gives out completely. I know what happens when people die—at my age, I've been to too many funerals to count. If I had the choice, I'd rather go in my sleep, back home in a comfortable bed. People who die like that look good at the viewing, which is why, if I feel the Grim Reaper tapping my shoulder, I've already decided to try to make my way to the backseat. The last thing I want is for someone to find me out here, frozen solid in a sitting position like some bizarre ice sculpture. How would they ever get my body out?

The way I'm wedged behind the wheel, it would be like trying to get a piano out of the bathroom. I can imagine some fireman chipping away at the ice and wobbling my body back and forth, saying things like "Swing the head this way, Steve," or "Wiggle the old guy's arms that way, Joe," while they try to manhandle my frozen body out of the car. Bumping and clunking, pushing and pulling, until, with one last big heave, my body thumps to the ground. Not for me, thanks. I still have my pride. So like I said, if it comes to that, I'll try my best to make my way to the backseat and just close my eyes. That way they can slide me out like a fish stick.

But maybe it won't come to that. Maybe someone will spot the tire tracks on the road, the ones heading straight over the embankment. Maybe someone will stop and call down, maybe shine a flashlight and realize there's a car down here. It isn't inconceivable; it could happen. It's snowing and people are already driving slowly. Surely someone's going to find me. They have to find me.

Right?

Maybe not.

The snow continues to fall. My breath comes out in little puffs, like a dragon, and my body has begun to ache with the cold. But it could be worse. Because it was cold—though not snowing—when I started out, I dressed for winter. I'm wearing two shirts, a sweater, gloves, and a hat. Right now the car is at an angle, nose pointed down. I'm still strapped into the seat belt, which supports my weight, but my head rests on the steering wheel. The air bag deployed, spreading white dust and the acrid scent of gunpowder throughout the car. It's not comfortable, yet I'm managing.

But my body throbs. I don't think the air bag worked properly, because my head slammed into the steering wheel and I was knocked unconscious. For how long, I do not know. The gash on my head continues to bleed, and the bones in my right arm seem to be trying to pop through my skin. Both my collarbone and my shoulder throb, and I'm afraid to move. I tell myself it could be worse. Though it is snowing, it is not bitterly cold outside. Temperatures are supposed to dip into the mid-twenties tonight but will climb into the high thirties tomorrow. It's also going to be windy, with gusts reaching twenty miles an hour. Tomorrow, Sunday, the winds will be even worse, but by Monday night, the weather will gradually begin to improve. By then, the cold front will have largely passed and the winds will be almost nonexistent. On Tuesday, temperatures are expected to reach the forties.

I know this because I watch the Weather Channel. It's less depressing than the news, and I find it interesting. It's not only about the expected weather; there are shows about the catastrophic effects of weather in the past. I've seen shows about people who were in the bathroom as a tornado ripped the house from its foundation, and I've seen people talk about being rescued after being swept away by flash flooding. On the Weather Channel, people always survive catastrophe, because these are the people who are interviewed for the program. I like knowing in advance that the people survived. Last year, I watched a story about rush-hour commuters who were surprised by a blizzard in Chicago. Snow came down so fast, the roads were forced to close while people were still on them. For eight hours, thousands of people sat on highways, unable to move while temperatures plummeted. The story I saw focused on two of the people who'd been in the blizzard, but what struck me while watching was the fact that neither of them seemed prepared for the weather. Both of them became almost hypothermic as the storm rolled through. This, I must admit, made no sense to me. People who live in Chicago are fully aware that it snows regularly; they experience the blizzards that sometimes roll in from Canada, they must realize it gets cold. How could they not know these things? If I lived in such a place, I would have had thermal blankets, hats, an additional winter jacket, earmuffs, gloves, a shovel, a flashlight, hand warmers, and bottled water in the trunk of my car by Halloween. If I lived in Chicago, I could be stranded by a blizzard for two weeks before I began to worry.

My problem, however, is that I live in North Carolina. And normally when I drive—except for an annual trip to the mountains, usually in the summer—I stay within a few miles of my home. Thus, my trunk is empty, but I'm somewhat comforted by the fact that even if I had a portable hotel in my trunk, it would do me no good. The embankment is icy and steep, and there's no way I could reach it, even if it held the riches of Tutankhamun. Still, I'm not altogether unprepared for what's happened to me. Before I left, I packed a thermos full of coffee, two sandwiches, prunes, and a bottle of water. I put the food in the passenger seat, next to the letter I'd written, and though all of it was tossed about in the accident, I'm comforted by the knowledge that it's still in the car. If I get hungry enough, I'll try to find it, but even now I understand that there's a cost to eating or drinking. What goes in must go out, and I haven't yet figured out how it will go out. My walker is in the backseat, and the slope would propel me to my grave; taken with my injuries, a call of nature is out of the question.

About the accident. I could probably concoct an exciting story about icy conditions or describe an angry, frustrated driver who forced me off the road, but that's not the way it happened. What happened was this: It was dark and it began to snow, then snow even harder, and all at once, the road simply vanished. I assume I entered a curve—I say *assume*, because I obviously didn't see a curve—and the next thing I knew, I crashed through the guardrail and began to career down the steep embankment. I sit here, alone in the dark, wondering if the Weather Channel will eventually do a show about me.

I can no longer see through the windshield. Though it sends up flares of agony, I try the windshield wipers, expecting nothing, but a moment later they push at the snow, leaving a thin layer of ice in their wake. It strikes me as amazing, this momentary burst of normalcy, but I reluctantly turn the wipers off, along with the headlights, though I'd forgotten they were even on. I tell myself that I should conserve whatever is left of the battery, in case I have to use the horn.

I shift, feeling a lightning bolt shoot from my arm up to my collarbone. The world goes black. Agony. I breathe in and out, waiting for the white-hot agony to pass. Dear God, please. It is all I can do not to scream, but then, miraculously, it begins to fade. I breathe evenly, trying to keep the tears at bay, and when it finally recedes, I feel exhausted. I could sleep forever and never wake up. I close my eyes. I'm tired, so tired.

Strangely, I find myself thinking of Daniel McCallum and the afternoon of the visit. I picture the gift he left behind, and as I slip away, I wonder idly how long it will be until someone finds me.

✤

"Ira."

I hear it first in my dream, slurry and unformed, an underwater sound. It takes a moment before I realize someone is saying my name. But that is not possible.

"You must wake up, Ira."

My eyes flutter open. In the seat beside me, I see Ruth, my wife.

"I'm awake," I say, my head still against the steering wheel. Without my glasses, which were lost in the crash, her image lacks definition, like a ghost.

"You drove off the highway."

I blink. "A maniac forced me off the road. I hit a patch of ice. Without my catlike reflexes, it would have been worse."

"You drove off the road because you are blind as a bat and too old to be driving. How many times have I told you that you are a menace behind the wheel?"

"You've never said that to me."

"I should have. You didn't even notice the curve." She pauses. "You are bleeding."

Lifting my head, I wipe my forehead with my good hand and it comes back red. There is blood on the steering wheel and the dash, smears of red everywhere. I wonder how much blood I've lost. "I know."

"Your arm is broken. And your collarbone, too. And there is something wrong with your shoulder."

"I know," I say again. As I blink, Ruth fades in and out.

"You need to get to the hospital."

"No argument there," I say.

"I am worried about you."

I breathe in and out before I respond. Long breaths. "I'm worried about me, too," I finally say.

My wife, Ruth, is not really in the car. I realize this. She died nine years ago, the day I felt my life come to a full stop. I had called to her from the living room, and when she didn't answer, I rose from my chair. I could move without a walker back then, though it was still slow going, and after reaching the bedroom, I saw her on the floor, near the bed, lying on her right side. I called for an ambulance and knelt beside her. I rolled her onto her back and felt her neck, detecting nothing at all. I put my mouth to hers, breathing in and out, the way I had seen on television. Her chest went up and down and I breathed until the world went black at the edges, but there was no response. I kissed her lips and her cheeks, and I held her close against me until the ambulance arrived. Ruth, my wife of more than fifty-five years, had died, and in the blink of an eye, all that I'd loved was gone as well.

"Why are you here?" I ask her.

"What kind of question is that? I am here because of you."

Of course. "How long was I asleep?"

"I do not know," she answers. "It is dark, though. I think you are cold."

"I'm always cold."

"Not like this."

"No," I agree, "not like this."

"Why were you driving on this road? Where were you going?"

I think about trying to move, but the memory of the lightning bolt stops me. "You know."

"Yes," she says. "You were driving to Black Mountain. Where we spent our honeymoon."

"I wanted to go one last time. It's our anniversary tomorrow."

She takes a moment to respond. "I think you are going soft in your head. We were married in August, not February."

"Not that anniversary," I say. I don't tell her that according to the doctor, I will not last until August. "Our other anniversary," I say instead.

"What are you talking about? There is no other anniversary. There is only one."

"The day my life changed forever," I say. "The day I first saw you."

For a moment, Ruth says nothing. She knows I mean it, but unlike me, she has a hard time saying such things. She loved me with a passion, but I felt it in her expressions, in her touch, in the tender brush of her lips. And, when I needed it most, she loved me with the written word as well.

"It was February sixth, 1939," I say. "You were shopping downtown with your mother, Elisabeth, when the two of you came into the shop. Your mother wanted to buy a hat for your father."

She leans back in the seat, her eyes still on me. "You came out of the back room," she says. "And a moment later, your mother followed you."

Yes, I suddenly recall, my mother did follow. Ruth has always had an extraordinary memory.

Like my mother's family, Ruth's family was from Vienna, but they'd immigrated to North Carolina only two months earlier. They'd fled Vienna after the *Anschluss* of Austria, when Hitler and the Nazis absorbed Austria into the Reich. Ruth's father, Jakob Pfeffer, a professor of art history, knew what the rise of Hitler meant for the Jews, and he sold everything they owned to come up with the necessary bribes to secure his family's freedom. After crossing the border into Switzerland, they traveled to London and then on to New York, before finally reaching Greensboro. One of Jakob's uncles manufactured furniture a few blocks from my father's shop, and for months Ruth and her family lived in two cramped rooms above the plant floor. Later, I would learn that the endless fumes from the lacquer made Ruth so sick at night, she could barely sleep.

"We came to the store because we knew your mother spoke German. We had been told that she could help us." She shakes her head. "We were so homesick, so hungry to meet someone from home."

I nod. At least I think I do. "My mother explained everything after you left. She had to. I couldn't understand a word that any of you were saying."

"You should have learned German from your mother."

"What did it matter? Before you'd even left the store, I knew that we would one day be married. We had all the time in the world to talk."

"You always say this, but it is not true. You barely looked at me."

"I couldn't. You were the most beautiful girl I'd ever seen. It was like trying to stare into the sun."

"Ach, Quatsch . . . ," she snorts. "I was not beautiful. I was a child. I was only sixteen."

"And I had just turned nineteen. And I ended up being right."

She sighs. "Yes," she says, "you were right."

I'd seen Ruth and her parents before, of course. They attended our synagogue and sat near the front, foreigners in a strange land. My mother had pointed them out to me after services, eyeing them discreetly as they hurried home.

I always loved our Saturday morning walks home from the synagogue, when I had my mother all to myself. Our conversation drifted easily from one subject to the next, and I reveled in her undivided attention. I could tell her about any problems I was having or ask any question that crossed my mind, even those that my father would have found pointless. While my father offered advice, my mother offered comfort and love. My father never joined us; he preferred to open the shop early on Saturdays, hoping for weekend business. My mother understood. By then, even I knew that it was a struggle to keep the shop open at all. The Depression hit Greensboro hard, as it did everywhere, and the shop sometimes went days without a single customer. Many people were unemployed, and even more were hungry. People stood in lines for soup or bread. Many of the local banks had failed, taking people's savings with them. My father was the type to set money aside in good times, but by 1939 times were difficult even for him.

My mother had always worked with my father, though seldom out front with the customers. Back then, men—and our clientele was almost exclusively men—expected another man to help them, in both the selection and the fitting of suits. My mother, however, kept the storeroom door propped open, which allowed her a perfect view of the customer. My mother, I must say, was a genius at her craft. My father would tug and pull and mark the fabric in the appropriate places, but my mother in a single glance would know immediately whether or not to adjust the marks my father had made. In her mind's eye, she could see the customer in the completed suit, knowing the exact line of every crease and seam. My father understood this—it was the reason he positioned the mirror where she could see it. Though some men might have felt threatened, it made my father proud. One of my father's *Rules for Life* was to marry a woman who was smarter than you. "I did this," he would say to me, "and you should do it, too. I say, why do all the thinking?"

My mother, I must admit, really was smarter than my father. Though she never mastered the art of cooking—my mother should have been banned from the kitchen—she spoke four languages and could quote Dostoyevsky in Russian; she was an accomplished classical pianist and had attended the University of Vienna at a time when female students were rare. My father, on the other hand, had never gone to college. Like me, he'd worked in his father's haberdashery since he was a boy, and he was good with numbers and customers. And like me, he'd first seen his wife-to-be at the synagogue, soon after she'd arrived in Greensboro.

There, however, is where the similarity ends, because I often wondered whether my parents were happy as a couple. It would be easy to point out that times were different back then, that people married less for love than for practical reasons. And I'm not saying they weren't right for each other in many ways. They made good partners, my parents, and I never once heard them argue. Yet I often wondered whether they were ever in love. In all the years I lived with them, I never saw them kiss, nor were they the kind of couple who felt comfortable holding hands. In the evenings, my father would do his bookkeeping at the kitchen table while my mother sat in the sitting room, a book open in her lap. Later, after my parents retired and I took over the business, I hoped they might grow closer. I thought they might travel together, taking cruises or going sightseeing, but after the first visit to Jerusalem, my father always traveled alone. They settled into separate lives, continuing to drift apart, becoming strangers again. By the time they were in their eighties, it seemed as though they'd run out of anything at all to say to each other. They could spend hours in the same room without uttering a single word. When Ruth and I visited, we tended to spend time first with one and then the other, and in the car afterward, Ruth would squeeze my hand, as if promising herself that we would never end up the same way.

Ruth was always more bothered by their relationship than either of them seemed to be. My parents seemed to have little desire to bridge the gap between them. They were comfortable in their own worlds. As they aged, while my father grew closer to his heritage, my mother developed a passion for gardening, and she spent hours pruning flowers in the backyard. My father loved to watch old westerns and the evening news, while my mother had her books. And, of course, they were always interested in the art-work Ruth and I collected, the art that eventually made us rich.

*

"You didn't come back to the shop for a long time," I said to Ruth.

Outside the car, the snow has blanketed the windshield and continues to fall. According to the Weather Channel, it should have stopped by now, but despite the wonders of modern technology and forecasting, weather predictions are still fallible. It is another reason I find the channel interesting.

"My mother bought the hat. We had no money for anything more."

"But you thought I was handsome."

"No. Your ears were too big. I like delicate ears."

She's right about my ears. My ears are big, and they stick out in the same way my father's did, but unlike my father, I was ashamed of them. When I was young, maybe eight or nine, I took some extra cloth from the shop and cut it into a long strip, and I spent the rest of the summer sleeping with the strip wrapped around my head, hoping they would grow closer to my scalp. While my mother ignored it when she'd check on me at night, I sometimes heard my father whispering to her in an almost affronted tone. *He has my ears,* he'd say to her. *What is so bad about my ears?*

I told Ruth this story shortly after we were married and she laughed. Since then, she would sometimes tease me about my ears like she is doing now, but in all our years together, she never once teased me in a way that felt mean.

"I thought you liked my ears. You told me that whenever you kissed them."

"I liked your face. You had a kind face. Your ears just happened to come with it. I did not want to hurt your feelings."

"A kind face?"

"Yes. There was a softness in your eyes, like you saw only the good in people. I noticed it even though you barely looked at me."

"I was trying to work up the courage to ask if I could walk you home."

"No," she says, shaking her head. Though her image is blurred, her voice is youthful, the sixteen-year-old I'd met so long ago. "I saw you many times at the synagogue after that, and you never once asked me. I even waited for you sometimes, but you went past me without a word."

"You didn't speak English."

"By then, I had begun to understand some of the language, and I could talk a little. If you had asked, I would have said, 'Okay, Ira. I will walk with you.'"

She says these last words with an accent. Viennese German, soft and musical. Lilting. In later years her accent faded, but it never quite disappeared.

"Your parents wouldn't have allowed it."

"My mother would have. She liked you. Your mother told her that you would own the business one day."

"I knew it! I always suspected you married me for my money."

"What money? You had no money. If I wanted to marry a rich man, I would have married David Epstein. His father owned the textile mill and they lived in a mansion."

This, too, was one of the running jokes in our marriage. While my mother had been speaking the truth, even she knew it was not the sort of business that would make anyone wealthy. It started, and remained, a small business until the day I finally sold the shop and retired.

"I remember seeing the two of you at the soda parlor across the street. David met you there almost every day during the summer."

"I liked chocolate sodas. I had never had them before."

"I was jealous."

"You were right to be," she says. "He was rich and handsome and his ears were perfect."

I smile, wishing I could see her better. But the darkness makes that impossible. "For a while I thought the two of you were going to get married."

"He asked me more than once, and I would tell him that I was too young, that he would have to wait until after I finished college. But I was lying to him. The truth was that I already had my eye on you. That is why I always insisted on going to the soda parlor near your father's shop."

I knew this, of course. But I like hearing her say it.

"I would stand by the window and watch you as you sat with him."

"I saw you sometimes." She smiles. "I even waved once, and still, you never asked to walk with me."

"David was my friend."

This is true, and it remained true for most of our lives. We were social with both David and his wife, Rachel, and Ruth tutored one of their children.

"It had nothing to do with friendship. You were afraid of me. You have always been shy."

"You must be mistaking me for someone else. I was debonair, a ladies' man, a young Frank Sinatra. I sometimes had to hide from the many women who were chasing me."

"You stared at your feet when you walked and turned red when I waved. And then, in August, you moved away. To attend university."

I went to school at William & Mary in Williamsburg, Virginia, and I didn't return home until December. I saw Ruth twice at the synagogue that month, both times from a distance, before I went

back to school. In May, I came home for the summer to work at
the shop, and by then World War II was raging in Europe. Hitler
had conquered Poland and Norway, vanquished Belgium, Lux-
embourg, and the Netherlands, and was making mincemeat of
the French. In every newspaper, in every conversation, the talk
was only of war. No one knew whether America would enter the
conflict, and the mood was grim. Weeks later, the French would
be out of the war for good.

"You were still seeing David when I returned."

"But I had also become friends with your mother in the year
you were gone. While my father was working, my mother and
I would go to the shop. We would speak of Vienna and our old
lives. My mother and I were homesick, of course, but I was angry,
too. I did not like North Carolina. I did not like this country. I
felt that I did not belong here. Despite the war, part of me wanted
to go home. I wanted to help my family. We were very worried for
them."

I see her turn toward the window, and in the silence, I know
that Ruth is thinking about her grandparents, her aunts and
uncles, her cousins. On the night before Ruth and her parents
left for Switzerland, dozens of her extended family members had
gathered for a farewell dinner. There were anxious good-byes and
promises to stay in touch, and although some were excited for
them, nearly everyone thought Ruth's father was not only overreacting, but foolish to have given up everything for an uncertain
future. However, a few of them had slipped Ruth's father some
gold coins, and in the six weeks it took to journey to North Carolina, it was those coins that provided shelter and kept food in
their stomachs. Aside from Ruth and her parents, her entire family had stayed in Vienna. By the summer of 1940, they were wearing the Star of David on their arms and largely prohibited from
working. By then, it was too late for them to escape.

My mother told me about these visits with Ruth and their
worries. My mother, like Ruth, still had family back in Vienna,

but like so many, we had no idea what was coming or just how terrible it would eventually be. Ruth didn't know, either, but her father had known. He had known while there was still time to flee. He was, I later came to believe, the most intelligent man I ever met.

"Your father was building furniture then?"

"Yes," Ruth said. "None of the universities would hire him, so he did what he had to do to feed us. But it was hard for him. He was not meant to build furniture. When he first started, he would come home exhausted, with sawdust in his hair and bandages on his hands, and he would fall asleep in the chair almost as soon as he walked in the door. But he never complained. He knew we were the lucky ones. After he woke, he would shower and then put on his suit for dinner, his own way of reminding himself of the man he once had been. And we would have lively conversations at dinner. He would ask what I had learned at school that day, and listen closely as I answered. Then he would lead me to think of things in new ways. 'Why do you suppose that is?' he would ask, or, 'Have you ever considered this?' I knew what he was doing, of course. Once a teacher, always a teacher, and he was good at it, which is why he was able to become a professor once again after the war. He taught me how to think for myself and to trust my own instincts, as he did for all his students."

I study her, reflecting on how significant it was that Ruth, too, had become a teacher, and my mind flashes once more to Daniel McCallum. "And your father helped you learn all about art in the process."

"Yes," she says, a mischievous lilt in her voice. "He helped me do that, too."

2

❧

Four Months Earlier
Sophia

Y ou've got to come," Marcia pleaded. "I want you to come. There's like thirteen or fourteen of us going. And it's not that far. McLeansville is less than an hour away, and you know we'll have a blast in the car."

Sophia made a skeptical face from her bed, where she was halfheartedly reviewing some Renaissance history notes. "I don't know...the *rodeo?*"

"Don't say it like that," Marcia said, adjusting a black cowboy hat in the mirror, tilting it this way and that. Sophia's roommate since sophomore year, Marcia Peak was easily her best friend on campus. "A, it's not the rodeo—it's only *bull riding.* And B, it's not even about that. It's about getting off campus for a quick road trip, and hanging out with me and the girls. There's a party afterwards, where they set up bars in this big, old-fashioned barn near the arena...there's going to be a band, and dancing, and I swear to God you'll never find so many cute guys in one place again."

Sophia looked up over the top of her notebook. "Finding a cute guy is the last thing I want right now."

Marcia rolled her eyes. "The point is, you need to get out of the house. It's already October. We're two months into school and you need to stop moping."

"I'm not moping," Sophia said. "I'm just...tired of it."

"You mean you're tired of seeing Brian, right?" She spun around to face Sophia. "Okay, I get that. But it's a small campus. And Chi Omega and Sigma Chi are paired this year. No matter what, it's going to be inevitable."

"You know what I mean. He's been following me. On Thursday, he was in the atrium of Scales Center after my class. That never happened while we were together."

"Did you talk to him? Or did he try to talk to you?"

"No." Sophia shook her head. "I headed straight for the door and pretended I didn't notice him."

"So no harm, no foul."

"It's still creepy—"

"So what?" Marcia gave an impatient shrug. "Don't let it get to you. It's not like he's psycho or anything. He'll figure it out eventually."

Sophia glanced away, thinking, *I hope so,* but when she didn't answer, Marcia crossed the room and took a seat on the bed beside her. She patted Sophia's leg. "Let's think about this logically, okay? You said he stopped calling and texting you, right?"

Sophia nodded, albeit with a feeling of reluctance.

"So okay, then," she concluded. "It's time to move on with your life."

"That's what I've been trying to do. But everywhere I go, he's there. I just don't understand why he won't leave me alone."

Marcia pulled her knees up, resting her chin on them. "Simple—Brian thinks that if he can talk to you, if he says the right things and pours on the charm, he'll convince you to change your mind. He honestly believes that." Marcia fixed her with an earnest expression. "Sophia, you have to realize that all guys think like this. Guys think they can talk their way out of anything, and they always want what they can't have. It's in their DNA. You dumped him, so now he wants you back. It's Guy 101." She winked at her friend. "He'll eventually accept that it's over. As long as you don't give in, of course."

"I'm not giving in," Sophia said.

"Good for you," Marcia said. "You were always too good for him."

"I thought you liked Brian."

"I *do* like him. He's funny and good-looking and rich—what's not to like? We've been friends since freshman year, and I still talk to him. But I also get that he's been a crappy boyfriend who cheated on my roommate. Not just once or twice, either, but three times."

Sophia felt her shoulders sag. "Thanks for reminding me."

"Listen, it's my job as your friend to help you move past this. So what do I do? I come up with this amazing solution to all your problems, a night out with the girls away from campus, and you're thinking of staying here?"

When Sophia still said nothing, Marcia leaned closer. "Please? Come with us. I need my wingman."

Sophia sighed, knowing how persistent Marcia could be. "Okay," she relented, "I'll go." And though she didn't know it then, whenever her thoughts drifted back toward the past, she would always remember that this was how it all began.

🌿

As midnight gradually approached, Sophia had to concede that her friend had been right. She'd needed a night out...she realized that for the first time in weeks, she was actually having fun. After all, it wasn't every night that she got to enjoy the aromas of dirt, sweat, and manure, while watching crazy men ride even crazier animals. Marcia, she learned, thought bull riders oozed sex appeal, and more than once, her roommate had nudged her to point out a particularly handsome specimen, including the guy who'd won it all. "Now that is definitely eye candy," she'd said, and Sophia had laughed in agreement despite herself.

The after-party was a pleasant surprise. The decaying barn, featuring dirt floors, wood plank walls, exposed beams, and gaping holes in the roof, was jammed. People stood three deep at the makeshift bars and clustered around a haphazard collection of tables and stools scattered throughout the cavernous interior. Even though she didn't generally listen to country-western music, the band was lively and the improvised wooden dance floor was thronged. Every now and then a line dance would start, which everyone except her seemed to know how to do. It was like some secret code; a song would end and another would begin, dancers streaming off the floor while others replaced them, choosing their places in line, leaving her with the impression that the whole thing had been choreographed in advance. Marcia and the other sorority girls would also join in, executing all the dance moves perfectly and leaving Sophia to wonder where they'd all learned how to do it. In more than two years of living together, neither Marcia nor any of the others had ever once mentioned they knew how to line dance.

Though she wasn't about to embarrass herself on the dance floor, Sophia was glad she'd come. Unlike most of the college bars near campus—or *any* bar she'd been to, for that matter—here the people were genuinely nice. Ridiculously nice. She'd never heard so many strangers call out, "Excuse me," or, "Sorry 'bout that," accompanied by friendly grins as they moved out of her path. And Marcia had been right about another thing: Cute guys were everywhere, and Marcia—along with most of the other girls from the house—was taking full advantage of the situation. Since they'd arrived, none of them had had to buy a single drink.

It all felt like the kind of Saturday night she imagined occurring in Colorado or Wyoming or Montana, not that she'd ever been to any of those places. Who knew that there were so many cowboys in North Carolina? Surveying the crowd, she realized they probably weren't real cowboys—most were there because they liked to watch the bull riding and drink beer on Saturday nights—but she'd never seen so many cowboy hats, boots, and belt buckles in one place before. And the women? They wore boots and hats, too, but between her sorority sisters and the rest of the women here, she noticed more short-shorts and bare midriffs than she'd ever seen in the campus quad on the first warm day of spring. It might as well have been a Daisy Duke convention. Marcia and the girls had gone shopping earlier that day, leaving Sophia feeling almost dowdy in her jeans and sleeveless blouse.

She sipped her drink, content to watch and listen and take it all in. Marcia had wandered off with Ashley a few minutes earlier, no doubt to talk to some guys she'd met. Most of the other girls were forming similar clusters, but Sophia didn't feel the need to join them. She'd always been a bit of a loner, and unlike a lot of people in the house, she didn't live and die by the rules of the sorority. Though she'd made some good friends, she was ready to move on. As scary as the prospect of *real life* seemed, she was excited at the thought of having her own place. She vaguely imagined a loft in some city, with bistros and coffeehouses and bars nearby, but who knew how realistic that was. The truth was that even living in a dumpy apartment off the highway in Omaha, Nebraska, would be preferable to her current situation. She was tired of living in the sorority house, and not just because Chi Omega and Sigma Chi were paired again. It was her third year in the house, and by now the drama of sorority life was wearing thin. No, scratch that. In a house with thirty-four girls, the drama was *endless*, and though she'd done her best to avoid it, she knew this year's version was already under way. The new crop of sophomore girls fretted endlessly about what everyone else thought of them and how best to fit in as they vied for a higher place in the pecking order.

Even when she'd joined, Sophia hadn't really cared about any of that stuff. She'd become a member of the sorority partly because she hadn't gotten along with her freshman roommate and partly because all the other freshmen were rushing. She was curious to find out what it was all about, especially since the

social life at Wake was defined largely by the Greek system. The
next thing she knew, she was a Chi Omega and putting a deposit
down on the room in the house.

She'd tried to get into the whole thing. Really. During her
junior year, she'd briefly considered becoming an officer. Marcia
had burst out laughing as soon as Sophia had mentioned it, and
then Sophia had begun to laugh as well, and that had been the
end of it. A good thing, too, because Sophia knew she would
have made a lousy officer. Even though she'd attended every
party, formal, and mandatory meeting, she couldn't buy into the
whole "sisterhood will change your life" ethos, nor did she believe
that "being a Chi Omega will bestow lifelong benefits."

Whenever she heard those slogans at the chapter meetings,
she'd wanted to raise her hand and ask her fellow sisters if they
honestly believed that the amount of spirit she showed during
Greek Week really mattered in the long run. No matter how hard
she tried, she couldn't imagine sitting in an interview and hearing her future boss say, *I notice here that you helped choreograph the
dance number that helped to put Chi Omega at the top of the sorority
rankings your junior year. Frankly, Miss Danko, that happens to be
exactly the skill set we've been searching for in a museum curator.*

Please.

Sorority life was part of her college experience and she didn't
regret it, but she never wanted it to be the *only* part. Or even the
major part. First and foremost, she'd come to Wake Forest because
she'd wanted a good education, and her scholarship required that
she put her studies first. And she had.

She rotated her drink, reflecting on the past year. Well...
almost, anyway.

Last semester, after she'd learned that Brian had cheated on
her for the second time, she'd been a wreck. She'd found it impossible to study, and when finals rolled around, she'd had to cram
like crazy to maintain her GPA. She'd made it...barely. But it
was just about the most stressful thing she'd ever gone through,

and she was determined not to let it happen again. If it hadn't
been for Marcia, she wasn't sure how she could have gotten
through last semester at all, and that was reason enough to be
grateful she'd joined Chi Omega in the first place. To her, the
sorority had always been about individual friendship, not some
rah-rah group identity; and to her, friendship had nothing to
do with anyone's place in the pecking order. And so, as she had
since the beginning, she would do what she had to in the house
during her senior year, but no more than that. She'd pay her fees
and dues and ignore the cliques that were no doubt already forming, especially the ones that believed that being a Chi Omega
was the be-all and end-all of existence.

Cliques that worshipped people like Mary-Kate, for instance.

Mary-Kate was the chapter president, and not only did she
ooze sorority life, but she looked the part as well—with full lips
and a slightly turned-up nose, set off by flawless skin and well-
defined bone structure. With the added allure of her trust fund—
her family, old tobacco money, was still one of the wealthiest in
the state—to many people, she *was* the sorority. And Mary-Kate
knew it. Right now, at one of the larger circular tables she was
holding court, surrounded by younger sisters who clearly wanted
to grow up to be just like her. As always, she was talking about
herself.

"I just want to make a difference, you know?" Mary-Kate was
saying. "I know I'm not going to be able to change the world, but
I think it's important to try to make a difference."

Jenny, Drew, and Brittany hung on her every word. "I think
that's amazing," Jenny agreed. She was a sophomore from
Atlanta, and Sophia knew her well enough to exchange greet-
ings in the mornings, but not much more than that. No doubt
she was thrilled to be spending time with Mary-Kate.

"I mean, I don't want to go to Africa or Haiti or anything like
that," Mary-Kate went on. "Why go all the way over there? My
daddy says that there are plenty of opportunities to help people

right around here. That's why he started his charitable foundation in the first place, and that's why I'm going to work there after
graduation. To help eliminate local problems. To make a difference right here in North Carolina. Do you know that there are
some people in this state who still have to use outhouses? Can
you imagine that? Not having any indoor plumbing? We need to
address these kinds of problems."

"Wait," Drew said, "I'm confused." She was from Pittsburgh,
and her outfit was nearly identical to Mary-Kate's, even down
to the hat and boots. "You're saying that your dad's foundation
builds bathrooms?"

Mary-Kate's shapely brows formed a V. "What are you talking
about?"

"Your dad's foundation. You said it builds bathrooms."

Mary-Kate tilted her head, inspecting Drew as if she were a
mental midget. "It provides scholarships to needy children. Why
on earth would you think it builds bathrooms?"

Oh, I don't know, Sophia thought, smiling to herself. *Maybe
because you were talking about outhouses? And you made it sound
that way?* But she said nothing, knowing Mary-Kate wouldn't
appreciate the humor. When it came to her *plans for the future,*
Mary-Kate had no sense of humor. The future was serious business, after all.

"But I thought you were going to be a newscaster," Brittany
said. "Last week, you were telling us about your job offer."

Mary-Kate tossed her head. "It's not going to work out."

"Why not?"

"It was for the morning news. In Owensboro, Kentucky."

"So?" asked one of the younger sorority sisters, clearly puzzled.

"Hello? Owensboro? Have you ever heard of Owensboro?"

"No." The girls exchanged timid glances.

"That's my point," Mary-Kate announced. "I'm *not* moving to
Owensboro, Kentucky. It's barely a blip on the map. And I'm not
getting up at four in the morning. Besides, like I said, I want to make

a difference. There are a lot of people out there that need help. I've been thinking about this for a long time. My daddy says…"

By then, Sophia was no longer listening. Wanting to find Marcia, she rose from her seat and scanned the crowd. It really *was* packed in here, and it was getting more crowded as the evening wore on. Squeezing past a few of the girls and the guys they were talking to, she began to slip through the crowd, searching for Marcia's black cowboy hat. Which was hopeless. There were black hats *everywhere*. She tried to remember the color of Ashley's hat. Cream colored, yes? With that, she was able to narrow down the choices until she spotted her friends. She had started in their direction, squeezing past clusters of people, when she caught something from the corner of her eye.

Or, more accurately, some*one*.

She stopped, straining for a better sight line. Usually, his height made him easy to find in crowds, but there were so many tall hats in the way that she couldn't be sure it was him. Even so, she suddenly felt uneasy. She tried to tell herself that she'd been mistaken, that she was just imagining things.

Despite herself, she couldn't stop staring. She tried to ignore the sinking feeling in her stomach as she searched the faces in the moving crowd. *He's not here*, she told herself again, but in that instant she saw him again, swaggering through the crowd, flanked by two friends.

Brian.

She froze, watching as the three of them moved toward an open table, Brian muscling his way through the crowd the way he did on the lacrosse field. For a second, she couldn't believe it. All she could think was, *Really? You followed me here, too?*

She felt a flush rising in her cheeks. She was with her friends, off campus…what was he thinking? She'd made it plain that she didn't want to see him; she'd told him point-blank that she didn't want to talk to him. She was tempted to march right up and tell him—again, right to his face—that it was over.

But she didn't, because she knew that *it wouldn't make any difference*. Marcia was right. Brian believed that if he could just talk to her, he could change her mind. Because he thought that at his most *charming* and *apologetic*, he was irresistible. She'd forgiven him before, after all. Why not again?

Turning away, she worked her way through the crowd toward Marcia, thanking God she'd left the tables when she had. The last thing she needed was for him to saunter up, feigning surprise at finding her. Because no matter what the facts were, she'd end up being painted as the heartless one. Why? Because Brian was the Mary-Kate of his fraternity. An all-American lacrosse player blessed with startlingly good looks and a wealthy investment banker father, Brian ruled their social circle effortlessly. Everyone in the sorority revered Brian, and she knew for a fact that half the girls in the house would hook up with him given the slightest encouragement.

Well, they could have him.

Sophia continued to weave through the crowd as the band finished one song and rolled into the next. She glimpsed Marcia and Ashley near the dance floor, talking to three guys wearing tight jeans and cowboy hats, who she guessed were a couple of years older than them. Sophia made her way in that direction, and when she reached for Marcia's arm, her roommate turned, looking almost flustered. Or, more accurately, drunk.

"Oh, hey!" she drawled, dragging out the words. She maneuvered Sophia forward. "Guys, this is my roommate, Sophia. And this is Brooks and Tom...and..." Marcia squinted at the guy in the middle. "Who are you again?"

"Terry," he offered.

"Hi," Sophia said, the word automatic. She turned back to Marcia. "Can I talk to you alone?"

"Right now?" Marcia frowned. She cut her eyes toward the cowboys as she turned to face Sophia, not bothering to hide her irritation. "What's up?"

"Brian's here," Sophia hissed.

Marcia squinted at her, as if trying to make sure she'd heard her right, before finally nodding. The two of them retreated to a place farther removed from the dance floor. It wasn't quite as deafening, but Sophia still had to raise her voice to be heard.

"He followed me. Again."

Marcia peered over Sophia's shoulder. "Where is he?"

"Back by the tables, with everyone else from school. He brought Jason and Rick."

"How did he know you'd be here?"

"It's not exactly a secret. Half the campus knew we were coming tonight."

As Sophia fumed, Marcia's interest flickered to one of the guys she'd been talking to, then she turned back to Sophia with a trace of impatience.

"Okay...he's here." She shrugged. "What do you want to do?"

"I don't know," Sophia said, crossing her arms.

"Did he see you?"

"I don't think so," she said. "I just don't want him to start anything."

"Do you want me to go talk to him?"

"No." Sophia shook her head. "Actually, I don't know what I want."

"Then just relax. Ignore him. Hang with me and Ashley for a while. We don't have to go back to the tables. Maybe he'll leave. And if he finds us here, I'll just start flirting with him. Distract him." Her mouth curved into a provocative smile. "You know he used to have a thing for me. Before you, I mean."

Sophia pulled her arms tighter. "Maybe we should just go."

Marcia waved a hand. "How? We're an hour from campus, and neither of us has a car here. We rode with Ashley, remember? And I know for a fact that she's not going to want to leave."

Sophia hadn't thought of that.

"Come on," Marcia cajoled. "Let's get a drink. You'll like these guys. They're in graduate school at Duke."

Sophia shook her head. "I'm not really in the mood to talk to any guys right now."

"Then what do you want to do?"

Sophia caught sight of the night sky at the far end of the barn and suddenly felt the overwhelming desire to get out of this sweaty, densely packed scene. "I think I just need some fresh air."

Marcia followed her gaze, then looked at Sophia again. "Do you want me to come with you?"

"No, that's okay. I'll find you again. Just hang around here, okay?"

"Yeah, sure," Marcia agreed with obvious relief. "But I can go with you..."

"Don't worry about it. I'm not going to be long."

As Marcia headed back to her new friends, Sophia started toward the rear of the barn, the crowd thinning out as she moved farther from the dance floors and the band. A few men tried to catch her attention as she maneuvered past them, but Sophia pretended not to notice, refusing to be sidetracked.

The oversize wooden doors had been propped open, and as soon as she stepped outside, she felt a wave of relief wash over her. The music wasn't nearly as loud, and the crisp autumn air felt like a cool balm on her skin. She hadn't realized how hot it was inside the barn. She looked around, hoping to find a place to sit. Off to the side was a massive oak tree, its gnarled limbs stretching in all directions, and here and there, people were standing in small groups, smoking and drinking. It took a second for her to realize that they were all inside a large enclosure bounded by wooden rails radiating from either side of the barn; no doubt it had once been a corral of sorts.

There weren't any tables. Instead, knots of people mostly sat on or leaned against the rails; one group perched on what she thought was an old tractor tire. Farther off to the side, a solitary man in a cowboy hat stared out over the neighboring pasture, his face in shadow. She wondered idly whether he, too, was in graduate school at Duke, but she doubted it. Somehow, cowboy hats and Duke graduate school just didn't go together.

She started toward an empty section of the railings a few fence posts down from the solitary cowboy. Above her, the sky was as clear as a glass bell, the moon hovering just over the distant tree line. She propped her elbows on the rough wooden rails and took in her surroundings. Off to the right were the rodeo stands, where she had watched the bull-riding contests earlier; directly behind them was a series of small enclosed pastures, which held the bulls. Though the corrals weren't lit, a few of the arena lights were still on, casting the animals in a spectral glow. Behind the pens were twenty or thirty pickups and trailers, surrounded by their owners. Even from a distance, she could see the glowing tips of the cigarettes some of them were smoking and hear the occasional clink of bottles. She wondered what the place was used for when the rodeos weren't in town. Did they use this place for horse shows? Dog shows? County fairs? Something else? There was a desolate, ramshackle feel to the place, suggesting that it sat empty much of the year. The rickety barn reinforced that impression, but then what did she know? She'd been born and raised in New Jersey.

That's what Marcia would have said, anyway. She'd been saying it since they were sophomores, and it had been funny at first, then had worn thin after a while, and now was funny again, a kind of long-running joke just between the two of them. Marcia was from Charlotte, born and raised only a few hours from Wake Forest. Sophia could still remember Marcia's bewildered reaction when she said she'd grown up in Jersey City. For all intents and purposes, Sophia might as well have said she'd been raised on Mars.

Sophia had to admit that Marcia's reaction hadn't been completely off base. Their backgrounds couldn't have been more different. Marcia was the second of two; her father was an orthopedic surgeon, and her mother was an environmental attorney.

Her older brother was in his last year of law school at Vanderbilt, and although the family wasn't on the Forbes list, it definitely resided comfortably in the upper crust. She was the kind of girl who took equestrian and dance lessons as a girl and who received a Mercedes convertible on her sixteenth birthday. Sophia, on the other hand, was the child of immigrants. Her mother was French, her father was from Slovakia, and they'd arrived in the country with little more than the money they had in their pockets. Though educated—her father was a chemist, her mother a pharmacist—their English skills were limited and they spent years working menial jobs and living in tiny, run-down apartments until they saved enough to open their own delicatessen. Along the way, they had three more kids—Sophia was the oldest—and Sophia grew up working alongside her parents at the deli after school and on weekends.

The business was moderately successful, enough to provide for the family but never much more than that. Like many of the better students in her graduating class, until a few months before graduation she'd expected to attend Rutgers. She'd applied to Wake Forest on a whim because her guidance counselor had suggested it, but never in a million years could she have afforded it, nor did she really know much about the place beyond the beautiful photos that were posted on the university's website. But surprising no one more than her, Wake Forest had come through with a scholarship that covered tuition, and in August Sophia had boarded the bus in New Jersey, bound for a virtually unknown destination where she'd spend much of the next four years.

It had been a great decision, at least from an educational standpoint. Wake Forest was smaller than Rutgers, which meant the classes were, too, and the professors in the Art History Department were passionate about teaching. She'd already had one interview for an internship at the Denver Art Museum—and no, they hadn't asked a thing about her role at Chi Omega—which she thought had gone well, but she hadn't heard back yet. Last summer, she'd also managed to save enough to buy her first car. It wasn't much—an eleven-year-old Toyota Corolla with more than a hundred thousand miles on the engine, a dent in the rear door, and more than a few scrapes—but for Sophia, who'd grown up walking or riding the bus everywhere, it was liberating to be able to come and go as she pleased.

At the railing, she grimaced. Well, except for tonight, anyway. But that was her fault. She could have driven, but...

Why did Brian have to come here tonight? What did he think was going to happen? Did he honestly believe that she'd forget what he'd done to her—not once or twice, but three times? That she'd take him back just as she had previously?

The thing was, she didn't even miss him. She wasn't going to forgive him, and if he hadn't been following her, she doubted she'd be thinking about him at all. Yet he was still able to ruin her night, and that bothered her. Because she was *allowing* it to happen. Because she was giving him that power over her.

Well, not anymore, she decided. She'd head back inside and hang with Marcia and Ashley and those Duke boys, and so what if Brian found her and wanted to talk? She'd simply ignore him. And if he tried to interfere with her good time? Well, she might even kiss one of the guys to make sure he knew she had moved on, period.

Smiling at the image, she turned from the railing, bumping into someone and almost losing her balance.

"Oh...excuse me," she said automatically as she reached out to brace herself. As her hand met his chest and she looked up, she felt a burst of recognition and she recoiled.

"Whoa," Brian said, catching her by the shoulders.

By then, she'd regained her balance and she assessed the situation with a sickening sense of predictability. He'd found her. They were face-to-face and alone together. Everything she'd been trying to avoid since the breakup. Great.

"Sorry about sneaking up on you like that." Like Marcia's, his words were slurred, which didn't surprise her—Brian never missed an opportunity to tie one on. "I didn't find you at the tables, and I had a hunch that you might be out here—"

"What do you want, Brian?" she demanded, cutting him off.

He flinched visibly at her tone. But as always, he recovered quickly. Rich people—*spoiled* people—always did.

"I don't want anything," he said, tucking one hand into the pocket of his jeans. When he staggered slightly, she realized he was well on his way to being falling-down drunk.

"Then why are you here?"

"I saw you out here all alone and thought I'd come over to make sure you were doing okay." He cocked his head, trying on his "I'm so wholesome" routine, but his bloodshot eyes undermined his efforts.

"I was fine until you got here."

He raised an eyebrow. "Wow. That's harsh."

"I have to be. You've been following me like a stalker."

He nodded, acknowledging the truth of her words. And, of course, to show that he accepted her disdain. He could probably star in a video entitled *How to Get Your Ex-Girlfriend to Forgive You . . . Again.*

"I know," he offered, right on cue. "I'm sorry about that."

"Are you?"

He shrugged. "I didn't want it to end the way it did . . . and I just wanted to tell you how ashamed I am about everything that happened. You didn't deserve it and I don't blame you for ending it. I realize that I've been . . ."

Sophia shook her head, already tired of listening to him. "Why are you doing this?"

"Doing what?"

"This," she said. "This whole phony show. Coming out here, pretending to be so abject and apologetic. What do you want?"

Her question seemed to catch him off guard. "I'm just trying to say sorry—"

"For what?" she asked. "For cheating on me for the third time? Or for lying to me ever since I've known you?"

He blinked. "Come on, Sophia," he said. "Don't be like this. I don't have any kind of agenda—really. I just don't want you to go through the whole year feeling like you have to avoid me. We've been through too much for that."

Despite the occasional slurring, he sounded almost credible. Almost. "You don't get it, do you?" She wondered if he honestly thought she'd forgive him. "I know I don't *have* to avoid you. I *want* to avoid you."

He stared at her, plainly confused. "Why are you acting like this?"

"Are you kidding?"

"After you broke up with me, I knew I'd made the biggest mistake of my life. Because I need you. You're good for me. You make me a better person. And even if we can't be together, I'd like to think we could get together and talk sometime. Just talk. The way we used to. Before I screwed things up."

She opened her mouth to reply, but his bravado left her speechless. Did he really think she'd fall for this again?

"Come on," he said, reaching for her hand. "Let's get a drink and talk. We can work through this—"

"Don't touch me!" Her voice rang out sharply.

"Sophia..."

She slid farther down the railing, away from him. "I said don't touch me!"

For the first time, she glimpsed a flash of anger in his expression as he lunged for her wrist. "Calm down..."

She yanked her arm, trying to free it. "Let go of me!"

Instead, he drew close enough for her to smell the stale beer on his breath. "Why do you always have to make such a scene?" he demanded.

As she struggled to break free, she looked up at him and felt a cold blade of fear. This wasn't a Brian she recognized. His brow was furrowed, almost wrinkled, his jaw ropy and distended. She froze, leaning away from his hot, labored breath. Later, she would recall only how paralyzed with fear she was, until she heard the voice behind her.

"You need to let her go," the voice said.

Brian looked over and back to her again, squeezing harder. "We're just talking," he said, his teeth clenched, the muscle in his jaw flexing.

"It doesn't look like you're just talking to me," the voice said. "And I'm not asking you to let her go. I'm telling you."

There was no mistaking the warning in the tone, but unlike the adrenaline-charged exchanges she'd sometimes witnessed at the frat houses, this stranger's voice sounded calm.

It was a beat before Brian even registered the threat, but he clearly wasn't intimidated. "I've got it handled. Why don't you mind your own business?"

"Last chance," came the voice. "I don't want to have to hurt you. But I will."

Too nervous to turn around, Sophia couldn't help noticing bystanders outside the barn beginning to turn their way. From the corner of her eye, she watched two men rise from the tractor tire and start toward them; another pair pushed off a section of the railing, their hats shadowing their faces as they approached.

Brian's bloodshot eyes flickered toward them, then he glared over Sophia's shoulder at the man who had just spoken. "What? You calling in your friends now?"

"I don't need them to deal with you," the stranger said, his voice even.

At the comment, Brian pushed Sophia aside, releasing the viselike grip on her arm. He turned and took a step toward the voice. "You seriously want to do this?"

When she turned, it was easy to understand the reason for

Brian's swagger. Brian was six and a half feet tall and over two hundred pounds; he worked out at the gym five times a week. The guy who'd threatened him was more than half a foot shorter and wiry; he wore a cowboy hat, though it had definitely seen better days.

"Go along now," the cowboy said, backing up a step. "There's no reason to make this any worse."

Brian ignored him. With surprising speed, he lunged toward the smaller man, his arms wide, intending to take him down. She recognized the move, had watched Brian flatten countless people on the lacrosse field, and knew exactly what was going to happen: He'd lower his head and drive hard with his legs, felling the other man like an axed tree. And yet...while Brian did just what she'd expected, it didn't end the way she'd seen it happen before. As Brian closed in, the man kept one leg in place as he leaned to the opposite side, his arms sweeping as he used Brian's momentum to throw him off balance. A moment later, Brian was facedown in the dirt with the smaller man's scuffed cowboy boot on the back of his neck.

"Just calm down, now," the cowboy said.

Brian began to struggle beneath the boot, preparing to push himself up, but with a quick hop—while still keeping one boot planted firmly on Brian's neck—the cowboy's other foot slammed down on Brian's fingers, then quickly moved aside. On the ground, Brian retracted his hand and screamed while the boot on his neck pressed down even harder.

"Stop moving or it's only going to get worse." The cowboy's words were clear and slow, as if he were addressing a dimwit.

Still stunned by the rapidity of the events, Sophia stared at the cowboy. Recognizing him as the figure she'd noticed standing alone by the railing when she'd first walked out, she noted that he had yet to look at her. Instead, he seemed intent on keeping his boot in the proper place, as if warily pinning a rattlesnake to the canyon floor. Which, in a way, he was.

On the ground, Brian began to struggle again. Again, his fingers were stomped while the other boot remained fixed on his neck. Brian stifled a wail, his body gradually growing still. Only then did the cowboy look up at Sophia, his blue eyes piercing in the reflected lights outside the barn.

"If you want to go," he offered, "I'll be glad to hold him for a bit."

He sounded unconcerned, as if the circumstances were nothing out of the ordinary. As she struggled for an appropriate response, she took in the messy brown hair poking out from beneath his hat and realized that he wasn't much older than her. He looked vaguely familiar, but not because she'd seen him at the railing earlier. She'd seen him somewhere else, maybe inside, but that wasn't quite right. She couldn't put her finger on it.

"Thanks," she said, clearing her throat. "But I'll be okay."

As soon as he heard her voice, Brian resumed his struggle; again it ended with Brian jerking his hand back amid howls of pain.

"You sure?" the cowboy asked. "I'm sensing he's a bit angry."

That's an understatement, she thought. She had no doubt that Brian was *furious*. She couldn't suppress the tiniest of smiles.

"I think he's learned his lesson."

The cowboy seemed to evaluate her answer. "Maybe you should check with him," he suggested, pushing his hat back on his head. "Just to make sure."

Surprising herself, she smiled at him before leaning over. "Are you going to leave me alone, Brian?"

Brian gave a muffled yelp. "Get him off me! I'm going to kill him..."

The cowboy sighed, putting even more pressure on the back of Brian's neck. This time, Brian's face was pressed hard into the dirt.

She turned to the cowboy, then back to Brian again. "Is that a yes or a no, Brian?" she asked.

The cowboy laughed, revealing even white teeth and a boyish grin.

Although she hadn't noticed it earlier, four other cowboys had surrounded them in the meantime, and Sophia wondered if this whole incident could become any more surreal. She felt as though she'd stumbled onto the set of an old western, and all at once, she realized where she'd seen this cowboy before. Not inside the barn, but earlier, at the rodeo. The one Marcia had called eye candy. The bull rider who'd won it all.

"You doing okay, Luke?" one of the circle asked. "Need a hand?"

The blue-eyed cowboy shook his head. "I got it for now. But if he don't stop wiggling, his nose is gonna get broke whether he likes it or not."

She looked at him. "You're Luke?"

He nodded. "You?"

"Sophia."

He tipped his hat. "Nice to meet you, Sophia." Grinning, he glanced down at Brian again.

"You gonna leave Sophia alone if I let you up?"

Defeated, Brian stopped moving. Slowly but surely, the pressure eased off his neck and Brian cautiously turned his head. "Get your boot off my neck!" he grunted, his expression simultaneously surly and fearful.

Sophia shifted from one foot to the other. "You should probably let him up," she said.

After a beat, Luke lifted his boot and stepped back. In that instant, Brian leapt to his feet, his body tense. His nose and cheek were scraped, and he had dirt in his teeth. As the circle of other riders tightened, Brian turned from one bull rider to the next, his head swiveling back and forth.

Though drunk, Brian wasn't stupid, and after glaring at Sophia, he took a step backward. The five cowboys stayed put, appearing not to care one way or the other, but Sophia sensed it was only an illusion. They were prepared for whatever Brian might do, but Brian again took another step backward before pointing at Luke.

"You and I aren't finished yet," he spat. "You understand that?"

He let the words hang before focusing on Sophia. There was anger in his expression and betrayal as well, and with that, he turned and started back toward the barn.

3

Luke

Ordinarily, he wouldn't have gotten involved.

Hell, anyone who went to bars had been confronted with this scenario before, the events unfolding with an almost ridiculous predictability: a couple enjoying a night out, both of them drinking, when—no doubt fueled by too much booze—an argument begins. One starts yelling at the other, the other yells back, the anger escalates, and nine times out of ten, the man ends up grabbing the woman. By the hand, the wrist, the arm, whatever. And then?

That's where things got trickier. A few years ago, when he was riding in Houston, he'd been in much the same situation. He'd been decompressing at a local bar when a man and woman began arguing. After a minute or so, with their voices rising, it turned physical and Luke had intervened then, too—only to be turned on by both the man and the woman, each screaming at him to leave them the hell alone and to mind his own business. The next thing he knew, the woman was clawing at his face and latching on to his hair while he scuffled with the man. Fortunately, no real damage had been done—others had quickly intervened to separate the three of them. Luke had walked away shaking his head and swearing that from then on, he would stick to his own affairs. Hell, if they wanted to act like idiots, why try to stop them?

Which was exactly what he'd intended to do in this instance. He hadn't even wanted to join the after-party in the first place, but he'd been talked into it by a few fellow riders who wanted to celebrate his comeback and drink to his victory. He'd ended up winning the event, after all—both the short go and the event total. Not because he'd ridden particularly well, but simply because no one else had completed his ride in the final round. He won essentially by default, but sometimes that was how things played out.

He was glad no one had noticed his hands shaking beforehand. The tremors were a first for him, and although he wanted to believe that it was because of the long hiatus, he knew the real reason. His mom did, too, and she'd made it clear that she opposed his return to the ring. Ever since he'd mentioned the possibility of riding again, things had been strained between them. Ordinarily, he'd call her after he finished an event, but not tonight. She wouldn't care that he'd won. Instead, he'd simply texted her after the event that he was fine. She hadn't responded.

After a couple of beers, he was only just feeling the acidic rush of fear ebb away. He'd retreated to his truck after each of his first two rides, needing to be alone and settle his nerves. Despite his advantageous standings, he'd actually considered forfeiting. But he'd crushed that instinct and gone back out for his last ride of the night. He'd heard the announcer talking about his injury and subsequent hiatus as he was getting ready in the chute. The bull he'd drawn—a rank bull named Pump and Dump—spun wildly as soon as he broke free, and Luke had been barely able to hold on until the buzzer. He'd landed hard after freeing himself from the wrap, but there'd been no damage done, and he'd waved his hat while the crowd roared its approval.

After that came the backslaps and congratulations, and he couldn't very well say no when so many people wanted to buy him a drink. He wasn't ready to go home yet anyway. He needed some time to unwind, to replay the rides in his head. In his mind, he was always able to make the adjustments he hadn't been able to during the ride, and he needed to think through those steps if he planned to continue. Though he'd won, his balance was nowhere near what it once had been. He still had a long way to go.

He was replaying the second ride when he first noticed the girl. It was hard not to appreciate the cascade of blond hair and deep-set eyes; he had the sense that, like him, she was wrapped up in her own thoughts. She was pretty, but beyond that there was something wholesome and natural about her appearance, the kind of girl who probably looked equally at home in jeans or a formal gown. This was no dolled-up buckle-bunny, hoping to hook up with one of the riders. They were everywhere on tour and easy to find—a pair of them had sidled up to him in the barn and introduced themselves earlier—but he'd had no interest in encouraging them. He'd had a few one-night stands over the years, enough to know they inevitably left him feeling empty.

But the girl on the railing interested him. There was something different about her, though he couldn't pinpoint what. Maybe, he thought, it was the unguarded, almost vulnerable way she stared into the distance. Whatever it was, he sensed that right now what she really needed was a friend. He considered going over to talk to her, but he pushed aside the idea as he focused on the bulls in the distance. Despite the arena lights, it was too dark to make out all the details, but he searched for Big Ugly Critter anyway. They would forever be linked, he thought, and he wondered idly whether the bull had already been loaded up. He doubted the owner of the bull had planned to drive all night, which meant the animal was here, but it still took some time before he was able to locate him.

It was while he was staring at Big Ugly Critter that the drunk ex-boyfriend had walked up. It was impossible not to overhear their conversation, but he reminded himself not to get involved. And he wouldn't have, at least until the huge brute had grabbed her. By then, it was obvious she didn't want anything to do with him, and when he heard the blonde's anger give way to fear, Luke found himself pushing away from the railing. He knew his decision would probably backfire on him, but as he stepped toward the two of them, he thought again of the way she'd looked earlier, and he knew he didn't have a choice.

❧

Luke watched as the drunk ex-boyfriend stalked off, and he turned to thank his fellow riders for coming over. One by one they drifted away, leaving Luke and Sophia alone.

Above them, the stars had multiplied in the ebony sky. In the barn, the band finished one song and eased into another, an older classic by Garth Brooks. With a deep sigh, Sophia let her arms fall to her sides, the autumn breeze lifting her hair gently as she turned to face him.

"I'm sorry you were dragged into all this, but I want to thank you for what you did," Sophia said, a little sheepish.

Closer now, Luke registered the unusual green color of her eyes and the soft precision of her speech, a sound that made him think of faraway places. For a moment, he found himself tongue-tied.

"I was glad to help," he managed.

When he said nothing more, she tucked a loose strand of hair behind her ear. "He's...not always as crazy as you probably imagine he is. We used to go out and he's not too happy I broke up with him."

"I figured," Luke said.

"Did you...hear everything?" Her face was a mixture of embarrassment and fatigue.

"It was kind of hard not to."

Her lips tightened. "That's what I thought."

"If it makes you feel any better, I promise to forget," he offered.

She gave a genuine laugh, and he thought he heard relief in it. "I'm going to try my best to forget all about it, too," she said. "I just wish..."

When she trailed off, Luke finished her thought for her. "It's over and done, I'd guess. At least for tonight, anyway."

She turned, taking her time as she examined the barn. "I sure hope so."

Luke's feet scraped at the ground, as if trying to unearth words in the dust. "I assume your friends are inside?"

Her gaze flickered over the figures milling around the barn doors and beyond. "A bunch of us are here," she said. "I go to Wake Forest and my roommate at the sorority decided that what I really needed was a girls' night out."

"They're probably wondering where you are."

"I doubt it," she said. "They're having too much fun for that."

From a tree bordering the corral came the sound of an owl calling from a low-hanging branch, and both of them turned at the sound.

"Do you want me to walk you back inside? In case there's any trouble, I mean?"

She surprised him by shaking her head. "No. I think it's best if I stay out here for a little longer. It'll give Brian a chance to cool off."

Only if he quits drinking, Luke thought. *Let it go. It's not your business*, he reminded himself. "Would you rather be alone, then?"

A look of amusement flashed across her face. "Why? Am I boring you?"

"No," he said, shaking his head. "Not at all. I just didn't want—"

"I'm kidding." She stepped to the railing and propped her elbows on the fence. She leaned forward and turned toward him, smiling. Hesitantly, Luke joined her at the railing.

In the distance, she took in the view, appreciating the gently rolling hills common to this part of the state. Luke studied her features silently, noting the small stud in her earlobe, trying to figure out what to say.

"What year are you in college?" he finally asked. He knew it was an inane question, but it was all he could come up with.

"I'm a senior."

"That makes you ... twenty-two?"

"Twenty-one." She half turned in his direction. "And you?"

"Older than that."

"Not by much, I'd guess. Did you go to college?"

"It wasn't really my thing." He shrugged.

"And you ride bulls for a living?"

"Sometimes," he answered. "When I stay on, that is. But other times, I'm just a toy the bull gets to play with until I can get away."

She raised an eyebrow. "You were pretty impressive out there today."

"You remember me?"

"Of course. You were the only one who rode them all. You won, right?"

"I had a pretty good night," he admitted.

She brought her hands together. "So it's Luke ..."

"Collins," he finished.

"That's right," she said. "The announcer was going on and on about you before your ride."

"And?"

"To be honest, I wasn't paying much attention. At the time, I didn't know you'd end up coming to my rescue."

He listened for traces of sarcasm but detected none, which surprised him. Hooking a thumb toward the tractor tire, he pointed out, "Those other guys came over to help, too."

"But they didn't intervene. You did." She let the comment sink in for a moment. "Can I ask you a question, though?" she went on. "I've been wondering about it all night."

Luke picked at a sliver on the railing. "Go ahead."

"Why on earth would you ride bulls? It seems like you could get killed out there."

That's about right, he thought. It's what everyone wanted to know. As usual, he answered it the way he always did. "It's just something I've always wanted to do. I started when I was a little kid. I think I rode my first calf when I was four years old, and I was riding steers by the third grade."

"But how did you start in the first place? Who got you into it?"

"My dad," he said. "He was in rodeo for years. Saddle bronc."

"Is that different than bulls?"

"It's pretty much the same rules, except that it's on a horse. Eight seconds, holding on with one hand while the animal tries to throw you."

"Except that horses don't have horns the size of baseball bats. And they're smaller and not as mean."

He considered it. "That's about right, I'd guess."

"Then why don't you compete in saddle bronc instead of riding bulls?"

He watched her brush her hair back with both hands, trying to capture the flyaways. "That's kind of a long story. Do you really want to know?"

"I wouldn't have asked if I didn't."

He fiddled with his hat. "It's just a hard life, I guess. My dad would drive a hundred thousand miles a year going from rodeo to rodeo just to qualify for the National Finals Rodeo. That kind of travel is hard on the family, and not only was he gone almost all the time, but back then, it didn't pay much. After travel expenses and entry fees, he probably would have been better off working minimum wage. He didn't want that for me, and when he heard that bull riders were about to start their own tour, he thought it had a pretty good chance to be successful. That's when he got me into it. There's still a lot of travel, but the events are on weekends and usually I can get in and out pretty quick. The purses are bigger too."

"So he was right."

"He had great instincts. About everything." The words came out without thinking, and when he saw her expression, he knew she'd picked up on it. He sighed. "He passed away six years ago."

Her gaze didn't waver, and impulsively she reached out, touching his arm. "I'm sorry," she said.

Though her hand barely grazed his arm, the sensation lingered. "It's okay," he said, straightening up. Already he could feel the post-ride soreness settling in, and he tried to concentrate on that instead. "Anyway, that's the reason I ride bulls."

"And you like it?"

That was a tough one. For a long time, it was how he'd defined himself, no question about it. But now? He didn't know how to answer, because he wasn't sure himself. "Why are you so interested?" he countered.

"I don't know," she said. "Maybe because it's a world I know nothing about? Or maybe I'm just naturally curious. Then again, I might just be making conversation."

"Which one is it?"

"I could tell you," she said, her green eyes seductive in the moonlight. "But how much fun would that be? The world needs a little mystery."

Something stirred in him at the veiled challenge in her voice. "Where are you from?" he asked, feeling himself being reeled in and liking it. "I take it you're not from around here."

"Why would you think that? Do I have an accent?"

"I suppose that depends on where you're from. Up north, I'd be the one with the accent. But I can't really tell where you're from."

"I'm from New Jersey." She paused. "No jokes, please."

"Why would I joke? I like New Jersey."

"Have you ever been there?"

"I've been to Trenton. I rode in a few events at the Sovereign Bank Arena. Do you know where that is?"

"I know where Trenton is," she answered. "It's south of where I live, closer to Philadelphia. I'm up north, by the city."

"Have you been to Trenton?"

"A handful of times. But I've never been to the arena. Or to a rodeo, for that matter. This is my first time."

"What did you think?"

"Other than being impressed? I thought you were all crazy."

He laughed, charmed by her frankness. "You know my last name, but I didn't catch yours."

"Danko," she said. Then, anticipating his next question: "My dad is from Slovakia."

"That's near Kansas, right?"

She blinked. Her mouth opened and closed, and just as she was about to explain the concept of Europe to him, he raised his hands.

"Joking," he said. "I know where it is. Central Europe, part of what was once Czechoslovakia. I just wanted to see your reaction."

"And?"

"I should've taken a picture to show my friends."

She scowled before nudging against him. "That's not nice."

"But it was funny."

"Yeah," she admitted. "It was funny."

"So if your dad is from Slovakia..."

"My mom is French. They moved here a year before I was born."

He turned toward her. "No kidding..."

"You sound surprised."

"I don't know if I've ever met a French Slovakian before." He paused. "Hell, I don't know if I've ever met someone from New Jersey before."

When she laughed, he felt something relax in him, and he knew he wanted to hear the sound again. "And you live close by?"

"Not too far. A little north of Winston-Salem. I'm right outside of King."

"Sounds fancy."

"That's one thing it isn't. It's a small town with friendly people, but that's about it. We have a ranch up there."

"We?"

"My mom and I. Well, actually it's her ranch. I just live and work there."

"Like...a real ranch? With cows and horses and pigs?"

"It's even got a barn that makes this one here look new."

She surveyed the barn behind them. "I doubt that."

"Maybe I'll show you one day. Take you horseback riding and everything."

Their eyes met, holding for a beat, and again she reached out to touch his arm. "I think I'd like that, Luke."

4

Sophia

Sophia wasn't sure exactly why she'd said it. The words had simply come out before she could stop them. It occurred to her to try to backtrack or play it off somehow, but for whatever reason, she realized that she didn't want to.

It had less to do with his appearance, despite the fact that Marcia had been exactly right. He was unmistakably good-looking in a boyish kind of way, with a friendly, open smile highlighted by dimples. He was lean and wiry, too, his broad shoulders a contrast to his narrow hips, and the unruly mass of brown curls under his battered hat was definitely sexy. What really stood out were his eyes, though—she'd always been a sucker for beautiful eyes. His were a summer blue, vivid and bright enough to make you suspect colored contacts, as ludicrous as she knew Luke would have found such things.

She had to admit, it helped that he so obviously found her attractive. Growing up, she'd always been gawky, with long skinny legs, zero in the hips department, and prone to the occasional bout of acne. It wasn't until she was a junior in high school that she'd needed more than a training bra. All that had begun to change during her senior year, although it mostly made her feel self-conscious and awkward. Even now, when evaluating herself in the mirror, she still sometimes caught sight of the teenage girl she used to be, and it surprised her to realize that no one else could.

As flattering as Luke's appreciation was, what appealed to her most was the way he made everything appear easy, from the unflappable way he'd handled Brian to their meandering conversation. She never had the sense that he was trying to impress her, but his quiet self-possession made him come across as very different from the guys she met at Wake—especially Brian.

She also liked that he was comfortable leaving her alone with her thoughts. A lot of people felt the need to fill every silence, but Luke simply watched the bulls, content to keep his own counsel. After a while, she realized that the music from the barn had stopped temporarily—the band on a short intermission, no doubt—and she wondered whether Marcia would try to find her. She found herself hoping that she wouldn't—not yet, anyway.

"What's it like living on a ranch?" she asked, breaking the silence. "What do you do all day?"

She watched as he crossed one leg over the other, the toe of his boot in the dirt. "A bit of everything, I guess. There's always something to do."

"Such as?"

He absently massaged one hand with the other as he thought about it. "Well, for starters, horses and pigs and chickens need to be fed first thing in the morning and their stalls need to be cleaned. The cattle have to be monitored. I have to check the herd every day to make sure they're okay—no eye infections, no cuts from the barbed wire, things like that. If one is hurt or sick, I try to take care of it right away. After that, there are pastures to irrigate, and a few times a year, I have to move all the cattle from one pasture to the next, so they always have good grass. Then, a couple of times a year, I have to vaccinate the herd, which means roping them one by one and keeping them separated afterwards. We also have a pretty good-sized vegetable garden for our own use, and I've got to keep that going, too..."

She blinked. "That's all?" she joked.

"Not quite," he continued. "We sell pumpkins, blueberries,

honey, and Christmas trees to the public, so sometimes I spend part of my day planting or weeding or watering, or collecting the honey from the hives. And when the public comes out, I have to be there to tie down the trees or help carry pumpkins to the car, or whatever. And then, of course, there's always something broken that needs repairs, whether it's the tractor or the Gator or the fencing or the barn or the roof on the house." He offered a rueful expression. "Trust me, there's always something to do."

"You can't possibly do all that alone," Sophia said in disbelief.

"No. My mom does quite a bit, and we have a guy who's been working for us for years. José. He handles what we can't, essentially. And then when we have to, we'll bring in crews for a couple of days to help shape the trees or whatever."

She frowned. "What do mean by 'shape the trees'? You mean the Christmas trees?"

"In case you were wondering, they don't grow in pretty triangles. You have to prune them as they're growing to make them come out the way they do."

"Really?"

"And you have to roll the pumpkins, too. You want to keep them from rotting on the bottom, but you also want them to be round, or at least oval, or no one will buy them."

She wrinkled her nose. "So you literally roll them?"

"Yep. And you have to be careful not to break the stem."

"I never knew that."

"A lot of people don't. But you probably know a lot of things that I don't."

"You knew where Slovakia was."

"I always liked history and geography. But if you ask me about chemistry or algebra, I'd probably be lost."

"I never liked math that much, either."

"But you were good at it. I'll bet you were among the best in your class."

"Why would you say that?"

"You go to Wake Forest," he answered. "I'd guess you aced every subject growing up. What are you studying there?"

"Not ranching, obviously."

He flashed those dimples again.

She picked at the railing with her fingernail. "I'm majoring in art history."

"Is that something you were always interested in?"

"Not at all," she said. "When I first got to Wake, I had no idea what I wanted to do with my life, and I took the kind of classes that all freshmen take, hoping I'd stumble on something. I wanted to find something that made me feel...passionate, you know?"

When she paused, she could feel his attention on her, focused and sure. His genuine interest reminded her again of how different he was from the guys she knew on campus.

"Anyway, when I was a sophomore, I signed up for a class in French Impressionism, mostly to fill out my schedule, not for any particular reason. But the professor was amazing—intelligent and interesting and inspirational, everything a professor should be. He made art come alive and feel *relevant*, somehow...and after a couple of classes, it just clicked for me. I knew what I wanted to do, and the more art history classes I took, the more I knew how much I wanted to be part of that world."

"I'll bet you're glad you took the class, huh?"

"Yeah...my parents, not so much. They wanted me to major in pre-med or pre-law or accounting. Something that will lead to a job when I graduate."

He tugged at his shirt. "As far as I know, it's having a degree that's important. You can probably get a job doing almost anything."

"That's what I tell them. But my real dream is to work in a museum."

"So do it."

"It's not as easy as you might think. There are a lot of art history majors out there and only a handful of entry-level positions to go around. Plus a lot of museums are struggling, which means they're cutting back on their staff. I was lucky enough to get an interview with the Denver Art Museum. It's not a paid position, it's more of an internship thing, but they said that there's a possibility it could evolve into a paying position. Which, of course, begs the question as to how I'd be able to pay my bills while working there. And I wouldn't want my parents to support me, not that they could afford it. I have a younger sister at Rutgers, and two more starting college soon and..."

She said nothing, momentarily daunted. Luke seemed to read her mind and didn't press. "What do your parents do?" he asked instead.

"They own a deli. Specialty cheeses and meats. Fresh-baked bread. Homemade sandwiches and soups."

"Good food?"

"Great food."

"So if I ever go in there, what should I order?"

"You can't go wrong with anything. My mom makes an amazing mushroom soup. That's my favorite, but we're probably best known for our cheesesteaks. At lunch, there's always a long line and that's what most people order. It even won an award a couple of years back. Best sandwich in the city."

"Yeah?"

"Oh, yeah. The newspaper ran a contest and people voted and everything. My dad framed the certificate and it hangs right by the register. Maybe I'll show it to you one day."

He brought his hands together, mimicking her earlier stance. "I think I'd like that, Sophia."

She laughed, acknowledging his comeback and liking how he said her name. It came out slower than she was used to, but also smoother, the syllables rolling off his tongue in a pleasing, unrushed cadence. She reminded herself that they were strangers, but somehow it didn't feel that way. She leaned back against the fence post.

"So those other guys who came over...did you come here with them?"

He peered in their direction, then turned back to her. "No," he said. "Actually, I only knew one of them. My friends are inside. Probably ogling your friends, if you want to know the truth."

"How come you're not in there with them?"

He used a finger to push the brim of his hat back. "I was. For a while, anyway. But I wasn't in the mood to do much talking, so I came out here."

"You seem to be talking fine right now."

"I guess I am." He gave a sheepish grin. "There's not much to tell, other than what I've already said. I ride bulls and work on the family ranch. My life ain't all that interesting."

She studied him. "Then tell me something you don't usually tell people."

"Like what?" he said.

"Anything," she said, lifting her hands. "What were you thinking about earlier, when you were standing out here all alone?"

Luke shifted uncomfortably and glanced away. He said nothing at first. Instead, buying time, he folded his hands before him on the railing. "To really understand, I think you'd need to see it," he said. "But the problem is, it's not exactly here."

"Where is it?" she asked, puzzled.

"Over there," he said, motioning toward the corrals.

Sophia hesitated. Everyone knew the stories: *Girl meets guy who comes across as nice and pleasant, but as soon as he gets her alone* . . . And yet, as she regarded him, she didn't hear any warning bells. For some reason she trusted him, and not simply because he'd come to her aid. It just didn't feel like he was coming on to her; she even had the sense that if she asked him to leave, he'd walk away and she'd never talk to him again. Besides, he'd made her laugh tonight. In the short time they'd spent together, she'd forgotten all about Brian.

"Okay," she responded. "I'm game."

If he was surprised by her answer, he didn't show it. Instead he simply nodded, and putting both hands on the top railing, he hopped gracefully over the fence.

"Show-off," she teased. Bending down, she squeezed through the rails, and a moment later, they started toward the corrals.

As they crossed the pasture toward the fence on the far side, Luke maintained a comfortable distance. Sophia studied the undulations of the fence line as it rode the contours of the land, marveling at how different this place was from where she'd grown up. It occurred to her that she'd come to appreciate the quiet, almost austere beauty of this landscape. North Carolina was home to a thousand small towns, each with its own character and history, and she'd come to understand why many locals would never leave. In the distance, the pines and oaks, scrabbled together, formed an impenetrable scrim of blackness. Behind them, the music gradually faded, the distant sound of meadow crickets emerging in its wake. Despite the darkness, she felt Luke appraising her, though he was trying not to be obvious about it.

"There's a shortcut after the next fence," he said. "We can get to my truck from there."

The comment caught her off guard. "Your truck?"

"Don't worry," he said, raising his hands. "We're not leaving. We're not even getting in. It's just that I think you'll be able to see better from the bed. It's higher and more comfortable. I've got a couple of lawn chairs in the bed that I can set up."

"You have lawn chairs in the bed of your truck?" She squinted in disbelief.

"I've got a lot of stuff in the bed of my truck."

Of course he did. Didn't everyone? Marcia would have a *field day* with this.

By then, they'd reached the next fence, and the glow from the arena lights was growing stronger. Again, he hopped over it effortlessly, but this time the slats were placed too narrowly for her to squeeze through. Instead, she climbed up, perching on top before swinging her legs over. She took his hands as she jumped down, liking their callused warmth.

They trekked to a nearby gate and veered toward the trucks.

Luke angled toward a shiny black one with big tires and a rack of lights across the roof, the only one parked with the nose in the opposite direction. He opened the tailgate and hopped up into the back. Again, he held out his hands, and with a quick lift, she was standing next to him in the bed of the truck.

Luke turned around and began rummaging, moving things aside, his back to her. She crossed her arms, wondering what Marcia was going to think of all this. She could imagine her questions already: *We're talking about the cute one, right? He took you where? What were you thinking? What if he was crazy?* Meanwhile, Luke continued to sort through various items. She heard a metallic clunk as he finally reappeared beside her with the chair, the kind that most people brought to the beach. After opening it, he set it down in the bed of the truck and motioned toward it. "Go ahead and sit. It'll be ready in just a bit."

She stood without moving—again picturing Marcia's skeptical face—but then decided, Why not? The whole night had felt slightly surreal, so finding herself sitting in a lawn chair in the bed of a pickup owned by a bull rider was an almost natural extension. She reflected on the fact that aside from Brian, the last time she'd been alone with a guy was the summer before she first came to Wake, when Tony Russo had taken her to the prom. They'd known each other for years, but past graduation, it hadn't amounted to much. He was cute and smart—he was heading to Princeton in the fall—but he was all hands by their third date, and—

Luke set the other chair beside her, interrupting her thoughts. Instead of sitting, however, he hopped down from the bed and went around to the driver's-side door and leaned inside the cab. A moment later, the radio came on. Country-western.

Of course, she thought to herself, amused. What else would it be?

After rejoining her, he took a seat and stretched out his legs in front of him, crossing one leg over the other.

"Comfy?" he asked.

"Getting there." She squirmed a bit, conscious of how close they were to each other.

"Do you want to trade chairs?"

"It's not that. It's...this," she said with an all-encompassing wave. "Sitting in chairs in the back of your truck. It's new to me."

"You don't do this in New Jersey?"

"We do stuff. Like see movies. Go out to eat. Hang out at a friend's house. I take it you didn't do any of those things growing up?"

"Of course I did. I still do."

"What was the last movie you went to?"

"What's a movie?"

It took her a second to realize he was teasing, and he laughed at her rapidly changing expression. Then he motioned toward the rails. "They're bigger up close, don't you think?" he asked.

When Sophia turned, she saw a bull lumbering slowly toward them, not more than a few feet away, chest muscles rippling. Its size took her breath away; up close, it was nothing like viewing them in the arena.

"Holy crap," she said, not hiding the wonder in her tone. She leaned forward. "It's...huge." She turned toward him. "And you ride those things? Voluntarily?"

"When they let me."

"Was this what you wanted me to see?"

"Kind of," he said. "Actually, it's that one over there."

He pointed into the pen beyond, where a cream-colored bull stood, his ears and tail switching, but otherwise unmoving. One horn was lopsided, and even from a distance she could make out the web of scars on his side. Though he wasn't as large as some of the others, there was something wild and defiant in the way he stood, and she had the sense that he was challenging any of the others to come near him. She could hear his rough snorts breaking the silence of the night air.

When she turned back to Luke, she noticed a change in his

expression. He was staring at the bull, outwardly calm, but there was something else there, something she couldn't quite put her finger on.

"That's Big Ugly Critter," he said, his attention still on the bull. "That's what I was thinking about when I was standing out there. I was trying to find him."

"Is he one of the bulls you rode tonight?"

"No," he said. "But after a while, I realized that I couldn't leave here tonight without getting right up close to him. Which was strange, because when I got here, he was the last bull I wanted to see. That's why I parked my truck backwards. And if I had drawn him tonight, I don't know what I would have done."

She waited for him to continue, but he didn't. "I take it you've ridden him before."

"No," he said, shaking his head. "I've tried, though. Three times. He's what you call a rank bull. Only a couple of people have ever ridden him, and that was a few years back. He spins and kicks and shifts direction, and if he throws you, he tries to hook you for even trying to ride him in the first place. I've had nightmares about that bull. He scares me." He turned toward her, his face half in shadow. "That's something almost no one knows."

There was something haunted in his expression, something she hadn't expected.

"Somehow, I just can't imagine you being afraid of anything," she said quietly.

"Yeah, well... I'm human." He grinned. "I'm not too fond of lightning, either, if you're curious."

She sat up straighter. "I *like* lightning."

"It's different when you're out in the middle of a pasture, without any cover."

"I'll take your word on that."

"My turn now. I get to ask a question. Anything I want."

"Go ahead."

"How long were you dating Brian?" he asked.

She almost laughed, relieved. "That's it?" she asked, not waiting for an answer. "We started going out when I was a sophomore."

"He's a big fellow," he observed.

"He's on a lacrosse scholarship."

"He must be good."

"At lacrosse," she admitted. "Not so much in the boyfriend department."

"But you still went out with him for two years."

"Yeah, well..." She pulled her knees up and wrapped her arms around them. "Have you ever been in love?"

He raised his head, as if trying to find the answers in the stars. "I'm not sure."

"If you're not sure, then you probably weren't."

He considered this. "Okay."

"What? No argument?"

"Like I said, I'm not sure."

"Were you upset when it ended?"

He pressed his lips together, weighing his response. "Not really, but Angie wasn't either. It was just a high school thing. After graduation, I think both of us understood that we were on different paths. But we're still friends. She even invited me to her wedding. I had a lot of fun at the reception, hanging out with one of her bridesmaids."

Sophia looked toward the ground. "I loved Brian. I mean, before him, I had these little crushes, you know? Like when you write a boy's name on your folder and draw little hearts around it? I guess people tend to put their first loves on pedestals, and in the beginning, I was no different. I wasn't even sure why he wanted to go out with me—he's good-looking and a scholarship athlete, and he's popular and rich...I was so shocked when he singled me out for attention. And when we first started going out, he was so funny and charming. By the time he kissed me, I was already falling for him. I fell hard, and then..." She trailed off, not wanting to go into the details. "Anyway, I broke up with him right after school started up this year. Turns out he was sleeping with another girl from back home, all summer long."

"And now he wants you back."

"Yeah, but why? Is it because he wants me, or is it because he can't have me?"

"Are you asking me?"

"I'm asking for your perspective. Not because I'll take him back, because I won't. I'm asking you as a guy."

When he spoke, his words were measured. "A bit of both, probably. But from what I can tell, I'd guess it's because he realized he made a big mistake."

She absorbed the unspoken compliment in silence, appreciating his understated ways. "I'm glad I got to watch you ride tonight," she said, knowing she meant it. "I thought you did really well."

"I got lucky. I felt pretty rusty out there. It's been a while since I've ridden."

"How long?"

He brushed at his jeans, buying time before he answered. "Eighteen months."

For an instant, she thought she'd heard him wrong. "You haven't ridden in a year and a half?"

"No."

"Why not?"

She had the sense he was debating how to answer. "My last ride before tonight was a bad one."

"How bad?"

"Pretty bad."

At his response, Sophia felt it click into place. "Big Ugly Critter," she said.

"That's the one," he admitted. Warding off her next question, he focused on her again. "So you live in a sorority, huh?"

She noted the change of subject but was content to follow his lead. "It's my third year in the house."

His eyes glinted mischievously. "Is it really like people say? All pajama parties and pillow fights?"

"Of course not," she said. "It's more like negligees and pillow fights."

"I think I'd like living in a place like that."

"I'll bet." She laughed.

"So what's it really like?" he asked with genuine curiosity.

"It's a bunch of girls who live together, and most of the time, it's okay. Other times, not so much. It's a world with its own set of rules and hierarchy, which is fine if you buy into those things. But I've never really drunk the Kool-Aid... I'm from New Jersey, and I grew up working in a struggling family business. The only reason I can even afford to go to Wake is because I'm on a full academic scholarship. There aren't a lot of people in the house like me. I'm not saying that everyone else is rich, because they aren't. And a lot of the girls in the house had jobs in high school. It's just that..."

"You're different," he said, finishing for her. "I bet many of your sorority sisters wouldn't be caught dead checking out a bull in the middle of a cow pasture."

I wouldn't be so sure about that, she thought. He was the winner of tonight's rodeo, and he definitely qualified as eye candy, in Marcia's words. For some of the girls in the house, that would have been more than enough.

"You said you have horses at your ranch?" she asked.

"We do," he said.

"Do you ride them a lot?"

"Most days," he answered. "When I'm checking on the cattle. I could use the Gator, but I grew up doing it on horseback, and that's what I'm used to."

"Do you ever just ride for fun?"

"Every now and then. Why? Do you ride?"

"No," she said. "I've never ridden. There aren't too many

horses in Jersey City. But growing up, I always wanted to. I think all little girls do." She paused. "What's your horse's name?"

"Horse."

Sophia waited for the joke, but it didn't come. "You call your horse 'Horse'?"

"He doesn't mind."

"You should give him a noble name. Like Prince or Chief or something."

"It might confuse him now."

"Trust me. Anything is better than Horse. It's like naming a dog Dog."

"I have a dog named Dog. Australian Cattle Dog." He turned, his expression utterly matter-of-fact. "Great herder."

"And your mom didn't complain?"

"My mom named him."

She shook her head. "My roommate is never going to believe this."

"What? That my animals have—in your mind—strange names?"

"Among other things," she teased.

"So tell me about college," he said, and for the next half hour, she filled in the details about her daily life. Even to her ears, it sounded dull—classes, studying, social life on the weekends—but he seemed interested, asking questions now and then, but for the most part allowing her to ramble. She described the sorority—especially Mary-Kate—and a little about Brian and how he'd been behaving since school started. As they talked, people began to drift through the lot, some threading among the trucks with a tip of their hats, others stopping to congratulate Luke on his rides.

As the evening rolled on and the temperature dropped, Sophia felt goose bumps form on her arms. She crossed her arms, hunkering down in her chair.

"I've got a blanket in the cab if you need it," he offered.

"Thanks," she said, "but that's okay. I should probably be getting back. I don't want my friends to leave without me."

"I figured," he said. "I'll walk you back."

He helped her down from the pickup and they retraced their earlier path, the music growing louder as they approached. Soon they were standing outside the barn, which was only slightly less crowded than it had been when she'd left. Somehow it felt as though she'd been gone for hours.

"Do you want me to come in with you? In case Brian is still around?"

"No," she said. "I'll be fine. I'll stick close to my roommate."

He studied the ground, then raised his eyes. "I had a nice time talking to you, Sophia."

"Me too," she said. "And thanks again. For earlier, I mean."

"I was glad to help."

He nodded and turned, Sophia watching as he started away. It would have ended there—and later she would wonder whether she should have let it—but instead she took a step after him, the words coming out automatically.

"Luke," she called. "Wait."

When he faced her, she raised her chin slightly. "You said you were going to show me your barn. Supposedly, it's more rickety than this one."

He smiled, flashing his dimples. "One o'clock tomorrow?" he asked. "I've got some things to do in the morning. How about if I pick you up?"

"I can drive," she said. "Just text me the directions."

"I don't have your number."

"What's yours?"

When he told her, she dialed it, hearing the ring a few feet away. She ended the call and stared at him, wondering what had gotten into her.

"Now you do."

5

Ira

It's growing even darker now, and the late winter weather has continued to worsen. The winds have risen to a shriek, and the windows of the car are thick with snow. I am slowly being buried alive, and I think again about the car. It is cream colored, a 1988 Chrysler, and I wonder whether it will be spotted once the sun has come up. Or whether it will simply blend into the surroundings.

"You must not think these things," I hear Ruth say. "Someone will come. It won't be long now."

She's sitting where she'd been before, but she looks different now. Slightly older and wearing a different dress...but the dress seems vaguely familiar. I am struggling to recall a memory of her like this when I hear her voice again.

"It was the summer of 1940. July."

It takes a moment before it comes back. *Yes*, I think to myself. *That's right. The summer after I'd finished my first year of college.* "I remember," I say.

"Now you remember," she teases. "But you needed my help. You used to remember everything."

"I used to be younger."

"I was younger once, too."

"You still are."

"Not anymore," she says, not hiding the echo of sadness. "I was young back then."

I blink, trying and failing to bring her into focus. She was seventeen years old. "This is the dress you wore when I finally asked you to walk with me."

"No," she says to me. "This is the dress I wore when I asked you."

I smile. This is a story we often told at dinner parties, the story of our first date. Over the years, Ruth and I have learned to tell it well. Here in the car, she begins the story in the same way she'd always done for our guests. She settles her hands in her lap and sighs, her expression alternating between feigned disappointment and confusion. "By then, I knew you were never going to say a word to me. You had been home from university for a month, and still you never approached me, so after Shabbat services had ended, I walked up to you. I looked you right in the eyes and I said, 'I am no longer seeing David Epstein.'"

"I remember," I say.

"Do you remember what you said to me? You said, 'Oh,' and then you blushed and looked at your feet."

"I think you're mistaken."

"You know this happened. Then I told you that I would like you to walk me home."

"I remember that your father wasn't happy about it."

"He thought David would become a fine young man. He did not know you."

"Nor did he like me," I interject. "I could feel him staring at the back of my head while we walked. That's why I kept my hands in my pockets."

She tilts her head, evaluating me. "Is that why, even when we were walking, you said nothing to me?"

"I wanted him to know my intentions were honorable."

"When I got home, he asked if you were mute. I had to remind him again that you were an excellent student in college, that your marks were very high, and that you would graduate in only

three years. Whenever I spoke with your mother, she made sure
I knew that."

My mother. The matchmaker.

"It would have been different had your parents not been following us," I say. "If they hadn't been acting as chaperones, I
would have swept you off your feet. I would have taken your hand
and serenaded you. I would have picked you a bouquet of flowers.
You would have swooned."

"Yes, I know. The young Frank Sinatra again. You have said
this already."

"I'm just trying to keep the story accurate. There was a girl at
school who had her eye on me, you know. Her name was Sarah."

Ruth nods, looking unconcerned. "Your mother told me about
her, too. She also said that you had not called or written to her
since you had returned. I knew it was not serious."

"How often did you talk to my mother?"

"In the beginning, not too much, and my mother was always
there. But a few months before you came home, I asked your mother
if she would help me with my English and we began to meet once
or twice a week. There were still many words I did not know, and
she could explain their meaning in a way that I could understand.
I used to say that I became a teacher because of my father, and that
was true, but I also became a teacher because of your mother. She
was very patient with me. She would tell me stories, and that is
another way she helped me with the language. She said I must learn
to do this myself, because everyone in the South tells stories."

I smile. "What stories did she tell?"

"She told stories about you."

I know this, of course. There are few secrets left in any long
marriage.

"Which was your favorite?"

She thinks for a moment. "The one from when you were a
little boy," she finally says. "Your mother told me that you found

an injured squirrel, and despite the fact that your father refused to let you keep it in the store, you hid it in a box behind her sewing machine and nursed it back to health. Once it was better, you released it in the park, and even though it ran off, you returned every day to look for it, in case it needed your help again. She would tell me that it was a sign that your heart was pure, that you formed deep attachments, and that once you loved something—or someone—you would never stop."

Like I said, the matchmaker.

It was only after we were married that my mother admitted to me that she'd been "teaching" Ruth by telling her stories about me. At the time, I felt ambivalent about this. I wanted to believe that I'd won Ruth's heart on my own, and I said as much to her. My mother laughed and told me she was only doing what mothers have always done for their sons. Then she told me that it was my job to prove that she hadn't been lying, because that's what sons were supposed to do for their mothers.

"And here I thought I was charming."

"You became charming, once you were no longer afraid of me. But that did not happen on that first walk. When we finally reached the factory where we lived, I said, 'Thank you for walking with me, Ira,' and all you said was, 'You are welcome.' Then you turned around, nodded at my parents, and left."

"But I was better the next week."

"Yes. You talked about the weather. You said, 'It sure is cloudy,' three times. Twice you added, 'I wonder if it will rain later.' Your conversational skills were dazzling. By the way, your mother taught me the meaning of that word."

"And yet, you still wanted to walk with me."

"Yes," she says, looking right at me.

"And in early August, I asked if I could buy you a chocolate soda. Just like David Epstein used to do."

She smooths an errant tendril of her hair, her eyes holding

steady on my own. "And I remember telling you that the choco-late soda was the most delicious that I had ever tasted."

That was our beginning. It's not a thrilling tale of adventure or the kind of fairy-tale romance portrayed in movies, but it felt like divine intervention. That she saw something special in me made no sense at all, but I was bright enough to seize the opportunity. After that, we spent most of our free time together, although there wasn't much left of it. By then, the end of summer was already approaching. Across the Atlantic, France had already surrendered and the Battle of Britain was under way, but even so, the war in those last few weeks seemed far away. We went for walks and talked endlessly in the park; as David once did, I continued to buy her chocolate sodas. Twice, I brought Ruth to a movie, and once, I took both her and her mother to lunch. And always, I would walk her home from the synagogue, her parents trailing ten paces behind, allowing us a bit more privacy.

"Your parents eventually came to like me."

"Yes." She nods. "But that is because I liked you. You made me laugh, and you were the first to help me do that in this country. My father would always ask what you had said that I found so funny, and I would tell him that it was less about what you said than the way you would say things. Like the face you made when you described your mother's cooking."

"My mother could burn water and yet never learned how to boil an egg."

"She was not that bad."

"I grew up learning how to eat and hold my breath at the same time. Why do you think my father and I were as thin as straws?"

She shakes her head. "If your mother only knew you said such terrible things."

"It wouldn't have mattered. She knew she wasn't a good cook."

She is quiet for a moment. "I wish we could have had more time that summer. I was very sad when you left to go back to university."

"Even if I'd stayed, we couldn't have been together. You were leaving, too. You were heading off to Wellesley."

She nods, but her expression is distant. "I was very fortunate for the opportunity. My father knew a professor there, and he helped me in many ways. But the year was still very hard for me. Even though you had not written to Sarah, I knew you would see her again, and I worried that you might still develop feelings for her. And I was afraid that Sarah would see the same things in you that I did, and that she would use her charms to take you away from me."

"That would have never happened."

"I know this now, but I did not know it then."

I shift my head slightly, and all at once there are flashes of white in the corners of my eyes, a railroad spike near my hairline. I close my eyes, waiting for it to pass, but it seems to take forever. I concentrate, trying to breathe slowly, and eventually it begins to recede. The world comes back in bits and pieces, and I think again about the accident. My face is sticky and the deflated air bag is coated with dust and blood. The blood scares me, but despite this, there is magic in the car, a magic that has brought Ruth back to me. I swallow, trying to wet the back of my throat, but I can make no moisture and it feels like sandpaper.

I know Ruth is worried about me. In the lengthening shadows, I see her watching me, this woman I have always adored. I think back again to 1940, trying to distract her from her fears.

"And yet despite your concerns about Sarah," I say, "you didn't come home in December to see me."

In my mind's eye, I see Ruth roll her eyes—her standard response to my complaint. "I did not come home because I could not afford the train ticket," she says. "You know this. I was working at a hotel, and leaving would have been impossible. The scholarship only covered tuition, so I had to pay for everything else."

"Excuses," I tease.

She ignores me, as always. "Sometimes, I would work at the desk all night and still have to go to class in the morning. It was all I could do not to fall asleep with my book open on the desk. It was not easy. By the time I finished my first year, I was very much looking forward to coming home for the summer, if only to go straight to bed."

"But then I ruined your plans by showing up at the train station."

"Yes." She smiles. "My plan was ruined."

"I hadn't seen you in nine months," I point out. "I wanted to surprise you."

"And you did. On the train, I wondered whether you would be there, but I did not want to be disappointed. And then, when the train pulled into the station and I saw you from the window, my heart gave a little jump. You were very handsome."

"My mother had made me a new suit."

She emits a wistful laugh, still lost in the memory. "And you had brought my parents with you."

I would shrug, but I am afraid to move. "I knew they'd want to see you, too, so I borrowed my father's car."

"That was gallant."

"Or selfish. Otherwise, you might have gone straight home."

"Yes, maybe," she teases. "But of course, you had thought of that, too. You had asked my father if you could take me to dinner. He said that you had come to the factory while he was working to ask his permission."

"I didn't want to give you a reason to say no."

"I would not have said no, even if you had not asked my father."

"I know this now, but I didn't know it then," I say, echoing her earlier words. We are, and always have been, the same in so many ways. "When you stepped off the train that night, I remember thinking that the station should have been filled with photographers, waiting to snap your picture. You looked like a movie star."

"I had been in the train for twelve hours. I looked terrible."

This is a lie and we both know it. Ruth was beautiful, and even well into her fifties, men's eyes would follow her when she walked into a room.

"It was all I could do not to kiss you."

"That is not true," she counters. "You would never have done such a thing in front of my parents."

She's right, of course. Instead, I stood back, allowing her parents to greet and visit with her first; only then, after a few minutes, did I approach her. Ruth reads my thoughts. "That night was the first time my father really understood what I saw in you. Later, he told me that he had observed that you were not only hardworking and kind, but a gentleman as well."

"He still didn't think I was good enough for you."

"No father thinks any man is good enough for his daughter."

"Except David Epstein."

"Yes," she teases. "Except for him."

I smile, even though it sends up another electric flare inside me. "At dinner, I couldn't stop staring at you. You were so much more beautiful than I remembered."

"But we were strangers again," she says. "It took some time for the conversation to be easy, like it was the summer before. Until the walk home, I think."

"I was playing hard to get."

"No, you were being you," she says. "And yet, you were not you. You had become a man in the year we had been apart. You even took my hand as you walked me to the door, something you had never done before. I remember because it made my arm tingle, and then you stopped and looked at me and I knew then exactly what was going to happen."

"I kissed you good night," I say.

"No," Ruth says to me, her voice dipping to a seductive register. "You kissed me, yes, but it was not just good night. Even then, I could feel the promise in it, the promise that you would kiss me just like that, forever."

In the car, I can still recall that moment—the touch of her lips against my own, the sense of excitement and pure wonder as I hold her in my arms. But suddenly the world begins to spin. Hard spins, as if I'm on a runaway roller coaster, and all at once, Ruth vanishes from my arms. Instead, my head presses hard against the steering wheel and I blink rapidly, willing the world to stop spinning. I need water, sure that a single sip will be enough to stop it. But there is no water and I succumb to the dizziness before everything goes black.

When I wake, the world comes back slowly. I squint in the darkness, but Ruth is no longer in the passenger seat beside me. I am desperate to have her back. I concentrate, trying to conjure her image, but nothing comes and my throat seems to close in on itself.

Looking back, Ruth had been right about the changes in me. That summer, the world had changed and I understood that any time I spent with Ruth should be regarded as precious. War, after all, was everywhere. Japan and China had been at war for four years, and throughout the spring of 1941, more countries had fallen to the Wehrmacht, including Yugoslavia and Greece. The English had retreated in the face of Rommel's Afrika Korps all the way to Egypt. The Suez Canal was threatened, and though I didn't know it then, German panzers and infantry were in position to lead the imminent invasion of Russia. I wondered how long America's isolation would last.

I had never dreamed of being a soldier; I had never fired a gun. I was not, nor ever had been, a fighter of any sort, but even so, I loved my country, and I spent much of that year trying to imagine a future distorted by war. And I wasn't alone in trying to come to grips with this new world. Over the summer, my father read two or three newspapers a day and listened to the radio continuously; my mother volunteered for the Red Cross. Ruth's parents were especially frightened, and I often found them huddled at the table, speaking in low voices. They had not heard from anyone in their family for months. It was because of the war, others would whisper. But even in North Carolina, rumors had begun to circulate about what was happening to the Jews in Poland.

Despite the fears and whispers of war, or maybe because of them, I always regarded the summer of 1941 as my last summer of innocence. It was the summer in which Ruth and I spent nearly all our free time together, falling ever more deeply in love. She would visit me in the shop or I would visit her at the factory—she answered phones for her uncle that summer—and in the evenings, we would stroll beneath the stars. Every Sunday, we picnicked in the park near our home, nothing extravagant, just enough to hold us over until we had dinner together later. In the evenings, she would sometimes come to my parents' home or I would visit hers, where we would listen to classical music on the phonograph. When the summer drew to a close and Ruth boarded the train for Massachusetts, I retreated to a corner of the station, my face in my hands, because I knew that nothing would ever be the same. I knew the time was coming when I would eventually be called up to fight.

And a few months later, on December 7, 1941, I was proven right.

🌱

Throughout the night, I continue to fade in and out. The wind and snow remain constant. In those moments when I am awake, I wonder if it will ever be light; I wonder if I will ever see a sunrise again. But mostly I continue to concentrate on the past, hoping that Ruth will reappear. Without her, I think to myself, I am already dead.

When I graduated in May 1942, I returned home, but I did

not recognize the shop. Where once there were suits hanging from the racks out front, there were thirty sewing machines and thirty women, making uniforms for the military. Bolts of heavy cloth were arriving twice a day, filling the back room entirely. The space next door, which had been vacant for years, had been taken over by my father, and that space was large enough to house sixty sewing machines. My mother oversaw production while my father worked the phones, kept the books, and ensured delivery to the army and marine bases that were springing up throughout the South.

I knew I was about to be drafted. My order number was low enough to make selection inevitable, and that meant either the army or the marines, battles in the trenches. The brave were drawn to do such things, but as I mentioned, I was not brave. On the train ride home, I'd already decided to enlist in the U.S. Army Air Corps. Somehow, the idea of fighting in the air seemed less frightening than fighting on the ground. In time, however, I would be proven wrong about this.

On the evening I arrived home, I told my parents as we stood in the kitchen. My mother immediately began to wring her hands. My father said nothing, but later, as he jotted entries into his bookkeeping ledger, I thought I saw the gleam of moisture in his eyes.

I had also come to another decision. Before Ruth returned to Greensboro, I met with her father, and I told him how much his daughter meant to me. Two days later, I drove her parents to the station just as I had the previous year. Again, I let them greet her first, and again, I took Ruth out to dinner. It was there, while eating in a largely empty restaurant, that I told her my plans. Unlike my parents, she didn't shed a tear. Not then.

I didn't bring her home right away. Instead, after dinner we went to the park, near the spot where we'd shared so many picnics. It was a moonless night, and the lights in the park had been shut off. As I slipped my hand into hers, I could barely make out her features.

I touched the ring in my pocket, the one I had told her father I wanted to offer his daughter. I had debated long about this, not because I wasn't sure about my own intentions, but because I wasn't sure about hers. But I was in love with her, and heading off to war, and I wanted to know she would be here when I returned. Dropping to one knee, I told her how much she meant to me. I told her that I couldn't imagine life without her, and I asked her to be my wife. As I spoke the words, I offered Ruth the ring. She didn't say anything right away, and I'd be lying if I said I wasn't scared in that moment. But then, reading my thoughts, she took the ring and slipped it on before reaching for my hand. I rose, standing before her under a star-filled sky. She slipped her arms around me. "Yes," she whispered. We stood together, just the two of us, holding each other for what seemed like hours. Even now, almost seventy years later, I can feel her warmth despite the chill in the car. I can smell her perfume, something floral and delicate. I draw a long breath, trying to hold on to it, just as I held on to her that night.

Later, our arms entwined, we strolled through the park, talking about our future together. Her voice brimmed with love and excitement, yet it is this part of the evening that has always filled me with regret. I am reminded of the man I was never able to be; of the dreams that never came true. As I feel the familiar wave of shame wash over me, I catch the scent of her perfume once more. It is stronger now, and it occurs to me that it's not a memory, that I can smell it in the car. I am afraid to open my eyes, but I do so anyway. At first, everything is blurry and dark and I wonder if I will be able to see anything at all.

But then, finally, I see her. She is translucent, ghostlike again, but it is Ruth. She is here—she came back to me, I think—and my heart surges inside my chest. I want to reach for her, to take her in my arms, but I know this is impossible, so I concentrate instead. I try to bring her into better focus, and as my eyes adjust, I notice that her dress is the color of cream, with ruffles down the front. It is the dress she wore the night I proposed.

But Ruth is not happy with me. "No, Ira," she suddenly says. There is no mistaking the warning in her tone. "We must not talk about this. The dinner, yes. The proposal, yes. But not this."

Even now, I can't believe she's come back. "I know it makes you sad—," I begin.

"It does not make me sad," she objects. "You are the one who is sad over this. You have carried this sadness with you ever since that night. I should never have said the things I did."

"But you did."

At this, she bows her head. Her hair, unlike mine, is brown and thick, rich with the possibilities of life.

"That was the first night I told you that I loved you," she says. "I told you that I wanted to marry you. I promised that I would wait for you and that we would marry as soon as you returned."

"But that's not all you said…"

"It is the only thing that matters," she says, lifting her chin. "We were happy, yes? For all the years we were together?"

"Yes."

"And you loved me?"

"Always."

"Then I want you to hear what I am saying to you, Ira," she says, her impatience barely in check. She leans forward. "I never once regretted that we married. You made me happy and you made me laugh, and if I could do it all over again, I would not hesitate. Look at our life, at the trips we took, the adventures we had. As your father used to say, we shared the longest ride together, this thing called life, and mine has been filled with joy because of you. Unlike other couples, we did not even argue."

"We argued," I protest.

"Not real arguments," she insists. "Not the kind that mean anything. Yes, I would become upset when you forgot to take out the garbage, but that is not a real argument. That is nothing. It passes like a leaf blown by the window. It is over and done and it is forgotten quickly."

"You forget—"

"I remember," she says, cutting me off, knowing what I was about to say. "But we found a way to heal. Together. Just as we always did."

Despite her words, I still feel the regret, a deep-seated ache I've carried with me forever.

"I'm sorry," I finally say. "I want you to know that I've always been sorry."

"Do not say these things," she says, her voice beginning to crack.

"I can't help it. We talked for hours that night."

"Yes," she admits. "We talked about the summers we spent together. We talked about school, we talked about the fact that you would one day take over your father's shop. And later that night, when I was at home, I lay awake in bed looking at the ring for hours. The next morning, I showed it to my mother and she was happy for me. Even my father was pleased."

I know she's trying to distract me, but it does no good. I continue to stare at her. "We also talked about you that night. About your dreams."

When I say this, Ruth turns away. "Yes," she says. "We talked about my dreams."

"You told me that you planned to become a teacher and that we'd buy a house that was close to both of our parents."

"Yes."

"And you said that we would travel. We would visit New York and Boston, maybe even Vienna."

"Yes," she says again.

I close my eyes, feeling the weight of an ancient sorrow. "And you told me you wanted children. That more than anything, you wanted to be a mother. You wanted two girls and two boys, because you always wanted a home like that of your cousins, which was busy and noisy all the time. You used to love to visit them because you were always happy there. You wanted this more than anything."

At this, her shoulders seem to sag and she turns toward me. "Yes," she whispers, "I admit I wanted these things."

The words nearly break my heart, and I feel something crumble inside me. The truth is often a terrible thing, and I wish again that I were someone else. But it is too late now, too late to change anything. I am old and alone and I'm dying a little more with each passing hour. I'm tired, more tired than I've ever been.

"You should have married another man," I whisper.

She shakes her head, and in an act of kindness that reminds me of our life together, she inches closer to me. Gently, she traces a finger along my jaw and then kisses the top of my head. "I could never have another," she says. "And we are done talking about this. You need to rest now. You need to sleep again."

"No," I mumble. I try to shake my head but can't, the agony making it impossible. "I want to stay awake. I want to be with you."

"Do not worry. I will be here when you wake."

"But you were gone before."

"I was not gone. I was here and I will always be here."

"How can you be so sure?"

She kisses me again before answering. "Because," she says, her voice tender, "I am always with you, Ira."

6

Luke

Getting out of bed had been painful earlier in the morning, and as he reached up to brush Horse's neck and withers, he felt his back scream in protest. The ibuprofen had taken some of the pain's sharp edge away, but he still found it difficult to lift his arm any higher than his shoulder. While he had been checking the cattle at dawn, even turning his head from side to side had made him wince, making him glad that José was there to help around the ranch.

After hanging the brush, he poured some oats in a pail for Horse and then started toward the old farmhouse, knowing that it would take another day or two before he recovered fully. Aches and pains were normal after any ride, and he'd certainly been through worse. It wasn't a question of *if* a bull rider got injured, but rather *when* and *how badly*. Over the years, not counting his ride on Big Ugly Critter, he'd had his ribs broken twice and his lung collapsed, and he'd torn both his ACL and MCL, one in each knee. He'd shattered his left wrist in 2005, and both his shoulders had been dislocated. Four years ago, he'd ridden in the PBR World Championships—Professional Bull Riders—with a broken ankle, using a special-formed cowboy boot to hold the still-broken bones in place. And of course, he'd sustained his share of concussions from being thrown. For most of his life, however, he'd wanted nothing more than to keep riding.

Like Sophia said, maybe he was crazy.

Peering through the kitchen window above the sink, he saw his mom hurry past. He wondered when things would get back to normal between them. In recent weeks, she'd nearly finished her own breakfast before he showed up, in what was an obvious attempt to avoid talking to him. She was using his presence to demonstrate that she was still upset; she wanted him to feel the weight of her silence as she picked up her plate and left him alone at the table. Most of all, she wanted him to feel guilty. He supposed he could have had breakfast at his own place—he'd built a small house just on the other side of the grove—but he knew from experience that denying her those opportunities would have only made things worse. She'd come around, he knew. Eventually, anyway.

He stepped up on the cracked concrete blocks as he gave the place a quick scan. The roof was good—he'd replaced it a couple of years back—but he needed to get around to painting the place. Unfortunately, he'd have to sand every plank first, almost tripling the amount of time that it would take, time he didn't have. The farmhouse had been built in the late 1800s, and over the years it had been painted and repainted so many times that the coating was probably thicker than the wood itself. Now, it was peeling pretty much all over and rotting beneath the eaves. Speaking of which, he'd have to get around to fixing those, too.

He entered the small screened-in mudroom and wiped his boots on the mat. The door opened with the usual squeak, and he was struck by the familiar aroma of freshly cooked bacon and fried potatoes. His mom stood over the stove, stirring a pan of scrambled eggs. The stove was new—he'd bought that for her for Christmas last year—but the cabinets were original to the house, and the countertop had been around for as long as he could remember. So had the linoleum floor. The oak table, built by his grandfather, had dulled with age; in the far corner, the ancient woodstove was radiating heat. It reminded him that he needed to split some firewood. With cold weather coming, he needed to replenish the stack sooner rather than later. The woodstove warmed not only the kitchen, but the entire house. He decided he'd get to it after breakfast, before Sophia came by.

As he hung his hat on the rack, he noted that his mom appeared tired. No wonder—by the time he'd gotten Horse saddled and ridden out, his mom had already been hard at work cleaning the stalls.

"Morning, Mom," he said, moving to the sink, keeping his voice neutral. He began scrubbing his hands. "Need some help?"

"It's just about ready," she answered without looking up. "But you can put some bread in the toaster. It's on the counter behind you."

He dropped the bread slices in the toaster, then poured himself a cup of coffee. His mom kept her back to him, but he could feel her radiating the same aura he'd come to expect in recent weeks. *Feel guilty, you bad son. I'm your mother. Don't you care about my feelings?*

Yes, of course I care about your feelings, he thought to himself. *That's why I'm doing what I'm doing.* But he said nothing. After almost a quarter century on the ranch together, they'd become masters in the art of silent conversation.

He took another sip of coffee, listening to the clink of the spatula in the pan.

"No problems this morning," he said instead. "I checked the stitches on the calf that got caught up in the barbed wire, and she's doing fine."

"Good." Having set aside the spatula, she reached up into the cabinets and pulled down some plates. "Let's just serve up at the stove, okay?"

He set his coffee cup on the table, then retrieved the jelly and the butter from the refrigerator. By the time he'd served up, his mom was already at the table. He grabbed the toast, handed her one of the pieces, then moved the coffeepot to the table as well.

"We need to get the pumpkins ready this week," she reminded him, reaching for the pot. No eye contact, no morning hug...not that he'd expected it. "And we've got to get the maze set up, too. The hay will be arriving Tuesday. And you have to carve a bunch of pumpkins."

Half of the pumpkin crop had already been sold to the First Baptist Church in King, but they opened the ranch on the weekends for people to buy the remainder. One of the highlights for the kids—and thus a draw for the adults—was a maze built out of hay bales. His father had sparked to the idea when Luke was young, and over the years the maze had grown increasingly complex. Walking through had become something of a local tradition.

"I'll take care of it," he said. "Is the layout still in the desk drawer?"

"Assuming you put it back last year, it should be."

Luke buttered and jellied his toast, neither of them saying anything.

In time, his mother sighed. "You got in late last night," she said. She reached for the butter and jelly when he was finished with them.

"You were up? I didn't notice any lights on."

"I was sleeping. But I woke up just as your truck was pulling in."

He doubted that was the complete truth. The windows in her bedroom didn't face the drive, which meant she would have been in the living room. Which also meant she'd been waiting up, worried about him.

"I stayed late with a couple of friends. They talked me into it."

She kept her focus on her plate. "I figured."

"Did you get my text?"

"I got it," she said, adding nothing more. No questions about how the ride went, no questions about how he felt, no concern about the aches and pains she knew he was experiencing.

Instead, her aura expanded, filling the room. Heartache and anger dripped from the ceiling, seeped from the walls. He had to admit, she was pretty good at administering the guilt trip.

"Do you want to talk about it?" he finally asked.

For the first time, she looked across the table at him. "Not really."

Okay, he thought. But despite her anger, he still missed talking to her. "Can I ask you a question, then?"

He could practically hear the gears beginning to turn as she readied herself for battle. Ready to leave him alone at the table while she ate on the porch.

"What size shoe do you wear?" he asked.

Her fork froze in midair. "My shoe size?"

"Someone might be coming by later," he said. He shoveled some eggs onto his fork. "And she might need to borrow some boots. If we go riding."

For the first time in weeks, she couldn't hide her interest. "Are you talking about a girl?"

He nodded, continuing to eat. "Her name is Sophia. I met her last night. She said she wanted to check out the barn."

His mom blinked. "Why does she care about the barn?"

"I don't know. It was her idea."

"Who is she?" Luke detected a flicker of curiosity in his mother's expression.

"She's a senior at Wake Forest. She's from New Jersey. And if we go riding, she might need boots. That's why I was asking about your shoe size."

Her confusion let him know that for the first time in forever, she was thinking about something other than the ranch. Or bull riding. Or the list of things she wanted to finish before the sun went down. But the effect was only temporary, and she concentrated on her plate again. In her own way, she was just as stubborn as he was. "Seven and a half. There's an old pair in my closet she's welcome to use. If they fit."

"Thanks," he said. "I was going to split some wood before she gets here, unless there's something else you want me to do."

"Just the irrigation," she said. "The second pasture needs some water."

"I got it going this morning. But I'll turn it off before she gets here."

She pushed a pile of eggs around on her plate. "I'm going to need your help next weekend with the customers."

It was the way she said it that made him realize she'd been planning to bring it up all along, that it was the reason she'd stayed at the table with him. "You know I'm not going to be here on Saturday," he said deliberately. "I'll be in Knoxville."

"To ride again," she said.

"It's the last event of the year."

"Then why go? It's not like the points are going to matter." Her voice was starting to acquire a bitter edge.

"It's not about the points. I don't want to head into next season feeling unprepared." Again, the conversation died away, leaving only the sounds of forks against plates. "I won last night," he remarked.

"Good for you."

"I'll put the check in your account on Monday."

"Keep it," she snapped. "I don't want it."

"And the ranch?"

When she looked at him, he saw less anger than he'd expected. Instead he saw resignation, maybe even sadness, underlined by a weariness that made her look older than she really was. "I don't care about the ranch," she said. "I care about my son."

*

After breakfast, Luke chopped wood for an hour and a half, replenishing the pile on the side of his mom's house. Since breakfast, she'd been avoiding him again, and though it bothered him, the simple activity of swinging the ax made him feel better, loosening his muscles and freeing him to think about Sophia.

Already, she had a hold on him—he couldn't remember the last time that happened. Not since Angie, at least, but even that wasn't the same. He'd cared about Angie, but he couldn't remember dwelling on her the way he was on Sophia. Until last night, in fact, he couldn't even imagine it happening. After his dad died, it took everything he had to concentrate enough to ride at all. When the grief eventually faded to the point where he could go a day or two without thinking about his dad, he poured himself into becoming the best rider he could. During his years on the tour, it had been all he could think about, and with every success, he'd raised the bar, becoming even more intense in his pursuit to win it all.

That kind of commitment didn't leave a lot of room for relationships, except the short-term, meaningless kind. The past year and a half had changed that. No more travel, no practice, and although there was always something to do on the ranch, he was used to that. Those who succeeded in the business of ranching were good at prioritizing, and he and his mom had a pretty good handle on it. That had given him more time to think, more time to wonder about the future, and for the first time in his life, he sometimes finished his day yearning for someone to talk to over dinner, other than his mom.

While it didn't dominate his thoughts, he couldn't deny the urge to try to find someone. The only problem was that he hadn't the slightest idea how to go about doing such a thing...and now that he was riding again, he'd gotten busy and distracted.

Then, out of the blue and when he'd least expected it, he'd met Sophia. Although he'd spent most of the morning thinking about her and wondering what it would feel like to run his hands through her hair, he suspected it wouldn't last. They had nothing in common. She was in college—studying art history, of all things—and after graduation, she'd move away to work in a museum in some faraway city. On its face, they had no chance at all, but the image of her sitting in the bed of his truck under the stars kept replaying in his mind, and he found himself wondering if maybe, just maybe, there was a chance that they could somehow make it work.

He reminded himself that they barely knew each other and that he was probably reading too much into it. Nonetheless, he had to admit he was nervous at the prospect of her visit.

After chopping the firewood, he straightened up around the house and rode the Gator out to turn off the irrigation, then made a quick trip to the store to restock the fridge. He wasn't sure if she'd come inside, but if she did, he wanted to be prepared.

Even as he got into the shower, though, he found he couldn't stop thinking about her. Lifting his face into the spray, he wondered what on earth had gotten into him.

✦

At a quarter past one, Luke was sitting in a rocker on the front porch of his home when he heard the sound of a car slowly pulling up the long dirt drive, dust rising into the treetops. Dog was at his feet, next to the cowboy boots Luke had found in his mom's closet. Dog sat up, his ears cocked before glancing at Luke.

"Go get 'em," he urged, and Dog immediately trotted off. Luke grabbed the boots and stepped off the porch onto the grass. He waved his hat as he approached the main drive, hoping she'd spot him through the shrubbery that lined the drive. Heading straight would lead her to the main farmhouse; to get to his place, she'd need to turn off through an opening in the trees and follow a worn grassy track. It was hard to spot unless you knew where it was, and it would have benefited from some gravel surfacing, but that was yet another item on the to-do list he'd never quite gotten around to. At the time, he hadn't thought it all that important, but now, with Sophia approaching and his heart beating faster than usual, he wished he had.

Thankfully, Dog knew what to do. He'd run ahead and was standing in the main drive like a sentry until Sophia brought the car to a stop, then he barked authoritatively before trotting back toward Luke. Luke waved his hat again, eventually catching Sophia's attention, and she turned the car. A moment later, she pulled to a stop beneath a towering magnolia tree.

She stepped out, wearing tight faded jeans that were torn at the knees, looking as fresh as summer itself. With almost catlike eyes and faintly Slavic bone structure, she was even more striking in sunlight than she'd been the night before, and all he could do was stare at her. He had the strange feeling that in the future, whenever he thought about her, this would be the image he recalled. She was too beautiful, too refined and exotic, for this country setting, but when she broke into that wide, friendly smile, he felt something clear inside, like the sun breaking through the mist.

"Sorry I'm late," she called out as she closed the door, sounding nowhere near as nervous as he felt.

"It's all right," he said, replacing his hat and shoving his hands in his pockets.

"I made a wrong turn and had to backtrack a bit. But I had a chance to drive around King."

He shuffled his feet. "And?"

"You were right. It's not all that fancy, but the people are nice. An old guy on a bench got me headed in the right direction," she said. "How are you?"

"I'm good," he said, finally looking up.

If she could tell how unnerved he was, she gave no sign. "Did you finish all you needed to get done?"

"I checked the cattle, split some firewood, picked up a few things at the store."

"Sounds exciting," she said. Shading her eyes, she turned slowly in a circle, surveying her surroundings. By then, Dog had trotted up and introduced himself, twining around her legs. "I take it this is Dog."

"The one and only."

She squatted down, scratching behind his ears. His tail thumped in appreciation. "You have a terrible name, Dog," she whispered, lavishing attention on him. His tail only thumped harder. "It's beautiful here. Is it all yours?"

"My mom's. But yes, it's all part of the ranch."

"How big is it?"

"A little more than eight hundred acres," he said.

She frowned. "That means nothing to me, you know. I'm from New Jersey. City girl? Remember?"

He liked the way she said it. "How about this?" he offered. "It starts at the road where you turned in and goes a mile and a half in that direction, ending at the river. The land is shaped kind of like a fan, narrower at the road and getting wider toward the river, where it's more than two miles wide."

"That helps," she said.

"Does it?"

"Not really. How many city blocks is that?"

Her question caught him off guard and she laughed at his expression. "I have no idea."

"I'm kidding," she said, rising. "But this is impressive. I've never been on a ranch before." She motioned toward the house behind her. "And this is your house?"

He turned, following her gaze. "I built it a couple of years ago."

"And when you say you built it..."

"I did most of it, except for the plumbing and the electrical. I don't have a license for those things. But the layout and the framing, that was all me."

"Of course it was you," she said. "And I'll bet that if my car breaks down, you'll know how to fix that, too."

He squinted toward her car. "Probably."

"You're like...old-fashioned. A real man's man. A lot of guys don't know how to do that stuff anymore."

He couldn't tell whether she was impressed or teasing him, but he realized that he liked the way she kept him slightly off balance. Somehow it made her seem older than most of the girls he knew.

"I'm glad you're here," he said.

For a moment, it seemed as if she weren't quite sure what to make of his comment. "I'm glad I'm here, too. Thanks for inviting me."

He cleared his throat, thinking about that. "I had an idea that maybe I'd show you around the place."

"On horseback?"

"There's a nice spot down by the river," he said, not answering her question directly.

"Is it romantic?"

Luke wasn't quite sure how to answer that, either. "I like it, I guess," he said in a faltering voice.

"Good enough for me," she said, laughing. She pointed toward the boots he was holding. "Am I supposed to wear those?"

"They're my mom's. I don't know if they'll fit, but they'll help with the stirrups. I put some socks in there. They're mine and they're probably too big, but they're clean."

"I trust you," she said. "If you can fix cars and build houses, I'm sure you know how to run a washer and dryer. Can I try them on?"

He handed them to her and tried not to marvel at the fit of her jeans as she walked to the porch. Dog trailed behind her, his tail wagging and tongue hanging out, as if he'd discovered his new best friend. As soon as she sat, Dog began to nuzzle at her hand again, and he took that as a good sign—Dog wasn't normally so friendly. From the shade, he watched as Sophia slipped off her flats. She moved with a fluid grace, pulling on the socks and sliding her feet comfortably into the boots. She stood and took a few tentative steps.

"I've never worn cowboy boots before," she said, staring at her feet. "How do they look?"

"You look like you're wearing boots."

She gave an easy, rolling laugh, then began pacing the porch, staring again at the boots on her feet. "I guess I do," she said, and turned to face him. "Do I look like a cowgirl?"

"You'd need a hat for that."

"Let me try yours on," she said, holding out her hand.

Luke walked toward her and removed his hat, feeling less in control than he'd felt on the bulls last night. He handed it to her and she slipped it on, tilting it back on her head. "How's this?"

Perfect, he thought, as perfect as any girl he'd ever seen. He smiled through the sudden dryness in his throat, thinking, I'm in serious trouble.

"Now you look like a cowgirl."

She grinned, obviously pleased by that. "I think I'll keep this today. If it's okay with you."

"I've got plenty," he said, barely hearing himself. He shuffled his boots again, trying to stay centered. "How was it last night?" he asked. "I've been wondering if you had any more trouble."

She stepped down from the porch. "It was fine. Marcia was right where I'd left her."

"Did Brian bother you?"

"No," she answered. "I think he was worried you might still be around. Besides, we didn't stay long. Only another half hour or so. I was tired." By then, she'd drawn close to him. "I like the boots and hat. They're comfortable. I should probably thank your mom. Is she here?"

"No, she's at the main house. I can tell her later, though."

"What? You don't want me to meet her?"

"It's not that. She's kind of angry with me this morning."

"Why?"

"It's a long story."

Sophia tilted her head up at him. "You said the same thing last night when I asked you why you rode bulls," she remarked.

"I think you say 'It's a long story' when what you really mean is 'I don't want to talk about it.' Am I right?"

"I don't want to talk about it."

She laughed, her face flushing with pleasure. "So what's next?"

"I guess we can head to the barn," he said. "You said you wanted to see it."

She lifted an eyebrow. "You know I really didn't come here to see the barn, right?"

7

Sophia

Okay, she thought to herself as soon as the words left her mouth. Maybe that was a little too forward.

She blamed it on Marcia. If only Marcia hadn't pestered her with questions last night and all morning about what had happened the night before and the fact that she was going to the ranch today; if only she hadn't vetoed the first two outfits that Sophia had selected, all the while repeating, "I can't believe you're going riding with that hottie!" then Sophia wouldn't have been so nervous. Eye candy. Hot. Hottie. Marcia insisted on using those words instead of his name. As in, "So Mr. Eye Candy swooped in and saved you, huh?" or, "What did you and the hottie talk about?" or simply, "He's so hot!" It was no wonder she'd missed the turn after getting off the highway; by the time she'd pulled in the drive, she could feel a tiny bead of sweat trickling down her rib cage. She wasn't necessarily anxious, but she was definitely on edge, and whenever that happened she talked a lot and found herself taking cues from people like Marcia and Mary-Kate. But then sometimes her old self would come barreling through and she'd blurt out things better left unsaid. Like today. And last night, when she said she'd like to go horseback riding.

And Luke hadn't helped matters. He'd walked up to her car in that soft chambray work shirt and jeans, his brown curls trying to escape his hat. He'd barely raised those long-lashed blue eyes, surprising her with his shyness, when she felt her stomach do a little flip. She liked him...*really* liked him. But more than that, for whatever reason, she trusted him. She had the impression that his world was ordered by a sense of right and wrong, that he had integrity. He wasn't preoccupied with pretending to be something he wasn't, and his face was an open book. When she surprised him, she could see it instantly; when she teased him, he laughed easily at himself. By the time he finally mentioned the barn...well, she just couldn't help herself.

Although she thought she detected something that resembled a blush, he just ducked his head and popped inside to grab another hat. When he returned, they set off side by side, falling into an easy rhythm. Dog ran ahead and then came rushing back to them before darting off in yet another direction, a moving bundle of energy. Little by little, she felt her anxiety dissipate. They skirted the grove of trees that surrounded his house, angling toward the main drive. As the vista opened before her, she took in the main house, with its big covered porch and black shutters, backed by a copse of towering trees. Beyond it stood the aging barn and lush pastures nestled amid green rolling hills. In the distance, the banks of a small lake were dotted with cattle, smoky blue-tipped mountains near the horizon framing the landscape like a postcard. On the opposite side of the drive stood a grove of Christmas trees, planted in neat, straight rows. A breeze moved through the grove, making a soft fluting sound that resembled music.

"I can't believe you grew up here," she breathed, taking it all in. She motioned toward the house. "Is that where your mom lives?"

"I was actually born in that farmhouse."

"What? No horses fast enough to get to the hospital?"

He laughed, seemingly more relaxed since they'd left his house. "A lady on the next ranch over used to be a midwife. She's a good friend of my mom's, and it was a way to save some money. She's like that—my mom, I mean. She's kind of a hawk when it comes to expenses."

"Even for childbirth?"

"I'm not sure she was fazed by childbirth. Living on a farm, she'd been around a lot of births. Besides, she was born in the house, too, so she was probably thinking, What's the big deal?"

Sophia felt the gravel crunching beneath her boots. "How long has your family owned the ranch?" she asked.

"A long time. My great-grandfather bought most of it in the 1920s, and then, when the Depression hit, he was able to add to it. He was a pretty good businessman. From there, it became my grandfather's, and then my mom's. She took over when she was twenty-two."

As he answered, she looked around, amazed at how remote it felt despite its proximity to the highway. They passed the farmhouse, and on the far side there were smaller weather-beaten wooden structures surrounded by fencing. When the wind shifted, Sophia caught the scent of conifer and oak. Everything about the ranch was a refreshing change from the campus where she spent most of her time. Just like Luke, she thought, but she tried not to dwell on the observation. "What are those buildings?" she asked, pointing.

"The closest one is the henhouse, where we keep the chickens. And behind that is where we keep the hogs. Not many, only three or four at a time. Like I mentioned last night, we mainly do cattle here."

"How many do you have?"

"More than two hundred pair," he said. "We also have nine bulls."

She furrowed her brow. "Pair?"

"A mature cow and her calf."

"Then why don't you just say you have four hundred?"

"That's just the way they're counted, I guess. So you know

the size of the herd you can offer for sale that year. We don't sell the calves. Others do—that's veal—but we're known for our grass-fed, organic beef. Our customers are mainly high-end restaurants."

They followed the fence line, approaching an ancient live oak with massed limbs that spread in all directions like a spider. As they passed beneath the canopy of its limbs, they were greeted with a shrill assortment of bird cries, sounding their warnings. Sophia lifted her gaze to the barn as they neared it, realizing that Luke hadn't been kidding. It looked abandoned, the entire structure listing slightly and held together by rotting boards. Ivy and kudzu crawled up the sides, and a section of the roof appeared entirely stripped of shingles.

He nodded toward it. "What do you think?"

"I'm wondering if you ever think of razing it, just to show mercy?"

"It's sturdier than it looks. We just keep it this way for effect."

"Maybe," she said with a skeptical expression. "Either that, or you've never gotten around to fixing it."

"What are you talking about? You should have seen it before the repairs."

She smiled. He thought he was so funny. "Is that where you keep the horses?"

"Are you kidding? I wouldn't put them in that death trap."

This time, she laughed despite herself. "What do you use the barn for, then?"

"Storage, mostly. The mechanical bull is in there, too, and that's where I practice, but other than that, it's mainly filled with broken stuff. A couple of broken-down trucks, a tractor from the fifties, used well pumps, broken heat pumps, stripped engines. Most of it is junk, but like I said, my mom is funny about expenses. Sometimes I can find a part that I need to fix whatever needs fixing."

"Does that happen a lot? That you find something?"

"Not too much. But I can't order a part until after I check. It's one of my mom's rules."

Beyond the barn stood a small stable, open on one side to a medium-size corral. Three big-chested horses studied them as they approached. Sophia watched as Luke opened the door to the stable and produced three apples from the sack he'd been carrying.

"Horse! Get over here!" he called out, and at his command a chestnut-colored horse ambled in his direction. The two darker horses followed. "Horse is mine," he explained. "The others are Friendly and Demon."

She hung back, knitting her brows in concern. "I think I should probably ride Friendly, huh?" she said.

"I wouldn't," he said. "He bites and he'll try to throw you. He's awful for anyone but my mom. Demon, on the other hand, is a sweetheart."

She shook her head. "What is it with you and animal names?" By the time she turned toward the pasture again, Horse had sidled up close, dwarfing her. She stepped back quickly, though Horse— focused on Luke and the apples—didn't appear to notice her.

"Can I pet him?"

"Of course," he said, holding out the apple. "He likes his nose rubbed. And scratch him behind the ears."

She wasn't ready to touch his nose, but she ran her fingers gently behind the ears, watching as they tilted in pleasure, even as the horse continued to chomp on the apple.

Luke led Horse to a stall, and Sophia watched as he readied it for the ride: bridle, pad, and eventually the saddle, every movement practiced and unconscious. As he worked, his jeans pulling tight as he bent over, Sophia felt the heat rise in her cheeks. Luke was just about the sexiest thing she'd ever seen. She quickly turned away, pretending to study the rafters as he finished up and turned to saddle Demon.

"Okay," he said, adjusting the stirrup lengths. "You ready?"

"Not really," she admitted. "But I'll try. You're sure he's a sweetheart?"

"He's like a baby," Luke assured her. "Just put your hand on the horn and put your left boot in the stirrup. Then just swing your leg over."

She did as he told her, climbing onto the horse even as her heart began to race. As she tried to get comfortable, it occurred to her that the horse beneath her was like a giant muscle ready to flex.

"Umm...it's higher than I thought it would be."

"You'll be fine," he said, handing her the reins. Before she had time to protest, he was already on Horse, obviously at ease.

"Demon doesn't need much," he said. "Just touch the reins against his neck and he'll turn for you, like this. And to make him go, just tap his sides with your heels. To make him stop, pull back." He demonstrated a couple of times, making sure she understood.

"You do remember that this is my first time, right?" she asked.

"You told me."

"And just so you know, I have no desire to do anything crazy. I don't want to fall off. One of my sorority sisters broke her arm on one of these animals, and I don't want to be stuck wearing a cast while I have to write papers."

He scratched at his cheek, waiting. "Are you finished?" he asked.

"I'm just setting the ground rules."

He sighed, shaking his head in amusement. "City girls," he said, and with a flick of his wrist, Horse turned and began walking away. A moment later, Luke had leaned over and lifted the gate latch, allowing it to swing open. He made his way through it, the stall blocking her line of sight. "You're supposed to follow me," he called out.

With her heart still beating fast and her mouth dry as sawdust, she took a deep breath. There was no reason she couldn't do this.

She could ride a bike, and this wasn't all that different, right? People rode horses every day. *Little kids* rode horses, so how hard could it be? And even if it was hard, so what? She could do hard. English lit with Professor Aldair was hard. Working fourteen hours in the deli on Saturdays when all her friends were going to the city was hard. Letting Brian run her through the wringer— now that had been hard. Steeling herself, she fluttered the reins and tapped Demon on the sides.

Nothing.

She tapped again.

His ear twitched, but otherwise he remained as immobile as a statue.

Okay, not so easy, she thought. Demon obviously wanted to stay home.

Luke and Horse wandered back into view. He lifted the brim of his hat. "Are you coming?" he asked.

"He doesn't want to move," she explained.

"Tap him and tell him what you want him to do. Use the reins. He needs to feel that you know what you're doing."

Fat chance, she thought. I have no idea what I'm doing. She tapped again, and still nothing.

Luke pointed at the horse like a schoolteacher reprimanding a child. "Quit messing around, Demon," he finally barked. "You're scaring her. Get over here." Miraculously, his words were enough to get the horse moving without Sophia doing anything at all. But because she was caught off guard, she rocked backward in the saddle and then, trying to keep her balance, instinctively lunged forward.

Demon's ear twitched again, as if he were wondering if the whole thing was some sort of practical joke.

She held the reins with both hands, ready to make him turn, but Demon didn't need her. He passed through the gate, snorting at Horse as he passed, and then stopped while Luke shut the gate behind her and returned to her side.

He kept Horse at a slow but steady walk, and Demon was content to walk beside him without any work at all on her part. They crossed the drive and veered onto a path that skirted the last row of Christmas trees.

The scent of evergreen was stronger here, reminding her of the holidays. As she gradually grew used to the rhythm of the horse's gait, she felt small weights lifting from her body and her breathing returning to normal.

The far end of the grove gave way to a thin strand of forest, maybe a football field wide. The horses picked their way through an overgrown trail, almost on autopilot, uphill and then downhill, winding deeper into an untamed world. Behind them, the ranch slowly drifted from view, gradually making her feel as if she were in a distant land.

Luke was content to leave her alone with her thoughts as they made their way deeper into the trees. Dog ran ahead, nose to the ground, vanishing and reappearing as he veered this way and that. She ducked beneath a low-hanging branch and watched from the corner of her eye as Luke leaned to avoid another, the ground becoming rockier and densely carpeted. Thickets of blackberries and holly bushes sprouted in clumps, hugging the moss-covered trunks of oak trees. Squirrels darted along the branches of hickory trees, chattering a warning, while shafts of fractured sunlight cut through the foliage, lending her surroundings a dreamlike quality.

"It's beautiful out here," Sophia said, her voice sounding strange to her own ears.

Luke turned in his saddle. "I was hoping you'd like it."

"Is this your land, too?"

"Some of it. We share it with a neighboring ranch. It acts as a windbreak and property border."

"Do you ride out here often?"

"I used to. But lately, I'm only out here when one of the fences is broken. Sometimes, the cattle wander out this way."

"And here I was, thinking this is something you do with all the girls."

He shook his head. "I've never brought a girl out here."

"Why not?"

"I just never thought of it, I guess."

He seemed as surprised by the realization as she was. Dog trotted up, checked to make sure they were okay, then wandered off again. "So tell me about this old girlfriend. Angie, was it?"

He shifted slightly, no doubt surprised that she remembered. "There's not really much to tell. Like I told you, it was just a high school thing."

"Why did it end?"

He seemed to reflect on the question before answering. "I went on the tour the week after I graduated from high school," he said. "Back then, I couldn't afford to fly to the events, so I was on the road an awful lot. I'd leave on Thursday and wouldn't get home until Monday or Tuesday. Some weeks, I never made it home at all, and I don't blame her for wanting something different. Especially since it wasn't likely to change."

She digested this. "So how does it work?" she asked, shifting in her saddle. "If you want to be a bull rider, I mean? What do you have to do to get into it?"

"There's not much to it, really," he answered. "You buy your card with the PBR—"

"PBR?" she asked, cutting him off.

"Professional Bull Riders," he said. "They run the events. Basically, you sign up and pay your entry fee. When you get to the event, you draw a bull and they let you ride."

"You mean anyone can do it? Like if I had a brother and he decided that he wanted to start riding tomorrow, he could?"

"Pretty much."

"That's ridiculous. What if someone has no experience at all?"

"Then they'd probably get hurt."

"Ya think?"

He grinned and scratched under the brim of his hat. "It's always been like that. In rodeo, most of the prize money comes from the competitors themselves. Which means that people who are good at it like it when the other riders aren't so good. It means they have a better chance to walk away from an event with cash in their pocket."

"That seems kind of heartless."

"How else would you do it? You can practice all you want, but there's only one way to know whether you can ride and that's to actually try it."

Thinking back, she wondered how many of the riders last night were first timers. "Okay, someone enters an event and let's say he's like you and he happens to win. What happens next?"

He shrugged. "Bull riding is a little different than traditional rodeo. Bull riders have their own tour these days, but actually it's two tours. You have the big one, which is the one on television all the time, and you have the little tour, which is kind of like the minor leagues. If you earn enough points in the minor leagues, you get promoted to the major leagues. In this sport, that's where the real money is."

"And last night?"

"Last night was an event on the little tour."

"Have you ever ridden in the big tour?"

He reached down, patting Horse's neck. "I rode in it for five years."

"Were you good?"

"I did all right."

She evaluated his answer, remembering that he'd said the same thing last night—when he'd won. "Why do I get the sense that you're a lot better than you're implying?"

"I don't know."

She scrutinized him. "You might as well tell me how good you were. I can always Google you, you know."

He sat up straighter. "I made the PBR World Championships

four years in a row. To do that, you have to be in the top thirty-five in the standings."

"So you're one of the best, in other words."

"I was. Not so much anymore. I'm pretty much starting over again."

By then, they'd reached a small clearing near the river and they brought the horses to a halt on the high bank. The river wasn't wide, but Sophia had the sense that the slow-moving water was deeper than it appeared. Dragonflies flitted over the surface, breaking the stillness, causing tiny ripples that radiated to the edge. Dog lay down, panting from his exertions, his tongue hanging out the side of his mouth. Beyond him, in the shade of a gnarled oak tree, she noticed what seemed to be the remains of an old camp, with a decaying picnic table and an abandoned fire pit.

"What is this place?" she asked, adjusting her hat.

"My dad and I used to come fishing here. There's a submerged tree under the water just over there, and it's a great place to catch bass. We used to stay out here all day. It was kind of our place, just for the two of us. My mom hates the smell of fish, so we'd catch them and clean and cook them out here before bringing them back to the farmhouse. Other times, my dad would bring me out here after practice and we'd just stare at the stars. He never graduated from high school, but he could name every constellation in the sky. I had some of the best times of my life out here."

She stroked Demon's mane. "You miss him."

"All the time," he said. "Coming out here helps me remember him the right way. The way he should be remembered."

She could hear the loss in his tone, sense the tightness in his posture. "How did he die?" she asked, her voice soft.

"We were coming home from an event in Greenville, South Carolina. It was late and he was tired and a deer suddenly tried to dart across the highway. He didn't have time to even jerk the wheel, and the deer went through the windshield. The truck ended up rolling three times, but even before then, it was too late. The impact broke his neck."

"You were with him?"

"I dragged him out of the wreckage," he said. "I can remember holding him and frantically trying to get him to wake up until the paramedics got there."

She paled. "I can't even imagine something like that."

"Neither could I," he said. "One minute, we're talking about my rides, and the next minute, he was gone. It didn't seem real. It still doesn't. Because he wasn't just my dad. He was my coach and partner and friend, too. And..." He trailed off, lost in thought, then slowly shook his head. "And I don't know why I'm telling you all this."

"It's okay," she said, her voice soft. "I'm glad you did."

He acknowledged her words with a grateful nod. "What are your parents like?" he asked.

"They're...passionate," she finally said. "About *everything*."

"What do you mean?"

"You'd have to live with us to understand. They can be crazy about each other one minute and screaming at each other in the next, they have deep opinions on everything from politics to the environment to how many cookies we should have after dinner, even what language to speak that day—"

"Language?" he asked, breaking in.

"My parents wanted all of us to be multilingual, so on Mondays we spoke French, Tuesdays was Slovak, Wednesdays was Czech. It used to drive me and my sisters crazy, especially when we had friends come over, because they couldn't understand anything that anyone was saying. And they were perfectionists when it came to grades. We had to study in the kitchen, and my mom would quiz us before every test. And let me tell you, if I ever brought home a score that wasn't absolutely perfect, my mom and dad acted like it was the end of the world. My mom would wring her hands and my dad would tell me how disappointed he was and I'd end up feeling so guilty that I'd study again for a test that I'd already taken. I know it's because they never wanted me to struggle like they did, but it could be a little oppressive at times. On top of that, all of us had to work in the deli, which meant that we were pretty much always together...let's just say that by the time college rolled around, I was looking forward to making my own decisions."

Luke lifted an eyebrow. "And you chose Brian."

"Now you sound like my parents," she said. "They didn't like Brian from the beginning. As nuts as they are about some things, they're actually pretty smart. I should have listened to them."

"We all make mistakes," he said. "How many languages do you speak?"

"Four," she answered, pushing up the brim of her hat in the same way he did. "But that includes English."

"I speak one, including English."

She smiled, liking his comment, liking him. "I don't know how much good it will do me. Unless I end up working at a museum in Europe."

"Do you want to do that?"

"Maybe. I don't know. Right now, I'd be willing to work anywhere."

He was quiet when she finished, absorbing what she'd said to him. "Listening to you makes me wish I had been more serious about school. I wasn't a bad student, but I wasn't brilliant, either. I didn't work very hard at it. But now, I can't help thinking that I should have gone to college."

"I'd think it's a lot safer than riding bulls."

Though she meant it as a joke, he didn't smile. "You're absolutely right."

After leaving the clearing by the river, Luke took her on a leisurely tour of the rest of the ranch, their conversation wandering from one subject to the next, Dog always roaming in their vicinity. They rode between the Christmas trees and skirted past the beehives, and he led her through the rolling pastureland used by the cattle. They talked about everything from the kind of music they liked to their favorite movies to Sophia's impressions of North Carolina. She told him about her sisters and what it was like to grow up in a city, and also about life on the cloistered campus at Wake. Though their worlds were entirely different, she was surprised to discover that he seemed to find her world just as fascinating as she found his.

Later, when she had gained a bit more confidence in the saddle, she brought Demon to a trot and eventually to a canter. Luke rode beside her the whole time, ready to grab her if she was about to fall, telling her when she was leaning too far forward or back and reminding her to keep the reins loose. She hated trotting, but when the horse cantered, she found it easier to adjust to the steady, rolling rhythm. They rode from one fence to the next and back again, four or five times, moving a little faster with every lap. Feeling a little more sure of herself, Sophia tapped Demon and urged him to go even faster. Luke was caught unawares and it took a few seconds for him to catch up, and as they raced beside each other, she reveled in the feel of the wind in her face, the experience terrifying and exhilarating. On the way back, she urged Demon to go even faster, and when they finally brought the horses to a halt a few minutes later, she started to laugh, the surge of adrenaline and fear spilling out of her.

When the giddy waves of laughter eventually passed, they slowly made their way back to the stables. The horses were still breathing hard and sweating, and after Luke removed the saddles, she helped him brush them down. She fed Demon an apple, already feeling the first twinges of soreness in her legs but not caring in the slightest. She'd ridden a horse—actually ridden!—and in a burst of pride and satisfaction, she looped her arm through Luke's as they strolled back to the house.

They walked leisurely, neither of them needing to talk. Sophia replayed the events of the day in her head, glad that she'd come. From what she could tell, Luke shared her sense of peace and contentment as well.

As they neared the house, Dog darted ahead toward the water bowl on the porch; he lapped at it between pants, then collapsed onto his belly.

"He's tired," she said, startled at the sound of her own voice.

"He'll be fine. He follows me when I ride out every morning." He took off his hat and wiped the perspiration from his brow. "Would you like something to drink?" he asked. "I don't know about you, but I could really use a beer."

"Sounds great."

"I'll be back in a minute," he promised, and headed into the house.

As he walked away, she studied him, trying to make sense of her undeniable attraction to him. Who could make sense of any of this? She was still trying to figure it out when he emerged with a pair of ice cold bottles.

He twisted off a cap and handed her a bottle, their fingers brushing slightly. He motioned to the rockers.

She took a seat and leaned back with a sigh, her hat tilting forward. She'd almost forgotten that she'd been wearing it. She took it off, setting it in her lap before taking a sip. The beer was icy and refreshing.

"You rode really well," he said.

"You mean I rode well for a beginner. I'm not ready for the rodeo yet, but it was fun."

"You have naturally good balance," he observed.

But Sophia wasn't listening. Instead she was staring past him at the little cow that had appeared from around the corner of his house. It seemed to be taking an inordinate interest in them. "I think one of your cows got loose." She pointed. "A little one."

He followed her gaze, his expression turning to fond recognition. "That's Mudbath. I don't know how she does it, but she ends up here a couple of times a week. There's got to be a gap in the fencing somewhere, but I haven't found it yet."

"She likes you."

"She *adores* me," he said. "Last March, we had a wet, cold streak and she got trapped in the mud. I spent hours trying to pull her out and I had to bottle-feed her for a few days. Ever since then, she's been coming around here regularly."

"That's sweet," she said, trying not to stare at him but finding it hard to avoid. "You have an interesting life here."

He took off his hat and combed his fingers through his hair before taking another sip. When he spoke, his voice lost some of the customary reserve she'd grown used to. "Can I tell you something?" A long moment passed before he continued. "And I don't want you to take this the wrong way."

"What is it?"

"You make it seem a lot more interesting than it really is."

"What are you talking about?"

He began to pick at the label on his bottle, peeling the paper back with his thumb, and she had the impression that he wasn't so much searching for the answer as waiting for it to come to him before he turned to face her. "I think you're just about the most interesting girl I've ever met."

She wanted to say something, anything, but she felt as if she were drowning in those blue eyes, her words seeming to dry up. Instead, she watched as he leaned toward her, hesitating for an instant. His head tilted slightly, and the next thing she knew, she was tilting her head, too, their faces growing closer.

It wasn't long, it wasn't heated, but as soon as their lips came together, she knew with sudden certainty that nothing had ever felt so easy and so right, the perfect ending to an unimaginably perfect afternoon.

8

Ira

Where am I?

I wonder this for only a moment before I shift in the seat, pain providing me with an answer. It is a waterfall, white hot, as my arm and shoulder explode. My head feels like splintered glass, and my chest has begun to throb as if something heavy has just been lifted off me.

Overnight, the car has become an igloo. The snow on the windshield has begun to glow, which means that sunrise has come. It is Sunday morning, February 6, 2011, and according to the watch face that I have to squint to make out, it is 7:20 a.m. Last night, sunset occurred at 5:50 p.m., and I'd been driving in the darkness for an hour before I went off the highway. I have been here for over twelve hours, and though I am still alive, there is a moment when I feel nothing but terror.

I have felt this kind of terror before. Strangers would not know this by looking at me. As I worked at the shop, customers were often surprised to learn that I had been in the war. I never mentioned it; and only once did I talk to Ruth about what happened to me. We never spoke of it again. Back then, Greensboro was not the city it would eventually become—in many ways, it was still a small town, and many of the people I'd known growing up were aware that I'd been wounded while fighting in Europe.

And yet they, like me, had little desire to discuss the war after it ended. For some, the memories were simply too unbearable; for others, the future simply held more interest than the past.

But if anyone had asked, I would have said that my story was not worth the time it would take to listen to it. If nonetheless pressed for details, I would have told them that I'd enlisted in the U.S. Army Air Corps in June 1942, and after being sworn in, I boarded a train filled with other cadets bound for the Army Air Corps Reception Center in Santa Ana, California. It was my first trip out west. I spent the next month learning how to follow orders, clean bathrooms, and march properly. From there, I was sent to Primary Flight School at Mira Loma Flight Academy in Oxnard, where I learned the basics of meteorology, navigation, aerodynamics, and mechanics. During this time, I also worked with an instructor and was gradually taught to fly. I flew my first solo there, and within three months I had accumulated enough hours in the air to move to the next stage of training at Gardner Field in Taft. From there, it was off to Roswell, New Mexico, for even more flight training and then back to Santa Ana, where I finally began my formal training as a navigator. Yet even when I completed the training there, I still wasn't done. I was sent to Mather Field near Sacramento, where I attended Advanced Navigation School, to learn how to navigate by the stars, with dead reckoning, through the use of visual references on the ground. Only then did I receive my commission.

It was another two months before I was sent to the European theater. First, the crew was sent to Texas, where we were assigned to the B-17, and then finally to England. By the time I flew my first combat mission in October 1943, I'd been training stateside for almost a year and a half, as far from action as someone in the military could possibly be.

This is not what people would have wanted to hear, but this was my experience of the war. It was training and transfers and even more training. It was about weekend passes and my first visit to a California beach, where I laid eyes on the Pacific for the very first time. It was having the chance to see the giant sequoias in northern California, trees so large they seemed beyond comprehension. It was about the feeling of awe that overcame me when soaring over the desert landscape as dawn was breaking. And it was also, of course, about Joe Torrey, the best friend I ever had.

We had little in common. He was a Catholic from Chicago, a baseball player with a gap-toothed smile. He had trouble stringing a single sentence together without cursing, but he laughed a lot and poked fun at himself, and everyone wanted him along when weekend passes were handed out. They wanted him to join their poker games and to cruise downtown with them, since women also seemed to find him irresistible. Why he often chose to spend time with me has always been a mystery, but it was because of Joe that I ever felt included at all. It was with Joe that I drank my first beer while sitting on the Santa Monica Pier, and it was with Joe that I smoked the first and only cigarette of my life. It was Joe that I spoke with on those days I particularly missed Ruth, and Joe would listen in a way that made me want to keep talking until I finally began to feel better. Joe, too, had a fiancée back home—a pretty girl named Marla—and he admitted that he didn't particularly care what happened in the war as long as he was able to get back to her.

Joe and I ended up on the same B-17. The captain was Colonel Bud Ramsey, a genuine hero and a genius as a pilot. He'd already flown one round of combat missions and had been assigned a second. He was calm and collected under the most harrowing circumstances, and we knew we were lucky to have him as our commander.

My actual war experiences began on October 2, when we raided a submarine base in Emden. Two days later, we were part of a squadron of three hundred bombers converging on Frankfurt. On October 10, we bombed a railway junction at Münster, and on October 14, on a day that became known as Black Thursday, the war came to an end for me.

The target was a ball-bearing plant in Schweinfurt. It had been bombed once a few months earlier, but the Germans were making good headway in repairs. Because of the distance from base, our formation bombers had no fighter support, and this time the bombing run was anticipated. German fighters showed up at the coastline, dogging various squadrons all the way, and by the time we were within striking range, flak bursts had already formed a dense fog over the entire city. German rockets exploded all around us at high altitude, the shock waves shaking the plane. We had just dropped our payload when a number of enemy fighters suddenly closed in. They came from every direction, and all around us, bombers began to fall from the sky, enveloped in fire as they spiraled toward the earth. Within minutes, the formation was in tatters. Our gunner was struck in the forehead and fell back into the aircraft. On instinct, I climbed into his seat and began to fire, loosing close to five hundred rounds without doing any appreciable damage to the enemy. At that moment, I did not think that I would survive, but I was too terrified to stop firing.

We were strafed by enemy fire on one side and then the other. From my vantage point, I could see gigantic holes being ripped into the wing. When we lost an engine to enemy fire, the plane began to shimmy, the roar louder than anything I'd ever heard before as Bud struggled with the controls. The wing suddenly dipped, and the plane started to lose altitude, smoke billowing behind us. The fighters closed in for the kill, and more flak tore through the fuselage. We dropped a thousand feet, then two thousand. Five thousand. Eight thousand. Bud somehow managed to straighten the wings and, like a mythological creature, the nose of the plane somehow began to rise. Miraculously, the plane was still aloft, but we were separated from the formation, alone above enemy territory—and still the flak pursued us.

Bud had turned us toward home in a desperate bid to make our escape, when flak shattered the cockpit. Joe was struck, and instinctively, he turned toward me. I saw his eyes go wide in disbelief and his lips form my name. I lunged toward him, wanting to do something—anything—when suddenly I fell, my body losing all its strength. I couldn't understand what had happened. At the time, I didn't know I'd been hit, and I tried and failed again to get to my feet to help Joe when I felt a series of sharp, stinging burns. I looked down and saw large blooms of red spreading across the lower half of my body. The world seemed to telescope around me, and I passed out.

I don't know how we made it back to base, other than to say that Bud Ramsey performed a miracle. Later, at the hospital, I was told that people took photographs of the plane after we landed, marveling that it had been able to stay airborne. But I didn't look at the photographs, even when my strength had returned.

I was told that I should have died. By the time we'd reached England, I'd lost more than half my blood and I was as pale as a swan. My pulse rate was so low that they couldn't find it in my wrist, but they nonetheless rushed me into surgery. I wasn't expected to survive the night, or the night after that. A telegram was sent to my parents, explaining that I'd been wounded and that more information would be forthcoming. By "more information," the army air corps meant another, later telegram informing them of my death.

But the second telegram was never sent, because somehow I did not die. This was not the conscious choice of a hero; I was not a hero and remained unconscious. Later, I wouldn't remember a single dream or even whether I'd had any dreams at all. But somehow, on the fifth day after surgery, I woke, my body drenched in sweat. According to the nurses, I was delirious and screaming in agony. Peritonitis had set in and I was rushed into surgery once more. I do not remember this, either, or any of the days that followed. The fever lasted for thirteen days, and on each successive day, when asked about my prognosis, the doctor shook his head. Though I was unaware of it, I was visited by Bud Ramsey and surviving crew members before they were assigned to a new plane. Meanwhile, a telegram was sent to the home of Joe Torrey's parents, announcing his death. The RAF bombed Kassel, and the war continued.

The fever finally broke as the calendar turned to November. When I opened my eyes, I didn't know where I was. I couldn't remember what had happened, and I couldn't seem to move. I felt as though I'd been buried alive, and with all my strength, I was able to whisper only a single syllable.

Ruth.

The sun grows brighter and the winds have grown sharper, yet still no one comes. The terror I felt earlier has finally passed, and in its absence, my mind begins to wander. I note that being buried alive in a car by snowfall is not unique to me. Not too long ago on the Weather Channel, I saw a clip about a man in Sweden who, like me, was trapped in his car while snow gradually buried him alive. This was near a town called Umeå, near the Arctic Circle, where temperatures were well below zero. However, according to the broadcaster, the car became an igloo of sorts. Even though this man would not have survived long if exposed to the elements, the temperature inside the car could be tolerated for long periods, especially since the man was dressed appropriately and had a sleeping bag with him. But this is not the amazing part; what was amazing was how long the man survived. Though the man had no food or water and ate only handfuls of snow, the doctors said his body went almost into a sort of hibernation state. His bodily processes slowed down enough for him to be rescued after sixty-four days.

Good God, I remember thinking. *Sixty-four days.* When I saw the segment, I could barely imagine such a thing, but obviously it has taken on new meaning at the present time. Two months in the car, for me, would mean that someone would find me in early April. The azaleas will be blooming, the snow long since gone, and days will already begin to feel like summer. If I'm rescued in April, it will probably be by young people wearing hiking shorts and sunscreen.

Someone will find me before then, of this I'm sure. But even though it should make me feel better, it doesn't. Nor am I comforted by the fact that the temperature is nowhere near as cold or that I have two sandwiches in the car, because I am not the Swedish man. He was forty-four and uninjured; my arm and collarbone are broken, I've lost a lot of blood, and I'm ninety-one years old. I'm afraid that any movement at all will cause me to pass out, and frankly, my body has been in hibernation mode for the past ten years. If my bodily processes slow any further, I'll be permanently horizontal.

If there is a silver lining in any of this, it's that I'm not hungry yet. This is common for people my age. I haven't had much of an appetite in recent years, and I struggle to consume a cup of coffee and single piece of toast in the morning. But I am thirsty. My throat feels as though it has been clawed with nails, but I don't know what to do. Though there is a bottle of water in the car, I am afraid of the torture I will feel if I try to find it.

And I am cold, so cold. I have not endured this kind of shivering since my stay in the hospital a lifetime ago. After my surgeries, after the fever broke and I thought my body was beginning to heal, a fierce headache set in and the glands in my throat began to swell. The fever came back, and I felt a throbbing soreness in the place where no man wants to feel it. At first, the doctors were hopeful that the second fever was related to the first. But it wasn't. The man next to me had the same set of symptoms, and within days, three more in our ward became ill. It was mumps, a childhood disease, but in adults it's far more serious. Of all the men, I was hardest hit. I was the weakest and the virus raged through my body for almost three weeks. By the time it ran its course, I weighed only 115 pounds and I was so weak that I couldn't stand without help.

It was another month before I was finally released from the hospital, but I was not cleared to fly. My weight was still too low, and I had no crew to speak of. Bud Ramsey, I learned, had been shot down over Germany, and there were no survivors. Initially, the army air corps wasn't sure what to do with me, but they eventually decided to send me back to Santa Ana. I became a trainer for new recruits, working with them until the war finally came to an end. I received my discharge in January 1946, and after taking a train to Chicago to pay my respects to Joe Torrey's family, I returned to North Carolina.

Like veterans everywhere, I wanted to put the war behind me. But I couldn't. I was angry and bitter, and I hated what I had become. Aside from the night over Schweinfurt, I had few combat memories, yet the war stayed with me. For the rest of my life, I carried wounds that no man could see but were impossible to leave behind. Joe Torrey and Bud Ramsey were the best kind of men, yet they had died while I had survived, and the guilt never quite left me. The flak that tore through my body made it a struggle to walk on cold winter mornings, and my stomach has never been the same. I can't drink milk or eat spicy food, and I was never able to regain all the weight I lost. I have not been in an airplane since 1945, and I found it impossible to sit through movies that dealt with war. I do not like hospitals. For me, after all, the war—and my time in the hospital—had changed everything.

❧

"You are crying," Ruth says to me.

In another place, at another time, I would wipe the tears from my face with the back of my hand. But here and now, the task seems impossible.

"I didn't realize it," I say.

"You often cried in your sleep," Ruth says to me. "When we were first married. I would hear you at night and the sound would break my heart. I would rub your back and hush you and sometimes you would roll over and become silent. But other times, it would continue through the night, and in the mornings, you would tell me that you could not remember the reason."

"Sometimes I didn't."

She stares at me. "But sometimes you did," she finishes.

I squint at her, thinking her form is almost like liquid, as if I'm staring at her through shimmering heat waves that rise from the asphalt in summer. She wears a navy dress and a white hair band, and her voice sounds older. It takes a moment, but I realize she is twenty-three, her age when I returned from the war.

"I was thinking about Joe Torrey," I said.

"Your friend"—she nods—"the one who ate five hot dogs in San Francisco. The one who bought you your first beer."

I never told her about the cigarettes, for I know she would have disapproved. Ruth always hated their smell. It is a lie of omission, but I long ago convinced myself that it was the right thing to do. "Yes," I say.

The morning light surrounds Ruth in a halo.

"I wish I could have met him," she says.

"You would have liked him."

Ruth clears her throat, considering this, before turning away. She faces the snow-caked window, her thoughts her own. This car, I think, has become my tomb.

"You were also thinking about the hospital," she murmurs.

When I nod, she emits a weary sigh.

"Did you not hear what I told you?" she says, turning to me again. "That it did not matter to me? I would not lie to you about this."

"Not on purpose," I answer. "But I think that maybe, you sometimes lied to yourself."

She is surprised by my words, if only because I have never spoken so directly on this matter. But I know I am right.

"This is why you stopped writing me," she observes. "After you had been sent back to California, your letters became less frequent until they finally stopped coming at all. I did not hear from you for six months."

"I stopped writing because I remembered what you'd told me."

"Because you wanted to end it between us." There is an undercurrent of anger in her voice, and I can't meet her eyes.

"I wanted you to be happy."

"I was not happy," she snaps. "I was confused and heartbroken and I did not understand what had happened. And I prayed for you every day, hoping you would let me help you. But instead, I would go to the mailbox and find it empty, no matter how many letters I sent."

"I'm sorry. It was wrong of me to do that."

"Did you even read my letters?"

"Every one. I read them over and over, and more than once, I tried to write so you could know what happened. But I could never find the right words."

She shakes her head. "You did not even tell me when you were to arrive home. It was your mother who told me, and I thought about meeting you at the station, like you used to do when I came home."

"But you didn't."

"I wanted to see if you would come to me. But days passed and then a week, and when I did not see you at the synagogue, I understood that you were trying to avoid me. So I finally marched over to your shop and told you that I needed to speak to you. And do you remember what you said to me?"

Of all the things I've said in my life, these are the words I regret the most. But Ruth is waiting, her tense expression fixed on my face. There is a fierce challenge in the way she waits.

"I told you that the engagement was off, and that it was over between us."

She arches an eyebrow. "Yes," she says, "that is what you told me."

"I couldn't talk to you then. I was..."

When I trail off, she finishes for me. "Angry." She nods. "I could see it in your eyes, but even then, I knew you were still in love with me."

"Yes," I admit. "I was."

"But your words were still hurtful," she says. "I went home and cried like I had not since I was a child. And my mother finally came in and held me and neither of us knew what to do. I had lost so much already. I could not bear to lose you, too."

By this, she means her family, the family that had stayed behind in Vienna. At the time, I didn't realize how selfish my actions were or how Ruth might have perceived them. This memory, too, has stayed with me, and in the car, I feel an age-old shame.

Ruth, my dream, knows what I am feeling. When she speaks, it is with a new tenderness. "But if it was really over, I wanted to understand the reason, so the next day, I went to the drugstore across from your shop and ordered a chocolate soda. I sat next to the window and watched you as you worked. I know you saw me, but you did not come over. So I went back the next day and the day after that, and only then did you finally cross the street to see me."

"My mother made me go," I admit. "She told me that you deserved an explanation."

"That is what you have always said. But I think you also wanted to come, because you missed me. And because you knew that only I could help you heal."

I close my eyes at her words. She is right, of course, right about all of it. Ruth always did know me better than I knew myself.

"I took a seat across from you," I say. "And then, a moment later, a chocolate soda arrived for me."

"You were so skinny. I thought you needed my help to get fat again. Like you were when we met."

"I was never fat," I protest. "I barely made weight when I joined the army."

"Yes, but when you got back, you were all bones. Your suit hung from your frame like it was two sizes too big. I thought you would blow away as you crossed the street, and it made me wonder whether you would ever be yourself again. I was not sure you would ever again be the man I once loved."

"And yet you still gave me a chance."

She shrugs. "I had no choice," she says, her eyes glittering. "By then, David Epstein was married."

I laugh despite myself, and my body spasms, neurons blazing, nausea coming at me. I breathe through gritted teeth and gradually feel the wave begin to recede. Ruth waits for my breathing to steady before going on. "I admit that I was frightened about this. I wanted things between us to be the way they had been before, so I simply pretended that nothing had changed. I chattered about college and my friends and how much I had studied, and that my parents had surprised me by showing up at my graduation. I talked about my work as a substitute teacher at a school around the corner from the synagogue, but also mentioned that I was interviewing for a full-time position that fall at a rural elementary school on the outskirts of town. I told you also that my father was meeting with the dean of the Art History Department at Duke for the third time, and that my parents might have to move to Durham. And then I wondered aloud whether I would have to give up my new job and move to Durham, too."

"And I suddenly knew I didn't want you to go."

"That is why I said it." She smiles. "I wanted to see your expression, and for just an instant, the old Ira was back. And then I was no longer frightened that you were gone forever."

"But you didn't ask me to walk you home."

"You were not ready. There was still too much anger inside you. That is why I suggested that we meet once a week for chocolate sodas, just like we used to. You needed time, and I was willing to wait."

"For a while. Not forever."

"No, not forever. By the end of February, I had begun to wonder whether you would ever kiss me again."

"I wanted to," I say. "Every time I was with you, I wanted to kiss you."

"I knew that, too, and that was why it was so confusing to me. I could not understand what was wrong. I could not understand what was holding you back, why you did not trust me. You should have known that I would love you no matter what."

"I did know," I say. "And that was why I couldn't tell you."

I did eventually tell her, of course, on a cold evening in early March. I had called her at home, asking her to meet me in the park, where we had strolled together a hundred times. At the time, I wasn't planning to tell her. Instead, I convinced myself that I simply needed a friend to talk to, as the atmosphere at home had become oppressive.

My father had done well financially during the war, and as soon as it was over, he went back into business as a haberdasher. Gone were the sewing machines; in their place were racks of suits, and to someone walking past the shop, it probably looked the same as it did before the war. But inside, it was different. My father was different. Instead of greeting customers at the door as he used to, he would spend his afternoons in the back room, listening to the news on the radio, trying to understand the madness that had caused the deaths of so many innocent people. It was all he wanted to talk about; the Holocaust became the subject of every mealtime conversation and every spare moment. By contrast, the more he talked, the more my mother concentrated on her sewing, because she couldn't bear to think about it. For my father, after all, it was an abstract horror; for my mother—who, like Ruth, had lost friends and family—it was deeply personal. And in their divergent reactions to these shattering events, my parents gradually set in motion the largely separate lives they would lead from that point on.

As their son, I tried not to take sides. With my father I would listen and with my mother I would say nothing, but when the three of us were together, it sometimes struck me that we'd forgotten what it meant to be a family. Nor did it help that my father now accompanied my mother and me to synagogue; my intimate talks with my mother became a thing of the past. When my father informed me that he was bringing me in as a partner in the business—meaning the three of us would be together all the time—I despaired, sure that there would be no escaping the gloom that had infiltrated our lives.

"You are thinking about your parents," Ruth says to me.

"You were always kind to them," I say.

"I loved your mother very much," Ruth says. "Despite the difference in our ages, she was the first real friend I made in this country."

"And my father?"

"I loved him, too. How could I not? He was family."

I smile, recalling that in later years she was always more patient with him than I was.

"Can I ask you a question?"

"You can ask me anything."

"Why did you wait for me? Even after I stopped writing? I know you say that you loved me, but..."

"We are back to this? You wonder why I loved you?"

"You could have had anyone."

She leans closer to me, her voice soft. "This has always been your problem, Ira," she says. "You do not see in yourself what others see in you. You think you are not handsome enough, but you were very handsome when you were young. You think you are not interesting or smart enough, but you are these things, too, and that you are not aware of your best qualities is part of your charm. You always see so much in others—as you did in me. You made me feel special."

"But you are special," I insist.

She raises her hands in delight. "This is what I am talking

about," she says, laughing. "You are a man of deep feelings, who has always cared about others, and I am not alone in recognizing that. Your friend Joe Torrey sensed it. I am sure that is why he spent his free time with you. And my mother sensed it as well, which was why she held me when I thought I had lost you. Because we both knew that men like you are rare."

"I'm glad you came that night," I say. "I needed you."

"And you also knew, as soon as we fell into step at the park, that you were finally ready to tell me the truth. All of it."

I nod. In one of my final letters, I'd briefly told her about the bombing run over Schweinfurt and Joe Torrey. I mentioned the wounds I'd received and the infection that had followed, but I hadn't told her everything. On that night, however, I started at the beginning. I related every detail and I held nothing back. On the bench, she listened to my outpouring of words without speaking.

Afterward, she slipped her arms around me and I leaned into her. The emotions washed over me in waves, her whispered words of comfort unleashing memories I had tried too long to bury.

I don't know how long it took for the storm inside me to subside, but by that point, I was exhausted. Yet there was one thing remaining that I had not revealed, something that not even my parents knew.

In the car, Ruth is silent. I know she is replaying what I said to her that night.

"I told you that I got the mumps while I was in the hospital— the worst case the doctor had ever seen. And I told you what the doctor said to me."

Ruth remains quiet, but her eyes start to glisten.

"He said that mumps can cause sterility," I say. "That's why I tried to end it between us. Because I knew that if you ever married me, there was a good chance that we would never have children."

9

Sophia

And then what?" Marcia asked. She was standing in front of the mirror and applying a second coat of mascara while Sophia recounted her day at the ranch. "Don't tell me you slept with him." As she said it, she examined Sophia's reflection in the mirror.

"Of course not!" Sophia said. She crossed one leg beneath the other on the bed. "It wasn't like that. We just kissed and then we talked some more, and then when I left, he kissed me again at the car. It was...sweet."

"Oh," Marcia said, stopping in her attempt to dab on some mascara.

"Don't hide your disappointment. Really."

"What?" she announced. "The way you looked just now makes me think you wanted to."

"I barely know him!"

"That's not true. You were with him, what? More than an hour last night, and six or seven hours today? That's a lot of time together. That's *a lot* of talking. Horseback riding, a couple of beers...if it was me, I might have grabbed his hand and just dragged him inside."

"Marcia!"

"I'm just saying. He was seriously hot. You noticed that, right?"

Sophia really, truly, didn't want the whole "hot" thing to start up again. "He's a nice guy," she said, trying to head it off.

"Even better," Marcia said, giving her a wink. She applied a glossy coat of lipstick before reaching for a hair clip. "But okay, I get it. You're different than me. And I respect that—I really do. I'm just glad you're done with Brian."

"I've been done with him since I broke up with him."

"I could tell," she said, gathering her rich brown hair into a sleek ponytail and securing it with a glittery hair clip. "You know I talked to him, right?"

"When?"

"At the rodeo, when you were off with Mr. Hottie."

Sophia frowned. "Why didn't you tell me?"

"What was there to tell? I was just trying to distract him. The Duke guys hated him, by the way." She adjusted a few strands that she had artfully loosened from the ponytail, then met Sophia's gaze in the mirror. "You have to admit, I'm the best roommate ever, right? Convincing you to go out with us? If it wasn't for me, you'd still be moping around our room all day. All of which makes me wonder when I'm going to get the chance to meet your new stud."

"We didn't talk about getting together again."

Marcia's face was incredulous. "How could you not talk about it?"

Because we're different, Sophia thought. And because . . . she didn't really know why, other than that the dizzy way the kiss made her feel obliterated all practical thought.

"All I know is that he's going to be out of town next weekend. He's going to be riding in Knoxville."

"So call him. Invite him over to the house before he leaves."

Sophia shook her head. "I'm not going to call him."

"And if he doesn't call you?"

"He said he would."

"A lot of times, guys just say that and you never hear from them again."

"He's not like that," she said, and as if proving her point, her cell phone began to ring. Recognizing Luke's phone number, she grabbed it and jumped up from the bed.

"Don't tell me that's him, already."

"He said he would call to make sure I got home safely."

Sophia was already bounding to the door, barely noticing her roommate's surprise or the words she muttered to herself as Sophia slipped into the hallway. "I've really, really got to meet this guy."

On Thursday evening, an hour after the sun had gone down, Sophia was finishing up her hair when Marcia turned toward her. She'd been standing at the window and watching for Luke's truck, making Sophia feel even more nervous than she already was. She'd vetoed three of Sophia's outfits, had lent her a pair of gold, dangly earrings and a necklace that matched, and as she skipped toward Sophia, she didn't bother to hide her excitement.

"He's here. I'm going downstairs to meet him at the door."

Sophia let out a long breath. "Okay, I'm ready. Let's go."

"No, you stay in the room for a few minutes. You don't want him to think you were watching for him."

"I wasn't watching for him," Sophia said. "You were."

"You know what I mean. You need to make an entrance. He needs to see you coming down the stairs. The last thing you want is for him to think you're desperate."

"Why are you making this so complicated?" Sophia protested.

"Trust me," Marcia said. "I know what I'm doing. Come down in three minutes. Count to a hundred or something. I've got to go."

She fled, leaving Sophia alone with her nerves, her stomach feeling topsy-turvy. Which was strange, since they'd talked on the phone for an hour or more the last three nights, picking up each conversation exactly where they had left off. He would usually call around dusk, and she'd talk to him from the porch, trying to imagine how he looked at that moment and replaying their day together endlessly.

Spending time with him at the ranch was one thing. That was easy. But seeing Luke here? At the sorority house? He might as well be visiting Mars. In the three years she'd lived here, the only guys who'd ever come to the house—aside from brothers or fathers or boyfriends from back home—were either frat boys, or recently graduated frat boys, or frat boys from other colleges.

She'd gently tried to warn him but wasn't sure quite how to tell him that the girls in the house would probably regard him as an exotic specimen, a subject of endless chatter as soon as he left. She'd suggested meeting him off campus, but he'd said he'd never been to Wake and wanted to walk around. She fought the urge to race downstairs and hurry him out the door as quickly as possible.

Remembering Marcia's insistent advice, Sophia took a deep breath and gave herself the once-over in the mirror. Jeans, blouse, pumps: pretty much what she'd worn the last time they'd been together, but upgraded. She turned first one way and then the other, thinking, That's all I can do. Then she gave a coy smile and admitted, But not bad at all.

She checked her watch and let another minute pass before exiting the room. During the week, men were allowed entrance only to the foyer and the parlor. The parlor, which boasted couches and a gigantic flat-screen TV, was where a lot of her sisters liked to hang out. As she approached the steps at the end of the hall, she could hear Marcia laughing in an otherwise silent room. She walked a bit faster, praying that she and Luke could escape without being noticed.

She spotted him right away, standing in the center of the room next to Marcia, hat in hand. As always, he was wearing boots and jeans, his outfit completed by a belt with a shiny, oversize silver buckle. Sophia's heart sank as she realized that he and Marcia weren't alone in the parlor. In fact, it was more crowded than usual, but eerily silent. Three frat boys, dressed in cargo shorts, Polos, and

Top-Siders, gaped at Luke in the same way Mary-Kate did from the opposite couch. Likewise Jenny, Drew, and Brittany. Four or five more girls huddled silently in the far corner, all of them trying their best to figure out the unexpected stranger in their presence.

But as far as she could tell, their scrutiny had no effect on him. He seemed at ease, listening as Marcia chattered on, her hands gesturing flamboyantly. As she reached the entrance to the parlor, he glanced up and saw her. Breaking into a grin, his dimples flashing, he conveyed the impression that Marcia had vanished and that he and Sophia were the only two people in the room.

Sophia took a deep breath and stepped into the parlor, feeling everyone's attention swing to her. On cue, Jenny leaned toward Drew and Brittany and whispered something. Though they'd naturally heard about her breakup with Brian, it was clear that none of them had heard about Luke, and she wondered how quickly Brian would find out that a cowboy had come to pick her up. On Greek Row, word would get around fast. She could already imagine any number of them dialing their cell phones, even before she and Luke reached the truck.

Which meant that Brian would find out. It wouldn't take much for him to guess that it was the same cowboy who'd humiliated him the weekend before. He wasn't going to be happy about it, nor would his frat brothers. And depending on how much they'd been drinking—on Thursdays, everyone started early—they just might get it into their heads to exact revenge. Suddenly queasy, she wondered why she hadn't thought of it before.

"Hey there," she said, doing her best to disguise her anxiety.

Luke's smile deepened. "You look fantastic."

"Thank you," Sophia murmured.

"I like him," Marcia chimed in.

Luke glanced at her, startled, before turning back to Sophia. "Obviously, I had a chance to meet your roommate."

"I was trying to find out if he had any single friends," Marcia admitted.

"And?"

"He said he'd see what he could do."

Sophia motioned with her head. "You ready to go?" she asked.

Marcia was already shaking her head. "No, not yet. He just got here."

Sophia glared at Marcia, hoping she'd pick up on her cues. "We really can't stay."

"Come on," Marcia cajoled. "Let's get a drink first. Thursday night, remember? I want to hear about riding bulls."

Off to the side, Mary-Kate's expression was pinched as she put the pieces together. No doubt Brian had returned to the table last Saturday, regaling everyone with stories about how he'd been jumped by a gang of cowboys. Brian and Mary-Kate had always been friends, and when Mary-Kate grabbed her phone and rose from the couch and left the parlor, Sophia assumed the worst and didn't hesitate.

"We can't stay. We have reservations," she said firmly.

"What?" Marcia blinked. "You didn't tell me that. Where?"

Sophia blanked, unable to think of anything. She could feel Luke watching her before he cleared his throat. "Fabian's," he suddenly announced.

Marcia swiveled her attention from one to the other. "I'm sure they won't mind if you're a few minutes late."

"Unfortunately, we're already running late," Luke said. Then, to Sophia: "Do you have everything?"

Sophia felt a surge of relief and adjusted the purse strap on her shoulder. "I'm ready," she agreed.

Luke took her elbow gently as he led her toward the door. "Nice meeting you, Marcia."

"You too," she said, bewildered.

Opening the door, he stopped to put his hat back on. He wore an amused expression as he adjusted it, as if to acknowledge their confusion about the whole thing. With a grin, he stepped out with Sophia on his arm.

As the door swung shut behind them, Sophia heard the burst of excited chatter. If Luke heard it, he appeared to pay it no attention. Instead, he led her to the truck and opened the door, then walked around the front to his side. As he did, she noticed a row of eager faces—including Marcia's—at the parlor windows. She was debating whether to acknowledge them with a wave or simply ignore them when Luke crawled in, closing the door with a thud.

"I'm guessing you've made them curious," he said.

She shook her head. "It's not me they're wondering about."

"Oh, I get it," he said. "It's because I'm skinny, right?"

She laughed, and with that, she realized that she no longer cared about what the others were thinking or doing or saying about them. "Thanks for covering for me in there."

"What's going on?"

She told him about her concerns about Brian and her suspicions about Mary-Kate.

"I wondered about that," he said. "You mentioned that he'd been watching you. Part of me was expecting him to burst through the door any minute."

"And yet you came anyway?"

"I had to." He shrugged. "You invited me."

She leaned her head back against the headrest, liking the way he sounded. "I'm sorry that I'm not going to be able to show you the campus tonight."

"No big deal."

"We can do it another time," she promised. "When he doesn't know you're here, I mean. I'll show you all the cool places."

"It's a date," he said.

Up close, his eyes were a clear, unalloyed blue, striking in their purity. She plucked at an imaginary piece of lint on her jeans. "What would you like to do?"

He thought about it. "Are you hungry?"

"A little," she admitted.

"Do you want to go to Fabian's? I'm not sure we can get in, since we don't really have a reservation. But we can try."

She thought about it, then shook her head. "No, not tonight. I want to go someplace a little off the beaten track. How about sushi?"

He didn't respond right away. "Okay," he offered.

She regarded him. "Have you ever had sushi before?"

"I might live on a ranch, but I've left it every now and then."

And? she thought. "You didn't answer my question."

He fiddled with the keys before slipping the right one in the ignition. "No," he admitted, "I've never had sushi."

All she could do was laugh.

Following Sophia's directions, they drove to Sakura Japanese Restaurant. Inside, most of the tables were occupied, as was the sushi bar. While they waited for the hostess, Sophia looked around, praying she wouldn't bump into anyone she knew. It wasn't the kind of place regularly frequented by students—burgers and pizza were the favored foods of college students everywhere—but Sakura wasn't totally unknown, either. She'd come here occasionally with Marcia, and even though she didn't recognize anyone, she nonetheless requested a seat on the outdoor patio.

Heat lamps glowed in the corners of the patio, casting a blanket of warmth that took the edge off the evening chill. Only one other table was occupied by a couple finishing their meal, and it was blissfully quiet. The view wasn't much, but the soft yellow glow from the Japanese lantern overhead gave the place a romantic feel.

After they took their seats, Sophia leaned toward Luke. "What did you think of Marcia?"

"Your roommate? She seemed nice enough. Kind of touchy, though."

She tilted her head. "You mean like, irritable?"

"No, I mean she kept touching my arm when she talked."

Sophia waved it off. "That's just the way she is. She's like that with every guy. The world's biggest flirt."

"Do you know what the first thing she said to me was? Even before I entered the house?"

"I'm afraid to ask."

"She said, 'I hear you kissed my best friend.'"

No surprise there, Sophia thought. "That's Marcia, all right. She pretty much says whatever she's thinking. No filter."

"But you like her."

"Yeah," Sophia conceded. "I do. She's kind of taken me under her wing when I've needed it. She thinks I'm a little...naive."

"Is she right?"

"In some ways," Sophia admitted.

She reached for the chopsticks and broke them apart. "Before I came to Wake, I'd never even had a boyfriend before. In high school, I was kind of a nerd, and with work, I didn't have a lot of time to go to parties or anything like that. I mean, I wasn't a hermit and I knew what people did on the weekends. I knew there were drugs at school and sex and all that, but it was mainly rumors or whispers that I'd overhear. It's not like I ever saw any of it happening. During my first semester on campus, I was pretty shocked at how open everything was. I'd hear girls in the dorm talking about hooking up with guys they just met, and I wasn't even totally sure what that meant. Half the time, I'm still not sure, because it seems like different people mean different things. To some, it's just making out, but to others, it means sleeping with someone, and to others something in between, if you know what I mean. I spent a big chunk of my freshman year trying to unscramble the code."

He smiled as she went on.

"And then, Greek life in general isn't quite what I expected. There are parties all the time, and to a lot of people, that means booze and drugs or whatever. And I'll admit that I drank too much a couple of times, and I ended up sick and passing out in the bathroom at the house. I'm not proud of that, but there are people on campus who do that every weekend, all weekend long. And I'm not saying it's because of Greek life at all. It's in the dorms, in off-campus apartments, everywhere. But I'm just not that into it, and to a lot of people—Marcia included—that makes me naive. Added to that, I'm not part of the whole 'hookup' culture, and a lot of people think I'm some kind of prude. Even Marcia thinks that, a little. She's never understood why anyone would want a real boyfriend in college. She always tells me that the last thing she wants is anything serious."

He reached for his chopsticks, following her lead. "I can think of a few guys who would be very interested in a girl like that."

"No, don't...because even though she says that, I'm not sure it's true. I think she wants something more real, but she doesn't know how to find a guy who feels the same way. In college, there aren't that many guys like that, and why would there be? When girls just give it away for nothing? I mean, I can understand why you'd sleep with someone if you love them, but if you barely know them? What's the point? It just cheapens it."

She fell silent, realizing that he was the first person she'd ever admitted all this to. Which was strange. Wasn't it?

Luke toyed with his chopsticks, picking at the rough edges where he had broken them apart, taking his time to consider it. Then, leaning into the lamplight, he said, "Sounds kind of mature, if you ask me."

She raised the menu, a bit embarrassed by that. "Just so you know, you don't have to get sushi if you don't want that. They have chicken and beef teriyaki, too."

Luke studied his own menu. "What are you going to have?"

"Sushi," she answered.

"Where did you learn to like sushi?"

"In high school," she said. "One of my best friends was Japanese, and she kept telling me there was this great place in Edgewater where she went when she was homesick for good Japanese food. You can only eat at the deli so many times before you start to crave something new, so I went with her one day, and I ended up loving it. So sometimes, when we were studying, we'd get in her car and drive to Edgewater—just this little nondescript place. But we became regulars. And since then, I get these cravings for it every now and then. Like tonight."

"I get it," he agreed. "In high school, when I was competing in 4-H, I'd go to the state fair and I always had to have a fried Twinkie."

She stared at him. "You're comparing sushi to fried Twinkies?"

"Have you ever had a fried Twinkie?"

"It sounds disgusting."

"Yeah, well, until you try one, you're not allowed to comment. They're good. Eat too many and you'll probably have a heart attack, but every now and then, there's nothing like it. Way better than fried Oreos."

"Fried *Oreos?*"

"If you're trying to find a suggestion for your family deli, like I said, I'd go with the fried Twinkie."

At first, she couldn't formulate any response at all. Then, with a serious tone: "I don't think anyone in the Northeast would eat such a thing."

"You'd be surprised," he said. "It could be the next big thing up there—people lining up all day long."

With a tiny shake of her head, she turned to the menu again. "So 4-H, huh?"

"I started when I was a kid. Pigs."

"What is it, exactly? I mean, I've heard about it, but I don't know what it is."

"It's supposed to be about citizenship and responsibility and all that stuff. But when it comes to competing, it's more about learning how to choose a good pig when it's little. You check out its parents if you can or pictures or whatever, then you try to pick the one that you think has a chance to be a good show pig. You want a firm pig with a lot of muscle and not too much fat and no blemishes. And then, basically, you raise it for about a year. You feed it and care for it; in a way, they almost become like pets."

"Let me guess. You named all of them Pig."

"Actually, no. My first one was named Edith, the second one Fred, the third one was Maggie. I can go down the list if you'd like."

"How many were there? Over the years?"

He drummed his fingers on the table. "Nine, I think. I started when I was in the third grade and I did it until junior year in high school."

"And then, when they're grown, where do you compete?"

"At the state fair. The judges look them over and then you find out if you won."

"And if you win?"

"You get a ribbon. But win or lose, you still end up selling the pig," he said.

"What happens to the pig?"

"The same thing that usually happens to pigs," he answered. "They're sent to the slaughterhouse."

She blinked. "You mean you raise it from when it's little, you name it, you care for it for a year, and then you sell it so it can be killed?"

He looked at her, his expression curious. "What else would you do with a pig?"

She was dumbfounded, unable to respond. Finally, she shook her head. "I just want you to know that I have never, ever met anyone like you before."

"I think," he countered, "that I could say the same thing about you."

10

⬥

Luke

Even after studying the menu, he wasn't sure what to order. He knew he could have gone with something safe—like the chicken or beef teriyaki she'd mentioned—but he was reluctant to do that. He'd heard people rave about sushi and knew he should try it. Life was about experience, wasn't it?

The problem was that he didn't have the slightest idea what to choose. To his mind, raw fish was raw fish, and the pictures didn't help at all. As far as he could tell, he was supposed to order either the reddish one or the pinkish one or the whitish one, none of which hinted at how it might taste.

He peeked at Sophia over the top of his menu. She'd applied a bit more mascara and lipstick than she had on the day she'd come out to the ranch, reminding him of the night he'd first seen her. It seemed impossible that it had been less than a week ago. While generally a fan of natural beauty, he had to admit the makeup added a sophisticated touch to her features. On their way to the table, more than one man had turned to watch her pass.

"What's the difference between nigiri-sushi and maki-sushi?" he asked.

Sophia was still perusing the menu as well. When the waitress had come by, she'd ordered two Sapporos, a Japanese beer, one for each of them. He had no idea how that would taste, either.

"Nigiri means the fish is served on a pad of rice," she said. "Maki means it's rolled with seaweed."

"Seaweed?"

She winked. "It's good. You'll like it."

He compressed his lips, unable to hide his doubts. Beyond the windows, there were people at tables inside, enjoying whatever it was they'd ordered, all of them adept with their chopsticks. At least he was okay at that, his skills honed from eating Chinese food from thin cardboard boxes while on the road.

"Why don't you go ahead and order for me," he said, putting the menu aside. "I trust you."

"Okay," she agreed.

"What am I going to try?"

"A bunch of things," she said. "We'll try some anago, ahi, aji, hamachi . . . maybe some others."

He lifted his bottle, about to take a sip. "You do realize that sounds like gibberish to me."

"Anago is eel," she clarified.

The bottle froze in midair. "Eel?"

"You'll like it," she assured him, not bothering to hide her amusement.

When the waitress came by, Sophia rambled off the order like an expert; then they settled into easy conversation, interrupted only when their meal arrived. He gave her an abbreviated overview of his childhood, which despite his chores at the ranch had been fairly typical. His high school years included varsity wrestling for three years, all four homecoming dances, both proms, and a handful of memorable parties. He told her that in the summers, he and his parents would take the horses up to the mountains near Boone for a few days, where they'd go trail riding, the only family vacations they ever took. He talked a bit about his practices on the mechanical bull in the barn and how his father had tinkered with the bull to make the motion even more violent. The practice sessions had started when he was still in elementary school, his father critiquing his every move. He mentioned some of the injuries he'd suffered over the years and described the nerves he felt when riding in the PBR World Championships—once, he'd been in the running for the championship until the final ride, only to finish third overall—and through it all, Sophia listened raptly, interrupting him only occasionally to ask questions.

He felt the laserlike focus that she trained on him, absorbing every detail, and by the time the waitress had removed their plates, everything about her, from her easy laughter to her slight but discernible northern accent, struck him as charming and desirable. More than that, he felt like he could truly be himself despite their differences. When he was with her, he found it easy to forget the stress he felt whenever he thought about the ranch. Or his mom. Or what was going to happen if his plans didn't work out...

He was so absorbed in his thoughts, it took a moment before he realized she was staring at him.

"What are you thinking about?" she asked.

"Why?"

"You looked almost... lost there for a minute."

"Nothing."

"You sure? I hope it wasn't the anago."

"No. Just thinking about what I have to do before I leave this weekend."

She furrowed her brow, watching him. "Okay," she finally said. "When do you leave?"

"Tomorrow afternoon," he said, thankful she'd let it pass. "I'll drive to Knoxville after I finish up and spend the night. On Saturday night, I'll start driving back. I'll get in late, but it's the first weekend we're selling pumpkins. I got most of the Halloween stuff set up today—José and I built a great big maze out of hay bales, among other things—but a lot of people always show up. Even with José pitching in, my mom still needs extra help."

"Is that why she was mad at you? Because you'll be out of town?"

"Partly," he said, pushing a bright pink sliver of ginger around his plate. "She's mad because I'm riding, period."

"Isn't she used to it by now? Or is it because you got hurt on Big Ugly Critter?"

"My mom," he said, choosing his words with care, "is worried that something's going to happen to me."

"But you've been injured before. Lots of times."

"Yes."

"Is there something you're not telling me?"

He didn't answer right away. "How about this?" he said, laying his chopsticks down. "When the time is right, I'll tell you all about it."

"I could always ask your mom, you know."

"You could. But you'd have to meet her first."

"Well, maybe I'll just go out there on Saturday and try."

"Go ahead. But if you do, just be prepared to be put to work. You'll be carrying pumpkins all day."

"I've got muscles."

"Have you ever carried pumpkins all day?"

She leaned across the table. "Have you ever unloaded a truck filled with meat and sausage?" Her expression was victorious when he didn't answer. "See, we do have something in common. We're both hard workers."

"And we can both ride horses now, too."

She smiled. "That too. How did you like the sushi?"

"It was good," he said.

"I get the feeling you would have preferred pork chops."

"I can have pork chops anytime. It's one of my specialties."

"You cook?"

"On the grill," he said. "My dad taught me."

"I think I'd like for you to grill for me sometime."

"I'll make anything you want. As long as it's burgers, steaks, or pork chops."

She leaned closer. "So what's next? Would you like to risk

our luck and go to a frat party? I'm sure they're getting going about now."

"What about Brian?"

"We'll go to a party at a different house. One he never goes to. And we wouldn't have to stay long. You might have to ditch the hat, though."

"If you'd like to, I'm game."

"I can go anytime. I was asking for you."

"What are they like?" he asked. "Music, a bunch of drinking college kids, that kind of stuff?"

"Pretty much."

He thought about it for a second before shaking his head. "It's not really my thing," he admitted.

"I didn't think so. We could always do a tour of the campus if you'd like."

"I think I'd rather save that for another time. So you have to go out with me again."

She traced her finger around the rim of her water glass. "Then what do you want to do?"

He didn't answer right away, and for the first time, he wondered how different things might be had he not made the decision to ride again. His mom wasn't happy, and frankly, even he wasn't sure it was a good idea, but somehow it had led to a date with a girl he already knew he'd never forget.

"Are you up for a little drive? I know a place where I can promise you won't see anyone you know. It's quiet, but it's really pretty at night."

❧

Back at the ranch, the moon lent a silver wash to the world as they stepped out of the truck. Dog, a blur in the darkness, came racing out from beneath the porch, stopping at Sophia's side almost as though he'd been expecting them.

"I hope this is okay," he said. "I wasn't sure where else to go."

"I knew you were bringing me here," Sophia said, reaching down to pet Dog. "If it bothered me, I would have said something."

He motioned toward his house. "We could sit on the porch, or there's a great spot down by the lake."

"Not the river?"

"You've already been to the river."

She took in the surroundings, then turned to him again. "Are we going to sit in chairs in the back of the truck again?"

"Of course," he said. "Trust me, you wouldn't want to sit on the ground. It's a pasture."

He watched as Dog began to circle her legs. "Can we bring Dog?" she asked.

"Dog will follow whether I want him to come or not."

"Then the lake it is," she said.

"Let me just get some things from the house, okay?"

He left her, returning with a small cooler and some blankets beneath his arm, which he loaded into the back of the truck. They got in, the engine coming to life with a roar.

"Your truck sounds like a tank," she shouted over the noise. "I don't know if you're aware of that."

"Do you like it? I had to modify the exhaust system to make it sound the way it does. I added a second muffler and everything."

"You did not. No one does that."

"I did," he offered. "Lots of people do."

"People who live on ranches, maybe."

"Not just us. People who hunt and fish do it, too."

"Basically anyone with a gun and a passion for the outdoors, in other words."

"You mean there are other kinds of people in the world?"

She smiled as he backed out, turning onto the drive before heading past the farmhouse. There were lights blazing from inside the living room, and he wondered what his mom was doing. He thought then about what he'd said to Sophia and what he hadn't.

Trying to clear his thoughts, he rolled down the window, resting his elbow on the ledge. The truck bumped along, and from the corner of his eye, he could see Sophia's wheat-colored hair fanning out in the breeze. She was staring out the passenger window as they rode past the barn in comfortable silence.

At the pasture, he hopped out and opened a gate before nosing the truck through and closing the gate behind him. Turning the beams on high, he drove slowly to avoid damaging the grass. Near the lake, he stopped and turned the truck around, just as he had at the rodeo, and shut down the engine.

"Watch where you step," he warned. "Like I said, this is part of the pasture."

He opened her window and turned on the radio, then went around to the back of the truck. He helped Sophia climb up before setting up the chairs. And then, just as they had less than a week earlier, they sat in the bed of the truck, this time with a blanket draped over Sophia's lap. He reached for the cooler and pulled out two bottles of beer. He opened both, handing one to Sophia, watching as she took a sip.

Beyond them, the lake was a mirror, reflecting the crescent moon and the stars overhead. In the distance, on the other side of the lake, the cattle congregated near the bank were huddled together, their white chests flashing in the darkness. Every now and then one of them mooed and the noise floated across the water, mingling with the sounds of frogs and crickets. It smelled of grass and dirt and the earth itself, almost primordial.

"It's beautiful here," Sophia whispered.

He felt the same word could be used to describe her, but he kept his thoughts to himself.

"It's like the clearing at the river," she added. "Only more open."

"Kind of," he said. "But like I told you, I tend to go out there when I want to think about my dad. This place is where I come to think about other things."

"Like what?"

The water nearby was still and reflected the sky like a mirror. "Lots of things," he said. "Life. Work. Relationships."

She shot him a sidelong glance. "I thought you haven't been in a lot of relationships."

"That's why I have to think about them."

She giggled. "Relationships are tricky. Of course, I'm young and naive, so what do I know?"

"So if I was to ask you for advice..."

"I'd say there are better people out there to ask. Like your mom, maybe."

"Maybe," he said. "She got along pretty well with my dad. Especially after he gave up the rodeo circuit and was available to help out around the ranch. If he'd kept at it, I don't know if they would have made it. It was too much for her to handle on her own, especially with me to take care of. I'm pretty sure she told him exactly that. So he stopped. And growing up, whenever I asked him about it, he'd just say that being married to my mom was more important than riding horses."

"You sound proud of her."

"I am," he said. "Even though both my parents were hard workers, she's the one who really built up the business. When she inherited it from my grandfather, the ranch was struggling. Cattle markets tend to fluctuate a lot, and some years, you don't make much of anything. It was her idea to focus on the growing interest in organic beef. She was the one who'd get in the car and drive all over the state, leaving brochures and talking to restaurant owners. Without her, there would be no such thing as Collins Beef. To you, it might not mean much, but to high-end beef consumers in North Carolina, it means something."

Sophia took that in while she examined the farmhouse in the distance. "I'd like to meet her."

"I'd bring you by now, but she's probably already asleep. She goes to bed pretty early. But I'll be here on Sunday, if you'd like to come over."

"I think you just want me to help you haul pumpkins."

"I was thinking you could come by for dinner, actually. Like I said, during the day it's pretty busy."

"I'd like that, if you think your mom will be okay with that."

"She will."

"What time?"

"Around six?"

"Sounds great," she said. "By the way, where's that maze you were talking about?"

"It's near the pumpkin patch."

She frowned. "Did we go there the other day?"

"No," he said. "It's actually closer to the main road, near the Christmas trees."

"Why didn't I notice it when we drove in?"

"I don't know. Because it was dark, maybe?"

"Is it a scary maze? With spooky scarecrows and spiders and all that?"

"Of course, but it's not really spooky. It's mainly for little kids. One time, my dad went a little overboard and a few of the kids ended up crying. Since then, we try to keep it toned down. But there are a ton of decorations in there. Spiders, ghosts, scarecrows. Friendly-looking ones."

"Can we go?"

"Of course. I'll be happy to show you. But keep in mind it's not the same for big people, since you can see over the bales." He waved away a couple of gnats. "You didn't really answer my earlier question, by the way."

"What question?"

"About relationships," he said.

She adjusted the blanket again. "I used to think I understood the basics. I mean, my mom and dad have been married for a long time and I thought I knew what I was doing. But I guess I didn't learn the most important part."

"Which is?"

"Choosing well in the first place."

"How do you know if you're choosing well?"

"Well . . . ," she hedged. "That's where it starts getting tricky. But if I had to guess, I think it starts with having things in common. Like values. For instance, I thought it important that Brian be faithful. He was obviously operating under a different value system."

"At least you can joke about it."

"It's easy to joke when you don't care anymore. I'm not saying it didn't hurt me, because it did. Last spring, after I found out he hooked up with another girl, I couldn't eat for weeks. I probably lost fifteen pounds."

"You don't have fifteen pounds to lose."

"I know, but what could I do? Some people eat when they get stressed. I'm the other kind. And when I got home last summer, my mom and dad were panicked. They begged me to eat every time I turned around. I still haven't regained all the weight I lost. Of course, it hasn't been easy to eat since school started back up, either."

"I'm glad you ate with me, then."

"You don't stress me out."

"Even though we don't have a lot in common?"

As soon as he said it, he worried that she would hear the undercurrent of concern, but she didn't seem to detect it.

"We have more things in common than you'd think. In some ways, our parents were pretty similar. They were married for a long time, worked in a struggling family business, and expected the kids to chip in. My parents wanted me to do well in school, your dad wanted you to be a champion bull rider, and we both fulfilled their expectations. We're both products of our upbringing, and I'm not sure that's ever going to change."

Surprising himself, he felt a strange sense of relief at her answer. "You ready to check out that maze yet?"

"How about if we finish our beers first. It's too nice out here to leave just yet."

As they slowly drained their bottles, they chatted idly and watched the moonlight trace a path across the water. Though he felt the urge to kiss her again, he resisted it. Instead, he reflected on what she'd said earlier, about their similarities, thinking she was right and hoping that it was enough to keep her coming back to the ranch.

After a while their conversation lapsed into a peaceful lull, and he realized he had no idea what she was thinking. Instinctively, he reached toward the blanket. She seemed to realize what he was doing and wordlessly held his hand.

The night air was turning crisper, giving the stars a crystalline cast. He looked up at them, then over to her, and when her thumb gently began to trace the contours of his hand, he responded in kind. In that instant, he knew with certainty that he was already falling for her and that there was nothing on earth he could do to stop it.

As they strolled through the pumpkin patch toward the maze, Luke continued to hold her hand. Somehow, this simple gesture felt more significant than their earlier kisses, more permanent somehow. He could imagine holding it years into the future, whenever they were walking together, and the realization startled him.

"What are you thinking about?"

He walked a few paces before answering. "A lot of things," he finally said.

"Did anyone ever tell you that you have a tendency to be vague?"

"Does it bother you?" he countered.

"I haven't decided yet," she said, squeezing his hand. "I'll let you know."

"The maze is right over there." He pointed. "But I wanted to show you the pumpkin patch first."

"Can I pick one?"

"Sure."

"Will you help me carve it for Halloween?"

"We can carve it after dinner. And just so you know, I'm kind of an expert."

"Oh yeah?"

"I've already carved fifteen or twenty this week. Scary ones, happy ones, all kinds."

She gave him an appraising look. "You are obviously a man of many talents."

He knew she was teasing him, but he liked it. "Thanks."

"I can't wait to meet your mom."

"You'll like her."

"What's she like?"

"Let's just say that you shouldn't expect a lady in a flowered dress and pearls. Think more... jeans and boots with straw in her hair."

Sophia smiled. "Got it. Anything else I should know?"

"My mom would have been a great pioneer. When something has to be done, she just does it, and she expects the same from me. She's kind of no-nonsense. And she's tough."

"I would think so. It's not an easy life out here."

"I mean, she's really tough. Ignores pain, never complains, doesn't whine or cry. Three years ago, she broke her wrist falling off a horse. So what did she do? She said nothing, worked the rest of the day, cooked dinner, and then afterwards, she drove herself to the hospital. I didn't know a thing about it until I noticed her cast the next day."

Sophia stepped over some wayward vines, careful not to damage any of the pumpkins. "Remind me to be on my best manners."

"You'll be fine. She'll like you. You two are more alike than you'd think."

When she glanced over at him, he went on. "She's smart," he said. "Believe it or not, she was valedictorian of her high school class, and even now she reads, does all the bookkeeping, and stays on top of the business. She's opinionated, but she expects more from herself than from others. If she had one weakness, it was that she was a sucker for guys in cowboy hats."

She laughed. "Is that what I am? A sucker for cowboys?"

"I don't know. Are you?"

She didn't answer. "Your mom sounds pretty amazing."

"She is," he said. "And who knows, maybe if she's in one of her moods, she'll tell you one of her stories. My mom is big on stories."

"Stories about what?"

"Anything, really. But they always make me think."

"Tell me one," she said.

He stopped and then squatted down near an oversize pumpkin. "All right," he said as he shifted the pumpkin from one side to the other. "After I won the High School National Championship in Rodeo—"

"Wait...," she said, cutting him off. "Before you go on...they have rodeo in high school here?"

"They have it everywhere. Why?"

"Not in New Jersey."

"Of course they do. Contestants come from every state. You just have to be in high school."

"And you won?"

"Yes, but that's not the point," he said, standing up and taking her hand again. "I was trying to tell you that after I won—the *first* time, not the *second* time," he teased, "I was jabbering on about my goals and what I wanted to do, and of course, my dad was just lapping it up. But my mom started to clear the table, and after a while she interrupted my grand fantasy to tell me a story . . . and it's stayed with me ever since."

"What did she say?"

"A young man lives in a tiny, run-down cottage on the beach and he rows his boat out into the ocean every day to fish, not only because he needs to eat, but because he feels peaceful on the water. But more than that, he also wants to improve his life and that of his family, so he works hard at bringing in bigger and bigger catches. With his earnings, he eventually buys a bigger boat so he can make his business even more profitable. That leads to a third boat and then a fourth boat, and as the years pass and the business continues to grow, he eventually accumulates a whole fleet of boats. By then, he's rich and successful, with a big house and a thriving business, but the stress and pressure of running the company eventually take their toll. He realizes that when he retires, what he really wants more than anything is to live in a tiny cottage on the beach, where he can fish all day in a rowboat . . . because he wants to feel the same sense of peace and satisfaction he experienced when he was young."

She cocked her head. "Your mom's a wise woman. There's a lot of truth in that story."

"Do you think so?"

"I think," she said, "that the point is that people rarely understand that nothing is ever exactly what you think it will be."

By then, they'd reached the entrance to the maze. Luke led her through, pointing out openings that dead-ended after a series of turns and others that led much farther. The maze covered nearly an acre, which made it a huge draw for kids.

When they reached the exit, they strolled toward the harvested pumpkins. While many had been placed up front, some were stacked in bins, others clustered together in loose piles. Hundreds remained in the field beyond.

"That's it," he said.

"It's a lot. How long did it take you to set all this up?"

"Three days. But we had other things to do, too."

"Of course you did."

She sorted through the pumpkins, eventually picking out a medium-size one and handing it to Luke before they walked back to the truck, where he loaded it into the bed.

When he turned, Sophia was standing in front of him, her thick blond hair almost whitish in the starlight. Instinctively, he reached first for one hand and then the other, and the words came out before he could stop them.

"I feel like I want to know everything about you," he murmured.

"You know me better than you think," she said. "I've told you about my family and childhood, I've told you about college and what I want to do with my life. There's not much else to know."

But there was. There was so much more, and he wanted to know everything.

"Why are you here?" he whispered.

She wasn't sure what he meant. "Because you brought me here?"

"I mean why are you with me?"

"Because I want to be here."

"I'm glad," he said.

"Yeah? Why?"

"Because you're smart. And interesting."

Her head was tilted up, her expression inviting. "The last time you called me interesting, you ended up kissing me."

He said nothing to that. Instead, leaning in, he watched her eyes slowly close, and when their lips came together, he felt a sense of discovery, like an explorer finally reaching distant shores he'd only imagined or heard about. He kissed her again and then again, and when he pulled back, he rested his forehead against hers. He drew a deep breath, struggling to keep his emotions in check, knowing that he didn't love her simply in the here and now, but that he would never stop loving her.

11

Ira

It is now Sunday afternoon, and once it gets dark, I will have been here for more than twenty-four hours. The pain continues to wax and wane, but my legs and feet have gone numb from the cold. My face, where it rests against the steering wheel, has begun to ache; I can feel the bruises forming. My greatest torment, however, has become thirst. The thought of water is excruciating, my throat prickling with each breath. My lips are as dry and cracked as a drought-stricken field.

Water, I think again. Without it, I will die. I need it and can hear it calling to me.

Water.

Water.

Water.

The thought won't leave me, blocking out everything else. I have never in my life craved such a simple thing; I have never in my life spent hours wondering how to get it. And I do not need much. Just a little. Even a capful will make all the difference in the world. A single drop will make a difference.

Yet I remain paralyzed. I don't know where the bottle of water is, and I'm not sure I'd be able to open it even if I could find it. I'm afraid that if I unbuckle the seat belt, I might topple forward, too weak to stop my collarbone from smashing into the steering wheel. I might end up crumpled on the floor of the car, wedged into a position from which I can't escape. I can't even imagine lifting my head from the steering wheel, let alone rummaging through the car.

And still, my need for water calls to me. Its call is constant and insistent, and desperation sets in. I am going to die of thirst, I think to myself. I am going to die here, as I am. And there is no way I will ever get to the backseat. The paramedics will not slide me out like a fish stick.

"You have a morbid sense of humor," Ruth says, interrupting my thoughts, and I remind myself that she is nothing but a dream.

"I think the situation calls for it, don't you?"

"You are still alive."

"Yes, but for how much longer?"

"The record is sixty-four days. A man in Sweden. I saw it on the Weather Channel."

"No. I saw it on the Weather Channel."

She shrugs. "It is the same thing, yes?"

She has a point, I think. "I need water."

"No," she says. "Right now, we need to talk. It will keep your mind from fixating on it."

"Like a trick," I say.

"I am not a trick," she says. "I am your wife. And I want you to listen to me."

I obey. Staring at her, I allow myself to drift again. My eyes finally close and I feel as if I'm floating downstream in a river. Images coming and going, one right after the other as I am carried past on the current.

Drifting.

Drifting.

And then, finally, it solidifies into something real.

In the car, I open my eyes and blink, noticing how Ruth has changed from my last vision of her. But this memory, unlike the others, is sharp-edged and clear to me. She is as she was in June of 1946. I am certain of this, because it is the first time I've ever seen her wear a casual summer dress. She, like everyone else after the war, is changing. Clothes are changing. Later this year, the bikini will be invented by Louis Réard, a French engineer, and as I stare at Ruth, I notice a sinuous beauty in the muscles of her arms. Her skin is a smooth walnut hue from the weeks she'd just spent at the beach with her parents. Her father had taken the family to the Outer Banks to celebrate his official hiring at Duke. He had interviewed at a number of different places, including a small experimental art college in the mountains, but he felt most at home among the Gothic buildings at Duke. He would be teaching again that fall, a bright spot in what had otherwise been a difficult year of mourning.

Things had changed between Ruth and me since that night in the park. Ruth had said little about my revelation, but when I walked her home I didn't try to kiss her good night. I knew she was reeling, and even she would later admit that she was not herself for the next few weeks. The next time I saw her she was no longer wearing her engagement ring, but I didn't blame her for this. She was in shock, but she was also rightfully angry that I had not trusted her with the information until that night. Coming on the heels of the loss of her family in Vienna, it was undoubtedly a terrible blow. For it is one thing to declare one's love for someone and quite another to accept that loving that person requires sacrificing one's dreams. And having children— creating a family, so to speak—had taken on an entirely new significance for her in the wake of her family's losses.

I understood this intuitively, and for the next couple of months, neither of us pressed the other. We didn't speak of commitment, but we continued to see each other casually, perhaps two or three times a week. Sometimes I would take her to see a show or bring her to dinner, other times we would stroll downtown. There was an art gallery of which she'd grown particularly fond, and we visited regularly. Most of the artwork was unmemorable either in subject or in execution, but every now and then, Ruth would see something special in a painting that I could not. Like her father, she was most passionate about modern art, a movement given birth to by painters like Van Gogh, Cézanne, and Gauguin, and she was quick to discern the influence of these painters in even the mediocre work we examined.

These visits to the gallery, and her deep knowledge of art in general, opened up a world entirely foreign to me. However, I sometimes wondered whether our discussions about art became a means of avoiding conversation about our future. These discussions created a distance between us, but I was content to keep them going, longing even in those moments for both a forgiveness of the past and an acceptance of some kind of future for us, whatever that might be.

Ruth, however, seemed no closer to a decision than she'd been on that fateful night in the park. She wasn't cold to me, but she hadn't invited greater intimacy, either, and thus I was surprised when her parents invited me to spend part of their holiday at the beach with them.

A couple of weeks of quiet walks on the beach together might have been just what we needed, but unfortunately, it wasn't possible for me to be gone that long. With my father glued to the radio in the back room, I had by then become the face of the shop, and it was busier than ever. Veterans looking for work were coming in to buy suits they could barely afford, in the hopes of finding a job. But companies were slow to hire, and when these desperate men walked in the store, I thought of Joe Torrey and Bud Ramsey and I did what I could for them. I convinced my father to stock lower-priced suits with fractional markups, and my mother did the alterations free of charge. Word of our reasonable prices had gotten out, and though we were no longer open on Saturdays, sales were increasing every month.

Nonetheless, I was able to persuade my parents to lend me the car in order to visit Ruth's family toward the end of their vacation, and by Thursday morning, I was on the road. It was a long drive, the last hour of which was spent driving on the sand itself. There was a wild, untamed beauty to the Outer Banks in the years right after the war. Largely cut off from the rest of the state, it was populated by families who'd lived there for generations, making their living from the sea. Saw grass speckled the wind-blown dunes, and the trees looked like the twisted clay creations of a child. Here and there I saw wild horses, their heads sometimes rising as I passed, tails swishing to keep the flies at bay. With the ocean roaring on one side and the windswept dunes on the other, I rolled down the windows, taking it all in and wondering what I might find when I reached my destination.

When I finally pulled onto the sandy gravel drive, it was nearly sunset. I was surprised to see Ruth waiting for me on the front porch, barefoot and wearing the same dress she is wearing now. I stepped out of the car, and as I stared at her, all I could think was how radiant she looked. Her hair fell loosely around her shoulders and her smile seemed to hold a secret meant only for the two of us. When she waved at me, my breath caught at the sight of a tiny diamond flashing in the rays of the setting sun—my engagement ring, absent all these past months.

I stood momentarily frozen, but she skipped down the steps and across the sand as if she hadn't a care in the world. When she jumped into my arms, she smelled of salt and brine and the wind itself, a scent I have forever associated with her and that particular weekend. I pulled her close, savoring the feel of her body against my own, thinking how much I'd missed holding her for the past three years.

"I am glad you are here," she whispered into my ear, and after a long and gratifying embrace, I kissed her while the sound of ocean waves seemed to roar their approval. When she kissed me back, I knew instantly that she'd made her decision about me, and my world shifted on its axis.

It was not the first kiss we'd ever shared, but in many ways it has become my favorite, if only because it happened when I needed it most, marking the beginning of one of the two most wonderful, and life-altering, periods of my life.

*

Ruth smiles at me in the car, beautiful and serene in that summer dress. The tip of her nose is slightly red, her hair windblown and redolent of the ocean breeze.

"I like this memory," she says to me.

"I like it, too," I say.

"Yes, because I was a young woman then. Thick hair, no wrinkles, nothing sagging."

"You haven't changed a bit."

"*Unsinn*," she says with a dismissive wave. "I changed. I became old, and it is not fun to be old. Things that were once simple became difficult."

"You sound like me," I remark, and she shrugs, untroubled by the revelation that she is nothing but a figment of my imagination. Instead, she circles back to the memory of my visit.

"I was so happy that you were able to come on holiday with us."

"I regret that my visit was so short."

It takes her a moment to respond. "I think," she says, "that it was good for me to have a couple of weeks of quiet time alone. My parents seemed to know this, too. There was little to do other than sit on the porch and walk in the sand and sip a glass of wine while the sun went down. I had much time to think. About me. About us."

"Which is why you threw yourself at me when I showed up," I tease.

"I did not throw myself at you," she says indignantly. "Your memory is distorted. I walked down the steps and offered a hug. I was raised to be a lady. I simply greeted you. This embellishment is a product of your imagination."

Maybe. Or maybe not. Who can know after so long? But I suppose it doesn't matter.

"Do you remember what we did next?" she asks.

Part of me wonders if she's testing me. "Of course," I answer. "We went inside and I greeted your parents. Your mother was slicing tomatoes in the kitchen and your father was grilling tuna on the back porch. He told me that he'd bought it that afternoon from a fisherman tying up at the pier. He was very proud of that. He seemed different as he stood over the grill that evening... relaxed."

"It was a good summer for him," Ruth agrees. "By then, he was managing the factory, so the days were not so hard on him, and it was the first time in years that we had enough money to go on holiday. Most of all, he was ecstatic at the thought of teaching again."

"And your mother was happy."

"My father's good spirits were infectious." Ruth pauses for a moment. "And, like me...she had grown to like it here. Greensboro would never be Vienna, but she had learned the language and made some friends. She had also grown to appreciate the warmth and generosity of the people here. In a way, I think she had finally begun to think of North Carolina as her home."

Outside the car, the wind blows clumps of snow from the branches. None of them hits the car, but somehow it is enough to remind me again of exactly where I am. But it does not matter, not right now.

"Do you remember how clear the sky was when we ate dinner?" I say. "There were so many stars."

"That is because it was so dark. No lights from the city. My father noted the same thing."

"I've always loved the Outer Banks. We should have gone every year," I say.

"I think it would have lost its magic if we went every year," she responds. "Every few years was perfect—like we did. Because every time we went back, it felt new and untamed and fresh again. Besides, when would we have gone? We were always traveling in the summers. New York, Boston, Philadelphia, Chicago, even California. And always, Black Mountain. We had the chance to see this country in a way that most people never could, and what could be better?"

Nothing, I think to myself, knowing in my heart that she is right. My home is filled with keepsakes from those trips. Strangely, though, aside from a seashell we found the following morning, I had nothing to remind me of this place, and yet the memory never dimmed.

"I always enjoyed having dinner with your parents. Your father seemed to know something about everything."

"He did," she says. "His father had been a teacher, his brother was a teacher. His uncles were teachers. My father came from a family of scholars. But you were interesting to my father, too—he was fascinated by your work as a navigator during the war, despite your reluctance to speak of it. I think it increased his respect for you."

"But your mother felt differently."

Ruth pauses and I know she is trying to choose her words carefully. She toys with a windblown strand of hair, inspecting it before going on. "At that time, she was still worried about me. All she knew was that you had broken my heart only a few months earlier, and that even though we were seeing each other again, there was still something troubling me."

Ruth was talking about the consequences of my bout with mumps and what it would likely mean for our future. It was something she would tell her mother only years later, when her mother's puzzlement turned to sadness and anxiety over the fact that she hadn't become a grandmother. Ruth gently revealed that we couldn't have children, careful not to place the blame entirely on me, though she could easily have done so. Another of her kindnesses, for which I've always been thankful.

"She didn't say much at dinner, but afterwards, I was relieved that she smiled at me."

"She appreciated the fact that you offered to do the dishes."

"It was the least I could do. To this day, that was the best meal I've ever had."

"It was good, yes?" Ruth reminisces. "Earlier, my mother had found a roadside stand with fresh vegetables, and she had baked bread. My father turned out to be a natural with the grill."

"And after we finished the dishes, we went for a walk."

"Yes," she says. "You were very bold that night."

"I wasn't acting bold. I simply asked for a bottle of wine and a pair of glasses."

"Yes, but this was new for you. My mother had never seen that side of you. It made her nervous."

"But we were adults."

"That was the problem. You were a man and she knew that men have urges."

"And women don't?"

"Yes, of course. But unlike men, women are not controlled by their urges. Women are civilized."

"Did your mother tell you that?" My voice is skeptical.

"I did not need my mother to tell me. It was clear to me what you wanted. Your eyes were full of lust."

"If I recall correctly," I say with crisp propriety, "I was a perfect gentleman that night."

"Yes, but it was still exciting for me, watching you try to control your urges. Especially when you spread your jacket and we sat in the sand and drank the wine. The ocean seemed to absorb the moonlight and I could feel that you wanted me, even if you were trying not to show it. You put your arm around me and we talked and kissed and talked some more and I was a little tipsy..."

"And it was perfect," I finally offer.

"Yes," she agrees. "It was perfect." Her expression is nostalgic and a little sad. "I knew I wanted to marry you and I knew for certain we would always be happy together."

I pause, fully aware of what she was thinking, even then. "You were still hopeful that the doctor might be wrong."

"I think that I said that whatever happened would be in God's hands."

"That's the same thing, isn't it?"

"Maybe," she answers, then shakes her head. "What I do know is that when I was sitting with you that night, I felt like God was telling me that I was doing the right thing."

"And then we saw the shooting star."

"It blazed all the way across the sky," she says. Her voice, even now, is filled with wonder. "It was the first time I had ever seen one like that."

"I told you to make a wish," I said.

"I did," she says, meeting my eyes. "And my wish came true only a few hours later."

Though it was late by the time Ruth and I got back to the house, her mother was still awake. She sat reading near the window, and as soon as we walked in the door, I felt her eyes sweep over us, looking for an untucked or improperly buttoned shirt, sand in our hair. Her relief was apparent as she rose to greet us, though she did her best to disguise it.

She chatted with Ruth while I went back to the car to retrieve my suitcase. Like many of the cottages along this stretch of the beach, the house had two floors. Ruth and her parents had rooms on the lower level, while the room Ruth's mother showed me to was directly off the kitchen on the main floor. The three of us spent a few minutes visiting in the kitchen before Ruth began to yawn. Her mother began to yawn as well, signaling the end of the evening. Ruth did not kiss me in front of her mother—at that point, it wasn't something we'd yet done—and after Ruth wandered off, her mother soon followed.

I turned out the lights and retreated to the back porch, soothed by the moonlit water and the breeze in my hair. I sat outside for a long time as the temperature cooled, my thoughts wandering from Ruth and me, to Joe Torrey, to my parents.

I tried to imagine my father and mother in a place like this, but I couldn't. Never once had we gone on vacation—the shop had always anchored us in place—but even if it had been possible, it wouldn't have been a holiday like this. I could no more imagine my father grilling with a glass of wine in hand than I could imagine him atop Mt. Everest, and somehow the thought made me sad. My father, I realized, had no idea how to relax; he seemed to lead his life preoccupied by work and worry. Ruth's parents, on the other hand, seemed to enjoy each moment for what it was. I was struck by how differently Ruth and her parents reacted to the war. While my mother and father seemed to recede into the past—albeit in different ways—her parents embraced the future, as though seizing hold of their chance at life. They opted to make the most of their fortunate fates and never lost a sense of gratitude for what they had.

The house was silent when I finally came in. Tempted by the thought of Ruth, I tiptoed down the stairs. There was a room on either side of the hallway, but because the doors were closed, I did not know which was Ruth's. I stood waiting, looking from one to the other, then finally turned around and went back the way I'd come.

Once in my room, I undressed and crawled into bed. Moonlight streamed through the windows, turning the room silver. I could hear the rolling sound of the waves, soothing in its monotony, and after a few minutes, I felt myself drifting off.

Sometime later, and though I thought at first that I was imagining it, I heard the door open. I had always been a light sleeper—even more so since the war—and though only shadows were visible at first, I knew it was Ruth. Disoriented, I sat up in the bed as she stepped into the room, closing the door quietly behind her. She was wearing a robe, and as she approached the bed, she undid the knot in a single fluid motion and the robe slipped to the floor.

A moment later, she was in the bed. As she slid toward me, her skin seemed to radiate a crackling electricity. Our mouths came together and I felt her tongue push against my own as my fingers traced through her hair and down her back. We knew enough not to make a sound, the silence making everything even more exciting, and I rolled her onto her back. I kissed her cheek and trailed feverish kisses across and down her neck and then back to her mouth, lost in her beauty and in the moment.

We made love, then made love again an hour later. In between, I spooned her against my body, whispering into her ear how much I loved her and that there would never be another. Through it all, Ruth said little, but in her eyes and her touch I felt the echo of my words. Just before dawn, she kissed me tenderly and slipped back into her robe. As she opened the door, she turned to face me.

"I love you, too, Ira," she whispered. And with that, she was gone.

I lay in bed awake until the sky began to lighten, reliving the hours we'd just spent together. I wondered whether Ruth was sleeping or whether she, too, was lying awake. I wondered whether she was thinking of me. Through the window, I watched the sun rise as if being heaved from the ocean, and in all my life, I have never witnessed a more spectacular dawn. I did not leave my room when I heard low voices in the kitchen, her parents trying not to wake me. Finally I heard Ruth come into the kitchen, and still I waited for a little while before putting on my clothes and opening the door.

Ruth's mother stood at the counter, pouring a cup of coffee, while Ruth and her father were at the table. Ruth's mother turned to me with a smile.

"Sleep well?"

I did my best not to look at Ruth, but from the corner of my eye, I thought I saw the tiniest of smiles flash across her lips.

"Like a dream," I answered.

12

Luke

At Knoxville's arena, where Luke had last ridden six years ago, the bleachers were already nearly full. Luke was in the chute, experiencing the familiar rush of adrenaline, the world suddenly compressed. Only vaguely could he hear the announcer laying out the highs and lows of his career, even when the crowd grew silent.

Luke didn't feel ready. His hands had trembled earlier, and he could feel the fear bubbling up, making it hard to concentrate. Beneath him, a bull named Crosshairs thrashed and reared, forcing him to focus on the immediate. The rope beneath the bull was held taut by other cowboys, and Luke adjusted his wrap. It was the same suicide wrap he'd used for as long as he'd been riding, the one he'd used on Big Ugly Critter. As he finished adjusting the wrap, Crosshairs wedged his leg against the rails, leaning hard. The cowboys who'd helped tighten the rope pushed back against the bull. Crosshairs shifted and Luke quickly jammed his leg into position. He oriented himself, and as soon as he was ready, he said simply, "Let's go."

The chute gate swung open and the bull lunged forward with a savage buck, his head plunging down, hind legs reaching for the sky. Luke worked on staying centered, his arm held out as Crosshairs began to spin to the left. Luke cut with him, anticipating the move, and the bull bucked again before suddenly shifting direction.

That move Luke didn't anticipate and he went off center, his balance shifting slightly, but even then he stayed on. His forearms strained as he tried to right himself, holding on with everything he had. Crosshairs bucked once more and began to spin again just as the buzzer sounded. Luke reached for the wrap, freeing himself in the same instant he leapt from the bull. He landed on all fours and got quickly to his feet, heading toward the arena fence without turning around. When he reached the top, Crosshairs was already on his way out of the arena. Luke took a seat on the rails, waiting for his score as the adrenaline slowly drained from his system. The crowd roared when it was announced that he'd scored an 81—not good enough for the top four, but good enough to keep him in contention.

Yet even after he'd recovered, he spent a few minutes unsure whether he'd be able to ride again, the fear coming back hard. The next bull sensed his tension, and in the second round, he was tossed only halfway into the ride. While in the air, he felt a surge of panic. He landed on one knee and felt something twist sharply before he toppled to the side. He went dizzy for a second, but he was operating on instinct by then and again escaped without harm.

His first score was barely enough to keep him in the top fifteen, and in the short go, the final round, he rode again, finishing ninth overall.

Afterward, he didn't wait around. After texting his mom, he started the truck and peeled out of the parking lot, making it back to the ranch a little after four a.m. Seeing the lights on in the main house, he surmised that his mom had either risen early or, more likely, hadn't gone to bed.

He texted her again after turning off the engine, not expecting a reply.

As usual, he didn't get one.

❧

In the morning, after two hours of fitful sleep, Luke hobbled into the farmhouse just as his mom was finishing up at the stove. Eggs over medium, sausage links, and pancakes, the flavorful aroma filling the kitchen.

"Hey, Mom," he said, reaching for a cup. He hid the limp as best he could as he moved to the coffeepot, thinking he'd end up needing a lot more than a cup or two to wash down the ibuprofen he clutched in his hand.

His mom studied him as he poured. "You're hurt," she said, sounding less angry than he'd expected. More concerned.

"It's not too bad," he said, leaning on the counter, trying not to wince. "My knee swelled up a bit on the drive home, that's all. It just needs to loosen up."

She brought her lips together, obviously wondering whether she should believe him, before finally nodding. "Okay," she said, and after shifting the frying pan to a cold burner, she enveloped him in a hug, the first in weeks. The embrace lasted a beat longer than usual, as if she were trying to make up for lost time. When she pulled back, he noticed the bags under her eyes and he knew she was operating on as little sleep as he was. She patted him on the chest. "Go ahead and have a seat," she said. "I'll bring over your breakfast."

He moved slowly, taking care not to spill his coffee. By the time he'd straightened his leg beneath the table in an attempt to get comfortable, his mom had set the plate in front of him. She put the coffeepot on the table, then took a seat beside him. Her plate had exactly half the amount of food she'd put on his.

"I knew you'd be late getting in, so I went ahead and fed the animals and checked the cattle this morning."

That she didn't admit to waiting up didn't surprise him, nor would she complain about it.

"Thanks," he said. "How many people came by yesterday?"

"Maybe two hundred, but it rained a while in the afternoon, so there'll probably be more people today."

"Do I need to restock?"

She nodded. "José got some of it done before he went home, but we probably need some more pumpkins."

He ate a few bites in silence. "I got thrown," he said. "That's how I hurt my knee. I landed wrong."

She tapped her fork against her plate. "I know," she said.

"How would you know?"

"Liz, the gal from the arena office, called," she said. "She gave me a rundown on your rides. She and I go back a long way, remember?"

He hadn't expected that, and at first, he wasn't sure what to say. Instead, he speared a piece of the sausage and chewed, eager to change the subject.

"Before I left, I mentioned that Sophia will be coming by, right?"

"For dinner," she said. "I was thinking of blueberry pie for dessert."

"You don't have to do that."

"I already did," she said, pointing with her fork toward the counter. In the corner, beneath the cabinets, he spotted her favorite ceramic pie dish, rivulets of blueberry juice seared onto its sides.

"When did you do that?"

"Last night," she said. "I had some time after we finished up with the customers. Do you want me to toss together a stew?"

"No, that's okay," he said. "I was thinking I'd grill some steaks."

"So mashed potatoes, then," she added, already thinking ahead. "And green beans. I'll make a salad, too."

"You don't have to do all that."

"Of course I do. She's a guest. Besides, I've tried your mashed potatoes, and if you want her to come back, it's better if I make them."

He grinned. Only then did he realize that—in addition to baking the pie—she'd tidied up around the kitchen. Probably the house as well.

"Thanks," he said. "But don't be too hard on her."

"I'm not hard on anybody. And sit up straight when you're talking to me."

He laughed. "I take it you've finally forgiven me, huh?"

"Not at all," she said. "I'm still angry that you competed in those events, but I can't do anything about it now. And besides, the season's over. I figure you'll come to your senses before January. You might act dumb sometimes, but I'd like to think I raised you better than to act dumb all the time."

He said nothing, reluctant to start an argument. "You'll like Sophia," he said, changing the subject.

"I should think so. Since she's the first girl you've ever invited over."

"Angie used to come over."

"She's married to someone else now. And besides, you were a kid. It doesn't count."

"I wasn't a kid. I was a senior in high school."

"Same thing."

He cut another piece of pancake and swirled it in the syrup. "Even if I think you're wrong, I'm glad we're talking again."

She forked a piece of egg. "Me too."

🌿

For Luke, the rest of the day took on a strange cast. Ordinarily, after breakfast he'd immediately start work, doing his best to cross items off the to-do list and always prioritizing. Some things had to be taken care of immediately—like getting the pumpkins ready before the customers started rolling in or checking on an injured animal.

As a rule, time passed quickly. He'd move from one project to the next, and before he knew it, it would be time for a quick lunch. The same thing would happen in the afternoons. Most days, feeling a little frustrated that he hadn't quite finished a given task, he'd find himself walking into the farmhouse just as dinner was about to be served, wondering how the hours had escaped him.

Today promised to be no different, and as his mom had predicted, it was even busier than it had been on Saturday. Cars and trucks and minivans lined both sides of the drive, nearly back to the main road, and kids were everywhere. Despite the lingering soreness in his knee, he carried pumpkins, helped parents locate their kids in the maze, and filled hundreds of balloons with helium. The balloons were new this year, as were the hot dogs and chips and soda, at a table manned by his mom. But as he moved from one duty to the next, he would find himself thinking about Sophia. From time to time he checked his watch, sure that hours had passed, only to realize it had been a mere twenty minutes.

He wanted to see her again. He'd talked to her on the phone on Friday and Saturday, and each time he'd called her, he'd been nervous before she picked up. He knew how he felt about her; the problem was that he had no idea whether she felt the same way. Before dialing, he found it all too easy to imagine that she'd answer with only tepid enthusiasm. Even though she had been both cheerful and chatty, after hanging up, he'd replay the conversation, plagued by doubts about her true feelings.

It was just about the oddest thing he'd ever experienced. He wasn't some giddy, obsessive teenager. He'd never been like that, and for the first time in his life, he wasn't sure what to do. All he really knew for certain was that he wanted to spend time with her and that dinner couldn't come soon enough.

13

Sophia

You know what this means, right? Dinner with his mom?" Marcia said. As she spoke, she was nibbling from a box of raisins, which Sophia knew would comprise her breakfast, lunch, and dinner for the day. Marcia, like a lot of girls in the house, either saved her calories for cocktails later or made up for the extra cocktail calories from the night before.

Sophia was fastening a clip in her hair, just about ready to go.

"I think it means we're going to eat."

"You're being evasive again," Marcia noted. "You didn't even tell me what you two did on Thursday night."

"I told you we changed our minds and went out for some Japanese food. And then we drove to the ranch."

"Wow," she said. "I can practically imagine the whole night unfolding in high detail."

"What do you want me to say?" Sophia said, exasperated.

"I want details. Specifics. And since you're so obviously trying not to tell me, I'm just going to assume that you two got hot and heavy."

Sophia finished with the clip. "We didn't. Which makes me wonder why you're so interested..."

"Oh, gee, I don't know. Maybe because of the way you've been flitting around the room? Because when we went to the party on

Friday night, you didn't freak out even when you saw Brian? And during the football game, when your cowboy called, you wandered off to talk to him, even though the team was just about to score. If you ask me, it seems like things are already getting serious."

"We met last weekend. It's not serious yet."

Marcia shook her head. "No. I'm not buying it. I think you like this guy a lot more than you're saying. But I should also warn you that it's probably not a good idea."

When Sophia turned toward her, Marcia dumped the last of the raisins into her palm and crumpled the box. She tossed it toward the garbage and missed, as usual. "You just came off a relationship. You're on the rebound. And rebound relationships never work," she said with complete assurance.

"I'm not on the rebound. I broke up with Brian a long time ago."

"It wasn't so long ago. And just so you know, he's still not over you. Even after what happened last weekend, he still wants you back."

"So?"

"I'm just trying to remind you that Luke is the first guy you've gone out with since then. Which means that you haven't had time to figure out what it is you really want in a guy. You're still off-kilter. Can't you remember the way you were acting last weekend? You freaked out because Brian showed up. And now, while in this emotional state, you've found someone else. That's what rebound means, and rebound relationships don't work because you're not in the right frame of mind. Luke isn't Brian. I get that. All I'm trying to say is that, in a few months, you might want something more than simply, *He's not Brian*. And by then, if you're not careful, you'll get hurt. Or he will."

"I'm just going to dinner," Sophia protested. "It's not that big of a deal."

Marcia popped the last of the raisins into her mouth. "If you say so."

Sometimes, Sophia hated her roommate. Like right now, while driving out to the ranch. She'd been in a good mood for the past three days, even enjoying the party and Friday's football game. Earlier today, she'd gotten a big chunk done on a paper for her Renaissance art class, which wasn't due until Tuesday. All in all, an excellent weekend, and then, just as she was getting ready to cap it off in just the right way, Marcia had to open her mouth and put all these crazy thoughts in her head. Because one thing she knew for sure was that she *wasn't* on the rebound.

Right?

The thing was, she wasn't simply over Brian, she was glad about it. Since last spring, the relationship had made her feel like Jacob Marley, the ghost in *A Christmas Carol*, who had to carry forever the chains he'd forged in life. After Brian had cheated the second time, part of her had checked out emotionally, even though she didn't end it right away. She'd still loved him, just not in the same blind, innocent, all-consuming way. Part of her had known he wouldn't change, and that feeling only grew stronger over the summer, and her instincts were proven right. By the time they'd broken up, it felt as if it had already been over for a long time.

And yes, she admitted she'd been upset afterward. Who wouldn't be? They'd dated for almost two years; it would have been strange if she hadn't been upset. But she was far more upset by the other things he'd done: the calls, the texts, following her around campus. Why didn't Marcia understand that?

Satisfied that she'd sorted through everything, Sophia approached the exit that would lead to the ranch, feeling a little better. Marcia didn't know what she was talking about. She was doing fine emotionally, and she wasn't on the rebound. Luke was a nice guy and they were still getting to know each other. It wasn't like she was going to fall in love with him. It wasn't like the thought had even occurred to her.

Right?

🌱

As Sophia pulled up the drive, she was still trying to silence the irritating voice of her roommate, unsure whether she should park at Luke's or head on over to the farmhouse. It was already getting dark, and a thin layer of fog had drifted in. Despite her headlights, she had to lean over the wheel to see where she was going. She drove slowly, vaguely wondering if Dog would appear to direct her. Just then, she spotted him wandering into the road at the turnoff.

Dog trotted ahead of the car, occasionally glancing over his shoulder until she reached Luke's bungalow. She pulled to a stop and parked in the same location she had before. Lights were blazing inside, and she saw Luke in the window, standing in what she thought might be the kitchen. By the time she'd shut off the engine and climbed out, Luke was stepping off the porch and walking toward her. He wore jeans and boots and a white collared shirt with the sleeves rolled halfway up, his hat nowhere in sight. She took a deep breath, steadying herself, wishing again she hadn't talked to Marcia. Despite the darkness, she could tell he was smiling.

"Hey there," he called out. When he was close, he leaned in to kiss her, and she caught a whiff of shampoo and soap. It was short, just a kiss of greeting, but somehow he must have sensed her hesitation.

"Something's bothering you," he said.

"I'm okay," she demurred. She offered a quick smile but found it hard to look at him.

He said nothing for a beat, then nodded. "All right," he said. "I'm glad you're here."

Despite his unwavering gaze, she realized that she wasn't sure what he was thinking. "Me too."

He took a small step backward and tucked a hand in his pocket. "Did you get your paper written?"

The distance made it easier for her to think.

"Not all of it," she answered. "I got a good start, though. How did it go here?"

"Okay," he said. "We sold most of the pumpkins. The only ones left are those that are better for pies, anyway."

She noticed, for the first time, a trace of remaining dampness in his hair. "What will you do with those?"

"My mom will can them. And then, for the rest of the year, she'll make the tastiest pies and pumpkin bread in the world."

"Sounds like it could be another business."

"Not a chance. Not because she couldn't, but because she'd hate being in the kitchen all day. She's kind of an outdoor person."

"I guess she'd have to be."

For a moment, neither of them said anything, and for the first time since she'd met him, the silence felt awkward.

"You ready?" he asked, motioning toward the farmhouse. "I got the charcoal going just a few minutes ago."

"I'm ready," she said. As they walked, she wondered if he would reach for her hand, but he didn't. Instead, he left her alone with her thoughts as they rounded the grove of trees. The fog continued to thicken, especially in the distance, the pastures entirely hidden from view. The barn was nothing but a shadow, and the farmhouse, with its lights beckoning in the windows, resembled a glowing jack-o'-lantern.

She could hear the crunch of gravel beneath her feet. "I just realized you never told me your mom's name. Should I call her Mrs. Collins?"

The question seemed to stump him. "I don't know. I just call her Mom."

"What's her first name?"

"Linda."

Sophia mentally tried them out. "I think Mrs. Collins," she said. "Since it's my first time meeting her. I want her to like me."

He turned and, surprising her, she felt him take her hand in his. "She'll like you."

☙

Before they'd even had time to close the kitchen door, Linda Collins turned off the mixer and looked first to Luke, then scrutinized Sophia before turning back to Luke again. She set the mixer on the counter, the blades coated with mashed potatoes, and wiped her hands on her apron. As Luke had predicted, she was dressed in jeans and a short-sleeved shirt, though the boots had been replaced with walking shoes. Her graying hair was pulled back in a loose ponytail.

"So this is the young woman you've been hiding, huh?"

She opened her arms, offering Sophia a quick hug. "It's nice to meet you. Call me Linda."

Her face showed the effects of years spent working in the sun, though her skin was less weather-beaten than Sophia had expected. There was an underlying strength to her embrace, the kind of muscle tone that came from hard work.

"Nice to meet you. I'm Sophia."

Linda smiled. "I'm glad Luke finally decided to bring you over to say hello. For a while there, I couldn't help but think he was embarrassed about his old mom."

"You know that's not true," Luke said, and his mom winked before moving to hug him as well.

"Why don't you get the steaks going? They're marinating in the fridge, and it'll give Sophia and me a chance to get to know each other."

"All right. But remember that you promised to go easy on her."

Linda couldn't hide the mirth in her expression. "I honestly don't know why he'd say such a thing. I'm a nice person. Can I get you something to drink? I made some sun tea this afternoon."

"That would be great," Sophia said. "Thanks."

Luke flashed her a *good luck* expression before retreating to the porch, while Linda poured a glass of tea and handed it to Sophia. Her own glass was on the counter, and she moved back to the stove, where she twisted open a jar of green beans that Sophia guessed had come from the garden.

Linda put them in the pan with salt and pepper, along with butter. "Luke said that you go to Wake Forest?"

"I'm a senior there."

"Where are you from?" she asked, turning the burner on low. "I take it you're not from around here."

She'd asked in exactly the same way Luke had on the night they'd met—curious, but not judgmental. Sophia responded by filling Linda in on the whos, whats, wheres, and whens in her life, though only in broad strokes. At the same time, Linda shared some details about life on the ranch, and the conversation flowed as easily as it had with Luke. From what Linda described, it was clear that she and Luke were interchangeable when it came to chores—both could do it all, although Linda mostly handled the bookkeeping and cooking while Luke did a bit more of the out-door work and mechanical repairs, more out of preference than anything else.

By the time she'd finished cooking, Linda motioned toward the table just as Luke returned. He poured himself a glass of tea and went back outside to finish the steaks.

"There've been times when I wished I had gone to college," Linda went on. "Or, if not that, at least had taken some classes."

"What would you have studied?"

"Accounting. Maybe some classes in agriculture or cattle man-agement. I had to teach myself, and I made a lot of mistakes."

"You seem to be doing okay," Sophia observed.

Linda said nothing, merely reached for her glass and took another drink.

"You said you had younger sisters?"

"Three," Sophia said.

"How old are they?"

"Nineteen and seventeen."

"Twins?"

"My mother tells me that she was happy with two, but my dad really wanted a boy so they tried one more time. She swears she almost had a heart attack in the doctor's office when she heard the news."

Linda reached for her tea. "I'll bet it was fun growing up with so many of you in the house."

"Actually, it was an apartment. Still is. But it was fun, even if it was a little cramped at times. I miss sharing a room with my sister Alexandra. We slept in the same room until I went off to college."

"So you're close."

"We are," Sophia admitted.

Linda studied her in the acute way that Luke often did. "But?"

"But... it's different now. They're still my family and we'll always be close, but things changed when I left the state to come to Wake. Alexandra, even though she goes to Rutgers, still gets home every other weekend or so, sometimes more, and Branca and Dalena are living in the house and going to high school and working at the deli. Meanwhile, I'm down here eight months a year. In the summers, just when it begins to feel like things are getting back to normal, it's time for me to leave again." She ran her nail over the scuffed wooden table. "The thing is, I don't know what I can do to fit in again. I graduate in a few months, and unless I end up with a job in New York or New Jersey, I don't know how often I'll get back home. And what's going to happen then?"

Sophia could feel Linda's eyes on her, and she realized that it was the first time she'd ever shared those thoughts out loud. She wasn't sure why. Maybe because the conversation with Marcia had left her feeling off balance, or maybe it was because Linda seemed like someone she could trust. As she said the words though, she suddenly realized she'd wanted to say them for a long time to someone who would understand.

Linda leaned forward and patted the top of her hand. "It's hard, but keep in mind that it happens to almost every family. Kids move away from their parents, brothers and sisters drift apart because life gets in the way. But then often, after a while, they get closer again. The same thing happened to Drake and his brother..."

"Drake?"

"My late husband," she said. "Luke's father. He and his brother were close, and then when Drake went on the circuit, they barely talked for years. Later, though, after Drake retired, they started growing close again. That's the difference between family and friends. Family is always there, no matter what, even when it's not right next door. Which means that you'll find a way to keep the connection alive. Especially since you realize how important it is."

"I do," Sophia said.

Linda sighed. "I always wanted brothers and sisters," she confessed. "I always thought it would be fun. Having someone to play with, someone to talk to. I used to ask my mom about it all the time and she'd just say, 'We'll see.' What I didn't know until I was older was that my mom had a series of miscarriages and..." Her voice faltered before she went on. "She just couldn't have any more. Sometimes, things just don't work out the way you want them to."

As she said it, Sophia had the distinct feeling that Linda might have suffered some miscarriages as well. As soon as she realized it, however, Linda slid her chair back, obviously ending the subject. "I'm going to cut up some tomatoes for the salad," she announced. "The steaks should be ready any minute."

"Do you need some help?"

"You could help me set the table," she agreed. "The plates

are there, and utensils are in the drawer over there," she said, pointing.

Sophia retrieved them and finished setting the table. Linda diced tomatoes and cucumbers and shredded the lettuce, then tossed everything together in a brightly colored bowl just as Luke returned with the steaks.

"We need to let these sit for a couple of minutes," Luke said, putting the platter of steaks on the table.

"Perfect timing," his mom said. "Let me just get the beans and potatoes in bowls, and dinner will be ready."

Luke took a seat. "So what were y'all talking about in here? From outside, I got the sense that you two were knee-deep in serious conversation."

"We were talking about you," his mom said, turning around, a bowl in each hand.

"I hope not," he said. "I'm not that fascinating."

"There's always hope," his mom quipped, making Sophia laugh.

Dinner passed easily, punctuated by laughter and stories. Sophia told them about some of the antics that went on at the sorority house—including the fact that the plumbing had to be replaced because too many girls were bulimic, which corroded the pipes—and Luke told a few stories about some of the more colorful events on tour, one of which included a friend—who went nameless—and a woman he picked up at the bar who turned out to be...not quite what he imagined. Linda regaled her with stories of Luke's boyhood as well as some of his stunts from high school, none of which were too outrageous. Like many of the kids she'd known in high school, he'd gotten in trouble, but she also learned that he'd won the state championship in wrestling—in addition to the rodeo stuff—in both his junior and senior years. No wonder Brian hadn't intimidated him.

Through it all, Sophia watched and listened, Marcia's warnings becoming fainter with every passing minute. Having dinner with Linda and Luke was easy. They listened and talked in the

same informal, spirited way her own family did—entirely different from the socially self-conscious interactions at Wake.

When they'd finished their meal, Linda served the pie she'd
baked, which was just about the best thing Sophia had ever
tasted. Afterward, the three of them cleaned up the kitchen,
Luke washing the dishes while Sophia dried and Linda wrapped
the extra food and put it away.

The pattern was so comfortingly similar to what went on
back home, making Sophia think about her own family, and
for the first time she wondered what her parents would think of
Luke.

🌿

On the way out the door, Sophia hugged Linda, as did Luke,
Sophia noticing again the muscle definition on her arms as she
squeezed. When she pulled back, Linda winked. "I know you two
are going to go visit, but just remember that Sophia's got school
tomorrow. You don't want her up too late. And you yourself have
an early day."

"I always have an early day."

"You slept in this morning, remember?" Then she turned to
Sophia. "It was a pleasure meeting you, Sophia. Come by again
soon, okay?"

"I will," Sophia promised.

As Luke and Sophia walked into the cold night air, the fog,
even thicker now, had given the landscape a dreamlike quality.
Sophia's breaths came out in little puffs, and she looped her arm
through Luke's as they made their way to his house.

"I like your mom," she said. "And she wasn't at all like I imagined, based on how you described her."

"What did you imagine?"

"I thought I'd be afraid of her, I guess. Or that she wouldn't
show any emotion at all. I don't meet many people who ignore a
broken wrist all day."

"She was on her best behavior," Luke explained. "Trust me. She's not always like that."

"Like when she's angry with you."

"Like when she's angry with me," he agreed. "And other times, too. If you watch her dealing with suppliers or when the cattle go to market or whatever, she can be pretty ruthless."

"So you say. I think she's sweet and smart and funny."

"I'm glad. She liked you, too. I could tell."

"Yeah? How?"

"She didn't make you cry."

She nudged him. "You be nice to your mom or I'll turn right around and tell her what you're saying about her."

"I am nice to my mom."

"Not always," she said, half-teasing, half-prodding. "Otherwise, she wouldn't have been mad at you."

❧

When they arrived at his house, he invited her inside for the first time. He went first to the fireplace in the living room, where split wood and kindling were already stacked on the grate. After taking a pack of matches from the mantel, he squatted down to light the kindling.

While he worked on getting the fire going, Sophia's gaze wandered from the living room to the kitchen, taking in her eclectic surroundings. Low-slung brown leather couches with modern lines were coupled with a rustic coffee table on a cow-skin rug. Mismatched end tables supported matching wrought-iron lamps. Above the fireplace, an antlered buck's head poked out from the wall. The room was functional and unpretentious, devoid of trophies or awards or laminated articles. Though she spotted a few photos of Luke riding bulls, they were sandwiched between more traditional photos: one of his mom and dad on what she guessed was an anniversary; another photo of a younger Luke and his father holding a fish they'd caught; a photo of his mom and one of the horses, his mom smiling into the camera.

Off to the side, the kitchen was harder to read. Like his mom's, it featured a table in the center of the room, but the maple cabinets and counters showed little wear. In the opposite direction, the short hallway off the living room led to a bathroom and what she suspected were the bedrooms.

With the fire beginning to blaze, Luke stood and brushed his hands against his jeans.

"How's that?"

She walked toward the fireplace. "It feels toasty."

They stood in front of the fire, letting it warm them, before finally moving to the couch. Sitting next to Luke, she could feel him watching her. "Can I ask you a question?" Luke said.

"Of course."

He hesitated. "Are you okay?"

"Why wouldn't I be?"

"I don't know. When you got here earlier, it seemed like something was bothering you."

For a moment Sophia said nothing, unsure whether or not to answer. Finally she decided, *Why not?* and she reached over, lifting his wrist. Knowing what she wanted, he slipped his arm over her shoulder, allowing her to lean against him.

"It was just something Marcia said."

"About me?"

"Not really. It was more about me. She thinks we're moving a little fast, and that I'm not emotionally ready for that. She's convinced I'm on the rebound."

He pulled back to study her. "Are you?"

"I have no idea," she admitted. "This is all new to me."

He laughed before growing more serious. He pulled her close again and kissed her hair. "Yeah, well, if it makes you feel better, all this is new to me, too."

As the evening wore on, they sat in front of the fire, talking quietly in the familiar way they had since they'd first met. Every now and then the fire made the wood snap, sending sparks up the fireplace, lending the room a cozy, intimate glow.

Sophia reflected that spending time with Luke not only was easy, but felt indefinably right. With him, she could be herself; it felt as though she could say anything to him and that he would intuitively understand. With their bodies nestled close, she felt a sense of wonder at how effortlessly they seemed to fit together.

It hadn't been like that with Brian. With Brian, she'd always worried that she wasn't quite good enough; worse, she'd sometimes doubted whether she really knew him. She'd always sensed he put on a facade of sorts, one she'd never been able to breach. She'd assumed that it had been she who was doing something wrong, unintentionally creating barriers between them. With Luke, however, it wasn't that way. She already felt as if she'd known him most of her life, and their immediate ease made her realize what she'd been missing.

As the fire burned steadily, Marcia's words continued to fade from her thoughts, until she no longer heard them at all. Whether or not things were moving too fast, she liked Luke and she enjoyed every minute she spent with him. She wasn't in love with him, but as she felt the gentle rise and fall of his chest, she found it strangely easy to imagine that her feelings might soon begin to change.

Later, when they moved to the kitchen to carve her pumpkin, she felt a distinct pang of regret that the evening was already coming to an end. She stood beside Luke, watching with rapt attention as he slowly but surely brought the jack-o'-lantern to life, the pattern more intricate than the ones she'd always made as a child. On the counter were knives of varying sizes, each with its own use, and she watched as he etched the pumpkin's grin by carving away the outer shell only, forming what appeared to be lips and teeth. Every now and then he would lean back, assessing his work. The eyes came next; again he carved away the shell, sculpting detailed pupils before carefully cutting away the rest. He grimaced as he reached into the pumpkin to pull out the pieces. "I've always hated that slimy feeling," he said, making her giggle. At last, he handed her the knife, asking if she wanted to take over. Luke showed her where to cut next, explaining what he wanted her to do, the warmth of his body pressed against her making her hands tremble. Somehow, the jack-o'-lantern nose turned out fine, but one of the eyebrows ended up crooked, which added a touch of insanity to its expression.

When the carving was completed, Luke inserted a small tea candle and lit it, then carried the pumpkin out to the porch. They sat in the porch rockers, talking quietly again as the glowing pumpkin grinned in approval. When Luke scooted his chair closer, it was easy for her to picture them sitting together on a thousand other nights like this one. Later, when he walked her to the car, she had the sense that he'd been imagining exactly the same thing. After putting the pumpkin on the passenger seat, he reached for her hand and gently pulled her close. She could sense the desire in his expression; she could feel in his embrace how much he wanted her to stay; and when their lips came together, she knew she wanted to stay as well. But she wouldn't. Not tonight. She wasn't ready for that just yet, but she felt in those hungry last kisses the promise of a future that she could barely wait to begin.

14

Ira

The late afternoon sun begins to sink below the horizon, and I should be concerned about the coming of night. But one thought dominates my consciousness.

Water, in any form. Ice. Lakes. Rivers. Waterfalls. Flowing from the faucet. Anything to alleviate the clot that has formed in my throat. Not a lump, but a clot that found its way there from somewhere else, something that doesn't belong there. It seems to grow with every breath.

I recognize that I have been dreaming. Not about the car wreck. This, the car wreck, is real and I know this. This is the only real thing. I close my eyes and concentrate, forcing myself to remember the details. But in my parched haze, it's hard to piece together what happened. I'd wanted to avoid the interstate—people drove too fast—and I'd highlighted the route heavy with single-lane highways on a map I'd found in the kitchen drawer. I remember pulling off the highway to get gas and then being momentarily unsure which direction to go. I vaguely recall passing a town called Clemmons. Later, once I realized I'd gotten turned around, I followed a dirt road, finally ending up on another highway called 421. I saw signs for a town called Yadkinville. The weather started to worsen, and by then I was too afraid to stop. Nothing looked familiar, but I kept on following the twists and turns of the highway until I found myself on yet another highway altogether, one that was leading directly into the mountains. I didn't know the number and by then it didn't matter because the snow was really coming down. And it was dark, so dark that I did not see the curve. I went through the guardrail and heard the twisting of metal before the car surged down the embankment.

And now: I am alone and no one has found me. I have been dreaming about my wife for almost a day as I lay trapped in the car. Ruth is gone. She died in our bedroom a long time ago and she is not in the seat beside me. I miss her. I have missed her for nine years and spent much of that time wishing that I had been the one to die first. She would have been better at living alone, she would have been able to move on. She was always stronger and smarter and better at everything, and I think again that of the two of us, I made the better choice so long ago. I still don't know why she chose me. While she was exceptional, I was average, a man whose major accomplishment in life was to love her without reservation, and that will never change. But I am tired and thirsty, and I can feel my strength draining away. It's time to stop fighting. It's time to join her, and I close my eyes, thinking that if I go to sleep, I will be with her forever—

"You are not dying," Ruth suddenly interrupts my thoughts. Her voice is urgent and tense. "Ira. It is not your time yet. You wanted to go to Black Mountain, remember? There is still something you must do."

"I remember," I say, but even whispering the words is a challenge. My tongue feels too big for my mouth, and the blockage in my throat has grown larger. It is hard to draw a breath. I need water, moisture, anything to help me swallow, and I need to swallow now. It's almost impossible to breathe. I try to draw a breath, but not enough air comes in and my heart suddenly hammers in my chest.

Dizziness begins to distort the sights and sounds around me. I am going, I think. My eyes are closed and I'm ready—

"Ira!" Ruth shouts, leaning toward me. She grabs my arm. "Ira! I am talking to you! Come back to me!" she demands.

Even from a distance, I hear her fear, though she is trying to hide it from me. I vaguely feel the shaking of my arm, but it stays frozen in place, another sign that this isn't real.

"Water," I croak.

"We will get water," she says. "For now, you have to breathe, and to do that you must swallow. There is blood clotting in your throat from the accident. It is blocking your airway. It is choking you."

Her voice sounds thin and distant, and I do not answer. I feel drunk, passing-out drunk. My mind is swimming and my head is on the steering wheel and all I want to do is sleep. To fade away—

Ruth shakes my arm again. "You must not think that you are trapped in this car!" she shouts.

"But I am," I mumble. Even in my fogginess, I know my arm hasn't moved at all and that her words are just another trick of my imagination.

"You are at the beach!" Her breath is in my ear, suddenly seductive, a new tack. Her face is so close, I imagine I can feel the brush of her long lashes, the heat of her breath. "It is 1946. Can you remember this? It is the morning after we first made love," she says. "If you swallow, you will be there again. You will be at the beach with me. Do you remember when you came out of your room? I poured you a glass of orange juice and I handed it to you. I am handing it to you now . . ."

"You're not here."

"I am here and I am handing you the glass!" she insists. When I open my eyes, I see her holding it. "You need to drink right now."

She moves the glass toward me and tilts it toward my lips. "Swallow!" she commands. "It does not matter if you spill some in the car!"

It's crazy, but it's the last comment—about spilling in the car—that gets to me most. More than anything, it reminds me of Ruth and the demanding tone she would use whenever she needed me to do something important. I try to swallow, feeling nothing but sandpaper at first and then...something else, something that stops my breathing altogether.

And for an instant, I feel nothing but panic.

The instinct to survive is powerful, and I can no more control what happens next than I can control my own heartbeat. At that moment, I swallow automatically, and after that I keep swallowing, the tender soreness giving way to a coppery, acidic taste, and I keep swallowing even after the taste finally passes to my stomach.

Throughout all this, my head remains pressed against the steering wheel, and I continue to pant like an overheated dog until finally my breathing returns to normal. And as my breath returns, so too do the memories.

Ruth and I had breakfast with her parents and then spent the rest of the morning at the beach while her parents read on the porch. Patches of clouds had begun to form on the horizon and the wind had picked up since the day before. As the afternoon wound down, Ruth's parents strolled down to see whether we would like to join them on an expedition to Kitty Hawk, where Orville and Wilbur Wright made history by flying the first airplane. I had been there when I was young, and though I was willing to go again, Ruth shook her head. She'd rather relax on her last day, she told them.

An hour later, they were gone. By then the sky had turned gray, and Ruth and I meandered back to the house. In the kitchen, I wrapped my arms around her as we stood gazing out the window. Then, without a word, I took her hand and led her to my room.

Though my vision is hazy, I can make out Ruth sitting beside me again. Perhaps it is wishful thinking, but I could swear she's wearing the robe she'd worn the night we first made love.

"Thank you," I say. "For helping me catch my breath."

"You knew what you had to do," she says. "I am just here to remind you."

"I couldn't have done it without you."

"You would have," she says with certainty. Then, toying with the neckline of her robe, she says almost seductively: "You were very forward with me that day at the beach. Before we were married. When my parents went to Kitty Hawk."

"Yes," I admit. "I knew we had hours to ourselves."

"Well...it was a surprise."

"It shouldn't have been," I say. "We were alone and you were beautiful."

She tugs at the robe. "I should have taken it as a warning."

"Warning?"

"Of things to come," she says. "Until that weekend, I was not sure you were...passionate. But after that weekend, I sometimes found myself wishing for the old Ira. The shy one, the one who always showed restraint. Especially when I wanted to sleep in."

"Was I that bad?"

"No," she says, tilting her head back to gaze at me through heavy-lidded eyes. "Quite the contrary."

We spent the afternoon tangled in the sheets, making love with even greater passion than the night before. The room was warm, and our bodies glistened with sweat, her hair wet near the roots. Afterward, as Ruth showered, the rain began, and I sat in the kitchen, listening as it pounded against the tin roof, as content as I had ever been.

Her parents returned soon after that, drenched by the downpour. By then, Ruth and I were busy in the kitchen, preparing dinner. Over a simple meal of spaghetti with meat sauce, the four of us sat around the table as her father talked about their day, the conversation somehow segueing as it often did into a discussion about art. He spoke of Fauvism, Cubism, Expressionism, and Futurism—words I'd never heard before—and I was struck not only by the subtle distinctions that he drew, but by the hunger with which Ruth devoured every word. In truth, most of it was beyond me, the knowledge slipping through my grasp, but neither Ruth nor her father seemed to notice.

After dinner, once the rain had passed and evening was descending, Ruth and I went out for a walk on the beach. The air was sticky and the sand packed under our feet as I gently traced my thumb along the back of her hand. I glanced toward the water. Terns were darting in and out of the waves, and just past the breakers, a school of porpoises swam by in leaping formation. Ruth and I watched them until they were obscured in the mist. Only then did I turn to face her.

"Your parents will be moving in August," I finally said.

She squeezed my hand. "They are going to look for a house in Durham next week."

"And you start teaching in September?"

"Unless I go with them," she said. "Then I will have to find a job there."

Over her shoulder, the lights in the house went on.

"Then I guess we don't have much choice," I said to her. I kicked at the packed sand briefly, drawing up the courage I needed before meeting her eyes. "We have to get married in August."

❧

At this memory, I smile, but Ruth's voice cuts through my reverie, her disappointment evident.

"You could have been more romantic," she tells me, sulking.

For a moment, I'm confused. "You mean...with my proposal?"

"What else would I be talking about?" She throws up her hands. "You could have dropped to one knee, or said something about your undying love. You could have formally asked for my hand in marriage."

"I already did those things," I said. "The first time I proposed."

"But then you ended it. You should have started all over. I want to recall the kind of proposal one reads about in storybooks."

"Would you like me to do that now?"

"It is too late," she says, dismissing the notion. "You missed your chance."

But she says this with such flirtatious overtones that I can hardly wait to return to the past.

We signed the *ketubah* soon after we got home from the beach, and I married Ruth in August 1946. The ceremony was held under the chuppah, as is typical in Jewish weddings, but there weren't many people in attendance. The guests were mostly friends of my mother's that we knew from the synagogue, but that was the way both Ruth and I wanted it. She was far too practical for a more extravagant wedding, and though the shop was doing well—which meant I was doing well—both of us wanted to save as much as we could for a down payment on the home we wanted to buy in the future. When I broke that glass beneath my foot and watched our mothers clap and cheer, I knew that marrying Ruth was the most life-changing thing I'd ever done.

For the honeymoon, we headed west. Ruth had never visited that part of the state before, and we chose to stay at the Grove Park Inn resort in Asheville. It was—and still is—one of the most storied resorts in the South, and our room overlooked the Blue Ridge Mountains. The resort also boasted hiking trails and tennis courts, along with a pool that had appeared in countless magazines.

Ruth, however, showed little interest in any of those things. Instead, soon after we arrived, she insisted on heading into town. Madly in love, I didn't care what we did as long as we were together. Like her, I had never been to this part of the state, but I knew that Asheville had always been a prominent watering hole for the wealthy during the summer months. The air was fresh and the temperatures cool, which is why during the Gilded Age, George Vanderbilt had commissioned the Biltmore Estate, which at the time was the largest private home in the world. Other moneyed Americans followed his lead, and Asheville eventually came to be known as an artistic and culinary destination throughout the South. Restaurants hired chefs from Europe, and art galleries lined the town's main street.

On our second afternoon in town, Ruth struck up a conversation with the owner of one of the galleries, and that was when I first learned about Black Mountain, a small, almost rural, town just down the highway from where we were honeymooning.

More accurately, I learned about Black Mountain College.

Though I'd lived in the state all my life up to that point, I'd never heard of the college; for most people who spent the rest of the century in North Carolina, a casual mention of the college would elicit blank stares. Now, more than half a century after it closed, there are few people who remember that Black Mountain College even existed. But by 1946, the college was entering a magnificent period—perhaps the most magnificent period of any college, anywhere, at any time, *ever*—and when we stepped out of the gallery, I could tell by Ruth's expression that the name of the college was already known to her. When I asked her about it over dinner that night, she told me that her father had interviewed there earlier in the spring and had raved about the place. More surprising to me was that its proximity was one of the reasons she had wanted to honeymoon in the area.

Her expression was animated over dinner as she explained that Black Mountain College was a liberal arts school founded in 1933, whose faculty included some of the most prominent names in the modern art movement. Every summer, there were art workshops—conducted by visiting artists whose names I did not recognize—and as she rattled off the names of the faculty, Ruth grew more and more excited at the thought of visiting the college while we were in the area.

How could I say no?

The following morning, under a brilliant blue sky, we drove to Black Mountain and followed the signs to the college. As fate would have it—and I have always believed it to be fate, for Ruth always swore she knew nothing about it beforehand—an artists' exhibition was being held in the main building, spilling out onto the lawn beyond. Though it was open to the public, the crowds were relatively sparse, and as soon as we pushed through the doors, Ruth simply stopped in wonder. Her hand tightened around my own, her eyes devouring the scene around her. I watched her reaction with curiosity, trying to understand what it was that had so captivated her. To my eyes, those of someone who knew nothing about art, there seemed to be little difference in the work displayed here from that at any of the countless other galleries we'd visited over the years.

"But there was a difference," Ruth exclaims, and I get the sense that she still wonders how I could have been so dense. In the car, she is wearing the same collared dress she wore on the day we first visited Black Mountain. Her voice rings with the same sense of wonder I'd witnessed back then. "The work...it was like nothing I had ever seen before. It was not like the surrealists. Or even Picasso. It was...new. Revolutionary. A giant leap of imagination, of vision. And to think that it was all there, at a small college in the middle of nowhere! It was like finding..."

She trails off, unable to find the word. Watching her struggle, I finish for her.

"A treasure chest?"

Her head snaps up. "Yes," she immediately says. "It was like discovering a treasure chest in the unlikeliest of places. But you did not understand that yet."

"At the time, most of the artwork I saw struck me as a collection of random colors and squiggly lines."

"It was Abstract Expressionism."

"Same thing," I tease, but Ruth is lost in the memory of that day.

"We must have spent three hours there, wandering from one work to the next."

"It was more like five hours."

"And yet you wanted to leave," she says reproachfully.

"I was hungry," I reply. "We didn't have lunch."

"How could you even think of food when we were seeing such things?" she asks. "When we had the chance to talk to such amazing artists?"

"I couldn't understand a thing you said to them. You and the artists were speaking a foreign language. You would talk about intensity and self-denial, while throwing around words like Futurism, Bauhaus, and synthetic Cubism. To a man who sold suits for a living, these words were gibberish."

"Even after my father explained it to you?" Ruth seems exasperated.

"Your father *tried* to explain it to me. There's a difference."

She smiles. "Then why did you not force me to leave? Why did you not take my arm and steer me to the car?"

This is a question she has wondered about before, whose answer she has never fully understood.

"Because," I reply as always, "I knew that staying was important to you."

Unsatisfied, she nonetheless presses on. "Do you recall who we met that first day?" she asks.

"Elaine," I say automatically. I may not have understood art, but people and faces were within my grasp. "And, of course, we met her husband, too, though we didn't know then that he would later teach at the college. And then later in the afternoon, we met Ken and Ray and Robert. They were students—or, in Robert's case, later would be—but you spent a lot of time with them as well."

By her expression, I know she's pleased. "They taught me many things that day. I was much better able to understand their primary influences after speaking with them, and it helped me to understand much more about where art would be headed in the future."

"But you liked them as people, too."

"Of course. They were fascinating. And each of them was a genius in his own right."

"Which is why we continued to go back, day after day, until the exhibition closed."

"I could not let this remarkable opportunity pass. I felt lucky to be in their presence."

In hindsight, I see that she was right, but at the time all that mattered to me was that her honeymoon be as memorable and fulfilling as I could make it.

"You were very popular with them as well," I point out. "Elaine and her husband enjoyed having dinner with us. And on the final night of the show, we were invited to that private cocktail party at the lake."

Ruth, replaying these treasured memories, says nothing for a moment. Her gaze is earnest when she finally meets my eyes.

"It was the best week of my life," she says.

"Because of the artists?"

"No," she answers with a tiny shake of her head. "Because of you."

❧

On the fifth and final day of the exhibition, Ruth and I spent little time together. Not because of any tension between us, but because Ruth was eager to meet even more faculty members, while I was content to wander among the works and chat with the artists we'd already had the chance to get to know.

And then it was over. With the exhibition closed, we devoted the next few days to activities more typical of newlyweds. In the mornings we walked the nature trails, and in the afternoons we read by the pool and went swimming. We ate in different restaurants every evening, and on our last day, after I made a phone call and loaded our suitcases in the trunk, Ruth and I got into the car, both of us feeling more relaxed than we had in years.

Our return trip would bring us past Black Mountain one last time, and as we approached the turnoff on the highway, I glanced over at Ruth. I could sense her desire to return. Deliberately, I took the exit, heading toward the college. Ruth looked at me, her eyebrows raised, obviously wondering what I was doing.

"Just a quick stop," I said. "I want to show you something."

I wound through the town and again made a turn she recognized. And just as she'd done back then, Ruth begins to smile.

"You were bringing me back to the lake by the main building," she says. "Where we attended the cocktail party on the last night of the exhibition. Lake Eden."

"The view was so pretty. I wanted to see it again."

"Yes." She nods. "That is what you said to me back then, and I believed you. But you were not telling the truth."

"You didn't like the view?" I ask innocently.

"We were not going there for the view," she says. "We were going there because of what you had done for me."

At this, it is my turn to smile.

When we arrived at the college, I instructed Ruth to close her eyes. Reluctantly she agreed, and I took her gently by the arm and walked her down the gravel path that led to the lookout. The morning was cloudy and cool, and the view had been better at the cocktail party, but it really didn't matter. Once I settled Ruth in exactly the right spot, I told her to open her eyes.

There, on easels, were six paintings, by those artists whose work Ruth had admired most. They were also the artists with whom she'd spent the most time—work by Ken, Ray, Elaine, Robert, and two by Elaine's husband.

"For a moment," Ruth says to me, "I did not understand. I did not know why you had set them up for me."

"Because," I said, "I wanted you to see the work in the natural light of day."

"You mean the art that you had bought."

That was, of course, what I had been doing while Ruth met with the faculty; the phone call that morning had been to make sure the paintings would be set up by the lake.

"Yes," I say. "The art that I bought."

"You know what you did, yes?"

I choose my words carefully. "I made you happy?" I ask.

"Yes," she says. "But you know what I am talking about."

"That wasn't why I bought the paintings. I bought them because you were passionate about them."

"And yet...," she says, trying to make me say it.

"And yet, it didn't cost me all that much," I say firmly. "They weren't who they later became, back then. They were simply young artists."

She leans toward me, daring me to continue. "And..."

I relent with a sigh, knowing what she wants to hear.

"I bought them," I say, "because I'm selfish."

&

I'm not lying about this. Though I bought them for Ruth because I loved her, though I bought them because she'd loved the paintings, I also bought them for me.

Quite simply, the exhibition changed Ruth that week. I had been to countless galleries with Ruth, but during our time at Black Mountain College something inside her was awakened. In a strange way, it magnified a sensual aspect of her personality, amplifying her natural charisma. As she studied a canvas, her gaze would sharpen and her skin would flush, her whole body reflecting a pose of such intense focus and engagement that others couldn't fail to notice her. For her part, she was completely unaware of how transformed she appeared in those moments. It was why, I became convinced, the artists responded so strongly to her. Like me, they were simply drawn to her, and it was also the reason they had been willing to part with the work I purchased.

This electric, intensely sensual aura would linger long after we left the exhibition and returned to the hotel. Over dinner, her gaze seemed to glitter with heightened awareness, and there was a marked grace to her movements that I hadn't seen before. I could barely wait to get her back to the room, where she proved especially adventurous and passionate. All I remember thinking is that whatever it was that had stimulated her this way, I wanted it never to end.

In other words, as I'd just told her, I was selfish.

❧

"You are not selfish," she says to me. "You are the least selfish man I have ever known."

To my eyes, she looks as stunning as she did on that last morning of the honeymoon, as we stood near the lake. "It's a good thing I've never allowed you to meet another man or you might think differently."

She laughs. "Yes, you can make a joke. You always liked to play the joker. But I tell you, it was not the art that changed me."

"You don't know that. You couldn't see yourself."

She laughs again before growing quiet. Suddenly serious, she wills me to pay attention to her words. "This is what I think. Yes, I loved the artwork. But more than the work, I loved that you were willing to spend so much time doing what I loved. Can you understand why that meant so much to me? To know that I had married a man who would do such things? You think it is nothing, but I will tell you this: There are not many men who would spend five or six hours a day on their honeymoon talking to strangers and looking at art, especially if they knew almost nothing about it."

"And your point is?"

"I am trying to tell you that it was not the art. It was the way *you* looked at *me* while I looked at the art that changed me. It is you, in other words, who changed."

We have had this discussion many times over the years, and obviously we are of different opinions on the matter. I will not change her mind, nor will she change mine, but I suppose it makes no difference. Either way, the honeymoon set in motion a summer tradition that would remain with us for nearly all our lives. And in the end, after that fateful article appeared in the *New Yorker*, the collection would, in many ways, define us as a couple.

Those six paintings—which I casually rolled and stored in the backseat of the car for the ride back home—were the first of dozens, then hundreds, then more than a thousand paintings that we would eventually collect. Though everyone knows of Van Gogh and Rembrandt and Leonardo da Vinci, Ruth and I focused on twentieth-century American modern art, and many of the artists we met over the years created work that museums and other collectors later coveted. Artists like Andy Warhol and Jasper Johns and Jackson Pollock gradually became household names, but other, then less well-known artists, like Rauschenberg, de Kooning, and Rothko, also created work that would eventually sell at auctions at Sotheby's and Christie's for tens of millions of dollars, sometimes more. *Woman III*, by Willem de Kooning, sold for over $137 million in 2006, but countless others, including work by artists like Ken Noland and Ray Johnson, also had sales prices that reached into the millions.

Of course, not every modern artist became famous, and not every painting we bought became exceptionally valuable, but that was never a factor in our decisions about whether or not to buy a piece of art in the first place. These days, the painting I treasure most is worth nothing at all. It was painted by a former student of Ruth's and hangs above the fireplace, an amateur piece that is special only to me. The *New Yorker* journalist ignored it completely, and I didn't bother to tell her why I treasured it, because I knew she wouldn't understand. After all, she did not understand what I meant when I explained that the monetary value of the art meant nothing to me. Instead, all she seemed to want to know was how we'd been able to select the pieces we did, but even after I explained it, she didn't seem satisfied.

"Why did she not understand?" Ruth suddenly asks me.

"I don't know."

"You said to her what we had always said?"

"Yes."

"Then what was so difficult about it? I would talk about the ways in which the work affected me..."

"And I would simply observe you as you talked," I finished for her, "and know whether or not to buy it."

It wasn't scientific, but it worked for us, even if the journalist was frustrated by this explanation. And on the honeymoon it worked flawlessly, even if neither of us would fully understand the consequences for another fifty years.

It isn't every couple, after all, who purchases paintings by Ken Noland and Ray Johnson on their honeymoon. Or even a painting by Ruth's new friend Elaine, whose work now hangs in the world's greatest museums, including the Metropolitan Museum of Art. And, of course, it's almost impossible to conceive that Ruth and I were able to pick up not only a spectacular painting by Robert Rauschenberg, but two paintings by Elaine's husband, Willem de Kooning.

15

Luke

Although he'd been preoccupied with thoughts of Sophia since the night they'd met, they didn't compare with the obsession he felt the following day. As he worked on some fencing in the far pasture, replacing posts that had begun to rot away, he occasionally found himself smiling as he thought about her. Even the rain, a cold autumn downpour that left him drenched, did little to dampen his mood. Later, when he had dinner with his mom, she didn't even attempt to hide a smirk that let him know she was fully aware of the effect that Sophia had on him.

After dinner, he called and they talked for an hour; the next three days followed the same pattern. On Thursday evening, he made the drive to Wake Forest, where they finally had a chance to walk around campus. She showed him Wait Chapel and Reynolds Hall, holding his hand as they strolled through Hearn and Manchester Plazas. It was quiet on campus, the classrooms long since emptied of students. Leaves had already begun to fall en masse, carpeting the ground beneath the trees. In the residence halls, lights were blazing and he heard faint strains of music as students began readying themselves for yet another weekend.

On Saturday, Sophia returned to the ranch. They went for a short ride on horseback, and afterward she followed him around as he worked, lending a hand whenever she could. Again they ate at his mother's place and then went back to his, the glowing fire as welcoming as it had been the week before. As had become usual, she headed back to the sorority once the fire began to burn lower—she wasn't yet ready to spend the night with him—but the following day, he drove with her to Pilot Mountain State Park. They spent the afternoon hiking up to Big Pinnacle, where they shared a picnic lunch and took in the view. They'd missed the pageant of autumn color by a week or so, but beneath the cloudless sky, the horizon stretched all the way to Virginia.

In the week following Halloween, Sophia invited Luke back to the sorority. They were having a party on Saturday night. The novelty of his profession and their dating status must have worn off since he'd first shown up at the house, since no one paid him much attention after the initial hellos. He kept a wary lookout for Brian, but he was nowhere to be found. On their way out, he remarked upon it.

"He went to the football game at Clemson," Sophia told him. "Which made tonight an ideal night to visit."

The following morning, he returned to the sorority house to pick her up, and they walked around Old Salem, taking in the sights, before returning to the ranch for their third weekend in a row at his mother's. Later, as they were saying good night beside her car, he asked if she was free the following weekend—he wanted to bring her to the place where he'd vacationed as a child, a place where they could ride trails amid breathtaking views.

Sophia kissed him then and smiled. "That sounds absolutely perfect."

By the time Sophia arrived at the ranch, Luke had already loaded the horses in the trailer and packed the truck. A few minutes later, they were heading west on the highway, Sophia fiddling with the radio. She settled on a hip-hop station, cranking up the volume until he couldn't take it any longer and switched to country-western.

"I wondered how long you'd be able to last," she said, smirking.

"I just think this fits the mood better, what with the horses and all."

"And I think you just never developed an appreciation for other kinds of music."

"I listen to other music."

"Oh, yeah? Like what?"

"Hip-hop. For the past thirty minutes. But it's a good thing I changed it. I could feel my dance moves coming on, and I'd hate to lose control of the truck."

She giggled. "I'm sure. Guess what? I bought some boots yesterday. My very own pair. See?" She lifted her feet, preening as he admired them.

"I noticed when I was putting your bag in the truck."

"And?"

"You're definitely turning country. Next thing you know, you'll be roping cattle like a pro."

"I doubt it," she said. "There aren't too many cows wandering around museums as far as I can tell. But maybe you'll show me how this weekend?"

"I didn't bring my rope. I did, however, remember to bring you an extra hat. It's one of my nice ones. I wore it in the PBR World Championships."

She looked at him. "Why do I sometimes get the sense you're trying to change me?"

"I'm just offering ... improvements."

"You better be careful, or I'll tell my mom what you said. Right now, I've got her believing you're a nice guy, and you'll want to stay on her good side."

He laughed. "I'll keep that in mind."

"So tell me where we're going. You said you used to go there as a boy?"

"My mom discovered it. She was out this way trying to drum up business, and she just kind of stumbled on it. It used to be a struggling summer camp, but the new owners got it in their heads that if they opened it up to riders, they could fill the rooms all year long. They made some improvements on the cabins and added some horse stalls in the back of each one, and my mom fell in love with the place. You'll see why when we get there."

"I can't wait. But how did you get your mom to agree to let you take off the whole weekend?"

"I got most everything done before I left and I offered José a little extra to come in to help while I'm gone. She'll be in good shape."

"I thought you said there's always something to do."

"There is. But it's nothing my mom can't handle. No emergencies pending."

"Does she ever get to leave the ranch?"

"All the time. She tries to visit our customers at least once a year and they're all over the state."

"Does she ever take a vacation?"

"She's not big on vacations."

"Everyone needs a break now and then."

"I know. And I've tried to tell her that. I even bought her cruise tickets once."

"Did she go?"

"She returned the tickets and got a refund. The week she was supposed to go, she drove to Georgia to check out a bull that was for sale, and she ended up buying him."

"To ride?"

"No. For breeding. He's still out there, by the way. Mean cuss. But he gets the job done."

She pondered this information. "Does she have friends?"

"Some. And she still visits them from time to time. For a while, she was in a bridge club with a few ladies from town. But lately, she's been trying to figure out how to increase the size of the herd and that's been taking a lot of her time. She wants to add another couple hundred pair, but we don't have enough pasture, so she's trying to find a place for us to keep them."

"Why? She doesn't think she's busy enough already?"

He shifted hands on the steering wheel before sighing. "Right now," he said, "we don't have much choice."

He could feel Sophia's questioning gaze, but he didn't want to talk about it and he changed the subject. "Are you going to be heading home for Thanksgiving?"

"Yes," she said. "Assuming my car makes it. There's a loud squeaking-whining sound when I start it. The engine sounds like it's screaming."

"It's most likely just a loose belt."

"Yeah, well, it'll probably be expensive to fix and I'm kind of on a budget."

"If you'd like, I can probably take care of it."

She turned toward him. "Why do I have no doubt about that?"

It took a little over two hours to reach the camp, the sky slowly filling with clouds that stretched to the blue-peaked mountains that dotted the horizon. In time, the highway began to rise, the air thinning and turning crisp, and they eventually stopped at a grocery store to pick up supplies. Everything went into the coolers in the bed of the truck.

Luke exited the main highway after leaving town, following a road that curved steadily and seemed carved into the mountain itself. It dropped off steeply on Sophia's side, the tops of trees visible through the windows. Fortunately there was little traffic, but whenever a car passed in the opposite direction, Luke had to grip the wheel with both hands as the trailer's wheels skirted the very edge of the asphalt.

Not having visited in years, he slowed the truck, searching for the turnoff, and just when he started thinking that he'd gone too far, he spotted it off the curve. It was a dirt road, even steeper in places than he remembered, and he put the truck into overdrive as he navigated slowly past trees that were pressing in from both sides.

When he reached the camp, his first thought was that it hadn't changed much, with twelve cabins spreading out in a semicircle from the general store, which also doubled as the office. Behind the store was the lake, sparkling with the kind of crystal blue water found only in the mountains.

After checking in, Luke unloaded the coolers and filled the water trough for the horses while Sophia wandered off toward the ravine. She took in the view of the valley more than a thousand feet below, and when Luke finished up, he joined her near the ravine, their vision wandering from one mountaintop to the next. Below them was a collection of farmhouses and gravel roads lined by oaks and maples, everything looking miniaturized, like models in a diorama.

As they stood together, he noticed the same wonder on her face he'd felt whenever he came here as a child. "I've never seen anything like this," she murmured, awestruck. "It makes me feel breathless."

He stared at her, wondering how she'd come to mean so much to him so quickly. Studying the graceful outline of her profile, he was certain he'd never seen anyone more beautiful.

"I was thinking exactly the same thing."

16

Sophia

They stayed inside only long enough for Sophia to put a few items in the refrigerator and notice the claw-foot tub in the bathroom, yet her initial impression was one of fraying but pleasant hominess, a perfectly cozy overnight getaway. Meanwhile, Luke busied himself making sandwiches to go with the fruit and chips and bottles of water he'd picked up from the store.

Luke packed their lunches in the saddlebags before they started off on one of the dozen trails that crisscrossed the property. As usual, he rode Horse and she was once more on Demon, whom she couldn't help thinking was slowly but surely getting used to her. He'd nuzzled her hand and nickered contentedly while Luke saddled him, and though it might have been because he was in an unfamiliar place, only the slightest touch of the reins was necessary to direct him.

The trail climbed ahead of them, weaving among trees that were so thick in some places, she doubted anyone had ever passed through before. At other times the trail opened up into the kind of expansive vista that she had seen only on postcards. They rode through lush green meadows of tall grass, and Sophia tried to picture them filled with wildflowers and butterflies every summer. She was grateful for her jacket and cowboy hat, as the trees kept most of the trail in shadow and the air was brisk as they rose to higher elevations.

Where the trail was too narrow to ride side by side, Luke motioned for her to take the lead, sometimes lagging a little behind. In those moments, she imagined that she was a settler gradually making her way out west, alone in a vast, unspoiled landscape.

They rode for a couple of hours before stopping for lunch at a clearing near the top. At the clearing's lookout, they sat on boulders and ate, watching a pair of hawks circling the valley below. After lunch, they followed the trail for another three hours on horseback, sometimes on tracks that ran to the edge of steep precipices, the danger heightening Sophia's senses.

They made it back to the cabin an hour before sundown and brushed down the horses before feeding each of them some apples along with their regular feed. By the time they finished, the moon had begun to rise, full-bodied and milky white, and the first stars were emerging.

"I think I'm in the mood for a bath before we eat," she said.

"Would you mind if I hopped in the shower first?"

"As long as you promise not to use all the hot water."

"I'll be fast. I promise."

Leaving the bathroom to Luke, she entered the kitchen and opened the refrigerator. Inside was a bottle of Chardonnay along with a six-pack of Sierra Nevada Pale Ale they'd picked up earlier, and she debated which one she wanted before searching through the drawers for the corkscrew.

There were no wineglasses in the cabinet, but she did find a jelly jar. It would have to do. She opened the wine bottle with a practiced motion and poured some into the jar.

Swirling the Chardonnay around in her jelly jar, she felt almost like a kid playing at being a grown-up. Come to think of it, she often felt that way, even though she was about to graduate from college. She'd never had to rent an apartment, for example. She'd never really worked for anyone other than her family. She'd never had to pay an electric bill, and even though she'd moved away, Wake wasn't real life. College wasn't real life. It was a fantasy world, she knew, entirely different from the world she would face in just a few months. Her classes, unlike work, started at ten in the morning and usually finished up around two. Nights and weekends, meanwhile, were devoted almost entirely to fun and socializing and defying boundaries. It had absolutely nothing in common with the lives her parents led, at least as far as she could tell.

As fun as college had been, she sometimes couldn't help feeling that her life had been on hold for the last few years. It wasn't until she'd met Luke that she realized how little she had really learned at school.

Unlike her, Luke seemed like an adult. He hadn't gone to college, but he understood real life: people and relationships and work. He'd been one of the best in the world at something—bull riding—and she had no doubt he would be again. He could fix anything, and he'd built his own house. By any measure, he had mastered many things in life already, and right now, it struck her as inconceivable that she would be able to claim as much—even in entirely different areas—over the next three years. Who knew if she'd even be able to get a job in her chosen field, one that actually paid her...

All she really knew was that she was here with Luke, and that spending time with him made her feel like she was finally, truly, moving forward somehow. Because whatever they had between them was based in the real world, not the fantasy bubble of college life. Luke was as real as anyone she'd ever met.

She heard the water shut off with a thump in the pipes, breaking the thread of her thoughts. Carrying her jelly jar of wine with her, she took a tour of the cabin. The kitchen was small and functional, with inexpensive cabinets. Though the countertop was peeling and rusty rings stained the sink, it smelled of Lysol and bleach. The floors had been recently swept, and the surfaces were dust-free.

Coming to Theaters This Spring

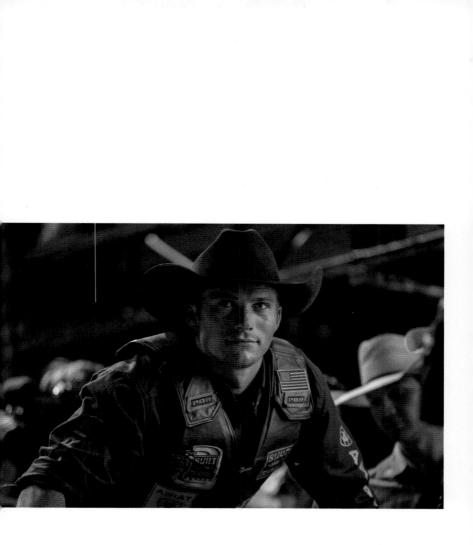

The small living area sported scuffed pine flooring and cedar wall planking with just enough room for a frayed plaid couch and a pair of rocking chairs. Blue curtains framed the window, and a single lamp stood in the corner. Sophia crossed the room to turn it on, only to discover that it was no brighter than the single bulb in the kitchen had been. Which no doubt explained the candles and matches on the coffee table. On a shelf opposite the windows lay a random assortment of books that she guessed had been left behind by other visitors, some hunting decoys—ducks—and a stuffed squirrel. A small television with rabbit-ear antennas sat in the center of the shelf, and though she didn't bother to turn it on, she doubted it received more than one or two channels, if that.

She heard the water come on again and when the bathroom door squeaked open, Luke stepped out, looking clean and fresh in jeans and a white button-down shirt with the sleeves rolled up. He was barefoot, and he looked as though he'd raked his fingers through his wet hair rather than using a comb. From across the room, she could see a small white scar on his cheek, one she'd never noticed before.

"It's all yours," he said. "I've already got the water going for you."

"Thank you," she said. She kissed him briefly as she passed him. "I'll probably be thirty or forty minutes."

"Take your time. I've got to get dinner going anyway."

"Another specialty?" she called from the bedroom, where she scooped up her overnight bag.

"I like it."

"Does anyone else?"

"That's a good question. I guess we'll find out soon, huh?"

As promised, the water was already filling in the tub. It was hotter than she'd expected, and she turned the other faucet, trying to cool it a bit, wishing for some bubble bath or scented baby oil.

She undressed, conscious of the soreness in her legs and lower back. She hoped she wouldn't be too stiff to walk tomorrow.

Reaching for her wine, she slipped into the water, feeling luxurious despite her modest surroundings.

The bathroom had a small separate shower stall, and Luke had slung his used towel over the rod. The fact that he'd been naked in here only a few minutes earlier made something flutter in her lower belly.

She'd known what might happen this weekend. For the first time, they wouldn't say good-bye near her car; tonight, she wouldn't return to the sorority house. But being with Luke felt natural. It felt right, even if she admitted to herself she wasn't all that experienced in these kinds of things. Brian had been the first and only guy she'd ever slept with. It had happened at the Christmas formal, when they'd already been dating for two months. She hadn't known it would happen that night, but like everyone else, she was having fun and probably drinking too much, and when he brought her up to the room, they ended up making out on the bed. Brian was insistent, the room was spinning, and one thing led to the next. In the morning, she wasn't sure quite what to think about it. Nor was Brian there to help her—she vaguely remembered him talking to some friends the night before about having Bloody Marys in one of their rooms the next morning. She stumbled to the shower with a headache the size of Wisconsin, and as the spray ricocheted off her, a million thoughts raced through her head. She was relieved to have finally done it—like everyone else, she'd wondered what it would be like—and was glad it had been with Brian, in a bed, as opposed to a backseat or something equally awkward. But for some reason, it also felt a little sad. She could imagine what her mom would think—or, God forbid, her dad—and frankly, she'd thought herself that it would be more... *something*. Meaningful. Romantic. Memorable. But really, what she wanted most of all just then was to head back to campus.

After that, Brian was like most guys, she supposed. Whenever they were alone, he wanted something physical, and for a while, she supposed she did, too. But then it began to feel as if it were all he ever wanted, and that began to bother her, even before he'd cheated on her.

And now here she was, alone with a guy overnight for the first time since Brian. She wondered why she wasn't nervous, but she wasn't. Instead, she soaped up the washcloth and ran it over her skin, imagining what Luke was doing in the kitchen. She wondered if he was thinking about her as she soaked in the tub, maybe even picturing what she looked like without clothing, and again, she felt a flutter in her lower belly.

She wanted this, she realized. She wanted to fall in love with someone she could trust. And she trusted Luke. Never once had he pressed her to do something she hadn't wanted; never once had he been anything less than a perfect gentleman. The more time she'd spent with him, the more convinced she became that he was by far the sexiest guy she'd ever met. Who else did she know who could work with his hands the way he did? Who could make her laugh? Who was smart and charming, self-reliant and tender? And who else would take her horseback riding in one of the most beautiful places in the world?

Soaking in the tub and sipping wine, she felt for the first time older than her years. She finished her wine, feeling warm and relaxed, and when the water began to cool, she climbed out of the tub and toweled off. She sorted through her bag, intending to throw on a pair of jeans, but then realized that it was all she ever wore when they were together. Changing her mind, she pulled out a skirt and a tight, form-fitting blouse and slipped them on. She styled her hair, feeling pleased that she'd remembered to bring both the curling iron and the dryer. Makeup came next; she added a touch more mascara and eye shadow than she usually did, wiping the old mirror more than once to clear away the steam. She completed the outfit with a pair of gold hoop earrings that her mother had bought her for Christmas last year. When she was done, she looked herself over one more time, then with a deep breath she picked up the empty jelly jar and stepped into the hallway. Luke stood in the kitchen, his back to her as he stirred a pot on the stove. On the counter next to him was a box of crackers and a beer, and she watched as he reached for the bottle, taking a long pull.

He hadn't heard her leave the bathroom, and for a while she simply watched him in silence, admiring the fit of his jeans and his smooth, unhurried actions as he cooked. Quietly, she moved toward the end table and bent down to light the candles. She stood back to survey the scene, then stepped over to turn off the lamp. The room darkened, becoming more intimate, the small candle flames flickering.

Luke, noticing the change in light, glanced over his shoulder. "Oh, hey," he called out as she approached. "I didn't realize you were finished..."

He trailed off as she emerged from the shadows into the soft yellow light of the kitchen. For a long moment, he drank in the sight of her, recognizing the hope and desire in the eyes that held his own.

"Sophia," he whispered, the sound so soft that she barely heard it. But in her name, she could hear everything he hadn't been able to say, and she knew in that moment that he was truly in love with her. And perhaps it was an illusion, but she also felt in that instant that he always would be, no matter what happened, with everything he had to give.

"I'm sorry for staring," Luke said. "You just look so beautiful..."

She smiled as she continued to approach him, and when he leaned in to kiss her, she knew then that if she hadn't been in love with him before, she was surely in love with him now.

🌾

After the kiss she felt unsettled, and she sensed that Luke did as well. He turned around, lowering the flame beneath the burner, and reached for his beer, only to realize that he'd finished it. He set it beside the sink and went to the refrigerator to get another when he noticed the jelly jar she was holding.

"Would you like some more wine?" he asked.

She nodded, not trusting herself to speak, and handed him the glass. Their fingers brushed, sending a pleasant jolt through her hand. He pulled out the cork and poured some wine into the jelly jar.

"We could eat now if you'd like," he said, handing it back to her and recorking the bottle. "But it'll taste better if we let it simmer for another half hour. I sliced up some of the cheese we bought earlier if you're hungry."

"Sounds good," she said. "Let's sit on the couch, though."

He replaced the wine and pulled out a second beer for himself, then picked up the plate of cheese. He'd added grapes to the plate and reached for the box of crackers on the counter as he followed her to the couch.

He put the food on the end table but held his beer as they took a seat next to each other. Luke opened one arm wide as she leaned into him, her back snug against his chest. She felt his arm go around her, just below her breasts, and she rested her arm on top of his. She could feel the rise and fall of his chest, his steady breaths, as the candles burned lower.

"It's so quiet up here," she remarked as he shifted his beer to the end table and wrapped his other arm around her as well. "I can't hear anything outside at all."

"You'll probably hear the horses later," he said. "They're not the quietest animals and they're right outside the bedroom. And sometimes, raccoons get onto the porch and they'll knock all sorts of stuff over."

"Why did you stop coming here?" she asked. "Was it because of your dad?"

When Luke spoke, his voice was subdued. "After my dad died, a lot of things changed. My mom was alone, and I was traveling on the circuit. When I was home, it always felt like we were so far behind...but I guess that's really an excuse. For my mom, this was their place. I'd spend so much time outside riding and swimming and playing that I'd just collapse in bed right after dinner. My mom and dad would have the place to themselves. Later, when I was in high school, they used to sometimes come up here without me...but now, she doesn't want to come. I've asked, but she just shakes her head. I think she wants to remember this place like it used to be. When he was still with us."

She took another sip of wine. "I was thinking earlier about how much you've been through. In some ways, it's like you've lived a full life already."

"I hope not," he said. "I'd hate for you to think I'm over-the-hill."

She smiled, conscious of the contact between her body and his, trying not to think about what might come later.

"Do you remember the first night we met? When we talked and you took me out to show me the bulls?"

"Of course."

"Could you ever have imagined that we'd end up here?"

He reached out for his beer and took a sip before resting it on the couch beside her. She could feel the chill from the bottle near her thigh. "At the time, I was just surprised you were talking to me at all."

"Why would you be surprised?"

He kissed her hair. "Do you really have to ask? You're perfect."

"I'm not perfect," she protested. "I'm far from it." She swirled the wine in her jar. "Just ask Brian."

"What happened with him had nothing to do with you."

"Maybe not," she said. "But..."

Luke said nothing, allowing her time to consider what she was going to say. She turned, looking directly at him.

"I told you that last spring I was a wreck, right? And that I lost a lot of weight because I couldn't eat?"

"You told me."

"All that's true. But I didn't tell you that for a while there, I also thought about suicide. It wasn't like I came close to actually doing anything about it; it was more like a *concept*, something that I latched on to, to feel better. I'd wake up and not care about anything and not be able to eat, and then I'd think that there was one sure way to stop the pain and that was to end it all. Even then, I knew it was crazy, and like I said, I never really thought I'd go through with it. But just knowing that the option was there made me feel like I still had some kind of control. And at the time, that's what I needed more than anything. To think that I was in control. And little by little, I was able to pull myself together. That's why, the next time Brian cheated on me, I was able to walk away." She closed her eyes, the memory of those days passing like a shadow over her face. "You're probably thinking you've made a big mistake right about now."

"Not at all," he said.

"Even if I'm crazy?"

"You're not crazy. You said yourself you never really considered going through with it."

"But why would I latch on to the idea? Why would I even think about it at all?"

"Do you still think about it?"

"Never," she said. "Not since last spring."

"Then I wouldn't worry too much. You're not the first person in the world to *think* about it. It's a big leap from thinking to considering, and an even bigger leap to attempting."

She weighed the comment, recognizing his point. "You're being too logical about the whole thing."

"That's probably because I have no idea what I'm talking about."

She squeezed his arm. "No one knows any of this, by the way. Not my mom or dad, or even Marcia."

"I won't tell," he said. "But if it happens again, you might consider talking to someone a whole lot smarter than I am. Someone who would know what to tell you, maybe help you navigate the whole thing."

"I plan on it. But hopefully it won't happen again."

They sat in silence, his body warm against hers. "I still think you're perfect," he offered, making her laugh.

"You're a sweet talker," she teased. She tilted her head up, kissing him on the cheek. "But can I ask you something?"

"Anything," he answered.

"You said that your mom wanted to double the size of the herd and when I asked why, you said she didn't have a choice. What does that mean?"

He traced a finger along the back of her hand. "It's a long story."

"That again? Then answer me this: Does it have anything to do with Big Ugly Critter?"

She felt his muscles tighten involuntarily, if only for an instant. "Why would you say that?"

"Call it a hunch," she said. "You never finished that story either, so I just assumed they might be related." She hesitated. "I'm right, aren't I?"

She felt him take a long breath and then release it slowly. "I thought I knew his tendencies," Luke began, "and I did—at first. Halfway through the ride, I made a mistake. I leaned too far forward just as Big Ugly Critter threw his head back and I was knocked unconscious. When I toppled off, Big Ugly Critter ended up dragging me around the arena. He dislocated my shoulder, but that wasn't the worst of it." Luke scratched at the stubble on his cheek, then continued, his voice matter-of-fact, almost distant. "As I lay there in the dirt, the bull came back at me. It was pretty bad. I ended up in the ICU for a while...but the doctors did amazing work and I got lucky. After I woke up, I recovered a lot faster than they thought I would. But I still had to stay in the hospital for a long time, and then there were months of rehab. And my mom..."

He trailed off, and though he was telling the story without emotion, Sophia could feel her own heart beginning to speed up as she tried to picture his injuries.

"My mom...she did what most moms would do, right? She did whatever she could to make sure I got the best care possible. But the thing is, I didn't have health insurance—bull riders can't really get it, because of how dangerous riding is. Or, at least, they couldn't back then. The tour provides minimal coverage, but it was nowhere near enough to cover the cost of my hospital care. So my mom had to mortgage the ranch." He paused, suddenly looking older than his years. "The terms weren't great, and the rates are going to readjust next summer. And the ranch doesn't have enough income to cover those upcoming loan payments. We can barely meet them now. We've been doing everything we can this past year to figure out how to squeeze some more money out of the place, but it's just not working. We're not even close."

"What does that mean?"

"It means we're going to have to sell it. Or in the end, the bank is going to take it. And this is the only life my mom knows. She built the business, and she's lived on the ranch her entire life..." He let out a long exhale before going on. "She's fifty-five years old. Where would she go? What would she do? Me, I'm young. I can go anywhere. But for her to lose everything? Because of me? I just can't do that to her. I won't."

"Which is why you started riding again," Sophia said.

"Yeah," he admitted. "It'll help cover the payments, and with a few good years, I can make a dent in what we owe, so that we can get the principal down to something manageable."

Sophia brought her knees up. "Then why doesn't she want you to ride?"

Luke seemed to choose his words carefully. "She doesn't want me to get hurt again. But what other choice do I have? I don't even want to ride anymore...it's not the same for me. But I don't know what else to do. As best I can figure, we can last until June, maybe July. And then..."

The guilt and anguish in his expression made her chest constrict.

"Maybe you'll find that other pasture you need."

"Maybe," he said, sounding less than sure. "Anyway, that's what's going on with the ranch. It's not all that pretty. That's one of the reasons I wanted to bring you here. Because being here with you meant that I didn't have to think about it. I didn't have to worry. All I've done since I've been here is think about you and how glad I am that you're with me."

Just as he'd predicted, one of the horses outside let out a long neigh. The room was growing cooler, the cold mountain air seeping through the windows and the walls.

"I should probably check our dinner," he said. "Make sure it's not burning."

With reluctance, Sophia sat up, letting Luke squeeze past. The guilt he felt at his role in jeopardizing the ranch was so genuine, so evident, that she found herself rising from the couch to follow. She needed him to know that she was here to comfort him, not because he needed her to, but because she wanted to. The love she felt for him altered everything, and she wanted him to feel that.

He was stirring the chili when she came up behind him and slipped her arms around his waist. He stood straighter and she squeezed him lightly before loosening her grip. He turned around and pulled her close. Their bodies came together then, and she leaned into him. For a long time, they simply held each other.

He felt so good to her. She could feel his heart beating in his chest, could hear the gentle rhythm of his breaths. She tucked her face into his neck, inhaling his scent, and as she did, she felt desire flooding her body in a way she had never experienced before. She slowly kissed his neck, listening to his rapid breath.

"I love you, Sophia," he whispered.

"I love you, too, Luke," she whispered back as his face inched closer to hers. Her only thought as they began to kiss was that this was the way it should always be, forever. Hesitant at first, their kisses became more passionate, and when she raised her eyes, she knew her desire was plain. She wanted all of him, more than she had ever wanted anyone, and after kissing him one more time, she reached behind him, turning off the burner. Without breaking his gaze, she reached for his hand and slowly began leading him to the bedroom.

17

Ira

Evening again, and still I am here. Cocooned in silence, interred by the white hard cold of winter, and unable to move.

I've lasted more than a day now. At my age and considering my plight, this should be cause for celebration. But I'm weakening now. Only my pain and thirst seem real. My body is failing, and it is everything I can do to keep my eyes open. They will close again in time, and part of me wonders whether they will ever open again. I stare at Ruth, wondering why she says nothing. She does not look at me. Instead, I see her in profile. With every blink, she seems to be changing. She is young and old and young again, and I wonder what she is thinking with each transformation.

As much as I love her, I admit that she has always remained somewhat of an enigma to me. In the mornings, as we sat at the breakfast table, I would catch her staring out the window. In those moments, she looked the same as she does right now, and my eyes would often follow hers. We would sit in silence, watching the birds as they flitted from one branch to the next, or gaze at the clouds as they slowly gathered shape. Sometimes I would study her, trying to intuit her thoughts, but she would offer only a slight smile, perfectly content to keep me in the dark.

I liked this about her. I liked the mystery she added to my life.

I liked the occasional silence between us, for ours was a comfortable silence. It was a passionate silence, one that had its roots in comfort and desire. I have often wondered whether this made us unique or whether it was something that couples often experience. It would sadden me to think that we were an exception, but I've lived long enough to conclude that what Ruth and I had was an uncommon blessing.

And still, Ruth says nothing. Perhaps she, too, is reliving the days that we once shared.

After Ruth and I returned from our honeymoon, we began the process of creating a life together. By then, her parents had already moved to Durham, and Ruth and I stayed with my parents while we looked for a home to buy. Though a number of new neighborhoods were springing up in Greensboro, Ruth and I wanted a home with character. We spent most of our time walking through homes in the historic district, and it was there that we found a Queen Anne that had been built in 1886, with a front-facing gable, a round tower, and porches gracing the front and back. My first thought was that it was far too large for us, with more space than we would ever need. It was also desperately in need of renovation. But Ruth loved the moldings and the craftsmanship and I loved her, so when she said she'd leave the decision up to me, I made an offer the following afternoon.

While the paperwork with the bank loan was being finalized— we would move in a month later—I went back to work at the shop while Ruth threw herself into her teaching job. I admit that I was nervous for her. The rural school where she'd been hired largely served students who'd grown up on farms. More than half of them lived in homes without indoor plumbing, and many wore the same clothes day after day. Two arrived in class on the first day without shoes. Only a handful seemed to care about learning, and more than a few were fundamentally illiterate. It was the kind of poverty she'd never before experienced, less about money than a poverty of dreams. In those first few months of teaching, I'd never seen Ruth more frazzled, nor would I ever see her that way again. It takes a teacher both time and experience to formalize lesson plans and to become comfortable in even the best schools, and I often saw Ruth working late into the evenings at our small kitchen table, thinking of new ways to engage her students.

But as harried as she was during that first semester, it became plain that teaching such students, even more than the artwork we eventually collected, was not only her calling, but her true passion. She took to the job with a single-minded intensity that surprised me. She wanted her students to learn, but more than that, she wanted them to treasure education in the same way she did. The challenge she faced with such disadvantaged students only fired her enthusiasm. Over dinner, she would talk to me about her students and would recount to me the "little victories" that could make her smile for days. And that is how she would describe them. *Ira*, she would tell me, *one of my students had a little victory in class today*, before she proceeded to tell me exactly what had happened. She would tell me when a child unexpectedly shared a pencil with another, or how much their penmanship had improved, or the pride that a student demonstrated at reading her first book. Beyond that, she cared for them. She would notice when one of them was upset and would speak to them as a mother would; when she learned that a number of her students were too poor to bring lunch to school, she began to make extra sandwiches in the morning. And slowly but surely, her students responded to her nurturing ways, like young plants to sun and water.

She had been worried about whether the children would accept her. Because she was Jewish in a school that was almost exclusively Christian, because she was from Vienna and had a German accent, she wasn't sure whether they would regard her as alien. She had never said this directly to me, but I knew it for certain one day in December, when I found her sobbing in the kitchen at the end of the day. Her eyes were swollen and raw, frightening me. I imagined that something terrible had happened to her parents or perhaps that she'd been in an accident of some sort. Then I noticed that the table was littered with an assortment of homemade items. She explained that her students—each and every one—had brought her gifts in celebration of Hanukkah. She would never be sure how it had come about; she hadn't told them about the holiday, nor was it clear that any of the students understood the meaning of the celebration. Later, she would tell me that she heard one of the students explaining to another that "Hanukkah is the way Jews celebrate the birth of Jesus," but the truth was less important than the meaning of what the children had done for her. Most of the gifts were simple—painted rocks, handmade cards, a bracelet made of seashells—but in every gift there was love, and it was in that moment, I later came to believe, that Ruth finally accepted Greensboro, North Carolina, as her home.

Despite Ruth's workload, we were slowly able to furnish our home. We spent many weekends during that first year shopping for antiques. In the same way she had an eye for art, she had a gift for selecting the kind of furniture that would make our home not only uniquely beautiful, but welcoming.

The following summer, we would begin renovations. The house needed a new roof, and the kitchen and bathrooms, though functional, were not to Ruth's liking. The floors needed to be sanded, and many windows had to be replaced. We had decided when purchasing the house to wait until the following summer to begin the repairs, when Ruth would have time to supervise the workers.

I was relieved that she was willing to assume this responsibility.

My mother and father had cut back further on the time they spent at work, but the shop had only grown busier in the year that Ruth had begun teaching. As my father had done during the war, I again took over the lease on the space next to ours. I expanded the store and hired three additional employees. Even then, I struggled to keep up. Like Ruth, I often worked late into the evenings.

The renovations on the house took longer, and cost more, than expected, and it went without saying that it was far more inconvenient than either of us imagined the process might be. It was the end of July 1947 before the final worker carried his toolbox to the truck, but the changes—some subtle, others dramatic—made the house finally seem really ours, and I have lived there for over sixty-five years now. Unlike me, the house is still holding up reasonably well. Water flows smoothly through the pipes, the cabinets swing open with ease, and the floors are as flat as a billiard table, whereas I can no longer move from room to room without the use of my walker. If I have one complaint, it's that the house seems drafty, but then I've been cold for so long that I've forgotten what it's like to feel warm. To me, the house is still filled with love, and at this point in my life, I could ask for nothing more.

"It is filled, all right," Ruth snorts. "The house, I mean."

I detect a note of disapproval in her tone and glance at her. "I like it the way it is."

"It is dangerous."

"It's not dangerous."

"No? What if there is a fire? How would you get out?"

"If there was a fire, I'd have trouble getting out even if the house stood empty."

"You are making excuses."

"I'm old. I might be senile."

"You are not senile. You are stubborn."

"I like to remember. There's a difference."

"This is not good for you. The memories sometimes make you sad."

"Maybe," I say, looking directly at her. "But memories are all that I have left."

❧

Ruth is right about the memories, of course. But she is also right about the house. It's filled, not with junk, but with the artwork we collected. For years, we kept the paintings in climate-controlled storage units that I rented by the month. Ruth preferred it that way—she always worried about fires—but after she died, I hired two workers to bring everything back home. Now, every wall is a kaleidoscope of paintings, and paintings fill four of the five bedrooms. Neither the sitting room nor the dining room has been usable for years, because paintings are stacked in every spare inch. While hundreds of pieces were framed, most of them were not. Instead, those are separated by acid-free paper and stored in a number of flat oak boxes labeled by the year that I had them built by a carpenter here in town. I'll admit that there's a cluttered extravagance to the house that some might find claustrophobic—the journalist who came to the house wandered from room to room with her mouth agape—but my home is clean. The cleaning service sends a woman to my house twice a week to keep the rooms I still use spotless, and though few, if any, of these women over the years spoke English, I know that Ruth would have been pleased I hired them. Ruth always hated dust or mess of any sort.

The clutter does not bother me. Instead, it reminds me of some of the best days of my marriage, including, and especially, our trips to Black Mountain College. After the renovations were completed, when both of us were in need of a vacation, we spent our first anniversary at the Grove Park Inn, the place we'd honeymooned. Again, we visited the college, but this time we were greeted by friends. Elaine and Willem weren't there, but Robert and Ken were, and they introduced us to Susan Weil and

Pat Passlof, two extraordinary artists whose work also hangs in numerous museums. That year, we came home with fourteen more paintings.

Even then, however, neither of us was thinking of becoming collectors. We were not rich, after all, and the purchase of those paintings had been a stretch, especially after the renovations on the house. Nor did we hang all of them right away. Instead, Ruth would rotate them from room to room, depending on her moods, and more than once I came home to a house that felt both the same and different. In 1948 and 1949, we found ourselves returning yet again to Asheville and Black Mountain College. We purchased even more paintings, and when we returned home, Ruth's father suggested that we take our hobby more seriously. Like Ruth, he could see the quality in the work we'd purchased, and he planted in us the seed of an idea—to build a true collection, one that might one day be worthy of a museum. I could tell that Ruth was intrigued by the idea. Though we made no official decision one way or the other, we began saving nearly all of Ruth's salary, and she spent much of the year writing letters to the artists we knew, asking their opinions about other artists they believed we might like. In 1950, after a trip to the Outer Banks, we traveled to New York for the first time. We spent three weeks visiting every gallery in the city, meeting owners and artists whom our friends had introduced us to. That summer, we laid the groundwork for a network that would continue to grow for the next four decades. At the end of that summer, we returned to the place where it had all begun, almost as though we had no other choice.

I'm not sure when we first began to hear the rumors that Black Mountain College might close—1952 or 1953, I think—but like the artists and the faculty we had come to think of as close friends, we wanted to dismiss them. In 1956, however, our fears came true, and when Ruth heard the news, she wept, recognizing the end of an era for us. That summer, we again traveled throughout the Northeast, and though I knew it wouldn't be the same, we concluded our travels by returning to Asheville for our anniversary. As always, we drove to the college, but as we stood by the waters of Lake Eden and stared at the now vacant buildings of the college, I couldn't help wondering whether our idyll at the college had been nothing more than a dream.

In time, we made our way to the spot where those first six paintings had once been displayed. We stood beside the silent blue water and I thought of how appropriate the name of the lake had been. To us, after all, this spot had always been like Eden itself. I knew that no matter where our lives took us, we would never leave this place behind. Surprising Ruth, I offered her a letter I'd written the night before. It was the first letter I'd written to Ruth since I'd been in the war, and after reading it, Ruth took me in her arms. In that moment, I knew what I had to do to keep this place alive in our hearts. The following year, on our eleventh anniversary, I wrote another letter to her, which she read under those very same trees on the shores of Lake Eden. And with that, a new tradition in our marriage began.

In all, Ruth received forty-five letters, and she saved every one. They are stored in a box that she kept atop her chest of drawers. Sometimes I would catch her reading them, and I could tell by her smile that she was reliving something she'd long since forgotten. These letters had become something of a diary to her, and as she grew older, she began to pull them out more frequently, sometimes reading them all in the course of a single afternoon.

The letters seemed to give her peace, and I think this is why much later, she decided to write to me. I did not find this letter until after she was gone, but in many ways, it saved my life. She knew I would need it, for she knew me better than I ever knew myself.

But Ruth has not read all the letters I've written to her. She couldn't. Though I wrote them for her, I also wrote them for me, after all, and after she passed away, I placed another box beside the original. In this box are letters written with a shaking hand, letters marked only by my tears, not hers. They are letters written on what would have been yet another anniversary. Sometimes I think about reading them, just as she used to, but it hurts me to think that she never had the chance. Instead, I simply hold them, and when the ache becomes too great, I'll wander the house and stare at the paintings. And sometimes, when I do, I like to imagine that Ruth has come to visit me, just as she has come to me in the car, because she knows, even now, that I can't live without her.

*

"You can live without me," Ruth says to me.

Outside the car, the winds have died down and the darkness seems less opaque. This is moonlight, I think to myself, and I realize that the weather is finally clearing. By tomorrow night, if I last that long, the weather will begin to improve, and by Tuesday the snow will be melting. For a moment, this gives me hope, but as quickly as it comes, the feeling fades away. I will not last that long.

I am weak, so weak that even focusing on Ruth is difficult. The inside of the car is moving in circles, and I want to reach for her hand to steady me, but I know that's impossible. Instead, I try to remember the feel of her touch, but the sensation eludes me.

"Are you listening to me?" she asks.

I close my eyes, trying to make the dizziness stop, but it only increases, colored spirals exploding behind my eyes. "Yes," I finally whisper, a dry rasp in the volcanic ash of my throat. My thirst claws at me with a vengeance. Worse than before. Infinitely worse. It's been more than a day since I've had anything to drink, and the desire for water consumes me, growing stronger with every labored breath.

"The water bottle is here," Ruth suddenly says to me. "I think it is on the floor by my feet."

Her voice is soft and lilting, like a melody, and I try to latch on to the sound to avoid thinking about the obvious. "How do you know?"

"I do not know for sure. But where else can it be? It is not on the seat."

She's right, I think to myself. It's likely on the floor, but there is nothing I can do to reach it. "It doesn't matter," I finally say in despair.

"Of course it matters. You must find a way to reach the bottle."

"I can't," I say. "I'm not strong enough."

She seems to absorb this and remains quiet for a moment. In the car, I think I hear her breathing before I realize that it is I who has begun to wheeze. The blockage in my throat has begun to form again.

"Do you remember the tornado?" she suddenly asks me. There is something in her voice imploring me to concentrate, and I try to figure out what she's referring to. The tornado. It means nothing at first, and then, slowly, the memory begins to acquire shape and significance.

I'd been home from work for an hour when all at once the sky turned an ominous shade of grayish green. Ruth stepped outside to investigate, and I remember seizing her by the hand to drag her to the bathroom in the center of the house. It was the first tornado she'd ever experienced, and though our house was unharmed, a tree down the street had been toppled, crushing a neighbor's car. "It was 1957," I say. "April."

"Yes," she says. "That is when it happened. I am not surprised you remember. You always remember the weather, even from long ago."

"I remember because I was frightened."

"But you remember the weather now, too."

"I watch the Weather Channel."

"This is good. There are many good programs on this channel. There is sometimes much to learn."

"Why are we talking about this?"

"Because," she says to me, urgency in her tone, "there is something you must remember. There is something more."

I don't understand what she means, and in my exhaustion, I realize I suddenly don't care. The wheeze grows worse and I close my eyes, beginning to float on a sea of dark, undulating waves. Toward a distant horizon, away from here. Away from her.

"You have seen something interesting lately!" she shouts.

And still, I drift. Outside the car. Flying now. Under the moon and stars. The night is clearing and the wind has died, and I'm so tired I know I will sleep forever. I feel my limbs relax and lose heft.

"Ira!" she shouts, the panic in her voice rising. "There is something you must remember! It was on the Weather Channel!"

Her voice sounds far away, almost like an echo.

"A man in Sweden!" she shouts. "He had no food or water!"

Though I can barely hear her, the words somehow register. Yes, I think, and the memory, like the tornado, also begins to take shape. *Umeå. Arctic Circle. Sixty-four days.*

"He survived!" she shouts. She reaches for me, her hand coming to rest on my leg.

And in that moment, I stop drifting. When I open my eyes, I'm back in the car.

Buried in his car in the snow. No food or water.

No water . . .

No water . . .

Ruth leans toward me, so close I can smell the delicate rose notes of her perfume. "Yes, Ira," she says, her expression serious. "He had no water. So how did he survive? You must remember!"

I blink and my eyes feel scaly, like those of a reptile. "Snow," I say. "He ate the snow."

She holds my gaze and I know she is daring me to look away. "There is snow here, too," she says. "There is snow right outside your window."

At her words, I feel something surge inside me despite my weakness, and though I am afraid of movement, I nonetheless raise my left arm slowly. I inch it forward on my thigh and then lift it, moving it to the armrest. The exertion feels mammoth and I take a moment to catch my breath. But Ruth is right. There is water close by and I stretch my finger toward the button. I'm afraid the window won't open, but still I stretch my finger forward. Something primal keeps me going. *I hope the battery still works.* It worked before, I tell myself again. *It worked after the accident.* Finally my finger meets the button and I push it forward.

And like a miracle, bitter cold suddenly invades the interior. The chill is brutal and a dab of snow lands on the back of my hand. So close now, but I am facing the wrong way. I must lift my head. The task seems insurmountable, but the water calls out to me and it is impossible not to answer.

I raise my head, and my arm and shoulder and collarbone explode. I see nothing but white and then nothing but black, but I keep on going. My face feels swollen, and for an instant, I don't think I'll make it. I want to put my head back down. I want the pain to end, yet my left hand is already moving toward me. The snow is already melting and I can feel the water dripping and my hand keeps moving.

And then, just when I'm on the brink of giving up, my hand meets my mouth. The snow is wonderful, and my mouth seems to come alive. I can feel the wetness on my tongue. It is cold and sharp and heavenly, and I feel the individual drops of water trace a path down my throat. The miracle emboldens me and I reach for another handful of snow. I swallow some more and the needles vanish. My throat is suddenly young like Ruth, and though the car is freezing, I do not even feel the cold. I take another handful of snow, and then another, and the exhaustion I felt just a minute ago has dissipated. I'm tired and weak, but this seems infinitely bearable by comparison. When I look at Ruth, I can see her clearly. She's in her thirties, that age when she was most beautiful of all, and she is glowing.

"Thank you," I finally say.

"There is no reason to thank me." She shrugs. "But you should roll up the window now. Before you get too cold."

I do as she tells me, my eyes never leaving hers. "I love you, Ruth," I croak.

"I know," she says, her expression tender. "That is why I have come."

The water has restored me in a way that seemed impossible even a few hours earlier. By this, I mean my mind. My body is still a wreck and I am still afraid to move, but Ruth seems comforted by my recovery. She sits quietly, listening to the chatter of my thoughts. Mostly I am preoccupied with the question of whether someone will ever find me...

In this world, after all, I've become more or less invisible. Even when I filled my tank with gasoline—which led to me getting lost, I now think—the woman behind the counter looked past me, toward a young man in jeans. I've become what the young are afraid of becoming, just another member of the nameless elderly, an old and broken man with nothing left to offer to this world.

My days are inconsequential, comprising simple moments and even simpler pleasures. I eat and sleep and think of Ruth; I wander the house and stare at the paintings, and in the mornings, I feed the pigeons that gather in my backyard. My neighbor complains about this. He thinks the birds are a disease-ridden nuisance. He may have a point, but he also cut down a magnificent maple tree that straddled our properties simply because he was tired of raking the leaves, so his judgment isn't something that I consider altogether trustworthy. Anyway, I like the birds. I like the gentle cooing noises they make and I enjoy watching their heads bob up and down as they pursue the seed I scatter for them.

I know that most people consider me to be a recluse. That's how the journalist described me. As much as I despise the word and what it implies, there is some truth to what she wrote about me. I've been a widower for years, a man without children, and as far as I know, I have no living relatives. My friends, aside from my attorney, Howie Sanders, have long since passed away, and since the media storm—the one unleashed by the article in the *New Yorker*—I seldom leave the house. It's easier that way, but I frequently wonder whether I should have ever talked to the journalist in the first place. Probably not, but when Janice or Janet or whatever her name was showed up at the door unannounced, her dark hair and intelligent eyes reminded me of Ruth, and the next thing I knew, she was standing in the living room. She didn't leave for the next six hours. How she found out about the collection, I still don't know. Probably from an art dealer up north—they can be bigger gossips than schoolgirls—but even so, I didn't blame her for all that followed. She was doing her job and I could have asked her to leave, but instead I answered her questions and allowed her to take photographs. After she left, I promptly put her out of my mind. Then, a few months later, a squeaky-voiced young man who described himself as a fact-checker for the magazine phoned to verify things that I had said. Naively, I gave him the answers he wanted, only to receive a small package in the mail several weeks later. The journalist had been thoughtful enough to send me a copy of the issue in which the article appeared. Needless to say, the article enraged me. I threw it away after reading what she'd written, but later after I'd cooled down, I retrieved it from the trash and read it once more. In retrospect, I realized it wasn't her fault that she hadn't understood what I'd been trying to tell her. In her mind, after all, the collection was the entirety of the story.

That was six years ago, and it turned my life upside down. Bars went up on the windows and a fence was installed that circled the yard. I had a security system put in, and the police began making a point to drive past my house at least twice a day. I was deluged with phone calls. Reporters. Producers. A screenwriter who promised to put the story on the big screen. Three or four lawyers. Two people who claimed to be related, distant cousins on Ruth's side of the family. Strangers down on their luck and looking for handouts. In the end, I simply unplugged the phone, for all of them—including the journalist—thought about the art only in terms of money.

What every last person failed to see was that it was not about money; it was about the memories they held. If Ruth had the letters I wrote her, I had the paintings and the memories. When I see the de Koonings and the Rauschenbergs and the Warhols, I recall the way Ruth held me as we stood by the lake; when I see the Jackson Pollock, I am reliving that first trip to New York in 1950. We were halfway through our trip, and on a whim we drove out to Springs, a hamlet near East Hampton on Long Island. It was a glorious summer day and Ruth wore a yellow dress. She was twenty-eight then and growing more beautiful with every passing day, something that Pollock did not fail to notice. I am convinced that it was her elegant bearing that moved him to allow two strangers into his studio. It also explains why he eventually allowed Ruth to purchase a painting he'd only recently completed, something he seldom, if ever, did again. Later that afternoon, on our way back to the city, Ruth and I stopped at a small café in Water Mill. It was a charming place with scuffed wood floors and sun-drenched windows, and the owner led us to a wobbly outdoor table. On that day, Ruth ordered white wine, something light and sweet, and we sipped from our glasses while gazing out over the Sound. The breeze was light and the day was warm, and when we spotted the occasional boat passing in the distance, we'd wonder aloud where it might be headed.

Hanging next to that painting is a work by Jasper Johns. We bought it in 1952, the summer that Ruth's hair was at its longest. The first faint lines were beginning to form at the corners of her eyes, adding a womanly quality to her face. She and I had stood atop the Empire State Building earlier that morning, and later in the quiet of our hotel room, Ruth and I made love for hours before she finally fell asleep in my arms. I could not sleep that day. Instead, I stared at her, watching the gentle rise and fall of her chest, her skin warm against my own. In the dim surroundings of that room, her hair splayed over the pillow, I found myself asking whether any man had ever been as lucky as I.

This is why I wander our house late at night; this is why the collection remains intact. This is why I've never sold a single painting. How could I? In the oils and pigments I store my memories of Ruth; in every painting I recall a chapter of our lives together. There is nothing more precious to me. They are all I have left of the wife I've loved more than life itself, and I will continue to stare and remember until I can do it no more.

Before she passed, Ruth sometimes joined me on these late-hour wanderings, for she, too, enjoyed being drawn back in time. She, too, liked to retell the stories, even if she never realized that she was the heroine in all of them. She would hold my hand as we wandered from room to room, both of us reveling as the past came alive.

My marriage brought great happiness into my life, but lately there's been nothing but sadness. I understand that love and tragedy go hand in hand, for there can't be one without the other, but nonetheless I find myself wondering whether the trade-off is fair. A man should die as he had lived, I think; in his final moments, he should be surrounded and comforted by those he's always loved.

But I already know that in my final moments, I will be alone.

18

Sophia

The next few weeks were one of those rare and wonderful interludes in which almost everything made Sophia believe nothing could be better.

Her classes were stimulating, her grades were excellent, and even though she hadn't heard from the Denver Art Museum, her adviser recommended her for an internship at the Museum of Modern Art in New York. She would interview there over Christmas break. It wasn't a paid position and she would probably have to commute from home if she got it, but it was MoMA. Never in her wildest dreams had she considered it a possibility.

In the limited time that she spent at the sorority house, she'd noticed that Marcia was developing a prance in her step—the same one she got whenever she'd focused on someone special. She was in a perpetually good mood, despite her denials that a guy had anything to do with it. At the same time, Mary-Kate had significantly reduced her responsibilities at the sorority—other than attending mandatory meetings, Sophia was for the most part exempt from sisterly obligations. Granted, this was probably the result of her own perfunctory attitude, but hey, whatever worked. Best of all, she hadn't run into Brian around campus—nor had he texted or called—making it easy to forget they'd ever dated.

And then, of course, there was Luke.

For the first time, she felt she understood what loving someone really meant. Since their weekend in the cabin—aside from Thanksgiving, when she'd gone home to visit her family—they'd spent every Saturday night together at the ranch, mostly in each other's arms. In between kisses, the feel of his bare skin electric against her own, she reveled in the sound of his voice telling her over and over how much he adored her and how much she'd come to mean to him. In the darkness, she would gently trace her finger over his scars, sometimes finding a new one that she hadn't noticed before; they would talk until the early hours of the morning, pausing only to make love once more. The passion they felt for each other was intoxicating, something entirely different from what she'd felt with Brian. It was a connection that transcended the physical act. She'd grown to appreciate the quiet way Luke would slip from the bed first thing on Sunday mornings to feed the animals and check the cattle, trying his best not to wake her. Usually she would doze again, only to be awakened later with a cup of hot coffee and his presence beside her. Sometimes they'd while away an hour or more on the porch or simply make breakfast together. Almost always they'd take the horses out, sometimes for an entire afternoon. The crisp winter air would turn her cheeks red and make her hands ache, yet in those moments she felt connected to Luke and the ranch in a way that made her wonder why it had taken her so long to find him.

As the holidays loomed closer, they would spend much of the weekend in the grove of Christmas trees. While Luke did the cutting, hauling, and tying up of the trees, Sophia worked the register. During lulls, she was able to study for finals.

Luke had also begun to practice in earnest on the mechanical bull again. Sometimes she'd watch him atop the hood of a rusting tractor in the rickety barn. The bull was set up in a makeshift ring thickly padded with foam to break his falls. Usually he started off slowly, riding just hard enough to loosen his muscles, before setting the bull on high. The bull would spin and dip and shift directions abruptly, yet somehow Luke would stay centered, holding his free hand up and away from his body. He would ride three or four times, then sit with her while he recovered. Then he would climb into the ring again, the practice session sometimes lasting up to two hours. Though he never complained, she could recognize his soreness in the way he occasionally winced while shifting position or altering his walk. Sunday nights often found him in his bedroom, surrounded by candles as Sophia kneaded his muscles, trying to work out his aches and pains.

Though they spent little time together on campus, they would sometimes go to dinner or a movie, and once they even visited a country bar, where they listened to the same band that had been playing on the night they'd met, Luke teaching her to line dance at last. Luke made the world more vivid somehow, more real, and when they weren't together, she inevitably found her thoughts drifting toward him.

The second week of December brought with it an early cold front, a heavy storm that blew down from Canada. It was the first snow of the season, and though most of it had melted by the following afternoon, Sophia and Luke spent part of the morning admiring the white-capped beauty of the ranch before hiking to the grove of Christmas trees on what ended up being the busiest day to that point.

Later, as had become their habit, they headed over to his mother's. While Luke worked on replacing the brake pads in his truck, Linda taught Sophia how to bake. Luke hadn't been lying about how good her pies were, and they passed an enjoyable afternoon in the kitchen, chatting and laughing, their aprons coated with flour.

Spending time with Linda reminded Sophia of her parents and all the sacrifices they'd made for her. Watching Linda and Luke tease and joke with each other made her wonder whether she'd have the same kind of relationship with her own parents someday. Gone would be the little girl they remembered; in her place would be not only their daughter, but perhaps a friend as well. Being part of Luke's life had made her feel more like an adult. With only a semester to go, she no longer wondered what the point of college had been. The ups and downs, the dreams and struggles, had all been part of the journey, she realized—a journey that led to a cattle ranch near a town called King, where she had fallen in love with a cowboy named Luke.

"Again?" Marcia whined. She crossed her legs on the bed, pulling her oversize sweater down over her tights. "What? Twelve weekends in a row at the ranch weren't enough for you?"

"You're exaggerating." Sophia rolled her eyes, adding a final coat of lip gloss. Next to her, her small bag was already packed.

"Of course I am. But it's our last weekend before Christmas break. We leave on Wednesday, and I've barely spent any time with you at all this semester."

"We're together all the time," Sophia protested.

"No," Marcia said. "We *used* to spend time together. Now you're at the ranch with him almost every weekend. You didn't even go to the winter formal last weekend. *Our* winter formal."

"You know I don't care for those kinds of events."

"Don't you mean *he* doesn't care for them?"

Sophia brought her lips together, not wanting to sound defensive but feeling the first hint of irritation in the way Marcia sounded. "Neither of us wanted to go, okay? He was working and he needed my help."

Marcia ran her hand through her hair, clearly exasperated. "I don't know how to say this without making you mad at me."

"Say what?"

"You're making a mistake."

"What are you talking about?" Sophia put down her tube of lip gloss and turned to face her friend.

Marcia tossed up her hands. "Think about how it looks—imagine what you'd say if our roles were reversed. Say I was in a relationship for two years—"

"Not likely," Sophia stopped her.

"Okay, and I know it's hard, but just pretend. I'm doing this for you. Say I went through a truly awful breakup and was hiding out in my room for weeks, then out of the blue, I meet this guy. So I talk to him and visit him the next day, and then talk to him on the phone and visit him the next weekend. Pretty soon, I'm treating him like he's my whole world and spending every free minute with him. What would you think? That it just so happened that I met Mr. Right while I was rebounding from a horrible breakup? I mean, what are the odds?"

Sophia could feel blood begin to pound in her veins. "I don't know what you're trying to say."

"I'm saying that you could be making a mistake. And that if you're not careful, you could end up getting hurt."

"I'm not making a mistake," Sophia snapped, zipping up the bag. "And I'm not going to get hurt. I *like* spending time with Luke."

"I know." Marcia softened, patting the bed beside her. "Sit down with me," she pleaded. "Please?"

Sophia debated before crossing the room and taking a seat on the bed. Marcia faced her.

"I get that you like him," she said. "I really do. And I'm glad you're happy again. But where do you see this going? I mean, if it were me, I'd be happy to hang out and have fun, just see where it goes and live for the day. But I'd never let myself think for one minute that I'm going to spend the rest of my life with the guy."

"I'm not thinking that either," Sophia interjected.

Marcia picked at her sweater. "Are you sure? Because that's not the impression I get." She paused, her expression almost sad. "You shouldn't have fallen in love with him. And every time you're with him, you're only making it worse for yourself."

Sophia flushed. "Why are you doing this?"

"Because you're not thinking clearly," Marcia answered. "If you were, you'd be thinking about the fact that you're a senior in college—an art history major from New Jersey, for God's sake—while Luke rides bulls and lives on a ranch in rural North Carolina. You'd be wondering what was going to happen in six months, once you graduate." She stopped, forcing Sophia to concentrate on what she was really saying. "Can you imagine living on a ranch for the next fifty years? Riding horses, herding cows, and cleaning out stalls for the rest of your life?"

She shook her head. "No—"

"Oh," Marcia said, cutting her off. "Then maybe you see Luke living in New York City while you work at a museum? Maybe you imagine the two of you spending every Sunday morning at the latest brunch hot spots, sipping cappuccinos and reading the *New York Times*? Is that how you picture your future together?"

When Sophia didn't answer, Marcia reached over and squeezed her hand.

"I know how much you care about him," she went on. "But your lives aren't just on different tracks, they're on different continents. And that means you're going to have to watch your heart from here on, because if you don't, it's going to end up breaking into all sorts of pieces."

"You've been quiet tonight," Luke said between sips of hot cocoa. Sophia held her hands around her cup, staring out from their spot on the couch at the snow flurries beyond the window, the second snow of the season, though this one wasn't likely to stick. As usual, Luke had the fireplace going, but she couldn't shake the chill she felt.

"I'm sorry," she said. "I'm just tired."

She could feel his attention, which tonight for some reason left her strangely unsettled.

"Do you know what I think?" he asked. "I think Marcia said something to you and it made you upset."

Sophia didn't answer right away. "Why would you say that?" she asked, her voice weaker than what she'd expected.

He shrugged. "When I called you to tell you that I was on my way, I could barely get you off the phone. By the time I got to the house, you'd gone silent. And I noticed the way you and Marcia kept glancing at each other. It was like the two of you had just shared some kind of confession, and neither of you was happy about it."

The warmth from the cup radiated into her hands. "You're very perceptive for a guy who can go a whole day without talking," she said, peering up at him.

"That's why I'm perceptive."

His answer reminded her of the reasons they'd become so close so fast. But whether that was such a good idea wasn't quite so clear anymore.

"You're thinking again," he chided. "And it's beginning to make me nervous."

Despite the tension, she laughed.

"Where do you think all this is going?" she suddenly asked, echoing Marcia's earlier question.

"Between us, you mean?"

"I'm going to be graduating in the spring. Just a few months from now. What's going to happen then? What happens when I move back home? Or get a job somewhere?"

He leaned forward, putting his cup on the coffee table before slowly turning to face her again. "I don't know," he said.

"You don't know?"

His face was unreadable. "I can't tell the future any more than you can."

"That sounds like an excuse."

"I'm not making excuses," he said. "I'm just trying to be honest."

"But you're not saying anything!" she cried, hearing her own desperation and hating it.

Luke kept his voice steady. "Then how about this? I love you. I want to be with you. We'll find a way to make it work."

"Do you really believe that?"

"I wouldn't have said it if I didn't."

"Even if that means you have to move to New Jersey?"

The firelight cast half his face in shadow. "You want me to move to New Jersey?"

"What's wrong with New Jersey?"

"Nothing," he said. "I told you that I've been there before and that I liked it."

"But?"

For the first time, his eyes dropped. "I can't leave the ranch until I know my mom's going to be okay," he said with a certain finality.

She understood his reasons, and yet...

"You want me to stay here," she said. "After graduation."

"No." He shook his head. "I would never ask you to do that."

She couldn't hide her exasperation. "Then, again, what are we going to do?"

He put his hands on his knees. "We're not the first couple to face something like this. My feeling is, if it was meant to be, we'll figure it out. No, I don't know the answers, and no, I can't tell you how it's all going to play out. And if you were leaving today, I'd be more worried about it. But we've got six months, and things might be different by then...Maybe I'll be riding well and I won't be so worried about the ranch, or maybe I'll be digging up one of the fence posts one day and discover some buried treasure. Or maybe we'll end up losing the ranch entirely and I'll have to move anyway. Or maybe you'll get a job in Charlotte, someplace close enough to commute. I don't know." He leaned closer, no doubt trying to underscore his words. "The only thing I do know for sure is that if we both want to, we'll find a way to make it work."

She knew it was the only thing he could say, but the question of their future still left her feeling unsettled. She didn't say that, though. Instead, she scooted closer and let him slip his arm around her, his body warm against hers. She drew a long breath, wishing that time could somehow stop. Or at least slow down. "Okay," she whispered.

He kissed her hair, then rested his chin on top of her head. "I love you, you know."

"I know," she whispered. "I love you, too."

"I'm going to miss you while you're gone."

"Me too."

"But I'm glad you'll spend some time with your family."

"Me too."

"Maybe I'll drive up to New Jersey and surprise you."

"I'm sorry," she said. "You can't do that."

"Why not?"

"I'm not saying you're not welcome to visit me. I'm just saying it won't be a surprise. You kind of ruined it."

He thought about that. "I guess I did, didn't I? Well, maybe I'll surprise you by not coming."

"You better come. My parents want to meet you. They've never met a cowboy before and I know they have this crazy picture in their heads in which you walk around with a six-shooter and say things like 'Howdy, pardner.'"

He laughed. "I guess I'll disappoint them."

"No," she said. "That's one thing you won't do."

At that, Luke smiled. "How about New Year's Eve? You doing anything?"

"I don't know. Am I?"

"Now you are."

"Perfect. But you can't show up at night. You're going to have to spend some time with my parents, like I said."

"Fair enough," he said. He nodded toward the corner. "Do you want to help me decorate the tree?"

"What tree?"

"It's out back. I picked it out yesterday and dragged it over. It's kind of small and sparse and it wasn't likely to sell, but I thought it might be nice in here. So you know what you'll be missing."

She leaned into him. "I already know what I'll be missing."

An hour later, Sophia and Luke stood back and admired their work.

"It's not quite right," Luke said, crossing his arms as he surveyed the tinsel-strewn tree. "It needs something more."

"There's not much more we can do with it," Sophia said, reaching out to adjust a strand of lights. "A lot of the branches are already sagging."

"It's not that," he said. "It's...Hold on. I'll be right back. I know exactly what it needs. Just give me a minute—"

Sophia watched him disappear into the bedroom and return with a medium-size gift box, tied with ribbon. He walked past her and set it beneath the tree, then joined her again.

"Much better," he said.

She looked over at him. "Is that for me?"

"As a matter of fact, it is."

"That's not fair. I didn't get you anything."

"I don't want anything."

"That may be, but now I feel bad."

"Don't. You can make it up to me later."

She studied him. "You knew I was going to say that, didn't you?"

"It was all part of my plan."

"What's in it?"

"Go ahead," he urged. "Open it."

She approached the tree and picked up the box. It was light enough for her to guess what was inside before she'd untied the ribbon and lifted the lid. She pulled it out and held it in front of her, examining it. Dyed black and made of straw, it was decorated with beads and a band that held in place a small feather.

"A cowboy hat?"

"A nice one," he said. "For girls."

"Is there a difference?"

"Well, I would never wear one with a feather or beads. And I figured that since you were coming out here so much, you really needed your own."

She leaned over and kissed him. "It's perfect. Thank you."

"Merry Christmas."

She put it on and peered up at him coquettishly. "How does it look?"

"Beautiful," he said. "But then again, you always look beautiful."

19

❧

Luke

With the beginning of the season less than a month away—and Sophia up in New Jersey—Luke stepped up his training regimen. In the days leading up to Christmas, he not only increased the duration of his rides on the mechanical bull by five minutes a day, but added strength training to the program. He'd never been fond of weight lifting, but no matter what he was doing in the way of work—which lately was primarily selling the remaining trees—he would duck away at the top of every hour and do fifty push-ups, sometimes finishing four or five hundred in a day. Finally, he added pull-ups and core work to strengthen his stomach and lower back. By the time he collapsed in bed at the end of the day, he would fall asleep within seconds.

Despite his sore muscles and exhaustion, he could gradually feel his skills coming back. His balance was improving, which made it easier to keep firmly seated. His instincts, too, were sharpening, allowing him to anticipate the reversals and pitches. In the four days following Christmas, he drove to Henderson County, where he rode live bulls. A guy he knew had a practice facility there, and though the bulls weren't of the highest quality, practicing on the mechanical bull could do only so much. Live animals were never predictable, and though Luke wore both a helmet and a flak jacket, he found himself as nervous before these encounters as he'd been in McLeansville back in October.

He pushed himself hard, and then even harder. The season began in mid-January, and he needed a strong start. He needed to win or place as high as possible in order to garner enough points to move up to the major league tour by March. By June, it might be too late.

His mom saw what he was doing, and little by little she began to withdraw again. Her anger was evident, but her sadness was, too, and he found himself wishing that Sophia were with them, if only to ease the growing awkwardness. Then again, he wished Sophia were here, period. With Sophia back in New Jersey for the holidays, Christmas Eve had been a quiet affair. Christmas Day was also subdued. He hadn't gone over to his mother's house until the early afternoon, and her tension was palpable.

He was glad to have the Christmas tree sales behind him. Though they'd done well, the month in the grove meant everything else on the ranch had deteriorated further, and the weather wasn't helping matters. Luke's to-do list grew longer, and it worried him, particularly because he knew he'd be traveling a lot in the coming year. His absence would only make things harder for his mom.

Unless, of course, he started winning right away.

Always, it came back to that. Despite the tree sales, which his mom used to add seven pair to the herd, the farm's income wasn't going to be near enough to cover their payments.

And with that in mind, Luke would trudge to the barn to practice, counting the days until New Year's Eve, when he'd finally see Sophia again.

❧

He left early in the morning, arriving in Jersey City a few minutes before lunch. After spending the afternoon with Sophia's parents and sisters, neither Luke nor Sophia had wanted to battle the crowds in Times Square for New Year's Eve celebrations. Instead, they had a quiet dinner at an unpretentious Thai restaurant before returning to Luke's hotel.

In the hours past midnight, Sophia lay on her stomach while Luke traced small circles on her lower back.

"Stop," she said, wiggling. "It's not going to work."

"What's not going to work?"

"I already told you that I can't stay. I have a curfew."

"You're twenty-one years old," he protested.

"But I'm at my parents' house, and they have rules. And actually, they were being extra permissive by letting me stay out until two. Normally, I have to be in by one."

"What would happen if you stayed?"

"They'd probably think we slept together."

"We did sleep together."

She turned her head to face him. "They don't have to know that. And I have no intention of making it obvious."

"But I'm only here for one night. I have to leave tomorrow afternoon."

"I know, but rules are rules. And besides, you don't want to get on my parents' bad side. They liked you. Although my sisters told me they were disappointed you weren't wearing your hat."

"I wanted to fit in."

"Oh, you did all right. Especially when you started talking about 4-H again. You noticed they had the same reaction I did when they found out you sell those poor little pigs for slaughter after raising them like pets."

"I've been meaning to thank you for bringing that up."

"You're welcome," Sophia said, her expression mischievous. "Did you see Dalena's face when I explained it? I thought her eyes were going to pop out of her head. How's your mom doing, by the way?"

"She's all right."

"I take it she's still mad at you?"

"You could say that."

"She'll come around."

"I hope so." He leaned down, kissing her. Although she returned his kiss, he felt her hands move toward his chest and gently push him away.

"You can kiss me all you want, but you still have to bring me back home."

"Can you sneak me into your room?"

"Not with my sister there. That would be too weird."

"If I'd known you wouldn't stay over, I might not have driven all the way up here."

"I don't believe you."

He laughed before becoming serious again. "I missed you."

"No, you didn't. You were too busy to miss me. Every time I called, you were always on the go. Between work and practice, you probably didn't even think about me."

"I missed you," he said again.

"I know. And I missed you, too." She reached up, touching his face. "But sadly, we're going to have to get dressed anyway. You're supposed to come over for brunch tomorrow, remember?"

Back in North Carolina, Luke made the decision to redouble his practice efforts. The first event of the season was less than two weeks away. The two days in New Jersey had given his body a chance to rest, and he felt good for the first time in weeks. The only problem was that it was as cold here as it had been in New Jersey, and he dreaded the chill of the barn even as he set out in its direction.

He had just turned on the barn lights and was stretching before his first ride of the night when he heard the door swing open. He turned around just as his mom emerged from the shadows.

"Hey, Mom," he said, surprised.

"Hi," she said. Like him, she wore a heavy jacket. "I went over to your house and when I realized you weren't there, I figured this is where you might be."

He said nothing. In the silence, his mom stepped into the foam-padded ring, sinking with every step until she stood on the opposite side of the bull from him. Unexpectedly, she reached out and ran her hand over it.

"I remember when your dad first brought this home," she said. "It was all the rage for a while, you know. People wanted to ride these things because of that old movie with John Travolta, and practically every country bar put one in, only to watch the interest die out within a year or two. When one of those bars was being torn down, your dad asked if he could buy the bull. It didn't cost much, but it was still more than we could afford at the time and I remember being furious with him. He'd been off in Iowa or Kansas or somewhere, and he drove all the way back here to drop it off before turning right around and heading to Texas for another set of rodeos. It wasn't until he got back that he realized it didn't work. He had to rebuild the thing pretty much from scratch, and it took him almost a year to get it working the way he wanted. But by then, you came along and he'd pretty much retired. It sat in the barn here collecting dust until he eventually put you on it...I think you were two years old at the time. I got pretty mad about that, too, even though it was barely moving. I somehow knew that you'd end up following in his footsteps. The thing is, I never wanted you to ride in the first place. I always thought it was a crazy way to try to make a living." In her voice, he heard an uncharacteristic trace of bitterness.

"Why didn't you say anything?"

"What was there to say? You were as obsessed as your dad. You broke your arm when you were five riding on a calf. But you didn't care. You were just mad because you couldn't ride for a few months. What could I do?" She didn't expect an answer, and she sighed. "For a long time, I hoped you'd grow out of it.

I was probably the only mother in the world who prayed that her teenager would get interested in cars or girls or music, but you never did."

"I liked those things, too."

"Maybe. But riding was your life. It was all you ever really wanted to do. It was all you really dreamed about, and..." She closed her eyes, an extended blink. "You had the makings of a star. As much as I hated it, I knew you had the ability and the desire and the motivation to be the best in the world. And I was proud of you. But even then, it broke my heart. Not because I didn't think you'd make it, but because I knew you'd risk everything to reach your dream. And I watched you get hurt over and over and try again and again." She shifted her stance. "What you have to remember is that to me, you'll always be my child, the one I held in my arms right after you were born."

Luke stayed silent, overcome by a familiar shame.

"Tell me," his mother said, searching his face. "Is it something you feel like you couldn't live without? Do you still burn with the desire to be the best?"

He stared at his boots before reluctantly lifting his head.

"No," he admitted.

"I didn't think so," she said.

"Mom—"

"I know why you're doing this. Just like you know why I don't want you to. You're my son, but I can't stop you and I know that, too."

He drew a long breath, noting her weariness. Resignation hung on her like a tattered shroud.

"Why did you come out here, Mom?" he asked. "It wasn't to tell me all that."

She gave a melancholy smile. "No. Actually, I came out here to check on you, to make sure you were okay. And to find out how your trip went."

There was more and he knew it, but he answered anyway.

"The trip was good. Short, though. I feel like I spent more time in the truck than I did with Sophia."

"That's probably right," she agreed. "And her family?"

"Nice people. Close family. There was a lot of laughing at the table."

She nodded. "Good." She crossed her arms, rubbing her sleeves. "And Sophia?"

"She's great."

"I see the way you look at her."

"Yeah?"

"It's pretty clear how you feel about her," his mom stated.

"Yeah?" he asked again.

"It's good," she said. "Sophia's special. I've enjoyed getting to know her. Do you think there's a future there?"

He shifted from one foot to the other. "I hope so."

His mom looked at him seriously. "Then you should probably tell her."

"I already have."

"No," his mom said, shaking her head. "You should *tell* her."

"Tell her what?"

"What the doctor told us," she said, not bothering to mince her words. "You should tell her that if you keep riding, you'll most likely be dead in less than a year."

20

Ira

When you wander the house at night," Ruth suddenly interjects, "you do not do as you say."

"What do you mean?" I am startled to hear her voice again after this long silence.

"They are not like the diary you made for me. I could read all my letters, but you do not see all the paintings. Many of them are stacked together in overcrowded rooms and you haven't seen them for years. And the ones you store in the oak boxes you do not look at either. It is impossible for you to even open the boxes these days."

This is true. "Perhaps I should call someone," I say. "I could hang different ones on the walls. Like you used to do."

"Yes, but when I did it, I knew how to arrange them to their best effect. Your taste is not so good. You simply had workers hang them in every open spot."

"I like the eclectic feel."

"It is not eclectic. It is tacky and cluttered and it is a fire hazard."

I smirk. "It's a good thing no one comes to visit, then."

"No," she says. "This is not good. You might have been shy, but you always drew strength from people."

"I drew strength from you," I say.

Though it's dark in the car, I see her roll her eyes.

"I am talking about your customers. You always had a special way with them. This is why they remained customers. And it is why the shop failed after you sold it. Because the new owners were more interested in money than in providing service."

Ruth might be right about this, but I sometimes wonder if the changing marketplace had more to do with it. Even before I retired, the shop had been drawing fewer customers for years. There were larger stores, with more selection, opening in other areas of Greensboro, while people began to flee the city for the suburbs and businesses downtown began to struggle. I warned the new owner about this, but he was intent on moving ahead, and I walked away knowing I had given him a fair deal. Even though the shop was no longer mine, I felt a strong pang of regret when I realized it was going out of business after more than ninety years. The old haberdasheries, the kind I ran for decades, have gone the way of covered wagons, buggy whips, and rotary-dial phones.

"My job was never like yours, though," I finally say. "I didn't love it the way you loved yours."

"I could take whole summers off."

I shake my head. Or rather, I imagine that I do. "It was because of the children," I say. "You may have inspired them, but they also inspired you. As memorable as our summers were, by the end, you were always excited at the thought of being back in the classroom. Because you missed the children. You missed their laughter and their curiosity and the innocent way they saw the world."

She looks at me, her eyebrow raised. "And how would you know this?"

"Because," I say, "you told me."

❧

Ruth was a third-grade teacher, and to her, it was one of the key educational periods in a student's life. Most of the students were eight or nine years old, an age she always considered an educational turning point. At that age, students are old enough to understand concepts that would have been foreign to them only a year earlier, but they are still young enough to accept guidance from adults with a near-unquestioning trust.

It was also, in Ruth's opinion, the first year in which students really began to differentiate academically. Some students began to excel while others fell behind; although there were countless reasons for this, in that particular school, in that era, many of her students—and their parents—simply didn't care. The students would attend school until the eighth or ninth grade, then drop out to work on the farm full-time. Even for Ruth, this was a challenge that was difficult to overcome. These were the kids that kept Ruth awake at night, the ones she worried endlessly about, and she tinkered with her lesson plan for years, searching for ways to get through to them and their parents. She would have them plant seeds in Dixie cups and label them in an effort to encourage them to read; she would have the students catch bugs and name those as well, hoping to spark intellectual curiosity about the natural world. Tests in mathematics always included something about the farm or money: *If Joe gathered four baskets of peaches from each tree, and there were five trees in each of the six rows, how many baskets of peaches will Joe be able to sell?* Or: *If you have $200 and you buy seed that costs $120, how much money do you have left?* This was a world the students understood to be important—and more often than not, she got through to them. While some still ended up dropping out, they would sometimes come to visit her in later years, to thank her for teaching them how to read and write and perform the basic math necessary to figure out their purchases at the store.

She was proud of this—and proud of the students who eventually ended up graduating and going to college, of course. But every now and then, she had a student who made her realize again why she'd wanted to be a teacher in the first place. And that brings me to the painting above the fireplace.

❧

"You are thinking about Daniel McCallum," she says to me.

"Yes," I say. "Your favorite student."

Her expression is animated, and I know her image of him is as vivid as the day she first met him. At the time, she'd been teaching for fifteen years. "He was very difficult."

"That's what you told me."

"He was very wild when he first arrived. His overalls were dirty all the time and he could never sit still. I scolded him every day."

"But you taught him to read."

"I taught them all to read."

"He was different, though."

"Yes," she says. "He was bigger than the other boys and he would punch the other students in the arm at recess, leaving bruises. It is because of Daniel McCallum that my hair began to turn gray."

To this day, I can remember her complaints about him, but her words, as they are now, had always been tinged with affection.

"He'd never been to school before. He didn't understand the rules."

"He knew the rules. But at first, he did not care. He sat behind a pretty young girl named Abigail, and would constantly pull her hair. I would say to him, 'You must not do this,' but he would do it anyway. I finally had to seat him in the front row where I could keep my eye on him."

"And it was then that you learned he couldn't read or write."

"Yes." Even now, her voice is grim.

"And when you went to talk to his parents, you discovered they'd passed away. It turned out that Daniel was being raised by an older stepbrother and his wife, neither of whom wanted him to attend school at all. And you saw that the three of them were living in what was essentially a shack."

"You know this because you went with me that day to the place he lived."

I nod. "You were so quiet on the drive home."

"It bothered me to think that in this rich country, there were people who still lived as they did. And it bothered me that he had no one in his life who seemed to care about him."

"So you decided not only to teach him, but to tutor him as well. Both before and after school."

"He sat in the front row," she says. "I would not be a good teacher if he learned nothing at all."

"But you also felt sorry for him."

"How could I not? His life was not easy. And yet, I eventually learned that there were many children like Daniel."

"No," I say. "For both of us, there was only one."

❦

It was early October when Daniel first entered our home, a gangly, towheaded boy with rough country mannerisms and a shyness I hadn't anticipated. He did not shake my hand on that first visit, nor did he meet my eyes. Instead, he stood with his hands in his pockets, his gaze fixed on the floor. Though Ruth had tutored him after school, she worked with him again that evening at the kitchen table while I sat in the living room, listening to the radio. Afterward, she insisted he stay for dinner.

Daniel wasn't the first student she'd invited to our home for dinner, but he was the only one who ever came regularly. It was due partly to the family's situation, Ruth explained. Daniel's step-brother and his wife could barely keep the farm afloat and were resentful that the sheriff had ordered them to send Daniel to school at all. All the same, it didn't seem as though they wanted him around the farm, either. On the day Ruth visited, they sat on the porch smoking cigarettes and responded to Ruth's questions with indifferent, single-syllable answers. The next morning, Daniel came to school with bruises on his cheek and one eye as red as a ruby. The sight of his face nearly broke Ruth's heart, making her all the more determined to help him.

But it wasn't simply the obvious signs of abuse that upset her. When tutoring him after school, she often heard his stomach rumble, though when asked, he denied that he was hungry. When Daniel finally admitted that he sometimes went days without eating, her first instinct was to call the sheriff. Daniel begged her not to, if only because he had nowhere else to go. Instead, she ended up inviting him to dinner.

After that initial visit to our home, Daniel began to eat with us two or three times a week. As he grew more comfortable with us, the shyness evaporated, replaced by an almost formal politeness. He shook my hand and addressed me as Mr. Levinson, always making a point of asking how my day had been. The seriousness of his demeanor both saddened and impressed me, perhaps because it seemed a product of his prematurely hard life. But I liked him from the beginning and grew more fond of him as the year progressed. For her part, Ruth would eventually come to love him like a son.

I know that in this day and age, it's considered inappropriate to use such a word when describing a teacher's feeling for a student, and perhaps it was inappropriate even then. But hers was a motherly love, a love born of affection and concern, and Daniel blossomed under Ruth's care. Over and over, I would hear her tell him that she believed in him and that he could be anything he wanted to be when he grew up. She emphasized that he could change the world if he wanted, make it a better place for himself and others, and he seemed to believe her. More than anything, he seemed to want to please her and he stopped acting up in class. He worked hard to become a better student, surprising Ruth with the ease with which he learned. Though uneducated, he was highly intelligent, and by January, he was reading as well as his classmates. By May, he was nearly two years ahead, not only in reading, but in all the other subjects as well. His memory was remarkable; he was a veritable sponge, soaking up everything that Ruth or I ever told him.

As if keen to know Ruth's heart, he showed an interest in the art that hung on our walls, and after dinner, Ruth often walked him through the house to show him the paintings we'd collected. He would hold Ruth's hand and listen as she described them, his eyes flickering from the paintings to her face and back again. He eventually came to know the names of all the artists, as well as their styles, and in this fashion I knew that he had come to care for Ruth as much as she cared for him. Once, Ruth asked me to take a photograph of them together. After she presented it to him, he clung to it for the rest of the afternoon and I saw him staring at it sometime later, his face etched with wonder. Whenever Ruth dropped him off back at home, he never once forgot to thank her for the time she spent with him. And on the last day of school, before he ran off to play with his friends, he told her that he loved her.

By then, the idea had taken root in her mind to ask Daniel if he wanted to live with us permanently. We talked about this, and in truth, I wouldn't have minded. Daniel was a pleasure to have around our home and I told her as much. But by the end of the school year, Ruth still wasn't sure how to broach the subject to him. She wasn't sure whether Daniel would agree or even if he desired such a thing, nor did she know how to suggest this to his stepbrother. There was no guarantee that such a thing would even be legally allowed, so for all these reasons, she said nothing on that final day. Instead, she decided to postpone the matter until after we returned from our summer trip. But during our travels, Ruth and I spoke of Daniel frequently. We resolved to do whatever we could to make such an arrangement possible. When we finally returned to Greensboro, however, the shack stood empty, apparently abandoned for weeks. Daniel didn't return to school in August, nor were there any requests for his records to be forwarded. No one seemed to know where he'd gone or what had happened to the family. Students and other teachers soon forgot about him, but for Ruth, it was different. She cried for weeks when she realized not only that he was gone, but that he might be gone forever. She made a point of visiting the neighboring farms, hoping that someone could tell her where the family had gone. At home, she would eagerly sort through the mail, hoping to find a letter from him, and she could never hide her disappointment when, day after day, none arrived. Daniel had filled a hole in Ruth that I could not, something that had been missing in our marriage. In that year, he'd become the child she'd always wanted, the child I could never give her.

I would love to tell you that Ruth and Daniel reconnected; that later in life, he contacted her, if only to let her know how he was doing. She worried about him for years, but with the passage of time, Ruth began to mention his name less frequently, until finally she stopped mentioning him at all. Yet I knew she never forgot about him and that part of her never stopped looking for him. It was Daniel she was looking for as we drove the quiet country roads, passing run-down farms; it was Daniel she hoped to see whenever she returned to school after a summer spent in distant studios and galleries. Once, she thought she spotted him on the streets of Greensboro during a Veterans Day parade, but by the time we were able to make our way through the crowds, he was already gone, if he'd ever really been there at all.

After Daniel, we never again had a student in our home.

There is a bone-chilling cold in the car, the aftereffect of the window I opened earlier. Frost glitters on the dashboard now, and every time I breathe, a cloud forms beyond my lips. Though I'm no longer thirsty, my throat and stomach remain chilled from the snow. The cold is inside and outside, everywhere, and I can't stop shivering.

Beside me, Ruth stares out the window and I realize that I can see starlight beyond the pane. It is not yet light, but the moonlight makes the snow on the trees glow silver, and I can tell that the worst of the weather has passed. Tonight, the snow on the car will crust as it continues to freeze, but sometime tomorrow or the next day, the temperature will rise and the world will shake off the white embrace of winter as the snow begins to melt.

This is both good and bad. My car may become visible from the road, which is good, but I need the snow to live, and within a day or two, it might be gone completely.

"You are doing fine for now," Ruth tells me. "Do not worry about tomorrow until you have to."

"Easy for you to say," I reply, sulking. "I'm the one in trouble here."

"Yes," she says matter-of-factly. "But it is your fault. You should not have been driving."

"We're back to this again?"

She turns to me with a wry grin. She is in her forties now and wears her hair short. Her dress is cut in simple lines, in the bright red hues she preferred, with oversize buttons and elegant pockets. Like every other woman in the 1960s, Ruth was a fan of Jacqueline Kennedy.

"You brought it up."

"I was looking for sympathy."

"You are complaining. You do this more now that you are older. Like with the neighbor who cut down the tree. And the girl at the gas station who thought you were invisible."

"I wasn't complaining. I was observing. There's a difference."

"You should not complain. It is not attractive."

"I'm many years removed from being attractive."

"No," she counters. "In this you are wrong. Your heart is still beautiful. Your eyes are still kind, and you are a good and honest man. This is enough to keep you beautiful forever."

"Are you flirting with me?"

She raises an eyebrow. "I do not know. Am I?"

She is, I think. And for the first time since the accident, if only for a moment, I actually feel warm.

◆

It's strange, I think, the way our lives turn out. Moments of circumstance, when later combined with conscious decisions and actions and a boatload of hope, can eventually forge a future that seems predestined. Such a moment occurred when I first met Ruth. I wasn't lying when I told Ruth that I knew in that instant we would one day be married.

Yet experience has taught me that fate is sometimes cruel and that even a boatload of hope is sometimes not enough. For Ruth, this became clear when Daniel entered our lives. By then, she was over forty and I was even older. It was another reason she couldn't stop crying after Daniel left. Back then, social expectations were different, and both of us knew that we were too old to adopt a child. When Daniel disappeared from our lives, I couldn't escape the conclusion that fate had conspired against her for the last and final time.

Though she knew about the mumps and had married me anyway, I knew that Ruth had always clung to a secret hope that the doctor had somehow been mistaken. There was no definite proof, after all, and I admit that I nurtured a slim hope as well. But because I was so deeply in love with my wife, it was seldom at the forefront of my thoughts. We made love frequently in our first years of marriage, and though Ruth was reminded every month of the sacrifice she had made by marrying me, she wasn't initially bothered by it. I think she believed that will alone, that her profound desire for a child, would somehow make it happen. Her unspoken belief was that our time would come, and this, I think, was the reason we never discussed adoption.

It was a mistake. I know that now, but I didn't know it then. The 1950s came and went and our house slowly filled with art. Ruth taught school and I ran the store, and even though she was growing older, part of her still held out hope. And then, like the long-awaited answer to a prayer, Daniel arrived. He became first her student and then the son she had always longed for. But when the illusion suddenly ended, only I remained. And it wasn't quite enough.

The next few years were hard for us. She blamed me, and I blamed myself as well. The blue skies of our marriage turned gray and stormy, then bleak and cold. Conversations became stilted, and we began to argue for the first time. Sometimes it seemed to be a struggle for her to sit in the same room with me. She spent many weekends at her parents' house in Durham—her father's health was declining—and there were times when we didn't speak for days. At night, the space between us in the bed felt like the Pacific, an ocean impossible for either of us to swim across. She did not want to and I was too afraid to try, and we continued to drift further apart. There was even a period when she wondered whether she wanted to remain married to me, and in the evenings, after she'd gone to bed, I would sit in the living room, wishing that I were someone else, the kind of man who'd been able to give her what she wanted.

But I couldn't. I was broken. The war had taken from me the only thing she'd ever wanted. I was sad for her and angry with myself, and I hated what was happening to us. I would have traded my life to make her happy again, but I didn't know how; and as crickets sounded on warm autumn nights, I'd bring my hands to my face and I would cry and cry and cry.

"I would never have left you," Ruth assures me. "I am sorry I made you think such things." Her words are leaden with regret.

"But you thought about it."

"Yes," she said, "but not in the way you think. It was not a serious idea. All married women think such things at times. Men too."

"I never did."

"I know," she says. "But you are different." She smiles, her hand reaching out for mine. She takes it, caressing the knots and bones. "I saw you once," she says to me. "In the living room."

"I know," I say.

"Do you remember what happened next?"

"You came over and held me."

"It was the first time I had seen you cry since that night in the park, after the war," she says. "It scared me very much. I did not know what was wrong."

"It was us," I say. "I didn't know what to do. I didn't know how to make you happy anymore."

"There was nothing you could do," she says.

"You were so...angry with me."

"I was sad," she says. "There is a difference."

"Does it matter? Either way, you weren't happy with me."

She squeezes my hand, her skin soft against my own. "You are a smart man, Ira, but sometimes, I think you do not understand women very well."

In this, I know she is right.

"I was devastated when Daniel went away. I would have loved for him to become part of our lives. And yes, I was sad that we never had children. But I was also sad because I was in my forties, even though that might not make sense to you. I did not mind my thirties. That was when I felt for the first time in my life that I was actually an adult. But for women, older than forty is not always so easy. On my birthday, I couldn't help but think that I had already lived half my life, and when I looked in the mirror, a young woman no longer stared back at me. It was vain, I know, but it bothered me. And my parents were getting older, too. That was why I went to visit them so often. By then, my father had retired, but he was not well, as you know. It was difficult for my mother to take care of him. In other words, there was no simple way to make things better for me back then. Even if Daniel had stayed with us, those still would have been hard years."

I wonder about this. She has said as much to me before, but I sometimes question whether she is being completely truthful.

"It meant a lot to me when you held me that night."

"What else could I do?"

"You could have turned and walked back to the bedroom."

"I could not do such a thing. It hurt me to see you like that."

"You kissed my tears away," I said.

"Yes," she says.

"And later, we held each other as we lay in bed. It was the first time in a long time."

"Yes," she says again.

"And things started to get better again."

"It was time," she said. "I was tired of being sad."

"And you knew how much I still loved you."

"Yes," she says. "I always knew that."

🦢

In 1964, on our trip to New York, Ruth and I experienced a second honeymoon of sorts. It wasn't planned, nor did we do anything extraordinary; it was more akin to a daily celebration that we had somehow put the worst of the past behind us. We held hands as we toured the galleries and began to laugh again. Her smile, I still believe, had never been more contagious in its joy than it was that summer. It was also the summer of Andy Warhol.

His art, so commercial and yet unique, didn't appeal to me. I found little interest in paintings of soup cans. Nor did Ruth, but she was taken with Andy Warhol at their initial meeting. I think this was the only instance in which she bought something simply due to the force of the artist's personality. She knew intuitively that he would somehow be an artist who would define the 1960s, and we purchased four original prints. By then, his work had already become expensive—it's all relative, of course, especially when considering their value now—and afterward, we had no money left. After only a week up north, we returned to North

Carolina and went to the Outer Banks, where we rented a cottage at the beach. Ruth wore a bikini that summer for the very first time, though she refused to wear it anywhere except on the back veranda, with towels draped over the railing to block others' sight lines. After our trip to the beach, we journeyed to Asheville, as always. I read her the letter I'd written as we stood by the lake, and the years continued to roll along. Lyndon Johnson was elected president and the civil rights law was passed. The war in Vietnam picked up steam, while at home we heard much about the War on Poverty. The Beatles were all the rage, and women entered the workforce in droves. Ruth and I were aware of all of it, but it was life inside our home that mattered most to us. We led our lives as we always had, both of us working and collecting art in the summers, having breakfast in the kitchen, and sharing stories over dinner. We bought paintings by Victor Vasarely and Arnold Schmidt, Frank Stella and Ellsworth Kelly. We appreciated the work of Julian Stanczak and Richard Anuszkiewicz and bought paintings by them as well. And I will never forget Ruth's expression as she picked out every one.

It was around that time that we began to make use of our camera. Until that point, strangely, it had never been a priority for us, and in the long span of our lives, we filled only four albums. But it is enough for me to turn the pages and watch as Ruth and I slowly grow older. There is a photo Ruth took of me on my fiftieth birthday in 1970, and another of her in 1972, when she celebrated the same milestone. In 1973, we rented the first of the storage units to house part of our collection, and in 1975, Ruth and I boarded the QE2 and sailed to England. Even then, I couldn't imagine flying. We spent three days in London and another two days in Paris before boarding a train to Vienna, where we spent the next two weeks. For Ruth, it was both nostalgic and painful to return to the city she had once called home; though I could usually discern what she was feeling, I spent much of that time wondering what to say.

In 1976, Jimmy Carter was elected president over Gerald Ford, who'd replaced Richard Nixon. The economy was in the dumps and there were long lines at the gas stations. Yet Ruth and I hardly heeded these developments as we fell in love with a new movement in art called Lyrical Abstractionism, which had its roots in both Pollock and Rothko. In that year—it was the year Ruth finally stopped coloring her hair—we celebrated our thirtieth anniversary. Though it cost a small fortune and I had to take out a loan to do so, I presented her with the only paintings I ever bought on my own: two small Picassos, one from the Blue Period and another from the Rose. That night, she hung them in the bedroom, and after making love, we lay in the bed staring at them for hours.

In 1977, with business at the shop nearly at a standstill, I began to build birdhouses in my spare time from kits I purchased at the hobby shop. This phase did not last long, maybe three or four years, but my hands remained clumsy and I eventually gave it up, just as the Reagan era began. Though the news informed me that debt wasn't a problem, I paid off the loan I'd used to buy the Picassos anyway. Ruth sprained her ankle and spent a month on crutches. In 1985, I sold the shop and started collecting Social Security; in 1987, after forty years in the classroom, Ruth did the same. The school and the district threw a party in her honor. During her career, she had been named "Teacher of the Year" three times. And in that time, my hair went from black to gray and then to white, thinning with every passing year. The lines on our faces grew deeper, and both of us realized that we could no longer see near or far without glasses. In 1990, I turned seventy, and in 1996, on our fiftieth anniversary, I presented Ruth with the longest letter I'd ever written. She read it aloud, and when she did, I realized I could barely hear her. Two weeks later, I would be fitted with a hearing aid. But I accepted this with equanimity.

It was time. I was growing old. Though Ruth and I never again experienced darkness in our marriage the way we had after Daniel disappeared, things were not always easy. Her father died in 1966, and two years later, her mother died from a stroke. In the 1970s, Ruth found a lump in her breast, and until it was biopsied and found negative, she thought she might have cancer. My parents passed away within a year of each other in the late 1980s, and Ruth and I stood over each of their graves, sobered by the realization that we were the last survivors in either of our families.

I could not foresee the future, but who can do such things? I do not know what I expected in the years we still had left together. I assumed we would continue just as we always had, for it was the only life I'd ever known. Maybe less travel—the trips and the walking were getting hard for us—but other than that, no difference at all. We had no kids or grandkids we needed to visit, no urge to travel abroad again. Instead, Ruth devoted more time to the garden and I began to feed the pigeons. We began to take vitamins, and neither of us had much of an appetite. Looking back, I suppose I should have given more thought to the fact that by our golden anniversary, Ruth had already outlived both her parents, but I was too afraid to consider the implications. I couldn't imagine a life without her, nor did I want one, but God had other plans. In 1998, like her mother, Ruth had a stroke, one that weakened the left side of her body. Though she was still able to get around the house, our collecting days were at an end and we never again purchased another piece of art. Two years later, on a cold spring morning as we sat in the kitchen, she trailed off in midsentence, unable to complete her thought, and I knew she'd had another stroke. She spent three days in the hospital undergoing tests, and though she came back home, we would never again have a conversation in which the words flowed freely.

The left side of her face lost even more movement, and she began to forget the most common of words. This upset Ruth more than it did me; to my eyes, she remained as beautiful as she'd been on the day I'd first seen her. I was certainly no longer the man I once had been. My face had become wrinkled and thin, and whenever I looked in the mirror, the size of my ears never ceased to astonish me. Our routines become even simpler, one day simply drifting to the next. I would make her breakfast in the morning and we would eat together as we browsed the newspaper; after breakfast, we would sit in the yard and feed the pigeons. We napped in the late morning and would spend the rest of the day reading or listening to music or going to the grocery store. Once a week, I would drive her to the beauty salon, where a hairdresser would wash and style her hair, something that I knew would make her happy. And then, when August came around, I would spend hours at my desk crafting a letter for my wife, and I'd drive the two of us to Black Mountain on our anniversary, where we'd stand by the lake, just as we always had, while she read the words I'd written.

By that point, our adventures were long behind us, but for me it was more than enough, for the longest ride continued. Even then, as we lay in bed, I would hold Ruth close, grateful for the blessing of this life, this woman. In those moments, I would selfishly pray that I would die first, for even then I could sense the inevitable.

In the spring of 2002, a week after the azaleas in the yard had begun to bloom in full, we spent our morning as we always had, and in the afternoon, we made plans to go out to dinner. It was something we seldom did, but both of us were in the mood, and I remember calling the restaurant to make an early reservation. In the afternoon, we went for a walk. Not long, just to the end of the block and back. Though there was a brisk edge to the air, Ruth did not seem to notice. We spoke briefly to one of our neighbors—not the angry man who cut down the tree—and after we returned home, we settled into what was until that point a relatively ordinary day. Ruth said nothing to me about having a headache, but in the early evening, before we'd made dinner, she slowly made her way to the bedroom. I thought nothing of it at the time—I was reading in the easy chair and must have dozed off for a few minutes. When I woke, Ruth still had not come back, and I called for her. She did not answer, and I rose from my chair. I called for her again as I made my way down the hallway. When I saw her crumpled near the bed, I felt my heart jump in my chest. She'd had another stroke, I immediately thought. But it was worse, and as I tried to breathe life back into her, I could feel my soul begin to wither.

The paramedics arrived a few minutes later. I heard them first knocking and then pounding at the door. By then, I was holding Ruth in my arms and I did not want to let go. I heard them enter and call out; I called back and they rushed to the bedroom, where they found an old man holding the woman he'd always loved.

They were kind and soft-spoken as one of them helped me to my feet while the other began to administer to Ruth. I begged them to help her, trying to elicit promises that she was going to be all right. They put her on oxygen and loaded her onto the stretcher, allowing me to sit in the ambulance as Ruth was rushed to the hospital.

When the doctor came out to speak with me in the waiting room, he was gentle. He held my arm as we walked down the corridor. The tiles were gray and the fluorescent lights made my eyes hurt. I asked if my wife was all right; I asked when I would be allowed to see her. But he didn't answer. Instead, he led me to an empty patient room and closed the door behind him. His expression was serious, and when he cast his eyes toward the floor, I knew exactly what he was going to say.

"I'm sorry to have to tell you this, Mr. Levinson, but there was nothing we could do . . ."

At these words, I gripped a nearby bed rail to keep from falling. The room seemed to close in as the doctor went on, my vision telescoping until I could see nothing but his face. His words sounded tinny and made no sense, but it did not matter. His expression was plain—I'd been too late. Ruth, my sweet Ruth, had died on the floor while I dozed in the other room.

I do not remember leaving the hospital, and the next few days are hazy. My attorney, Howie Sanders, a dear friend to both Ruth and me, helped with the funeral arrangements, a small, private service. Afterward, the candles were lit, cushions were spread through the house, and I sat shiva for a week. People came and went, people we had known over the years. Neighbors, including the man who'd cut down the maple tree. Customers from the shop. Three gallery owners from New York. Half a dozen artists. Women from the synagogue came every day to cook and clean. And on each of those days, I found myself wishing that I would wake from the nightmare that my life had just become.

But gradually the people drifted away, until no one was left at all. There was no one to call, no one to talk to, and the house descended into silence. I did not know how to live that kind of life, and time became merciless. Days crept by slowly. I could not concentrate. I would read the newspaper and remember nothing at all. I would sit for hours before realizing that I'd left the radio on in the background. Even the birds did nothing to cheer me; I would stare at them and think to myself that Ruth should have been sitting beside me, our hands brushing as we reached into the bag for birdseed.

Nothing made any sense, nor did I want to make sense of it. My days were spent in the quiet agony of heartbreak. Evenings were no better. Late at night, as I lay in the half-empty bed unable to sleep, I would feel the dampness trickling off my cheeks. I'd wipe my eyes and be struck anew by the finality of Ruth's absence.

21

Luke

It all went back to the ride on Big Ugly Critter.

The one he'd had nightmares about, the one that had kept him away from the arena for eighteen months. He'd told Sophia about the ride and a bit about the injuries he'd suffered.

But he hadn't told her everything. As he stood in the barn after his mother had left, Luke leaned against the mechanical bull, reliving the past he'd tried hard to forget.

It was eight days before he'd even known what had happened. Although he knew he had been hurt and, after some prompting, could vaguely remember the ride, he'd had no idea how close he'd come to dying. He'd had no idea that in addition to fracturing his skull, the bull had cracked his C1 vertebra and that his brain had swelled with blood.

He hadn't told Sophia that they didn't reset the bones in his face for almost a month, for fear of causing additional trauma. Nor had he mentioned that the doctors had returned to his bedside to tell him that he'd never completely recover from the head injury—and that in a section of his skull, there was now a small titanium plate. The doctors told him that another similar impact to his head, with or without a helmet, would most likely be enough to kill him. The plate they had grafted onto his shattered skull was too close to the brain stem to adequately protect him.

After that first meeting with the doctors, he'd had fewer questions than anyone anticipated. He'd decided right then to give up bull riding, and he'd told everyone as much. He knew he'd miss the rodeo and that he'd probably wonder forever what it would have felt like to win the championship. But he'd never entertained a death wish, and at the time, he'd thought he still had plenty of money in the bank.

And he had, but it wasn't enough. His mom had offered up the ranch as collateral for the loan she'd taken out to cover his monstrous medical bills. Though she'd told him repeatedly that she didn't care about the fate of the ranch, he knew that deep down, she did. The ranch was her life, it was all she knew, and everything she'd done since the accident had confirmed her feelings. In the past year, she'd worked herself to the point of exhaustion in an attempt to forestall the inevitable. She could say whatever she wanted, but he knew the truth...

He could save the ranch. No, he couldn't earn enough in the next year—or even three years—to pay off the loan, but he was a good enough rider to earn enough to meet the payments and then some, even if he rode only on the little tour. He admired his mom's efforts with the Christmas trees and the pumpkins and expanding the herd, but both of them knew it wasn't going to be enough. He'd heard enough about the cost of fixing this or that to know that things were tight even in the best of times.

So what was he supposed to do? He had to either pretend that everything was going to work out—which wasn't possible—or find a way to fix the problem. And he knew exactly how to fix the problem. All he had to do was ride well.

But even if he rode well, he still might die.

Luke understood the risks. That was the reason his hands shook every time he prepared to ride. It wasn't that he was rusty or that he was plagued with ordinary nerves. It was the fact that when he used the suicide wrap to hold on, a part of him wondered if this would be his last ride.

It wasn't possible to ride successfully with that kind of fear. Unless, of course, there was something greater at stake, and for him, it came down to the ranch. And his mom. She wasn't going to lose the ranch because of him.

He shook his head. He didn't want to think about these things. It was hard enough to find the confidence he knew he needed to last—and win—over the course of a season. The one thing that you didn't want to think about was not being able to ride.

Or dying in the process . . .

He hadn't been lying to the doctor when he said that he was ready to quit. He knew what a life of riding could do to a man; he'd watched his father wince and struggle in the mornings, and he'd felt the same pains himself. He'd lived through all the training and he'd given it his best, but it hadn't worked out. And eighteen months ago, he'd been okay with that.

But right now, standing beside the mechanical bull, he knew that he had no choice. He pulled on his glove, then he took a deep breath and climbed onto the bull. Hanging off the horn was the control, and he took it in his free hand. But maybe because the season was getting close, or maybe because he hadn't told the complete truth to Sophia, he couldn't press the button. Not yet, anyway.

He reminded himself that he knew what might happen, and he tried to convince himself he was ready. He was ready to ride, he was preparing to ride, no matter what might happen. He was a bull rider. He'd done it for as long as he could remember, and he would do it again. He'd ride, because he was good at riding, and then all their problems would be solved . . .

Except that if he landed wrong, he might die.

All at once, his hands began to tremble. But, steeling himself, he finally pressed the button anyway.

🌿

On her way back from New Jersey, Sophia made a detour to the ranch before returning to campus. Luke was expecting her and had tidied up both the house and the porch in anticipation.

It was dark when her car pulled to a stop in front of his house. He bounded down the porch steps to meet her, wondering if anything had changed since he'd last seen her. Those worries evaporated as soon as she stepped out of her car and rushed toward him.

He caught her as she jumped, feeling her legs wrap around him. As they held each other, he reveled in how good she felt, certain again of how much she meant to him, wondering what the future would hold.

🌿

They made love that evening, but Sophia couldn't stay the night. The new semester was beginning and she had an early class. Once her taillights vanished up the drive, Luke turned and walked toward the barn for yet another practice session. He wasn't in the mood, but with the first event in less than two weeks, he reminded himself of how much more he had to do.

On his way to the barn, he made the decision to keep the practice shorter than usual, no more than an hour. He was tired and it was cold and he missed Sophia's presence already.

Inside the barn, he went through a quick warm-up to get the blood flowing, then hopped on the bull. While rebuilding the bull, his dad had modified it to make the ride more intense at top speeds and had rigged the control switch so that Luke could hold it in his free hand. Out of habit, he kept his hand clenched in a half fist even when riding live bulls, though to this point no one had ever asked why or probably even noticed.

When he was ready, he started the machine at a low-medium speed, again just enough to loosen up. He then rode once on medium and once on medium-high. In his practice sessions, he rode in sixteen-second increments, exactly double the time he'd need to ride in the arena. His dad had calibrated the machine for these longer rides, saying that it would make the live rides easier by comparison. And maybe it did. But it was twice as hard on the body.

After each ride, he'd take a break to recover, and he took a longer break after every three. Usually, in those moments his mind was blank, but tonight he found himself flashing back to his ride on Big Ugly Critter. He wasn't sure why the images kept flooding his mind, but he couldn't stop them, and he felt his nerves jangle when his gaze fell on the mechanical bull. It was time for the real rides, the ones on high speed. His dad had calibrated fifty different rides to occur in a random sequence, so Luke would never know what to expect. Over the years it had served him well, but right now he wished he knew exactly what was coming.

When the muscles in his hand and forearm had recovered, he trudged back to the mechanical bull and climbed up. He rode three times, then three more. And three more after that. Of those nine, he made it to the end of the cycle seven times. Counting the recovery time, he'd been practicing for more than forty-five minutes. He decided then to do three more sets of three and call it a night.

He didn't make it.

In the second ride of the second set, he felt the ride getting away from him. In that instant, he wasn't unduly alarmed. He'd been thrown a million times, and unlike the arena, the area surrounding the bull was lined with foam padding. Even while in the air, he hadn't been afraid, and he shifted, trying to land the way he wanted to in the arena: either on his feet or on all fours.

He managed to land on his feet, and the foam absorbed the impact as it usually did, but for some reason the landing left him off balance and he found himself stumbling, instinctively trying to stay upright instead of simply falling. He took three quick steps as he fell forward, his upper body stretching past the foam floor-ing, and slammed his forehead against the hard-packed ground.

His brain chimed like a thumbed guitar string; slices of golden light shimmered as he tried to focus. The room began to spin, blotting to darkness and then brightening again. The pain started, sharp at first and then sharper. Fuller. Slowly rounding into agony. It took him a minute to summon the strength to stagger to his feet, holding on to the old tractor to stay upright. Fear raced through his system as he carefully examined the bump on his forehead with his fingers.

It was swollen and tender, but as he felt around, he convinced himself that there was no further damage. He hadn't cracked anything; he was sure of it. The other parts of his head were fine as far as he could tell. Standing straight, he took a deep breath and started gingerly for the doors.

Outside the door, his stomach abruptly turned and he dou-bled over. The dizziness came back and he vomited into the dirt. Only once, but it was enough to concern him. He'd vomited after receiving previous concussions, and he figured he had one again. He didn't need to go to the doctor to know that he would be told not to practice for a week, maybe longer.

Or, more accurately, he would be warned never to ride again.

He was okay, though. It was a close call—too close—but he'd survived. He'd take a few days off regardless of the approaching season, and as he limped back to his house, he tried to put a posi-tive spin on it. He'd been practicing hard, and a break might do him good. When he came back, he'd probably be stronger than ever. But despite his attempts to reassure himself, he couldn't shake the feeling of dread that dogged his every step.

And what was he going to tell Sophia?

❦

Two days later, he still wasn't sure. He went to visit her at Wake, and as they walked the campus byways in the late hours of the night, Luke kept his hat on to hide the bruising on his forehead. He considered telling her about the accident but was afraid of the questions she would ask and where they would lead. Questions he had no answers to. Finally, when she asked him why he was so quiet, he pleaded exhaustion over the long hours at the ranch— truthfully enough, as his mother had decided to bring the cattle to market in advance of bull-riding season, and they'd spent a couple of grueling days roping and herding the cattle onto trucks.

But by then, he suspected that Sophia knew him well enough to sense that he wasn't himself. When she showed up at the ranch the following weekend wearing the hat he'd bought her and a thick down jacket, she seemed to be evaluating him as they readied the horses, though she said nothing at the time. Instead, they made the same ride they had on their first day together, through the stands of trees, toward the river. Finally, she turned toward him. "Okay, enough of this," she announced. "I want to know what's bothering you. You've been . . . off all week long."

"I'm sorry," he said. "I'm still a little tired." The bright sunlight drove knife blades into his skull, aggravating the constant headache he'd had since he'd been thrown.

"I've seen you tired before. It's something else, but I can't help if I don't know what it is."

"I'm just thinking about next weekend. You know, first event of the year and all."

"In Florida?"

He nodded. "Pensacola."

"I've heard it's pretty there. White sand beaches."

"Probably. Not that I'll see any of them. I'll drive back after the event on Saturday." He thought back to his practice yesterday, his first since the accident. It had gone pretty well—his balance seemed unaffected—but the pounding in his head forced him to quit after forty minutes.

"It'll be late."

"This one's in the afternoon. I should be back around two or so."

"So...I can see you on Sunday, then?"

He tapped his hand against his thigh. "If you come out here. But I'll probably be wiped out."

She squinted at him from under the brim of her hat. "Gee, don't sound so excited about it."

"I want to see you. I just don't want you to feel like you have to come over."

"Are you going to come to campus instead? Do you want to hang out at the sorority house?"

"Not particularly."

"Then would you like to meet somewhere else?"

"Dinner with my mom, remember?"

"Then I'll come here." She waited for a response, growing frustrated when he said nothing at all. In time, she turned in her saddle to face him. "What's gotten into you? It's like you're mad at me."

It was the perfect opportunity to tell her everything. He tried to find the words, but he didn't know how to begin. *I've been meaning to tell you that I could die if I keep riding.*

"I'm not mad at you," he hedged. "I'm just thinking about the season ahead and what I have to do."

"Right now?" She sounded doubtful.

"I think about it all the time. And I'll be thinking about it through the whole season. And just so you know, I'll be traveling a lot starting next weekend."

"I know," she said with unusual sharpness. "You told me."

"When the tour heads west, I might not even make it home most weeks until late Sunday night."

"So what you're saying is that you're not going to be seeing me as often, and when we are together, you'll be distracted?"

"Maybe." He shrugged. "Probably."

"That's no fun."

"What else can I do?"

"How about this? Try not to think about your event next

weekend right now. Let's just try to enjoy ourselves today, okay? Since you're going to be traveling? Since I'm not going to see you as much? It might be our last full day together for a while."

He shook his head. "It's not like that."

"What's not like that?"

"I can't just ignore what's coming," he said, his voice rising. "My life isn't like yours. It's not about going to classes and hanging out on the quad and gossiping with Marcia. I live in the real world. I have responsibilities." He heard her gasp but pressed on, growing more righteous with every word. "My job is dangerous. I'm rusty, and I know I should have practiced more this past week. But I have to do well starting next weekend, no matter what, or my mom and I are going to lose everything. So of course I'm going to think about it—and yes, I'm going to be distracted."

She blinked, taken aback by his tirade. "Wow. Someone's in a bad mood today."

"I'm not in a bad mood," he snapped.

"You could have fooled me."

"I don't know what you want me to say."

For the first time, her expression hardened and he heard her struggling to keep her voice steady. "You could have said that you wanted to see me on Sunday, even if you were tired. You could have said that even though you might be distracted, that I shouldn't take it personally. You could have apologized and said, 'You're right, Sophia. Let's just enjoy today.' But instead, you tell me that what you do—in the real world—isn't like going to college."

"College isn't the real world."

"Don't you think I know that?" she cried.

"Then why are you so mad that I said it?" he countered.

She tugged the reins, forcing Demon to a halt. "Are you kidding?" she demanded. "Because you're acting like a jerk! Because you're implying that you have responsibilities, but I don't. Can you even hear yourself?"

"I was just trying to answer your question."

"By insulting me?"

"I wasn't insulting you."

"But you still think that what you do is more important than what I do?"

"It is more important."

"To you and your mom!" she shouted. "Believe it or not, my family is important to me, too! My parents are important! Getting an education is important! And yes, I do have responsibilities. And I feel pressure to be successful, just like you do. I have dreams, too!"

"Sophia..."

"What? Now you're ready to be civil? Well, you know what? Don't bother. Because the reality is that I drove up here to spend time with you, and all you're doing is trying to pick a fight!"

"I'm not trying to pick a fight," he mumbled.

But she wasn't hearing him. "Why are you doing this?" she demanded. "Why are you acting like this? What's going on with you?"

He didn't answer. He didn't know what to say, and Sophia watched him, waiting, before shaking her head in disappointment. With that, she jerked the reins and turned Demon, prodding him into a canter. As she disappeared in the direction of the stables, Luke sat alone amid the trees, wondering why he couldn't find the courage to tell her the truth.

22

Sophia

So you just rode off and left him?" Marcia asked.

"I didn't know what else to do," Sophia replied, propping her chin in her hands. Marcia sat beside her as she lay on her bed. "By then, I was so angry, I could barely look at him."

"Hmmm. I guess I'd be angry, too," Marcia said, sounding just a bit too sympathetic. "I mean, we both know that art history majors are absolutely critical to the modern functioning of society. If that's not a serious responsibility, I don't know what is."

Sophia scowled at her. "Shut up."

Marcia ignored the comment. "Especially if they've yet to land a job that actually pays anything."

"Didn't I just say shut up?"

"I'm just teasing you," Marcia said, nudging her with her elbow.

"Yeah, well, I'm not in the mood, okay?"

"Oh, hush. I don't mean anything by it. I'm just happy you're here. I had already resigned myself to the fact that I'd be alone all day. And most of the night, too."

"I'm trying to talk to you!"

"I know. I've missed our talks. We haven't had one in ages."

"And we're not going to have any more if you keep this up. You're making this a lot harder than you need to."

"What do you want me to do?"

"I want you to listen. I want you to help me figure this out."

"I am listening," she said. "I heard everything you said."

"And?"

"Well, frankly, I'm just glad you finally had an argument. It's about time. I'm of the opinion that it's not a meaningful relationship until you have a real argument. Up until then, it's just a honeymoon. After all, you don't know how strong something is until you actually test it." She winked. "I read that in a fortune cookie once."

"Fortune cookie?"

"It's still true. And it's good for you. Because once you two get past this, you'll be stronger as a couple. And the make-up sex is always great."

Sophia made a face. "Is it always about sex with you?"

"Not always. But with Luke?" She broke into a lascivious grin. "If I were you, I'd be trying to get past this as soon as possible. That is one good-looking man."

"Stop trying to change the subject. You need to help me figure this out!"

"What do you think I've been doing?"

"Trying your best to irritate me?"

Marcia offered an earnest expression. "You know what I think?" she asked. "Based on what you told me? I think he's nervous about what's going to happen between you two. He's going to be traveling most weekends, and before you know it, you'll have graduated and he thinks you're not going to stick around. So he's probably beginning to distance himself."

Maybe, Sophia thought. There was some truth there, but . . .

"It's more than that," she said. "He's never been like this before. Something else is going on."

"Is there anything you haven't told me?"

He might lose the ranch. But she hadn't told Marcia that, nor would she. Luke had confided in her, and she wouldn't violate his trust.

"I know he's feeling a lot of pressure," she said instead. "He wants to ride well. He's nervous."

"Well, there's your answer," Marcia said. "He's nervous and under pressure, and you kept telling him not to think about it. So he got a little defensive and lashed out because in his mind, you're indifferent to what he's going through."

Maybe, Sophia thought.

"Trust me," Marcia went on. "He's probably regretting it already. And I'll bet he'll be calling you to apologize any minute now."

He didn't call. Not that night, or the next or even the next. On Tuesday, Sophia spent most of the day alternately checking her phone to see if he'd texted and wondering whether she should call him. Though she attended classes and took notes, she was hard-pressed to recall anything her professors had said.

Between classes, she would walk from one building to the next, reviewing Marcia's words, acknowledging that they made sense. Yet she couldn't escape the memory of Luke's...what? Anger? Hostility? She wasn't sure if those were the right words, but she'd definitely felt as though he'd been trying to drive her away.

Why, after everything had been so easy and comfortable for so long, had everything so quickly gone wrong?

There was a lot that didn't add up. She should just pick up the phone and get to the bottom of all this, she decided. Depending on Luke's tone, she'd know almost immediately whether she was overreacting.

She reached into her purse and pulled out her phone, but just as she was about to dial, she happened to look across the quad, noticing the familiar ebb and flow of life on campus. People carrying backpacks, a student riding his bike to who knew where, a college tour that had stopped near the administration building, and in the distance, beneath a tree, a couple facing each other.

There was nothing unusual about any of it, but for whatever reason, something in the scene caught her attention and she lowered the phone. She found herself zeroing in on the couple. They were laughing, heads close together, the girl's hand caressing the boy's arm. Even from a distance, their chemistry crackled. She could almost feel it, but then again, she knew them both. What she was seeing was definitely more than a close friendship, a realization confirmed as soon as they kissed.

Sophia couldn't look away, every muscle tensing at once.

As far as she knew, he hadn't been to the house, nor had she heard their names mentioned together. Which was almost impossible on a campus devoid of secrets. Which meant that both of them had been trying to keep it secret until now—not only from her, but from everyone.

But Marcia and Brian?

Her roommate wouldn't do that to her, would she? Especially knowing what Brian had done to her?

Yet in hindsight it struck her that Marcia had mentioned him several times in recent weeks…and hadn't she admitted that she still talked to him? What had Marcia said about Brian? Even while he was still stalking her? *He's funny and good-looking and rich. What's not to like?* Not to mention that he'd had a "thing" for her, as Marcia liked to point out, before Sophia came along.

Sophia knew it shouldn't matter. She wanted nothing to do with Brian, and it had been over for a long time. Marcia could have him if she wanted. But when Marcia lifted her gaze in Sophia's direction, Sophia inexplicably felt tears spring to her eyes.

🌿

"I was going to tell you," Marcia said, uncharacteristically shamefaced.

They were back in their room and Sophia stood near the window with her arms crossed. It was everything she could do to keep her voice steady.

"How long have you been seeing him?"

"Not long," Marcia said. "He visited me at home over Christmas break and—"

"Why him? You remember how much he hurt me, right?" Sophia's voice started to crack. "You're supposed to be my best friend."

"I didn't plan for it to happen...," Marcia pleaded.

"But it did."

"You were gone every weekend and I'd see him at parties. We'd end up talking. Usually about you..."

"So you're saying this is my fault?"

"No," Marcia said. "It's no one's fault. I didn't mean for it to happen. But the more we talked and really got to know each other..."

Sophia tuned out the rest of Marcia's explanation, the knots in her stomach tight enough to make her wince. When the room fell silent, she tried to keep her voice steady.

"You should have told me."

"I did. I mentioned that we were talking. And I hinted that we were friends. That's all there was until a few weeks ago. I swear."

Sophia turned, facing her best friend and hating her at the same moment. "This is just... *wrong* on so many levels."

"I thought you were over him...," Marcia mumbled.

Sophia's expression was livid. "I am over him! I don't want anything to do with him. This is about us! You and me! You're sleeping with my ex-boyfriend!" She ran a hand through her hair. "Marcia, friends don't do this to each other. How can you even begin to justify this?"

"I'm still your friend," Marcia offered, her tone soft. "It's not like I'm going to be bringing him up to the room when you're here..."

Sophia could barely register what she was hearing. "He's going to cheat on you, you know. Just like he cheated on me."

Marcia shook her head vehemently. "He's changed. I know you won't believe that, but he has."

At this, Sophia knew she had to leave. She strode toward the door, grabbing her purse from the desk on the way out. At the door, she turned around.

"Brian hasn't changed," she said with utter certainty. "I can promise you that."

❧

Habit and desperation led her back to the ranch. As always, Luke stepped onto the porch just as she was getting out of the car. Even from a distance, he seemed to know something was wrong, and despite the fact that she hadn't heard from him in days, he walked toward her with arms opened wide.

Sophia went into them, and for a long time, he simply held her as she cried.

❧

"I still don't know what to do," she said, leaning back into Luke's chest. "It's not like I can stop her from going out with him."

Luke was holding her close on the couch, both of them staring into the fire. He had let her ramble on for hours, agreeing with her from time to time but mostly soothing her with his silent, comforting presence.

"No," he agreed. "You probably can't."

"But what am I supposed to do when we're together? Pretend that it's not happening?"

"That would probably be best. Since she's your roommate."

"She's going to get hurt," Sophia said for the hundredth time.

"Probably."

"Everyone in the house is going to be talking about it. Every time they see me, they're going to either whisper or snicker or act way too concerned, and I'm going to spend the rest of the semester dealing with it."

"Probably."

She was quiet for a moment. "Are you going to agree with everything I say?"

"Probably," he answered, eliciting a laugh.

"I'm just glad you aren't still mad at me."

"I'm sorry about that," he said. "And you were right to call me on it. You caught me on a bad day and I took it out on you. I was wrong to do that."

"Everyone's entitled to a bad day."

He squeezed her tighter without saying anything. Only later did it occur to her that he never did tell her what had really been bothering him that day.

※

After spending the night at the ranch, Sophia returned to the sorority house and took a deep breath before stepping into her room. She still wasn't ready to talk to Marcia, but a quick survey told her that she need not have worried about it.

Marcia wasn't in the room, nor had her bed been slept in.

She'd spent the night with Brian.

23

Luke

When Luke left for Pensacola a few days later, he did so with the uncomfortable knowledge that he hadn't practiced enough. The relentless, throbbing headache made thinking difficult and practice impossible. He told himself that if he could just survive these preliminaries in decent standing, he'd have a chance to fully recuperate in time for the next event.

He knew nothing at all about Stir Crazy, the first bull he drew in Pensacola. He hadn't slept well after the long drive, and his hands had begun to shake again. Though his headache was slightly diminished, he could still feel the thrumming between his ears, a vibration that felt like a living thing. He recognized only a handful of the riders, and half of the rest struck him as barely old enough to drive. All of them fiddled, trying to keep their nerves in check, all clinging to the same dream. Win or place, earn money and points—and whatever you do, don't get hurt so bad that you can't ride the following week.

As he'd done in McLeansville, Luke stayed near his truck, preferring to be alone. He could still hear the crowd from the parking lot, and when he heard the roar go up, followed a few seconds later by the announcer barking, "That's the way it goes sometimes," he knew the rider had been thrown. He was scheduled to ride fourteenth, and even though the rides were measured in seconds, there was usually a break of a few minutes between competitors. He figured he'd go over in fifteen minutes, if only to keep his nerves in check.

He didn't want to be here.

The thought came to him with unexpected clarity, even though deep down he'd known it all along. The undeniable conviction made him feel like the ground had just shifted under his feet. He wasn't ready for this. And maybe, just maybe, he'd never be ready.

Fifteen minutes later, however, he began a slow trek to the arena.

More than anything, it was the smell that enabled him to continue. It was familiar, triggering responses that had grown automatic over the years. The world compressed. He tuned out the sound of the crowd and the announcer, focusing his attention on the young handlers who were helping him get ready. Ropes were tightened. He worked the wrap until it felt exactly right in his hand. He centered himself on the bull. He waited for a split second, making sure everything was right, then nodded to the gateman.

"Let's go."

Stir Crazy came out with a weak buck and then a second, before twisting hard to the right, all four legs off the ground. But Luke had been ready and stayed low in his seat, keeping his balance as Stir Crazy bucked two more times and then began to spin.

Luke adjusted instinctively throughout all of it, and as soon as the buzzer sounded, he reached down with his free hand and undid the wrap. He jumped off, landing on both feet, and ran to the arena fence. He was out of harm's way before the bull had stopped bucking.

The crowd continued to cheer and the announcer reminded

them that he'd once placed third in the world standings. He removed his hat and waved it at the crowd before turning around and hiking back to his truck.

On the walk, his headache returned with punishing force.

※

Ride number two was a bull named Candyland. Luke was in fourth place in the standings.

Again, he went through the motions on autopilot, the world compressed to the narrowest of frames. Meaner bull this time. More showy. During the ride, he heard the crowd roar its approval. He rode successfully and again escaped the arena while the bull threw a temper tantrum.

His score on that ride moved him into second place.

He spent the next hour sitting behind the wheel of his truck, his head throbbing with every heartbeat. He supplemented a handful of ibuprofen with Tylenol, but it did little to blunt the pain. He wondered if his brain was swelling and tried not to think about what would happen if he got thrown.

※

With his last ride, he found himself in a position to win. Earlier, though, one of the other finalists had finished with the highest score of the day.

In the chute, he was no longer nervous. Not because he'd experienced a burst of hidden confidence, but because the agony and exhaustion had left him too tired to care one way or the other.

He just wanted to get it over with. Whatever happened, happened.

When he was ready, the chute gate swung open. It was a good bull, though not as tricky as the second one had been. More challenging than the first, though, and his score reflected that.

The winner would be decided by the leader's performance on his final ride. But the leader of the first two rounds lost his balance early on with the bull he'd drawn and couldn't regain it, landing in the dirt.

Although he had been second in the short go, he ended up winning the event. One event into the season, he was in first place, precisely where he needed to be.

He collected his check and texted both his mom and Sophia that he was on his way back. But as he started the long drive home, his head still throbbing, he wondered why he honestly didn't care about the points at all.

❧

"You look terrible," Sophia said. "Are you okay?"

Luke tried to force a reassuring grin. After collapsing into bed around three a.m., he'd awakened after eleven, his head and body a chorus of pain. Automatically, he'd reached for the painkillers and swallowed several before staggering to the shower, where he'd let the hot spray seep into his bruised and knotted muscles.

"I'm fine," he said. "It was a long drive, and ever since I got up, I've been working on repairing some broken fencing."

"Are you sure?" Sophia's concern reflected her skepticism at his reassurances. Ever since she had arrived at the ranch that afternoon, she'd been scrutinizing him like an anxious mother hen. "You're acting like you're coming down with something."

"Just tired, is all. It's been a long couple of days."

"I know. But you won, huh?"

"Yeah," he said. "I won."

"That's good. For the ranch, I mean." Sophia wrinkled her forehead.

"Yeah," he repeated, sounding almost numb. "It's good for the ranch."

24

❧

Sophia

Luke was off again. Not like last weekend, but something definitely wasn't right with him. And it wasn't just exhaustion, either. He was pale, his skin tone almost white, and though he'd denied it, she knew that he was in a lot more pain than usual. Sometimes, when he'd made a quick, unexpected movement, she'd noticed he'd wince or draw a sharp breath.

Dinner with his mom had been a stilted affair. Though Linda was happy to see her, Luke had stayed outside by the grill while she and Linda chatted the whole time, almost as if he were trying to avoid them. At the table, the conversation had been notable for all the subjects they studiously avoided. Luke didn't talk about his obvious pain, his mom asked nothing about the rodeo, and Sophia refused to mention Marcia or Brian or how awful the week had been at the house. And it had been awful, one of the worst weeks ever.

As soon as they returned to Luke's, he made straight for the bedroom. She heard him tap out some pills from one bottle, then another, then followed him as he walked to the kitchen, where he swallowed what she guessed was a handful of pills with a glass of water.

To her alarm, he leaned forward, resting both hands on the edge of the counter, his head hung low.

"How bad is it?" she whispered, her hands on his back. "Your headache, I mean?"

He drew a couple of long breaths before answering. "I'm okay," he said.

"Obviously, you're not," she said. "How much did you take?"

"A couple of each," he admitted.

"But I saw you take some before dinner—"

"It wasn't enough, obviously."

"If it's that bad, you should have gone to the doctor."

"There's no reason," he said in a dull voice. "I already know what's wrong."

"What's wrong?"

"I have a concussion."

She blinked. "How? Did you hit your head when you jumped off the bull?"

"No," he said. "I landed wrong in practice a couple of weeks ago."

"A couple of *weeks* ago?"

"Yeah," he admitted. "And I made the mistake of practicing again too soon."

"You mean your head's been hurting for two weeks?" Sophia tried to keep the rising panic out of her voice.

"Not like this. Riding yesterday aggravated it again."

"Why would you ride, then, if you have what sounds like a concussion?"

He kept his focus on the floor. "I didn't have a choice."

"Of course you had a choice. And that was a stupid thing to do. C'mon. Let's bring you to the emergency room—"

"No," he said.

"Why not?" she said, bewildered. "I'll drive. You need to see a doctor."

"I've had headaches like this before and I know what a doctor's going to tell me. He's going to tell me to take some time off, and I can't do that."

"You mean you're going to ride again next weekend?"

"I have to."

Sophia tried and failed to understand what he was saying. "Is that why your mom has been so mad at you? Because you're acting like an idiot?"

He didn't answer right away. Instead, he sighed. "She doesn't even know about it."

"You didn't tell her? Why wouldn't you tell her?"

"Because I don't want her to know. She'd just end up worrying."

She shook her head. "I just don't understand why you would continue to ride, when you know it's going to make your concussion worse. It's dangerous."

"I'm past worrying about it," he said.

"What do you mean by that?"

Luke slowly pushed himself upright and turned to face her with an expression of resignation, something akin to an apology.

"Because," he finally said, "even before the concussion, I was never supposed to ride again."

She wasn't sure she'd heard him right, and she blinked. "You're not supposed to ride at all? Ever?"

"According to the doctors, I'm taking a massive risk every single time."

"Because?"

"Big Ugly Critter," he said. "I didn't just get knocked out and dragged around. I told you he trampled me, but I didn't tell you that he fractured my skull, back near the brain stem. There's a small metal plate there now, but if I land wrong, it's not going to be enough to protect me."

As he spoke in a monotone, Sophia felt a chill spread through her body at his words. He couldn't be serious...

"Are you saying that you could die?" She didn't wait for an answer, feeling panic flood her system as she registered the truth. "That's what you're saying, isn't it? That you'll die? And you didn't tell me about this? How could you not tell me?"

It all clicked into place, the pieces fitting together: why he'd wanted to see the bull on their first night together; why his mom was so angry with him; his tense preoccupation before the start of the season.

"Well, that's it, then," she went on, trying to suppress the terror in her voice. "You're not riding anymore, okay? You're done. As of now, you're retired again."

Again he said nothing, but she could see in his face that she wasn't getting through. She moved in and encircled him with her arms, squeezing in desperation. She could feel his heart beating, could feel the strong muscles in his chest. "I don't want you to do this. You can't do this, okay? Please tell me that you're finished with all this. We'll figure some other way to save the ranch, okay?"

"There is no other way."

"There's always another way—"

"No," he said, "there isn't."

"Luke, I know the ranch is important, but it's not more important than your life. You know that, right? You'll start over. You'll get another ranch. Or you'll work on a ranch—"

"I don't need the ranch," he broke in. "I'm doing this for my mom."

She pushed away from him, feeling a swell of anger. "But she doesn't want you to do this either! Because she knows it's wrong—she knows how stupid it is! Because you're her son!"

"I'm doing it for her—"

"No, you're not!" Sophia interrupted. "You're doing it so that you won't have to feel guilty! You think you're being noble, but you're really being selfish! This is the most selfish thing—" She broke off, her chest heaving.

"Sophia..."

"Don't touch me!" she cried. "You're going to hurt me, too! Don't you get that? Did you ever stop for one minute to think that I might not want you to die? Or how it would make me feel? No, because it's not about me! Or your mom! This is all about you—and how you'll feel!"

She took a step backward. "And to think you lied about it...," she whispered.

"I didn't lie..."

"A lie of omission," she said, her voice bitter. "You lied because you knew I wouldn't agree with you! That I might walk away from someone who was willing to do something so...wrong. And why? Because you wanted to sleep with me? Because you wanted to have a good time?"

"No..." Luke's protest sounded weak to her ears.

She could feel hot tears spilling down her cheeks, beyond her control. "I...just can't handle this right now. Not this, too. It was a terrible week, all the girls talking and Marcia avoiding me...I needed you this week. I needed someone to talk to. But I understood that you needed to ride. I accepted it because it was your job. But now? Knowing that the only reason you were gone was because you were off trying to kill yourself?"

The words came out in a rush, almost as fast as her mind was racing, and she turned, reaching over and grabbing her purse. She couldn't be here. Not with him. Not now..."I can't take this..."

"Wait!"

"Don't talk to me!" she said. "I don't want to hear you try to explain why it's so important for you to die—"

"I'm not going to die."

"Yes, you are! I may not have been around long enough to know, but your mom has! And the doctors have! And you know what you're doing is wrong..." Her breaths were coming fast. "When you come to your senses, then we can talk. But until then..."

She didn't finish. Instead, flinging her purse over her shoulder, she stormed out of the house and ran to her car. After throwing it in gear, she almost backed into the porch as she turned it around and hit the accelerator hard, barely able to see through the blur of her tears.

🌿

Sophia was numb.

Luke had called twice since she returned to the sorority house, but she didn't answer. She sat in the room, alone, knowing that Marcia was with Brian but somehow missing her nonetheless. Since their argument, Marcia had spent every night at Brian's, but Sophia suspected it had less to do with Brian than the fact that Marcia felt too ashamed to face her.

She was still angry with Marcia—what she'd done was pretty crappy, and Sophia couldn't simply pretend it didn't bother her. A best friend didn't start dating an ex. Call it a cardinal rule or whatever, but friends just didn't do that to each other. Ever. But even though part of Sophia thought she should have told Marcia that their friendship was over, she hadn't been able to say the words, because in her heart she knew that Marcia hadn't done it on purpose. She hadn't schemed or plotted or purposely tried to hurt her. Marcia just wasn't wired that way, and Sophia knew firsthand how charming Brian could be when he put his mind to it. Which, she suspected, he probably had. Because Brian *was* wired that way. Brian had known exactly what he was doing, and she had no doubt that dating Marcia was his way of trying to get back at her. He wanted to hurt her one last time by destroying her relationship with Marcia.

And then, no doubt, he'd hurt Marcia, too. Marcia would end up learning the hard way what kind of guy Brian actually was. After that, she'd feel even worse than she was probably feeling right now. In a way, it would serve her right, and yet . . .

But now, Sophia wanted to talk to Marcia. Right now, she really needed her. To talk about Luke. And just to talk, period. Like her sisters were doing downstairs and in the hallway. She could hear the sound of their voices drifting through the door.

She didn't want to be anywhere near them, though, because

even if they said nothing, their expressions were plenty eloquent. Lately, every time she entered the house, the rooms and hallways would go quiet, and she could intuit exactly what each of them was thinking and wondering. *How do you think she feels? I hear that she and Marcia never see each other anymore. I feel bad for her. I can't imagine what she's going through.*

She couldn't face that right now, and despite everything, she found herself wishing that Marcia were there. Because right now, she was sure she'd never felt more alone.

❧

The hours passed. Outside, the sky slowly filled with wintry clouds, backlit by the silver glow of the moon. As Sophia lay on her bed, she remembered the evenings on which she and Luke had watched the sky. She remembered the horseback rides and making love, the dinners with his mom. She recalled in vivid detail how they'd sat in lawn chairs in the bed of his truck on the first night they met.

Why would he risk dying? As much as she tried, she couldn't understand it. She knew it was more about his guilt than anything else, but was it worth risking his life? She didn't think so, and she knew his mother didn't. But he seemed intent on sacrificing himself anyway. That's what she couldn't grasp, and when he called a third time, she still couldn't bring herself to answer.

It was getting late and the house had slowly but surely begun to quiet. Sophia was exhausted, yet she knew she wouldn't be able to sleep. As she tried to make sense of Luke's self-destructive path, she found herself wondering exactly what had happened on the night he'd first encountered Big Ugly Critter. He'd told her about the plate in his head, but she had the sense now that it had been even worse than that. Slowly, she crawled out of bed, making for the laptop on her desk. With equal parts foreboding and the urge to finally know everything, she typed his name into the search engine.

She wasn't surprised that there were quite a few listings, including a short bio on Wikipedia. He had, after all, been one of the top-ranked riders in the world. But she wasn't interested in a biography. Instead, she added the words *Big Ugly Critter* after his name and pressed the search button.

Instantly, a link to a video on YouTube appeared at the top of the screen. Before she lost her nerve, she pressed the button, watching anxiously as the YouTube screen came up.

The video was just shy of two minutes, and she saw with a sickening feeling that it had been viewed by over half a million people. She wasn't sure she wanted to watch, but she hit play nonetheless. As soon as it began, it took only a second to recognize Luke in the chute on top of the bull, the camera angled on him from somewhere above, obviously for the television audience. The stands were filled to capacity, and behind the chute there were signs and banners lining the arena wall. Unlike the McLeansville venue, this arena was indoors, which meant it was probably used for everything from basketball games to concerts. Luke wore jeans and a long-sleeved red shirt under a protective vest, along with his hat. The number 16 was embroidered on his vest.

She watched Luke adjust the wrap while other cowboys tried to tighten the rope beneath the bull. He pounded on his fist, then squeezed his legs, adjusting his position again. The announcers talked over the action in heavy twangs.

"Luke Collins has finished third overall in the PBR world standings and is considered one of the best riders in the world, but this is a bull he's never ridden before."

"Not many people have, Clint. Big Ugly Critter has only been ridden twice, and he was the PBR World Champion Bucking Bull last year. He's strong and mean and if Luke can stay on, he's just about assured of getting a score in the nineties . . ."

"He's getting ready . . ."

By then, Luke had grown strangely still, but the pause lasted only an instant. She watched the gate swing open and heard the roar of the crowd.

The bull came out hard, bucking, his rear legs pistoning into the air, his head pitched low to the ground. He half spun toward the left, kicking hard again, then literally jumped, all four legs coming off the ground, before suddenly beginning to spin in the opposite direction.

By then, four seconds had gone by and Sophia heard the crowd go berserk.

"He's doing it!" one of the announcers shouted.

It was at that instant that Sophia saw Luke jerk forward, his body off balance, just as the bull's head exploded backward.

The impact was horrific; Luke's head rocketed in the opposite direction, as if devoid of any muscle at all . . .

"Oh, my!"

Luke's body went suddenly limp as he toppled off the bull, his hand still tethered to the wrap.

But the bull appeared psychotic with rage, an animal out of control, and the bucking continued, fierce and unrelenting. Luke bobbed up and down like a rag doll, whipped in every direction. When the bull began to spin again, Luke followed in sickening motion, his feet skimming the ground like a whirligig.

By then the bullfighters and others had jumped into the ring, trying desperately to free Luke's grip, but the bull just wouldn't stop. He stopped spinning and charged at the new intruders, swinging his horns wildly, tossing one of the bullfighters aside as if he were weightless. Another tried and failed to free Luke's wrist from the wrap; another few seconds passed before a bullfighter was able to jump up and hold on long enough—while running with the bull—to free Luke's hand.

As soon as it happened, Luke toppled to the dirt and lay on his stomach, his head to the side, unmoving, while the bullfighter scurried away.

"He's hurt! They gotta get folks in here now!"

And still the bull wouldn't stop. Instead, as if realizing he was free of his rider but angry that Luke had even attempted to sit astride him in the first place, the bull turned around, oblivious to the others who were trying to distract him. Lowering his head, he charged Luke, gouging his horns at Luke's prone figure with murderous intent. Two bullfighters jumped in, slapping and hitting, but the bull would not be denied. Instead, he kept swinging his massive horns at Luke's inert figure, then suddenly lunged forward atop Luke's body, where he began to buck again.

No, not buck. Trample. And spin. In speechless terror, Sophia heard the announcer shout:

"Get that bull off him!"

Up and down, the enraged bull brought his hooves down with furious impact, crushing Luke beneath him. Smashing down on his back, his legs, his head.

His head...

Five people circled the bull by then, doing everything they could to stop the rampage, but Big Ugly Critter continued his single-minded attack.

Up and down, crushing Luke over and over...

The announcer saying:

"They gotta stop this!"

The bull seemingly possessed...

Until finally—*finally!*—he moved off of Luke and skittered sideways onto the dirt floor of the arena, still bucking wildly.

The camera followed the bull as he continued to buck away and then zeroed in on Luke's prone figure, his face bloody and unrecognizable, as others began to attend to him.

But by then, Sophia had covered her face, sobbing in horror and shock.

25

---- 🍃 ----

Luke

By Wednesday, Luke's headache had abated slightly, but he feared he wouldn't be well enough to compete in Macon, Georgia, over the coming weekend. After that, the next event was in Florence, South Carolina, and he wondered whether he'd be in better condition by then. From there, the tour moved to Texas, and the last thing he wanted was to head into that stretch of the season with a serious physical handicap.

Beyond that, he was beginning to worry about the expenses. Starting in February, the events required that he fly. It meant extra nights at the motels. Extra meals. Rental cars. In the past, when pursuing his dream, he'd viewed it as the cost of doing business. It still was, but now, with the loan repayment set to triple in six months, he'd found himself scouring the Web for the cheapest flights he could find, most of which had to be booked weeks in advance. As best as he could estimate, his winnings from the first event would cover the cost of travel to the next eight events. Which meant, of course, that not a dime would go toward meeting the upcoming loan payments. It wasn't about winning to chase a dream anymore. It was about winning regularly because he *had* to.

Even as the thought entered his mind, however, he could hear Sophia's words, contradicting him. That it wasn't about the ranch, or even about his mom. That it was all about the guilt he wanted to avoid.

Was he being selfish? Until she'd said it, he'd never even considered the idea. It wasn't about him. He'd be fine. It was about his mom, her heritage, her survival at an age at which her options were few. He didn't want to ride. He was doing it because his mom had risked everything to save him, and he owed her. He couldn't watch her lose everything because of him.

Otherwise he'd feel guilty. Which made it all about him. Or did it?

He'd called Sophia three times on Sunday night, another three times on Monday. Twice on Tuesday. He'd texted, too, once each day, without receiving a response. He remembered how upset she'd been by Brian's stalking, which kept him from texting or calling on Wednesday. But by Thursday, he could take the silence no longer. He climbed into his truck and drove to Wake Forest, pulling to a stop in front of the sorority house.

Two identically dressed girls were sitting in the porch rockers, one of them talking on the phone, the other texting. Both glanced up briefly, then did a double take when they saw who was walking toward them. As he knocked, he could hear laughter drifting from inside. A moment later, the door was opened by a pretty brunette with two piercings in each ear.

"I'll tell Sophia you're here," was all she said, moving aside to let him in.

Off to the side, three girls sat on the couch, craning their necks to get a glimpse of him. He guessed they were the same girls he'd heard from outside the door, but now they simply gawked at him, the television blaring in the background as he stood in the foyer, feeling out of place.

It was a couple of minutes before Sophia appeared at the top of the stairs, her arms crossed. She stared down at him, clearly debating what to do. Then, sighing, she approached reluctantly. Noticing everyone's attention, she said nothing to him; instead, she nodded toward the door. Luke followed her out.

She didn't stop at the porch but walked down the sidewalk out of sight of those in the house before turning to face him.

"What do you want?" she asked, her expression blank.

"I wanted to tell you that I'm sorry," Luke said, hands in his pockets. "For not telling you sooner."

"Okay," she said.

She added nothing, leaving him unsure what to say next. In the silence that followed, she turned away, studying the house across the street.

"I watched the video of your ride," she said. "On Big Ugly Critter."

He kicked at a few pebbles lodged in a crack in the sidewalk, afraid to face her. "Like I said, it was pretty bad."

She shook her head. "It was more than just *pretty bad*..." She turned to look at him, searching his face for answers. "I knew it was dangerous, but I never thought that it was a matter of life and death. I guess I didn't really understand how much you risk every time you step into the ring. And that bull and watching what he did to you. It was trying to kill you..."

She swallowed, unable to finish. Luke, too, had watched the video once, six months after his ride. Back when he'd sworn he'd never ride again. Back when he'd felt lucky simply to have survived.

"You should have died, but you didn't," Sophia stated. "You were given a second chance. Somehow, it was ordained that you should have the chance to live a normal life. And no matter what you say, I'll never understand why you'd want to risk that. It doesn't make sense to me. I told you once that I'd thought about killing myself but that I never really meant it. I knew I'd never go through with it. But you... it's like you want to do it. And you'll keep going until you succeed."

"I don't want to die," he insisted.

"Then don't ride," she said. "Because if you do, then I can't be part of your life. I'm not going to be able to pretend you're not trying to kill yourself. Because I'd feel like I was condoning it somehow. I just can't do that."

Luke could feel his throat close up, making it difficult to speak. "Are you saying you don't want to see me anymore?"

With his question, Sophia thought again about how much the tension had drained her, and she realized there were no tears left. "I love you, Luke. But I can't be part of this. I can't spend every minute that I'm with you wondering whether you'll live through the weekend. And I can't bear to imagine what it's going to be like if you don't."

"So it's over?"

"Yes," she said. "If you continue to ride, it's over."

✤

The following day, Luke sat at his kitchen table, truck keys on the table. It was Friday afternoon, and if he left in the next few minutes, he'd reach the motel before midnight. His truck was already loaded with the gear he needed.

His head still ached a little, but the real ache he felt was when he thought about Sophia. He wasn't looking forward to the drive or to the event; more than anything, he wanted to spend the weekend with Sophia. He wanted an excuse not to go. He wanted to take her horseback riding on the ranch, envelop her in his arms as they sat in front of the fire.

Earlier, he'd seen his mom, but their interaction remained strained. Like Sophia, she didn't want to talk to him. When work made it necessary to speak to him, her anger was palpable. He could feel the weight of her worries—about him, about the ranch. About the future.

Reaching for the keys, he heaved himself out of the chair and started toward his truck, wondering if he'd be able to drive it back home.

26

❦

Sophia

I thought you might be coming." Linda stood in the doorway of the farmhouse, her expression as weary and anxious as Sophia's own.

"I didn't know where else to go," Sophia said. It was Saturday night, and they both knew that the man they adored would be in the ring tonight, risking his life, perhaps at this very moment.

Linda waved her in and motioned for her to sit at the kitchen table. "Would you like a cup of hot cocoa?" she asked. "I was just about to make myself one." Sophia nodded, unable to say anything and noticing Linda's cell phone lying on the table. Linda must have noticed Sophia staring at it.

"He texts me when he's finished," Linda said, busying herself at the stove. "He's always done that. Well, actually, he used to call. He'd tell me how well he did, good or bad, and we'd talk for a while. But now he..." She shook her head. "He just texts to tell me that he's okay. And I can't do anything but sit here while I wait for it. Meanwhile, of course, time just slows down. Right now, I feel like I've been awake for a week. But even when I hear from him, I won't be able to sleep. Because I worry that even though he says he's okay, he's done something to further damage his brain."

Sophia picked at the table with her fingernail. "He said he was in the ICU after the accident."

"He was clinically dead when he arrived at the hospital," Linda said, stirring the heating milk slowly. "Even after they revived him, no one thought he'd survive. The back of his skull was just...shattered. Of course, I didn't know any of this at the time. I didn't get there until the following day, and when they brought me in to see him, I didn't even recognize him. The impact broke his nose and crushed his eye socket and his cheekbone—his face was swollen and just...wrecked. They couldn't do anything about it because of the other damage. His head was wrapped up and he was bolted down so he couldn't move at all." Linda took her time pouring the hot milk into the mugs, then spooned in the cocoa. "He didn't open his eyes for almost a week, and a few days after that, they had to rush him back into surgery. He ended up spending almost a month in the ICU."

Sophia accepted a mug from Linda and took a tentative sip. "He said he has a plate."

"He does," she said. "A small one. But the doctor said the bones in his skull might never heal completely because some of the pieces just couldn't be salvaged. He said that it's like a stained glass window back there, everything barely holding together. I'm sure it's better now than it was even last summer, and he's always been a strong rider, but..." She trailed off, unable to finish the thought. Instead, she shook her head.

"After he was released from the ICU and they thought he could handle the trip, he was transported to Duke University Hospital. By then, I felt like we'd put the worst behind us, because I knew he'd survive, maybe even recover fully." She sighed. "And then the bills started coming in, and I was looking at another three months at Duke, just to allow his body to heal, and all the reconstructive surgery on his face. Then, of course, he needed lots of rehab..."

"He told me about the ranch," Sophia said softly.

"I know," she said. "It's how he justifies what he's doing."

"It still doesn't justify it."

"No," Linda said. "It doesn't."

"Do you think he's okay?"

"I don't know," she said, tapping the phone. "I never know until he texts."

🌿

The next two hours passed in slow motion, elongated minutes stretching into eternity. Linda served up some slices of pie, but neither of them was hungry. Instead, they picked at the slices, waiting.

And waiting.

Somehow, Sophia thought that being here with Linda would reduce her anxiety, but if anything, she'd begun to feel worse. Seeing the video had been bad enough, but hearing about his injuries in detail made her almost nauseated.

Luke was going to die.

In her mind, there was no question about it. He would fall, the bull would swing his head the wrong way again. Or Luke would ride but the bull would go after him as he was exiting the arena...

He had no chance of survival, not if he kept riding. It was only a matter of time.

She stayed lost in these thoughts until finally Linda's phone vibrated on the table.

Linda lunged for it and read the message. Her shoulders suddenly relaxed and she let out a long breath. After sliding the phone to Sophia, she covered her face with her hands.

Sophia glanced at the words: *I'm OK and on my way home.*

27

Luke

The fact that he didn't win in Macon wasn't a reflection of how well he rode, but rather a function of the quality of the bulls. The bulls' performances made up half of every score, after all, meaning that every event was left somewhat in the hands of the gods.

His first bull was pretty much a flat spinner. Luke held on and the ride was no doubt exciting to the crowd, but when the scores came up, he found himself in ninth place. The second bull wasn't much better, but at least he managed to hold on while others ranked above him had been thrown, and he moved up to sixth. In the short go, he drew a decent bull, and he'd hopped off with a score good enough to move him into fourth place. It wasn't a stellar competition, but it was enough for him to retain, even extend, his lead in the overall points standings.

He should have been pleased. With one more good weekend, he'd practically be guaranteed a place on the big tour, even if he rode poorly in the events that followed. Despite the lack of practice, despite the concussion, he was in just the position he'd wanted to be.

Surprisingly, he didn't think that the rides had worsened his concussion. On the drive home, he kept waiting for his headache to intensify, but it didn't. Instead, it remained in low gear, a faint hum, nowhere close to the agony he'd felt earlier in the week. If anything, it seemed better than it had been this morning, and he had the sense that by morning, it might even be gone.

A good weekend, in other words. Everything was working out according to plan.

Except, of course, for Sophia.

He rolled home an hour before dawn and slept until almost noon. Only after his shower did he realize he hadn't reached for the painkillers. The headache, as he'd hoped, was gone.

Nor was his body as sore as it had been after the first event. There were the usual aches in his lower back, but nothing he couldn't handle. After getting dressed, he saddled Horse and went to check on the cattle. On Friday morning, before he'd left for Macon, he'd tended to a calf who'd had a run-in with some barbed wire and he wanted to make sure it was healing properly.

Sunday afternoon and Monday were spent working on the irrigation system, repairing leaks that had sprung up because of the cold weather, and beginning Tuesday morning, he tore off, and then, over the next two days, gradually replaced the shingles on his mom's roof.

It was a good week, the work physical and straightforward, and by Friday, he expected to feel a sense of accomplishment at everything he'd done. But he didn't. Instead, he ached for Sophia. He hadn't called or texted, nor had she, and her absence sometimes felt like a gaping hole where an essential limb used to be. He wanted things to go back to the way they were; he wanted to know that when he got home after the Florence event, he'd be able to spend the rest of the day with her.

But even as he began laying out the belongings he would need on his trip to South Carolina, he knew that she would never reconcile herself to the choice that he had made—and unlike his mother, she could walk away.

On Saturday afternoon, Luke stood watching the bulls behind the arena in Florence, South Carolina, and realized for the first time that his hands weren't shaking.

Under ordinary circumstances, that should have been a good sign, since it meant that his nerves had calmed. Yet he couldn't escape the feeling that it had been a mistake to come here. He'd felt a heavy sense of dread as he'd pulled up an hour earlier, and since then, the nameless black thoughts in his head had only grown louder, whispers that urged him to get back into the truck and go home.

Before it was too late.

He hadn't felt like this in either Pensacola or Macon. Granted, he hadn't wanted to ride in those events any more than he wanted to ride in this one, but that was mainly because he wasn't sure he was ready to rejoin the circuit at all. But the dread he felt now was different.

He wondered if Big Ugly Critter could sense it.

The bull was here, in Florence, South Carolina, which made no more sense than it had in McLeansville last October. The bull didn't belong on this qualifying tour. He belonged with the big boys, where he'd no doubt be in the running to win another World Champion Bucking Bull award. Luke couldn't figure out why the owner had consented to let him participate on the lower circuit. Most likely the promoter had made the owner a deal he couldn't refuse in conjunction with one of the auto dealers in town. That had become more common on the circuit— promotions like *If you can ride him, you'll drive off in a new truck!* While the crowd generally loved the added challenge, Luke would gladly excuse himself from that contest if he could. He wasn't close to being ready to ride him again, nor, most likely, was anyone else at the event. It wasn't the riding that was the concern. Nor was it the prospect of being thrown. It was the way Big Ugly Critter might react afterward.

He watched him for nearly an hour, thinking, *That bull shouldn't be here.*

And neither should he.

❧

The event began right on time, with the sun high enough to warm the day, if only slightly. In the stands, spectators were wearing jackets and gloves, and the lines for hot chocolate and coffee stretched nearly toward the entrance. As usual, Luke stayed in his truck, the heater blowing. He was surrounded by dozens of idling trucks in the parking lot as his competitors tried to do the same.

He ventured out once before his turn, as did a lot of the other competitors, to watch Trey Miller's attempt to ride Big Ugly Critter. As soon as the chute door opened, the bull ducked his head and launched into a twisting kick; Miller didn't have a prayer. When he landed, the bull turned, just as he had after Luke's ride, and rushed him, head down. Luckily Miller was able to make it to the arena fence in time to scramble away to safety.

The bull, as if aware how many people were watching him, stopped his charge and snorted hard. He stood in place, staring at the receding Miller, the cold air making it appear as though he were breathing smoke out of his nostrils.

For his draw, Luke had pulled Raptor, a young bull with a short history on the tour. He was supposed to be an up-and-comer, and he didn't disappoint. He spun and bucked and jumped, but Luke felt strangely in control throughout, and by the end of the ride, he'd earned his highest score of the season. After he'd jumped down, the bull—unlike Big Ugly Critter—ignored him.

❧

There were more competitors at this third event of the season, making the wait between rides that much longer. For his second bull, Luke drew Locomotive, and though his ride wasn't as high-scoring as the first, he remained in the lead.

Five rides later, Jake Harris had his turn on Big Ugly Critter. It didn't last long, but in a sense, he was either less or more lucky than Miller had been. He made it to the center of the arena before being thrown, and again, Big Ugly Critter turned and charged. There was nowhere to go. A younger rider might have been in trouble, but Harris was a veteran and was able to dart out of the way at the last instant, the bull's horns missing him by inches. Two bullfighters jumped in to distract Big Ugly Critter, offering a temporary reprieve that allowed Harris to reach the arena wall. He launched himself upward and threw his legs over just as the angry bull closed in, ready to gore.

Then, turning and squaring up, the bull set his sights on the bullfighters still in the arena. One made it to the safety of the arena fence, but the other had to hop into one of the barrels. Big Ugly Critter went after it, furious that his real prey had gotten away. He rammed the barrel, sending it careening across the arena, then rammed it again before pinning it against the wall, where he continued to savage it, swinging his horns and snorting, an animal gone insane.

Luke watched, feeling sick to his stomach, thinking again that the bull did not belong at the event. Or any event. One day soon, Big Ugly Critter was going to kill someone.

After the first two rounds, twenty-nine riders were on their way home. Fifteen remained. Luke was seeded first in the Championships round, the last rider of the day. There was a short break before the round started, and as the wintry sky darkened, the lights had been turned on.

His hands remained steady. His nerves were in check. He was riding well, and if his day so far was any indication, he would ride well again—which was strange, given how he'd felt at the beginning of the day. Nonetheless, the sense of dread he'd felt hadn't totally dissipated, despite his successful rides.

If anything, it had grown worse since he'd seen Big Ugly Critter go after Harris. The event promoters should have been aware of the danger, given the bull's history. They should have had five bullfighters in the ring, not just two. But even after Miller had ridden, they hadn't learned their lesson. The bull was dangerous. Psychotic, even.

Like the other finalists, Luke lined up for the last draw of the day, and one by one, he heard the bulls being assigned to the various riders. Raptor went third, Locomotive went seventh, and as the names continued, his sense of foreboding intensified. He couldn't look at the other competitors; instead, he closed his eyes, waiting for the inevitable.

And in the end, just as part of him had known would happen, he drew Big Ugly Critter.

🌿

Time slowed down in the final round. The first two riders stayed on, the next three were tossed. It went back and forth on the next two.

Luke sat in his truck, listening to the announcer. His heartbeat began to speed up as adrenaline flooded his system. He tried to convince himself he was ready, that he was up to the challenge, but he wasn't. He hadn't been when he'd been at his peak, let alone now.

He didn't want to go out there. He didn't want to hear the announcer mention the truck he could win or the fact that the bull hadn't been ridden successfully in the last three years. He didn't want the announcer to tell the crowd that Big Ugly Critter was the bull who'd almost killed him, turning his potential ride into some sort of grudge match. Because it wasn't. He didn't hold a grudge against the bull. He was just an animal, albeit the craziest, meanest one he'd ever come across.

He wondered whether he should simply withdraw. Take the scores from his first two rides and be done with it. He'd still finish in the top ten, maybe even the top five, depending on how well the other riders did after all was said and done. He might drop in the overall rankings, but he'd remain in position to make the big tour...

Where Big Ugly Critter would surely end up.

But what would happen the next time? If he drew the bull in the first round? When he was in California, for instance? Or Utah? After spending a small fortune on the flight and the motel and food? Would he be prepared to walk away then, too?

He didn't know. Right now, his mind was incoherent, filled with static, though when he glanced down, his hands were completely still. Odd, he thought, considering...

In the distance, the roar of the crowd went up, signaling a successful ride. A good one from the sound of it. Good for him, Luke thought, whoever it was. These days, he begrudged no one his success. He, more than anyone, knew the risks.

It was time. If he was going to go through with it, he had to make his decision. Stay or go, ride or withdraw, save the ranch or let the bank take it away.

Live or die...

He drew a long breath. Hands still good. He was as ready as he'd ever be. Pushing open the door, he stepped onto the hard-packed dirt and gazed upward at the darkening winter sky.

Live or die. That's what it all came down to. Steeling himself to the walk to the arena, he wondered which it would be.

28

Ira

When I wake, my first thought is that my body is weak and growing steadily weaker. Sleep, instead of giving me strength, has robbed me of some of the precious hours I have remaining.

Morning sunlight slants through the window, reflected bright and sharp by the snow. It takes a moment to realize that it's Monday. More than thirty-six hours now since the accident. Who could have imagined such a thing happening to an old man like me? This will to live. But I have always been a survivor, a man who laughs in the face of death and spits in the eye of mother fate. I fear nothing, not even the pain. It's time for me to open the door and scale the embankment, to flag down a passing car. If no one comes to me, I will have to go to them.

Who am I kidding?

I can do no such thing. The agony is so intense that it takes a concerted effort to bring the world back into focus. For a moment, I feel strangely dissociated from my body—I can see myself propped on the steering wheel, my body a broken wreck. For the first time since the accident, I am sure that it is no longer possible for me to move. The bells are tolling, and I do not have long. This should frighten me, but it doesn't. In no small way, I have been waiting to die for the last nine years.

I was not meant to be alone. I am not good at it. The years

since Ruth's passing have ticked by with the kind of desperate silence known only to the elderly. It is a silence underscored by loneliness and the knowledge that the good years are already in the past, coupled with the complications of old age itself.

The body is not meant to survive nearly a century. I speak from experience when I say this. Two years after Ruth died, I suffered a minor heart attack—I was barely able to dial for help before I fell to the floor, unconscious. Two years after that, it became difficult to maintain my balance, and I purchased the walker to keep from toppling into the rosebushes whenever I ventured outside.

Caring for my father had taught me to expect these kinds of challenges, and I was largely able to move past them. What I hadn't expected, however, was the endless array of minor torments—little things, once so easy, now rendered impossible. I can no longer open a jar of jelly; I have the cashier at the super-market do it before she slips it into the bag. My hands shake so much that my penmanship is barely legible, which makes it diffi-cult to pay the bills. I can read only in the brightest of lights, and without my dentures in place, I can eat nothing but soup. Even at night, age is torturous. It takes forever for me to fall asleep, and prolonged slumber is a mirage. There is medicine, too—so many pills that I've had to tack a chart on the refrigerator to keep them straight. Medicine for arthritis and high blood pressure and high cholesterol, some taken with food and some without, and I'm told that I must always carry nitroglycerine pills in my pocket, in the event I ever again feel that searing pain in my chest. Before the cancer took root—a cancer that will gnaw at me until I'm noth-ing but skin and bones—I used to wonder what indignity the future would bring next. And God, in his wisdom, provided the answer. *How about an accident! Let's break his bones and bury him in snow!* I sometimes think God has an odd sense of humor.

Had I said this to Ruth, she would not have laughed. She would say I should be thankful, for not everyone is blessed with a long life. She would have said that the accident was my fault.

And then, with a shrug, she would have explained that I had lived because our story was not yet finished.

What became of me? And what will become of the collection?

I've spent nine years answering these questions, and I think Ruth would have been pleased. I've spent these years surrounded by Ruth's passion; I have spent my years embraced by her. Everywhere I have looked, I've been reminded of her, and before I go to bed every night, I stare at the painting above the fireplace, comforted by the knowledge that our story will have precisely the kind of ending that Ruth would have wanted.

The sun rises higher, and I hurt even in the distant recesses of my body. My throat is parched and all I want is to close my eyes and fade away.

But Ruth will not let me. There is an intensity in her gaze that wills me to look at her.

"It is worse now," she says. "The way you are feeling."

"I'm just tired," I mumble.

"Yes," she says. "But it is not your time yet. There is more you must tell me."

I can barely make out her words. "Why?"

"Because it is the story of us," she says. "And I want to hear about you."

My mind spins again. The side of my face hurts where it presses against the steering wheel, and I notice that my broken arm looks bizarrely swollen. It has turned purple and my fingers look like sausages. "You know how it ends."

"I want to hear it. In your own words."

"No," I say.

"After sitting shiva, the depression set in," she goes on, ignoring me. "You were very lonely. I did not want this for you."

Sorrow has crept into her voice, and I close my eyes. "I couldn't help it," I say. "I missed you."

She is silent for a moment. She knows I am being evasive. "Look at me, Ira. I want to see your eyes as you tell me what happened."

"I don't want to talk about this."

"Why not?" she persists.

The ragged sound of my breath fills the car as I choose my words. "Because," I finally offer, "I'm ashamed."

"Because of what you did," she announces.

She knows the truth and I nod, afraid of what she thinks of me. In time, I hear her sigh.

"I was very worried about you," she finally says. "You would not eat after you sat shiva, after everyone went away."

"I wasn't hungry."

"This is not true. You were hungry all the time. You chose to ignore it. You were starving yourself."

"It doesn't matter now—," I falter.

"I want you to tell me the truth," she persists.

"I wanted to be with you."

"But what does that mean?"

Too tired to argue, I finally open my eyes. "It means," I say, "that I was trying to die."

🌿

It was the silence that did it. The silence that I still experience now, a silence that descended after the other mourners went away. At the time, I was not used to it. It was oppressive, suffocating— so quiet that it eventually became a roar that drowned out everything else. And slowly but surely, it leached me of my ability to care.

Exhaustion and habits further conspired against me. At breakfast, I would pull out two cups for coffee instead of one, and my throat would clench as I put the extra cup back in the cupboard. In the afternoon, I would call out that I was going out to retrieve the mail, only to realize that there was no one to answer me. My stomach felt permanently tense, and in the evenings, I couldn't fathom the idea of cooking a dinner that I would have to eat alone. Days would pass where I ate nothing at all.

I am no doctor. I do not know if the depression was clinical or simply a normal product of mourning, but the effect was the same. I did not see any reason to go on. I did not want to go on. But I was a coward, unwilling to take specific action. Instead, I took no action, other than a refusal to eat much of anything, and again the effect was the same. I lost weight and grew steadily weaker, my path preordained, and little by little, my memories became jumbled. The realization that I was losing Ruth again made everything even worse, and soon I was eating nothing at all. Soon, the summers we spent together vanished entirely and I no longer saw any reason to fend off the inevitable. I began to spend most of my time in bed, eyes unfocused as I gazed at the ceiling, the past and the future a blank.

*

"I do not think this is true," she says. "You say that because you were depressed, you did not eat. You say that because you could not remember, you did not eat. But I think that it is because you did not eat that you could not remember. And so you did not have the strength to fight the depression."

"I was old," I say. "My strength had long since evaporated."

"You are making excuses now." She waves a hand. "But this is not a time to make jokes. I was very worried about you."

"You couldn't be worried. You weren't there. That was the problem."

Her eyes narrow and I know I've struck a nerve. She tilts her head, the morning sunlight casting half her face in shadow. "Why do you say this?"

"Because it's true?"

"Then how can I be here now?"

"Maybe you aren't."

"Ira..." She shakes her head. She talks to me the way I imagine she once talked to her students. "Can you see me? Can you hear me?" She leans forward, placing her hand on my own. "Can you feel this?"

Her hand is warm and soft, hands I know even better than my own. "Yes," I say. "But I couldn't then."

She smiles, looking satisfied, as if I'd just proved her point. "That is because you were not eating."

A truth emerges in any long marriage, and the truth is this: Our spouses sometimes know us better than we even know ourselves.

Ruth was no exception. She knew me. She knew how much I would miss her; she knew how much I needed to hear from her. She also knew that I, not she, would be the one left alone. It's the only explanation, and over the years, I have never questioned it. If she made one mistake, it was that I did not discover what she had done until my cheeks had hollowed and my arms looked like twigs. I do not remember much about the day I made my discovery. The events have been lost to me, but this is not surprising. By that point, my days had become interchangeable, without meaning, and it wasn't until darkness set in that I found myself staring at the box of letters that sat upon Ruth's chest of drawers.

I had seen them every night since her passing, but they were hers, not mine, and to my misguided way of thinking, I simply assumed they would make me feel worse. They would remind me of how much I missed her; they would remind me of all that I had lost. And the idea was unbearable. I just could not face it. And yet, on that night, perhaps because I'd become numb to my feelings, I forced myself from the bed and retrieved the box. I wanted to remember again, if only for a single night, even if it hurt me.

The box was strangely light, and when I lifted the lid, I caught a whiff of the hand lotion Ruth had always used. It was faint, but it was there, and all at once, my hands began to shake. But I was a man possessed, and I reached for the first of the anniversary letters I'd written to her.

The envelope was crisp and yellowing. I'd inscribed her name with a steadiness that had long since vanished, and once again, I was reminded of my age. But I did not stop. Instead, I slid the brittle letter out of its sleeve as I maneuvered it into the light.

At first, the words were foreign to me, a stranger's words, and I did not recognize them. I paused and tried again, concentrating on bringing the words into focus. And as I did, I felt Ruth's presence gradually take shape beside me. She is here, I thought to myself; this is what she'd intended. My pulse began to race as I continued to read, the bedroom dissolving around me. Instead, I was back at the lake in the thin mountain air of late summer. The college, shuttered and forlorn, stood in the background as Ruth read the letter, her downcast eyes flickering across the page.

I've brought you here—to the place where art first took on true meaning for me—and even though it will never be the same as it once was, this will always be our place. It's here that I was reminded of the reasons I fell in love with you; it was here where we began our new life together.

When I finished the letter, I slipped it back into the envelope and set it aside. I read the second letter, then the next, then the one after that. The words flowed easily from one year to the next, and with them came memories of summers that in my depression I had been unable to recall. I paused when I read a passage that I'd written on our sixteenth anniversary.

I wish I had the talent to paint the way I feel about you, for my words always feel inadequate. I imagine using red for your passion and pale blue for your kindness; forest green to reflect the depth of your empathy and bright yellow for your unflagging optimism. And still I wonder: can even an artist's palette capture the full range of what you mean to me?

Later, I came across a letter I'd written in the midst of the dark years, after we'd learned that Daniel had moved away.

I witness your grief and I don't know what to do, other than wish that I could somehow wash away the traces of your loss. I want more than anything to make things better, but in this I am helpless and have failed you. I'm sorry for this. As your husband, I can listen and hold you; and kiss your tears away, if given the chance.

It went on, this lifetime in a box, one letter after another. Outside the window, the moon ascended and drifted and eventually climbed out of sight as I continued to read. Each letter echoed and reaffirmed my love for Ruth, burnished by our long years together. And Ruth, I learned, had loved me, too, for she left me a gift at the bottom of the stack.

I will admit: I didn't expect this. That Ruth could still surprise me, even from beyond, caught me off guard. I stared at the letter lying at the bottom of the box, trying to imagine when she'd written it and why she'd never told me.

I have read this letter often in the years since I first found it, so many times that I can recite it from memory. I know now that she'd kept it secret in the certainty that I would find it in the hour of my greatest need. She knew I would eventually read my letters to her; she predicted that a time would come when I could no longer resist the pull. And in the end, it worked out just as she'd planned.

On that night, however, I did not think of this. I simply reached for the letter with trembling hands and slowly began to read.

My Dearest Ira,

I write this letter as you are sleeping in the bedroom, uncertain where I should begin. We both know why you're reading this letter and what it means. And I am sorry for what you must be enduring.

Unlike you, I am not good at writing letters and there is so much I want to say. Perhaps if I wrote in German it might flow more easily, but then you could not read it, so what would be the point? I want to write you the kind of letter you always wrote to me. Sadly, unlike you I have never been good with words. But I want to try. You deserve it, not just because you're my husband, but because of the man you are.

I tell myself that I should begin with something romantic, a memory or gesture that captures the kind of husband you have been to me: the long weekend at the beach when we first made love, for example, or our honeymoon, when you presented me with six paintings. Or perhaps I should speak of the letters you wrote, or the feel of your gaze on me as I considered a particular piece of art. And yet, in truth it is in the quiet details of our life together where I have found the most meaning. Your smile at breakfast always made my heart leap, and the moment in which you reached for my hand never failed to reassure me of the rightness of the world. So you see, choosing a handful of singular events feels wrong to me—instead, I prefer to recall you in a hundred different galleries and hotel rooms; to relive a thousand small kisses and nights spent in the familiar comfort of each other's arms. Each of those memories deserves its own letter, for the way you made me feel in each and every instance. For this, I have loved you in return, more than you will ever know.

I know you are struggling, and I am so sorry that I am not able to comfort you. It feels inconceivable that I will never be able to do so again. My plea to you is this: despite your sadness, do not forget how happy you have made me; do not forget that

I loved a man who loved me in return, and this was the greatest gift I could ever have hoped to receive.

I am smiling as I write this, and I hope you can find it in yourself to smile as you read this. Do not drown yourself in grief. Instead, remember me with joy, for this is how I always thought of you. That is what I want, more than anything. I want you to smile when you think of me. And in your smile, I will live forever.

I know you miss me terribly. I miss you, too. But we still have each other, for I am—and always have been—part of you. You carry me in your heart, just as I carried you in mine, and nothing can ever change that. I love you, my darling, and you love me. Hold on to that feeling. Hold on to us. And little by little, you will find a way to heal.

Ruth

"You are thinking about the letter I wrote to you," Ruth says to me. My eyes flutter open, and I squint with weary effort, determined to bring her into focus.

She is in her sixties, wisdom now deepening her beauty. There are small diamond studs in her ears, a gift I'd bought her when she retired. I try and fail to wet my lips. "How do you know?" I rasp.

"It is not so difficult." She shrugs. "Your expression gives you away. You have always been easy to read. It is a good thing you never played poker."

"I played poker in the war."

"Perhaps," she says. "But I do not think you won much money."

I acknowledge the truth of this with a weak grin. "Thank you for the letter," I croak. "I don't know that I would have survived without it."

"You would have starved," she agrees. "You have always been a stubborn man."

A wave of dizziness washes over me, causing her image to flicker. It's getting harder to hold on to her. "I had a piece of toast that night."

"Yes, I know. You and your toast. Breakfast for dinner. This I never understood. And toast was not enough."

"But it was something. And by then, it was closer to breakfast anyway."

"You should have had pancakes. And eggs. That way, you would have had the strength to walk the house again. You could have looked at the paintings and remembered, just like you used to."

"I wasn't ready for that yet. It would have hurt too much. Besides, one of them was missing."

"It was not missing," she says. She turns toward the window, her face in profile. "It had not arrived yet. It would not come for another week." For a moment, she is silent, and I know she isn't thinking about the letter. Nor is she thinking of me. Instead, she is thinking about the knock at the door. The knock came a little more than a week later, revealing a stranger on the doorstep. Ruth's shoulders sag, and her voice is laced with regret. "I wish I could have been there," she murmurs, almost to herself. "I would have loved to talk to her. I have so many questions."

These final words are drawn from a deep, hidden well of sadness, and despite my plight, I feel an unexpected ache.

§

The visitor was tall and attractive, the creases around her eyes suggesting too many hours spent in the sun. Her blond hair was tucked into a messy ponytail, and she was dressed in faded jeans and a simple short-sleeved blouse. But the ring on her finger and the BMW parked at the curb spoke of a well-heeled existence far different from mine. Under her arm she carried a package wrapped in simple brown paper, of a familiar size and shape.

"Mr. Levinson?" she asked. When I nodded, she smiled. "My name is Andrea Lockerby. You don't know me, but your wife,

Ruth, was once my husband's teacher. It was a long time ago and you probably don't remember, but his name was Daniel McCallum. I was wondering if you have a few minutes."

For a moment, I was too surprised to speak, the name repeating in an endless loop. Only half-aware of what I was doing, I dumbly stepped aside to allow her to enter and guided her to the living room. When I sat in the easy chair, she took a seat on the couch kitty-corner to me.

Even then, I could think of nothing to say. Hearing Daniel's name after almost forty years, in the aftermath of Ruth's passing, still remains the greatest shock of my life.

She cleared her throat. "I wanted to come by to express my condolences. I know that your wife recently passed away and I'm sorry for your loss."

I blinked, trying to find words for the flood of emotion and memories that threatened to drown me. *Where is he?* I wanted to ask. *Why did he vanish? And why did he never contact Ruth?* But I could say none of those things. Instead, I could only croak out, "Daniel McCallum?"

She set the wrapped package off to the side as she nodded. "He mentioned a few times that he used to come to your house. Your wife tutored him here."

"And... he's your husband?"

Her eyes flashed away for an instant before coming back to me. "He was my husband. I'm remarried now. Daniel passed away sixteen years ago."

At her words, I felt something go numb inside. I tried to do the math, to understand how old he'd been, but I couldn't. The only thing I knew for sure was that he'd been far too young and that it didn't make any sense. She must have known what I was thinking, for she went on.

"He had an aneurysm," she said. "It occurred spontaneously— no prior symptoms at all. But it was massive and there was nothing the doctors could do."

The numbness continued to spread until it felt as though I couldn't move at all.

"I'm sorry," I offered. The words sounded inadequate even to my own ears.

"Thank you." She nodded. "And again, I'm sorry for your loss as well."

For a moment, silence weighed on us both. Finally, I spread my hands out before her. "What can I do for you, Mrs...."

"Lockerby," she reminded me, reaching for the package. She slid it toward me. "I wanted to give you this. It's been in my parents' attic for years, and when they finally sold the house a couple of months ago, I found it in one of the boxes they sent me. Daniel was very proud of it, and it just didn't feel right to throw his painting away."

"A painting?" I asked.

"He told me once that painting it had been one of the most important things he ever did."

It was hard for me to grasp her meaning. "You're saying that Daniel painted something?"

She nodded. "In Tennessee. He told me that he painted it while living at the group home. An artist who volunteered there helped him with it."

"Please," I said, suddenly raising my hand. "I don't understand any of this. Can you just start at the beginning and tell me about Daniel? My wife always wondered what happened to him."

She hesitated. "I'm not sure how much I can really tell you. I didn't meet him until we were in college, and he never talked much about his past. It's been a long time."

I stayed quiet, willing her to continue. She seemed to be searching for the right words, picking at a loose thread in the hem of her blouse. "All I know is the little he did tell me," she began. "He said his parents had died and that he lived with his stepbrother and his wife somewhere around here, but they lost the farm and ended up moving to Knoxville, Tennessee. The three of them lived in their pickup truck for a while, but then the stepbrother got arrested for something and Daniel ended up in a group home. He lived there and did well enough in school to earn an academic scholarship to the University of Tennessee...we started dating when we were seniors, both majoring in international relations. Anyway, a few months after graduation, before we headed off to the Peace Corps, we got married. That's really all I know. Like I said, he didn't talk much about his past—it sounded like a difficult childhood and I think it was painful for him to relive it."

I tried to digest all this, trying to picture the trajectory of Daniel's life. "What was he like?" I pressed.

"Daniel? He was...incredibly smart and kind, but there was a definite intensity to him. It wasn't anger, exactly. It was more like he'd seen the worst that life could offer, and was determined to make things better. He had a kind of charisma, a conviction that just made you want to follow him. We spent two years in Cambodia with the Peace Corps, and after that he took a job with the United Way while I worked at a free clinic. We bought a little house and talked about having kids, but after a year or so we sort of realized that we weren't ready for suburbia. So we sold our things, boxed up some personal items and stored them at my parents', and ended up taking jobs with a human rights organization based in Nairobi. We were there for seven years, and I don't think he'd ever been happier. He traveled to a dozen different countries getting various projects under way, and he felt like his life had true purpose, that he was making a difference."

She stared out the window, falling silent for a moment. When she spoke again, her expression was a mixture of regret and wonder. "He was just...so smart and curious about everything. He read all the time. Even though he was young, he was already in line to become the executive director of the organization, and he probably would have made it. But he died when he was only thirty-three." She shook her head. "After that, Africa just wasn't the same for me. So I came home."

As she talked, I tried and failed to reconcile all she had told me with the dusty country boy who'd studied at our dining room table. Yet I knew in my heart that Ruth would have been proud of the way he turned out.

"And you're remarried?"

"Twelve years now." She smiled. "Two kids. Or rather, stepchildren. My husband's an orthopedic surgeon. I live in Nashville."

"And you drove all the way here to bring me a painting?"

"My parents moved to Myrtle Beach—we were on our way to visit them. Actually, my husband's waiting for me at a coffee shop downtown, so I should probably get going soon. And I'm sorry to just drop in like this. I know it's a terrible time. But it didn't feel right to just throw the painting away, so on a whim, I looked up your wife's name on the Internet and saw the obituary. I realized that your house would be right on the way when we went to see my parents."

I had no idea what to expect, but after removing the brown paper, my throat seemed to close in on itself. It was a painting of Ruth—a child's painting, crudely conceived. The lines weren't exactly right and her features were rather out of proportion, but he'd been able to capture her smile and her eyes with surprising skill. In this portrait, I could detect the passion and lively amusement that had always defined her; there was also a trace of the enigma that had always transfixed me, no matter how long we were together. I traced my finger over the brushstrokes that formed her lips and cheek.

"Why . . . ," was all I could say, nearly breathless.

"The answer's on the back," she said, her voice gentle. When I leaned the painting forward, I saw the photograph I'd taken of Ruth and Daniel so long ago. It had yellowed with age and was curling at the corners. I tugged it free, staring at it for a long time.

"On the back," she said, touching my hand.

I turned the photograph over, and there, written in neat penmanship, I saw what he had written.

Ruth Levinson
Third grade teacher.
She believes in me and I can be anything I want when I grow up.
I can even change the world.

All I remember then is that I was overcome, my mind going blank. I have no recollection of what more we talked about, if anything. I do remember, however, that as she was getting ready to leave, she turned to me as she stood in the open doorway.

"I don't know where he kept it at the group home, but you should know that in college, the painting hung on the wall right over his desk. It was the only personal thing he had in his room. After college, it came with us to Cambodia, then back to the States. He told me he was afraid that something would happen to it if he brought it to Africa, and ended up leaving it behind. But after we got there, he regretted it. He told me then that the painting meant more to him than anything he owned. It wasn't until I found the photograph in the back that I really understood what he meant. He wasn't talking about the painting. He was talking about your wife."

In the car, Ruth is quiet. I know she has more questions about Daniel, but at the time, I had not thought to ask them. This, too, is one of my many regrets, for after that, I never saw Andrea again. Just as Daniel had vanished in 1963, she, too, vanished from my life.

"You hung the portrait above the fireplace," she finally says. "And then you removed the other paintings from storage and hung them all over the house and stacked them in the rooms."

"I wanted to see them. I wanted to remember again. I wanted to see you."

Ruth is silent, but I understand. More than anything, Ruth would have wanted to see Daniel, if only through his wife's eyes.

Day by day, after I'd read the letter and once the portrait of Ruth was hung, the depression began to lift. I began to eat more regularly. It would take over a year for me to gain back the weight I'd lost, but my life began to settle into a kind of routine. And in that first year after she died, yet another miracle—the third miracle in that otherwise tragic year—occurred that helped me find my way back.

Like Andrea, another unexpected visitor arrived at my doorstep—this time a former student of Ruth's who came to the house to express her condolences. Her name was Jacqueline, and though I did not remember her, she too wanted to talk. She told me how much Ruth had meant to her as a teacher, and before she left, she showed me a tribute that she'd written in Ruth's honor that would be published in the local paper. It was both flattering and revealing, and when it was published, it seemed to open the floodgates. Over the next few months, the parade of former students visiting my house swelled. Lindsay and Madeline and Eric and Pete and countless others, most of whom I'd never known existed, showed up at my door at unexpected moments, sharing stories about my wife's years in the classroom.

Through their words, I came to realize that Ruth had been a key who unlocked the possibilities of so many people's lives— mine was only the first.

The years after Ruth's death, I sometimes think, can be divided into four phases. The depression and recovery after Ruth's passing was the first of those phases; the period in which I tried to move on as best I could was the second. The third phase covered the years following the reporter's visit in 2005, when the bars went up on the windows. It wasn't until three years ago, however, that I finally decided what to do with the collection, which led to the fourth and final phase.

Estate planning is a complicated affair, but essentially, the question boiled down to this: I had to decide what to do with our possessions, or the state would end up deciding for me. Howie Sanders had been pressing Ruth and me for years to make a decision. He asked us whether there were any charities of which I was particularly fond or whether I wanted the paintings to go to a particular museum. Perhaps I wanted to auction them off, with the proceeds earmarked for specific organizations or universities? After the article appeared—and the potential value of the collection became a topic of heated speculation in the art world—he became even more persistent, though by then I was the only one who was there to listen.

It wasn't until 2008, however, that I finally consented to come to his office.

He had arranged meetings of a confidential nature with curators from various museums: New York's Metropolitan Museum of Art, the Museum of Modern Art, the North Carolina Museum of Art, and the Whitney, as well as representatives from Duke University, Wake Forest, and the University of North Carolina at Chapel Hill. There were individuals from the Anti-Defamation League and United Jewish Appeal—a couple of my father's favorite organizations—as well as someone from Sotheby's. I was ushered into a conference room and introductions were made, and on each of their faces, I could read an avid curiosity as they wondered how Ruth and I—a haberdasher and a schoolteacher—had managed to accumulate such an extensive private modern art collection.

I sat through a series of individual presentations, and in each instance, I was assured that any portion of the collection that I cared to put in their hands would be valued fairly—or, in the case of the auctioneer, maximized. The charities promised to put the money toward any causes that were special to Ruth and me.

I was tired by the time the day ended, and upon my return home, I fell asleep almost immediately in the easy chair in the

living room. When I woke, I found myself staring at the painting
of Ruth, wondering what she would have wanted me to do.

"But I did not tell you," Ruth says quietly. It has been a while
since she has spoken, and I suspect that she's trying to conserve
my strength. She, too, can feel the end coming.

I force my eyes open, but she is nothing but a blurry image
now. "No," I answer. My voice is ragged and slurry, almost unintelligible. "You never wanted to discuss it."

She tilts her head to look at me. "I trusted you to make the
decision."

I can remember the moment when I finally made up my mind. It
was early evening, a few days after the meetings at Howie's office.
Howie had called an hour earlier, asking if I had any questions or
wanted him to follow up with anyone in particular. After I hung up,
and with the help of my walker, I made my way to the back porch.

There were two rocking chairs flanking a small table, dusty
from disuse. When we were younger, Ruth and I used to sit out
here and talk, watching the stars emerge from hiding in the
slowly darkening sky. Later, when we were older, these evenings
on the back porch became less frequent, because both of us had
grown more sensitive to the temperature. The cold of winter and
the heat of summer rendered the porch unusable for more than
half the year; it was only during the spring and fall that Ruth and
I continued to venture out.

But on that night, despite the heat and the thick layer of dust
on the chairs, I sat just as we used to. I pondered the meeting and
everything that had been said. And it became clear that Ruth
had been right: No one really understood.

For a while, I toyed with the idea of bequeathing the entire
collection to Andrea Lockerby, if only because she, too, had
loved Daniel. But I didn't really know her, nor had Ruth. Besides,
I couldn't help feeling disappointed that despite the obvious

influence that Ruth had had on Daniel's life, he had never once tried to contact her. This I just could not understand, or entirely forgive, because I knew Ruth's heart had been irreparably broken.

There was no easy answer, because for us, the art had never been about the money. Like the reporter, these curators and collectors, these experts and salespeople, didn't understand. With the echo of Ruth's words in my head, I finally felt the answer begin to take shape.

An hour later, I called Howie at his home. I told him that my intention was to auction the entire collection, and like a good soldier, he did not debate my decision. Nor did he question me when I explained that I wanted the auction held in Greensboro. However, when I told him how I wanted the auction to be handled, he was stunned into silence to the point where I wondered whether he was still connected. Finally, after clearing his throat, he talked with me about the specifics of all that it would entail. I told him that secrecy was the foremost priority.

Over the next few months, the details were arranged. I went to Howie's office two more times and met with the representatives from Sotheby's. I met again with the executive directors of various Jewish charities; the sums they would receive obviously depended on the auction itself and how much money the collection would fetch. To that end, appraisers spent weeks cataloging and photographing the entire collection, estimating value, and establishing provenance. Eventually, a catalog was sent for my approval. The estimated value of the collection was mind-boggling even to me, but again it did not matter.

When all the arrangements for the initial and subsequent auctions were completed—it was impossible to sell all the art in a single day—I talked to both Howie and the appropriate representative from Sotheby's, outlining their responsibilities, and had them sign numerous legal documents, ensuring there could be no alteration to the plan I envisioned. I wanted to prepare for any contingency, and when everything was finally ready, I signed my will in front of four witnesses. I further specified that my will was final and not to be altered or modified under any circumstances.

Back at home, in the aftermath, I sat in the living room and gazed at the painting of Ruth, tired and satisfied. I missed her, maybe more in that instant than I ever had before, but even so, I smiled and said the words that I knew she would have wanted to hear.

"They will understand, Ruth," I said. "They will finally understand."

It is afternoon now, and I feel myself shrinking, like a sand castle slowly being washed away with every wave. Beside me, Ruth looks at me with concern.

"You should take a nap again," she says, her voice tender.

"I'm not tired," I lie.

Ruth knows that I am lying, but she pretends to believe me, chattering on with a forced insouciance. "I do not think I would have been a good wife to someone else. I think I am sometimes too stubborn."

"That's true," I concede with a smile. "You're lucky I put up with you."

She rolls her eyes. "I am trying to be serious, Ira."

I stare at her, wishing that I could hold her. Soon, I think to myself. Soon, I will join her. It is hard to keep talking, but I force myself to respond.

"If we'd never met, I think I would have known that my life wasn't complete. And I would have wandered the world in search of you, even if I didn't know who I was looking for."

Her eyes brighten at this, and she reaches over to run her hand through my hair, her touch soothing and warm. "You have said this to me before. I have always liked this answer."

I close my eyes and they nearly stay closed. When I force them open again, Ruth has dimmed, becoming almost translucent.

"I'm tired, Ruth."

"It is not time yet. I have not read your letter yet. The new one, the one you wanted to deliver. Can you remember what you wrote?"

I concentrate, recalling a tiny snippet, but only that and nothing more.

"Not enough," I mumble.

"Tell me what you can remember. Anything."

It takes a while to gather my strength. I breathe deliberately, hear the faint whistle of my labored exchange. I can no longer feel the dryness in my throat. All of it has been replaced by bone-deep exhaustion.

"'If there is a heaven, we will find each other again, for there is no heaven without you.'" I stop, realizing that saying even this much leaves me breathless.

I think she is touched, but I can no longer tell. Though I am looking at her, she is almost gone now. But I can feel the radius of her sadness, her regret, and I know that she is leaving. Here and now, she can't exist without me.

She seems to know this, and though she continues to fade, she scoots closer in the seat. She runs her hand through my hair and kisses me on my cheek. She is sixteen and twenty and thirty and forty, every age, all at once. She is so beautiful that my eyes begin to well with tears.

"I love what you have written to me," she whispers. "I want to hear the rest of it."

"I don't think so," I mumble, and I think I feel one of her tears splash onto my cheek.

"I love you, Ira," she whispers. Her breath is soft in my ear, like the murmurings of an angel. "Remember how much you always meant to me."

"I remember...," I begin, and when she kisses me again, my eyes close for what I think will be the very last time.

29

Sophia

On Saturday night, while the rest of the campus was celebrating yet another weekend, Sophia was writing a paper in the library when her cell phone buzzed. Though the use of phones was allowed only in designated areas, Sophia saw there was no one else around and reached over, frowning when she saw the text and the sender.

Call me, Marcia had written. *It's urgent.*

Minimal as it was, it was more communication than they'd had since the argument, and Sophia wondered what to do. Text back? Ask what was going on? Or do as Marcia had asked and call her?

Sophia wasn't sure. Frankly, she didn't want to talk to Marcia at all. Like the rest of her sorority, she was surely at a party or at a bar. She was most likely drinking, which opened the door to the possibility that she and Brian might be fighting, and the last thing Sophia wanted was to get involved in something like that. She didn't want to listen to Marcia cry about what a jerk he was, nor did she feel ready to rush over and support her, especially after the painstaking way in which Marcia had continued to avoid her.

Now, though, she wanted Sophia to *call her*. Because whatever was going on, it was *urgent*.

Now that was a word that was open to all sorts of interpretation, she thought to herself. She debated for another few seconds, making her decision, before finally saving her work and shutting down the computer. She slid it into her backpack, put on her jacket, and headed to the exit. As she pushed open the door, she was met unexpectedly by an arctic blast of air and a thickening layer of snow on the ground. The temperature must have dropped twenty degrees in the last few hours. She was going to freeze on the walk back...

But not yet. Brushing aside her better judgment, she reached for her phone and tucked back into the lobby. Marcia picked up on the first ring. In the background, she could hear music blaring and the cacophony of a hundred conversations.

"Sophia? Thank God you called!"

Sophia drew a tense breath. "What's so urgent?"

She could hear the background noise fading, Marcia no doubt in search of someplace more quiet. A door slammed, and she heard Marcia's voice more clearly.

"You need to get back to the house right now," Marcia said, a note of panic in her tone.

"Why?"

"Luke is there. He's parked on the street out front. He's been waiting there for the last twenty minutes. You need to get there right away."

Sophia swallowed. "We broke up, Marcia. I don't want to see him."

"Oh," Marcia said, not bothering to hide her confusion. "That's terrible. I know how much you liked him..."

"Is that it?" Sophia asked. "I've got to go..."

"No, wait!" Marcia called out. "I know you're mad at me and I know I deserve it, but that's not why I'm calling. Brian knows that Luke is there—Mary-Kate told him a few minutes ago. Brian's been drinking for hours and he's getting riled up. He's already getting some of the guys together to go after him. I've been trying to talk him out of it, but you know how he is. And Luke has no idea what's coming. You might be broken up, but I don't think you want him to get hurt..."

By then, Sophia was barely listening, the icy winds drowning out the sound of Marcia's voice as she hurried back toward the house.

*

The campus appeared deserted as she took every shortcut she could, trying to reach the house in time. As she ran, she called Luke repeatedly on his cell phone, but for whatever reason, he wasn't answering. She managed to send him a brief text as well but didn't get a response.

It wasn't far, but the cold February wind was bitter, stinging her ears and cheeks, and her feet kept sliding in the new-fallen snow. She hadn't worn boots, and melting snow seeped through her shoes, soaking her toes. Wet snow continued to fall, feathery and thick, the kind of snow that would turn instantly to ice, making the roads dangerous.

She broke into a flat-out run, autodialing Luke again to no avail. Off campus now, onto the streets. Then Greek Row, students clustered together behind brightly lit windows. A few people hurried down the sidewalks, bustling from one party to the next, the usual Saturday night ritual of abandon and excess. Her house was on the far end of the street, and peering into the snowy darkness, she faintly made out the outline of Luke's truck.

Just then, she glimpsed a group of guys leaving a fraternity house three doors down, on the other side of the street. Five or six of them, led by someone very tall. *Brian.* Another figure soon followed, and though she was illuminated only briefly as she ran across the porch and down the steps, Sophia easily recognized her roommate. Faintly, muffled by the winter weather, she heard Marcia calling for Brian to stop.

As she ran, her backpack thumped awkwardly and her feet continued to slip, making her feel clumsy. She was closing in, but not fast enough. Brian and his friends had already fanned out on either side of the truck. She was four houses away, unable to tell from the darkened interior of the truck whether Luke was in there at all. Marcia's screams cut the air again, angry this time. "This is stupid, Brian! Just forget about him!"

Three houses to go. She watched as Brian and his friend yanked open the door on the driver's side and reached in. A scuffle began and she screamed just as Luke was pulled from the truck.

"Leave him alone!" Sophia shouted.

"You've got to stop, Brian!" Marcia chimed in.

Brian—either buzzed or drunk—ignored them both. Off balance, Luke stumbled into the arms of Jason and Rick, the same two who had been with Brian at the rodeo in McLeansville. Four others crowded around, surrounding Luke.

Panicked, Sophia ran down the center of the street just as Brian reeled back and threw a punch, which sent Luke's head whipping back. Sophia felt a sudden flash of hard-formed terror as she remembered the video...

As Luke went wobbly, Rick and Jason released him, and he toppled onto the snow-covered asphalt. Finally closing in, still terrified, she watched for movement, not seeing any...

"Get up!" Brian shouted at him. "I told you it wasn't over!"

Sophia saw Marcia jump in front of Brian.

"Just stop!" she screamed at him, trying to hold him back. "You've got to stop!"

Brian ignored her as Sophia saw Luke finally beginning to struggle to all fours, trying to get to his feet.

"Get up!" Brian shouted again. By then, Sophia was able to break through the circle, elbowing past two frat boys to insert herself between Brian and Luke, next to Marcia.

"It's over, Brian!" she yelled. "Knock it off!"

"It's not over yet!"

"It is now!" Sophia responded.

"Come on, Brian," Marcia pleaded, reaching for Brian's hands. "Let's just go. It's cold out here. I'm freezing."

By then, Luke had risen to his feet, the bruise on his cheekbone evident. Brian was breathing hard, and, surprising Sophia, he shoved Marcia to the side. It wasn't a violent push, but Marcia hadn't expected it and she stumbled, falling to the ground. Brian didn't seem to notice. He took a menacing step forward, preparing to shove Sophia out of the way, too. Stepping aside, she whipped her phone from her pocket. By the time Brian grabbed Luke, Sophia was already pushing buttons and raising the phone.

"Go ahead! I'll record the whole thing! Go to jail for all I care! Get kicked off the team! You can all get kicked off for all I care!"

She continued to back away, recording, panning over everyone present. She was zooming in on their shocked and anxious expressions when Brian lunged at her, tearing the phone from her grasp and smashing it to the ground.

"You're not recording anything!"

"Maybe not," Marcia said from the opposite side of the circle, holding up her phone. "But I am."

❧

"I guess I probably deserved that," Luke said. "After what I did to him, I mean."

They'd climbed into the truck, Luke behind the wheel, Sophia beside him. The threats had worked. It was Jason and Rick who eventually convinced Brian to return with them to the frat house, where Brian was no doubt reliving the punch that had sent Luke crumpling to the ground. Marcia didn't go with them; instead, she retreated to the sorority house and Sophia had watched the light go on in their room.

"You didn't deserve it," she said. "As I recall, you never hit Brian. You just kind of...pinned him to the ground."

"In the dirt. Facedown."

"There was that," she admitted.

"Thanks for stepping in, by the way. With your phone. I'll buy you a new one."

"You don't have to. It was getting old anyway. Why didn't you answer?"

"Battery died on the drive home and I forgot to bring the car charger. I only packed the regular one. I didn't think it would be that big of a deal."

"Did you at least text your mom?"

"Yeah," he said. If he wondered how she'd known about his habit of doing that, he didn't ask. Sophia folded her hands in her lap.

"I guess you know what I'll ask next, right?"

Luke squinted at her. "Why am I here?"

"You shouldn't have come. I don't want you here. Especially right after you get back from an event. Because—"

"You can't live like this."

"No," she said. "I can't."

"I know," he said. He sighed before turning sideways in his seat to face her. "I came here to tell you that I can't either. As of tonight, I'm retired. For good, this time."

"You're quitting?" she asked, disbelief in her voice.

"I've already quit."

She wasn't sure how to respond. Should she congratulate him? Sympathize? Express her relief?

"I also came by to ask if you were doing anything this week-end. Or if you had anything pressing on Monday? Like tests or papers."

"I have a paper due next Thursday, but other than that, just a couple of classes. What did you have in mind?"

"Just a little break to get my head straight. Before my battery died, I called and talked to my mom about it, and she thinks it's a good idea." He let out a long breath. "I was thinking of driving up to the cabins, and I was wondering if you'd like to come with me."

She still had trouble absorbing everything he'd just said or figuring out whether to believe it. Could he be telling the truth? Had he really given up riding for good?

With his eyes fixed on her, she whispered, "Okay."

⚜

Upstairs in their room, she found Marcia packing a duffel bag.

"What are you doing?"

"I'm going to drive home tonight. I just need to sleep in my own bed, you know? I'll be out of here in a minute or two."

"It's okay," Sophia said. "It's your room, too."

Marcia nodded, continuing to throw items into her bag. Sophia shifted from one foot to the other. "Thanks for texting me. And for what you did with the phone down there."

"Yeah, well, he deserved it. He was acting... crazy."

"It was more than that," Sophia said.

Marcia looked up for the first time. "You're welcome."

"He probably won't remember much of it."

"It doesn't matter."

"It does if you like him."

Marcia debated that for an instant before shaking her head. Sophia had the sense she'd come to some sort of conclusion even if she wasn't quite sure what it was.

"Is Luke gone yet?"

"He went to get some gas and to pick up some supplies. He'll be back in a few minutes."

"Seriously? I hope he keeps the doors locked this time." She zipped up her bag and then focused on Sophia again. "Wait... why's he coming back? I thought you said you broke up with him."

"I did."

"But?"

"How about we talk about it next week—when you get back. Because right now, I'm not completely sure what's happening with us."

Marcia accepted that, then started toward the door before stopping again.

"I've been thinking," she said, "and I have the sense that everything is going to work out between you two. And if you want my opinion, I think that's a good thing."

🍃

In the mountains, the snowfall had been heavy and the roads were icy in places, which meant they didn't reach the cabins until nearly four in the morning. The grounds resembled a pioneer camp, long since abandoned. Despite the absence of light anywhere, Luke unerringly guided his truck to a stop in front of the same cabin where they'd stayed before, the key dangling from the lock.

Inside, the cabin was frigid, the thin plank walls doing little to keep the cold at bay. He'd told her to pack both a hat and mittens, and she wore them along with her jacket while Luke got the fireplace and the woodstove burning. The skidding, slipping drive had kept her on edge all night, but now that they had arrived, she felt exhaustion catching up with her.

They went to bed fully clothed in their jackets and hats, falling asleep within minutes. When Sophia woke hours later, the house had warmed considerably, though not enough for her to walk around without several layers of clothing. She reasoned that a cheap motel would have been more comfortable, but when she took in the scene outside the window, she was struck again by how beautiful it was here. Icicles hung from the branches, glittering in the sunlight. Luke was already in the kitchen, and the aroma of bacon and eggs filled the air.

"You're finally awake," he observed.

"What time is it?"

"It's almost noon."

"I guess I was just tired. How long have you been up?"

"A couple of hours. Trying to keep this place warm enough to be habitable isn't as easy as you think."

She didn't doubt that. Gradually, her attention was drawn toward the window. "Have you ever been here during the winter?"

"Just once. I was little, though. I spent the day building snowmen and eating roasted marshmallows."

She smiled at the image of him as a boy before growing serious. "Are you ready to talk yet? About what made you change your mind?"

He forked a piece of bacon and removed it from the pan. "Nothing, really. I guess I just finally got around to listening to common sense."

"That's it?"

He set down the fork. "I drew Big Ugly Critter in the short go. And when it came time to actually ride..." He shook his head, not finishing the thought. "Anyway, afterwards, I knew that it was time to hang up the spurs. I realized I was done with it. It was killing my mom little by little."

And me, she wanted to say. But didn't.

He glanced over his shoulder, as if hearing her unspoken words. "I also realized that I missed you."

"What about the ranch?" she asked.

He scooped the scrambled eggs onto two plates.

"We'll lose it, I guess. Then try to start over again. My mom's pretty well-known. I'm hoping she'll land on her feet. Of course, she told me not to worry about her. That I should be more concerned with what I'm going to do."

"And what are you going to do?"

"I don't know yet." He turned and brought both plates to the table. A pot of coffee was waiting, along with the utensils. "I'm hoping that this weekend is going to help me figure that out."

"And you think we can pick up right where we left off?"

"Not at all," he said. He arranged the plates on the table and pulled out her chair. "But I was hoping that we could maybe start over."

After they ate, they spent the afternoon building a snowman, just as he once did as a child. While they rolled the sticky snowballs into ever-larger boulders, they caught each other up on their lives. Luke described the events in Macon and South Carolina and what was happening at the ranch. Sophia explained that the state of affairs with Marcia had driven her to spend all her time at the library, leaving her so far ahead in her reading that she doubted she'd have to study for the next two weeks.

"That's one of the good things about trying to avoid your roommate," she commented. "It improves your study habits."

"She surprised me last night," Luke remarked. "I wouldn't have thought she'd do something like that. Based on the circumstances, I mean."

"I wasn't surprised," Sophia said.

"No?"

She thought about it, wondering how Marcia was doing. "Okay. Maybe I was a *little* surprised."

That evening, as they snuggled on the couch beneath a blanket, the fireplace roaring, Sophia asked, "Are you going to miss riding?"

"Probably a little," he said. "Not enough to do it again, though."

"You sound so sure of that."

"I'm sure."

Sophia turned to study his face, mesmerized by the reflection of firelight in his eyes. "I'm kind of sad for your mom," she said. "I know she's relieved that you stopped, but..."

"Yeah," he said. "I'm sad, too. But I'll make it up to her somehow."

"I think having you around is all she really wanted."

"That's what I told myself," he said. "But now, I've got a question for you. And I want you to think about it before you answer. It's important."

"Go ahead."

"Are you busy next weekend? Because if you're free, I'd like to take you to dinner."

"Are you asking me out on a date?" she asked.

"I'm trying to start over. That's what you do, right? Ask someone out?"

She leaned up, kissing him for the first time that day. "I don't think we have to start all the way over, do we?"

"Is that a yes or a no?"

"I love you, Luke."

"I love you, too, Sophia."

They made love that night, then again on Monday morning, after sleeping in late. They had a leisurely brunch, and after taking a walk, Sophia watched Luke load up the truck from the warmth of the cabin, sipping her coffee. They weren't the same as they once had been. She reflected that in the few months they'd known each other, their relationship had evolved into something deeper, something she hadn't anticipated.

They hit the road a few minutes later and settled into the drive, making their way down the mountain. The sun reflected against the snow and produced a harsh glare that caused Sophia to turn away, leaning her head against the truck's window. She glanced over at Luke in the driver's seat. She still wasn't sure what was going to happen when she graduated in May, but for the first time, she began to wonder whether Luke might be free to follow her. She hadn't voiced those thoughts to him, but she wondered whether her plans had played a role in his decision to walk away from his career.

She was musing over these questions in a warm and peaceful haze, on the verge of dozing, when Luke's voice broke the silence.

"Did you see that?"

She opened her eyes, realizing that Luke was slowing the truck. "I didn't see anything," she admitted.

Surprising her, Luke slammed on the brakes and pulled his truck to the side of the highway, his eyes glued to the rearview mirror. "I thought I saw something," he said. He put the truck into gear and shut off the engine, flicking on the flashers. "Give me a second, will you?"

"What is it?"

"I'm not sure. I just want to check something out."

He grabbed his jacket from behind his seat and hopped out of the truck, pulling it on as he walked toward the rear of the truck. Over her shoulder, she noted that they'd just rounded a curve. Luke checked in both directions, then jogged to the other side of the road, approaching the guardrail. Only then did she realize that it was broken.

Luke peered down the steeply sloping embankment, then quickly swiveled his head toward her. Even from a distance, she could sense the urgency in his expression and body language. Quickly, she hopped out of the truck.

"Grab my phone and call 911!" he shouted. "A car went off the road here, and I think someone's still in it!"

And with that, he climbed through the broken section of the guardrail, vanishing from sight.

30

Sophia

Later, she would recall the events that followed in a series of quick-flash images: Making the emergency call and then watching Luke descend the steep embankment. Running back to the truck in panic for a bottle of water after Luke said he thought the driver was still moving. Clinging to bushes and branches as she scrambled down the wooded incline and then noting the state of the wreck—the crumpled hood, quarter-panel nearly sheared off, the jagged cracks in the windshield. Watching Luke struggle to open the jammed driver's-side door while trying to keep his balance on the steep slope, a slope that became a sheer cliff face only several feet from the front of the car.

But most of all, she remembered her throat catching at the sight of the old man, his bony head pressed against the steering wheel. She noted the wisps of hair covering his spotted scalp, the ears that seemed too big for him. His arm was bent at an unnatural angle. A gash in his forehead, his shoulder cocked wrong, lips so dry they'd begun to bleed. He had to be in terrible pain, yet his expression was oddly serene. When Luke was eventually able to wrench the door open, she found herself moving closer, struggling to keep her balance on the slippery incline.

"I'm here," Luke was saying to the old man. "Can you hear me? Can you move?"

Sophia could hear the panic in Luke's voice as he reached over, gently touching the man's neck in search of a pulse. "It's weak," he said to her. "He's in really bad shape."

The old man's moan was barely audible. Luke instinctively reached for the water bottle and poured some water into the cap, then tilted it to the man's mouth. Most spilled, but the drops were enough to wet his lips and he was able to choke down a swallow.

"Who are you?" Luke inquired gently. "What's your name?"

The man made a sound that came out in a wheeze. His half-open eyes were unfocused. "*Ira.*"

"When did this happen?"

It took a long moment for the word to come. "*atur . . . day . . .*"

Luke glanced at Sophia in disbelief before focusing on Ira again. "We're getting you help, okay? The ambulance should be here soon. Just hold on. Do you want some more water?"

At first, Sophia wasn't sure Ira had heard Luke, but he opened his mouth slightly and Luke poured another capful, dribbling in a small amount. Ira swallowed again before mumbling something unintelligible. Then, with a slow rasp, the words separated by breaths: "*Edder . . . Fo . . . I . . . ife . . . Roof . . .*"

Neither Sophia nor Luke could make sense of it. Luke leaned in again.

"I don't understand. Can I call someone for you, Ira? Do you have a wife or kids? Can you tell me a phone number?"

"*Edder . . .*"

"Better?" Luke asked.

"*No . . . Edd . . . edder . . . in . . . car . . . roof . . .*"

Luke turned to Sophia, uncertain. Sophia shook her head, automatically running through the alphabet . . . getter, jetter, letter . . .

Letter?

"I think he's talking about a letter." She bent closer to Ira, could smell illness on his faint breath. "Letter? That's what you meant, right?"

"*Ess . . . ,*" Ira wheezed, his eyes closing again. His breaths rattled like pebbles in a jar. Sophia scanned the interior of the car, her gaze falling on several items strewn on the floor beneath the caved-in dashboard. Clinging to the side of the car, she worked herself around to the rear, making for the other side.

"What are you doing?" Luke called out.

"I want to find his letter..."

The passenger side was less damaged and Sophia was able to pull open the door with relative ease. On the floor lay a thermos and a misshapen sandwich. A small plastic bag filled with prunes. A bottle of water...and there, up in the corner, an envelope. She reached in, her feet sliding before she caught herself. She extended her reach with a grunt, grasping the envelope between two fingers. From across the car, she held it up, noting Luke's incomprehension.

"A letter for his wife," she said, closing the door and making her way back to Luke. "That's what he was saying earlier."

"When he was talking about the roof?"

"Not roof," Sophia said. She turned the envelope around so Luke could read it before sliding it into her jacket pocket. "Ruth."

❦

An officer with the highway patrol was the first to arrive. After scrambling down the slope, he and Luke agreed that it was too risky to move Ira. But it took forever for the EMTs and ambulance to arrive, and even when they did, it was clear that there wasn't a safe way to get him out of the car and up the snowy slope on a stretcher. They would have needed triple the manpower, and even then it would have been a challenge.

In the end, a large tow truck was called, which increased the delay. When it arrived and moved into the proper place, a cable was rolled out and hooked to the car's rear bumper while the EMTs—improvising with the seat belts—secured Ira in place to minimize any jostling. Only then was the car winched slowly up the slope and finally onto the highway.

While Luke answered the officer's questions, Sophia remained near the EMTs, watching while Ira was loaded onto the stretcher and given oxygen before he was rolled into the ambulance.

A few minutes later, Luke and Sophia were alone. He took her in his arms, pulling her close, both of them trying to draw strength from each other, when Sophia suddenly remembered that she still had the letter in her pocket.

Two hours later, they waited in the crowded emergency room of the local hospital, Luke holding Sophia's hand as they sat beside each other. In her other hand, she held the letter, and every now and then she'd study it, noting the shaky scrawl and wondering why she'd given the nurse their names and asked to be updated on Ira's condition, instead of simply handing over the letter to be placed with Ira's belongings.

It would have allowed them to continue the trip back to Winston-Salem, but when she recalled the look on Ira's face and the urgency he obviously felt about finding the letter, Sophia felt compelled to make sure the letter didn't get lost in the hustle and bustle of the hospital. She wanted to hand it to the doctor, or better yet, to Ira himself...

Or that was what she told herself, anyway. All she really knew was that the almost peaceful expression Ira had been wearing when they found him made her wonder what he'd been thinking or dreaming about. It was miraculous that he'd survived his injuries given his age and frail state. Most of all, she wondered why, to this point, no friends or family had come bursting through the doors of the emergency room, frantic with worry. He'd been conscious when they'd wheeled him in, which meant Ira probably could have told them to call someone. So where were they? Why weren't they here yet? At a time like this, Ira needed someone more than ever, and—

Luke shifted in his seat, interrupting her thoughts. "You know that we're probably not going to be able to see him, right?" he asked.

"I know," she said. "But I still want to know how he's doing."

"Why?"

She turned over the letter in her hands, still unable to put the reasons into words. "I don't know."

Another forty minutes passed before a doctor finally emerged from behind the swinging doors. He went first to the desk and then, after the nurse pointed them out, approached them. Luke and Sophia stood.

"I'm Dr. Dillon," he said. "I was told that you've been waiting for a chance to visit Mr. Levinson?"

"Do you mean Ira?" Sophia asked.

"You're the ones who found him, correct?"

"Yes."

"Can I ask what your interest is?"

Sophia almost told the doctor about the letter then but didn't. Luke sensed her confusion and cleared his throat. "I guess we just want to know that he's going to be okay."

"Unfortunately, I can't discuss his condition since you're not family," he said.

"But he's going to be okay, right?"

The doctor looked from one to the other. "By all rights, you shouldn't even be here. You did the right thing by calling the ambulance. And I'm glad you found him when you did, but you don't have any further responsibility. You're strangers."

Sophia looked at the doctor, sensing he had more to say, watching as he finally sighed.

"I don't really know what's going on here," Dr. Dillon said, "but for whatever reason, when Mr. Levinson heard you were here, he asked to see you. I can't tell you anything about his condition, but I must ask that you keep the visit as short as possible."

Ira appeared even smaller than he had in the car, as though he'd shrunk in the last few hours. He lay in the partially reclined hospital bed, his mouth agape, his cheeks hollow, IV lines snaking out of his arm. A machine next to his bed was beeping in rhythm to his heart.

"Not too long," the doctor warned, and Luke nodded before the two of them entered the room. Hesitating, Sophia moved to the side of the bed. From the corner of her eye, she saw Luke pull a chair away from the wall and slide it toward her before stepping back again. Sophia took a seat by the bed and leaned into his field of vision.

"We're here, Ira," she said, holding the letter in front of him. "I have your letter for you."

Ira inhaled with some effort, slowly rolling his head. His eyes went first to the letter and then to her. "Ruth..."

"Yes," she said. "Your letter to Ruth. I'm going to put it right here beside you, okay?"

At her comment, he stared without focus, uncomprehending. Then his face softened, becoming almost sad. He moved his hand slightly, trying to reach hers, and on instinct, she reached over and took it.

"Ruth," he said, tears beginning to form. "My sweet Ruth."

"I'm sorry...I'm not Ruth," she said softly. "My name is Sophia. We're the ones who found you today."

He blinked, then blinked again, his confusion evident.

"Ruth?"

The plea in his tone made her throat tighten.

"No," she said quietly, watching as he moved his hand and inched it toward the letter. She understood what he was doing and slid the letter toward him. He took it, lifting it as though it were an enormous weight, pushing it toward her hand. Only then did she notice Ira's tears. When he spoke, his voice sounded stronger, the words clear for the first time. "Can you be?"

She fingered the letter. "You want me to read this? The letter you wrote to your wife?"

His gaze met her eyes, a tear spilling down his shrunken cheek. "Please, Ruth. I want you to read it."

He exhaled a long breath, as if the effort of speaking had worn him out. Sophia turned toward Luke, wondering what she should do. Luke pointed toward the letter.

"I think you should read it, Ruth," he said to her. "It's what he wants you to do. Read it aloud, so he can hear you." Sophia stared at the letter in her hands. It felt wrong. Ira was confused. It was a personal letter. Ruth was supposed to read this, not her...

"Please," she heard Ira say, as if reading her mind, his voice weakening again.

With trembling hands, Sophia studied the envelope before lifting the seal. The letter was a single page long, written in the same shaky scrawl she'd noticed on the envelope. Though still uncertain, she found herself moving the letter into better light. And with that, she slowly began to read:

My darling Ruth,

It is early, too early, but as always it seems I'm unable to go back to sleep. Outside, the day is breaking in all its newfound glory and yet, all I can think about is the past. In this silent hour, I dream of you and the years we spent together. An anniversary is approaching, dear Ruth, but it is not the one we usually celebrate. It is, however, the one that set in motion my life with you, and I turn to your seat, wanting to remind you of this, even though I understand that you will not be there. God, with a wisdom I can't claim to understand, called you home a long time ago, and the tears I shed that night have never seemed to dry.

Sophia stopped to look at Ira, noting the way his lips had come together, tears still leaking into the crevices and valleys of his face. Though she tried to remain poised, her voice began to crack as she went on.

I miss you this morning, just as I have missed you every day for the last nine years. I'm tired of being alone. I'm tired of living without the sound of your laughter, and I despair at the thought that I can never hold you again. And yet it would please you to know that when these dark thoughts threaten to overtake me, I can hear your voice chiding me: "Do not be so gloomy, Ira. I did not marry a gloomy man."

When I think back, there is so much to remember. We had adventures, yes? These are your words, not mine, for this is how you always described our lives together. You said this to me while lying beside me in bed, you said this to me on Rosh Hashanah, every single year. I always detected a satisfied gleam in your eye whenever you said this, and in those moments, it was your expression, more than your words, that always filled my heart with joy. With you, my life felt indeed like a fantastic adventure—despite our ordinary circumstances, your love imbued everything we did with secret riches. How I was lucky enough to share a life with you, I still cannot understand.

I love you now, just as I have always loved you, and I'm sorry that I'm not able to tell you. And though I write this letter in the hope that you'll somehow be able to read it, I also know that the end of an era approaches. This, my darling, is the last letter I will write you. You know what the doctors have told me, you know that I'm dying, and that I will not visit Black Mountain in August. And yet, I want you to know that I'm not afraid. My time on earth is ending and I'm at peace with whatever comes. I'm not saddened by this. If anything, it fills me with peace, and I count the days with a sense of relief and gratitude. For every day that passes is one day closer to the moment I will see you again.

You are my wife, but more than that, you have always been my one true love. For nearly three-quarters of a century, you have given my existence meaning. It is time now to say good-bye, and on the cusp of this transition I think I understand why you were taken away. It was to show me how special you were and through this long process of grieving, to teach me again the meaning of love. Our separation, I now understand, has only been temporary. When I gaze into the depths of the universe, I know the time is coming when I will hold you in my arms once more. After all, if there is a heaven, we will find each other again, for there is no heaven without you.

I love you,

Ira

Through a blur of tears, Sophia watched Ira's face assume an expression of indescribable peace. Carefully, she reinserted the letter into the envelope. She slid it into his hand and felt him take it back. By then, the doctor was standing at the door and Sophia knew it was time to go. She rose from the chair and Luke returned it to its place against the wall, then slipped his hand into hers. As he turned his head on the pillow, Ira's mouth fell open, and his breathing became labored. Sophia turned to the doctor, who was already on his way to Ira's side. With one last glance back at Ira's frail figure, Sophia and Luke started down the corridor, on their way home at last.

31

Luke

As February passed and gradually wound down, Sophia edged toward graduation, while the ranch inched toward its inevitable foreclosure. Luke's winnings in the first three events had bought his mother and him another month or two before they defaulted, but at the end of the month his mother quietly began to approach their neighbors, exploring their interest in buying her out.

Sophia was beginning to worry concretely about her future. She hadn't heard from either the Denver Art Museum or MoMA yet, and she wondered whether she'd find herself working for her parents and living in her old bedroom. Similarly, Luke was having a hard time sleeping. He worried about his mother's options in the area and wondered how he could help support her until she landed something viable. For the most part, however, neither of them wanted to talk about the future. Instead, they tried to focus on the present, seeking comfort in each other's company and the certainty of the way they felt about each other. By March, Sophia was showing up at the ranch on Friday afternoons and staying until Sunday. Often she spent Wednesday nights there as well. Unless it was raining, they spent most of their time on horseback. Sophia usually assisted Luke with his farm duties, but occasionally she'd keep his mother company instead. It was the kind of life he'd always envisioned for himself . . . and then he'd remember that it was coming to an end and there was nothing he could do to stop it.

❧

One evening in mid-March, when the first hint of spring was noticeable in the air, Luke took Sophia to a club featuring a popular country-western band. Across the scuffed wooden table, he watched her grip her beer, her foot tapping along with the music.

"You keep that up," he said, nodding toward her foot, "and I'll think you like this music."

"I do like this music."

He smiled. "You've heard that joke, right? About what you get when you play country music backwards?"

She took a swallow of her beer. "I don't think so."

"You get your wife back, you get your dog back, you get your truck back..."

She smirked. "That's funny."

"You didn't laugh."

"It wasn't that funny."

That made him laugh. "You and Marcia still getting along?"

Sophia tucked a loose strand of hair behind her ear. "It was kind of awkward at first, but it's almost back to normal."

"Is she still dating Brian?"

She snorted. "No, that ended when she found out he was cheating on her."

"When did this happen?"

"A couple of weeks ago? Maybe a little more?"

"Was she upset?"

"Not really. By then, she was already seeing another guy, too. He's only a junior, so I'm not thinking it's going to last."

Luke picked absently at the label on his bottle of beer. "She's an interesting girl."

"She's got a good heart," Sophia insisted.

"And you're not mad about what she did?"

"I was. But I'm over it."

"Just like that?"

"She made a mistake. She didn't mean to hurt me. She's apologized a million times. And she came through when I needed her. So yes, just like that. I'm over it."

"Do you think you'll keep in contact with her? After you graduate?"

"Of course. She's still my best friend. And you should like her, too."

"Why's that?" He cocked an eyebrow.

"Because without her," she said, "I never would have met you."

A few days later, Luke accompanied his mom to the bank to propose a renegotiated payment plan that would allow them to keep the ranch. His mom presented a business plan that included selling nearly half the ranch, including the Christmas tree grove, the pumpkin patch, and one of the pastures, assuming a buyer could be found. They'd decrease the herd by a third, but according to her calculations, they'd be able to meet the reduced payments on the loan.

Three days later, the bank formally rejected the offer.

One Friday night at the end of the month, Sophia showed up at the ranch, visibly upset. Her eyes were red and swollen and her shoulders slumped in despair. Luke put his arms around her as soon as she reached the porch.

"What's wrong?"

He heard her sniff, and when she spoke, her voice shook. "I couldn't wait any longer," she said. "So I called the Denver Art Museum and I asked if they'd had a chance to review my application. They said that they had and that the internship had already been filled. And the exact same thing happened when I called MoMA."

"I'm sorry," he said, rocking her in his arms. "I know how much you were hoping for one of them."

Finally, she pulled back, anxiety etched on her face. "What am I going to do? I don't want to go back to my parents. I don't want to work at the deli again."

He was about to tell her that she could stay here with him for as long as she wanted, when he suddenly remembered that wasn't going to be possible, either.

In early April, Luke watched his mom give a tour of the property to three men. He recognized one of them as a rancher near Durham. They'd talked once or twice at cattle auctions and Luke didn't have any sense of the man, though it was obvious even from a distance that his mom didn't much care for him. Whether it was a personal dislike or the fact that the loss of the ranch was getting closer to reality, Luke couldn't tell. The other two, he suspected, were either relatives or business partners.

That night over dinner, his mom said nothing about it. And he didn't ask.

Although Luke had ridden in only three of the first seven events of the year, he'd earned enough points to find himself in fifth place by the cutoff date—enough to qualify him for the major league tour. The following weekend, in Chicago, there was an event with enough prize money at stake to keep the ranch afloat until the end of the year, assuming he rode as well as he had at the start of the season.

Instead, he kept his word to both Sophia and his mom. The mechanical bull in the barn stayed covered, and another rider went on to the big tour in his place, no doubt dreaming of winning it all.

"Any regrets?" Sophia asked him. "About not riding this weekend?"

On a whim, they'd driven to Atlantic Beach beneath a blue and cloudless sky. At the shore, the breeze was cool but not biting, and the beach was peppered with people walking or flying kites; a few intrepid surfers were riding the long, rolling waves to shore.

"None," he said without hesitation.

They walked a few steps, Luke's feet slipping in the sand.

"I'll bet you would have done okay."

"Probably."

"Do you think you could have won?"

Luke thought for a moment before answering, his eyes fixed on a pair of porpoises gliding through the water.

"Maybe," he said. "But probably not. There are some pretty talented riders on the circuit."

Sophia came to a stop and looked up at Luke. "I just realized something."

"What's that?"

"When you were riding in South Carolina? You said you'd drawn Big Ugly Critter in the finals."

He nodded.

"You never told me what happened."

"No," he said, still watching the porpoises. "I guess I didn't, did I?"

A week later, the three men who'd toured the ranch returned, then spent half an hour in his mom's kitchen. Luke suspected they were presenting an offer of some sort, but he didn't have the heart to go over and find out. Instead, he waited until they were gone. He found his mom still sitting at the kitchen table when he entered.

She looked up at him without saying anything.

Then she simply shook her head.

❧

"What are you doing next Friday?" Sophia asked. "Not tomorrow, but the one after that?" It was a Thursday night, just a month shy of graduation, the first—and probably last—time Luke would find himself at a club surrounded by a gaggle of sorority girls. Marcia was there, too, and though she'd greeted Luke, she was far more interested in the dark-haired boy who'd met them there. He and Sophia practically had to shout to be heard over the relentless bass of the music.

"I don't know. Working, I guess," he said. "Why?"

"Because the department chair, who also happens to be my adviser, snagged me invitations to an art auction and I want you to come."

He leaned over the table. "Did you say art auction?"

"It's supposed to be incredible, a once-in-a-lifetime thing. It'll be held at the Greensboro Convention Center and it's being run by one of the big auction houses from New York. Supposedly, some obscure guy from North Carolina accumulated a world-class collection of modern art. People are flying in from all over the world to bid. Some of the artwork is supposed to be worth a fortune."

"And you want to go?"

"Hello? It's art? Do you know the last time an auction of this caliber occurred around here? Never."

"How long's it going to last?"

"I have no idea. I've never been to an auction before, but just so you know, I'm going. And it would be nice if you came along. Otherwise, I'm going to have to sit with my adviser, and I know for a fact that he's bringing along another professor from the department, which means they'll spend the whole time talking to each other. And let's just say if that happens, I'll probably be in a bad mood and might have to stay at the sorority house all weekend just to recover."

"If I didn't know you better, I'd say you were threatening me."

"It's not a threat. It's just...something to keep in mind."

"And if I keep it in mind and still say no?"

"Then you're going to be in trouble, too."

He smiled. "If it's important to you, I wouldn't miss it for the world."

Luke wasn't sure why he hadn't noticed before, but it struck him at some point that getting started on the day's work had become more and more difficult as time passed. The maintenance work on the ranch had begun to suffer, not because it wasn't important, he realized, but because he had little motivation. Why replace the sagging porch railings at his mom's place? Why fill in the sinkhole that had formed near the irrigation pump? Why fill in the potholes in the long gravel drive that had grown deeper over the winter? Why do anything when they weren't going to be living here much longer?

He'd supposed that his mom had been immune to those sorts of feelings, that she had a strength he hadn't inherited, but as he'd ridden out to check the cattle that morning, something about his mom's property had caught his attention, and he had pulled Horse to a stop.

His mother's garden had always been a source of pride to her. Even as a toddler, he could remember watching as she readied it for the spring planting or weeded it with painstaking care during the summer, harvesting the vegetables at the end of a long day. But now, as he looked out at what should have been straight, neat rows, he realized that the plot was overrun by weeds.

"Okay, so about this Friday." Sophia rolled over in bed to face him. "Keep in mind that it's an art auction." It was only two days away, and he tried to come across as properly attentive.

"Yes. You told me."

"Lots of rich people there. Important people."

"Okay."

"I just wanted to make sure you weren't planning to wear your hat and boots."

"I figured."

"You're going to need a suit."

"I have a suit," he said. "A nice one, in fact."

"You have a suit?" Her eyebrows shot up.

"Why do you so sound so surprised?"

"Because I can't imagine you in a suit. I've only ever seen you in jeans."

"Not true." He winked. "I'm not wearing any jeans now."

"Get your mind out of the gutter," she said, not wanting even to acknowledge his comment. "That's not what I'm talking about and you know it."

He laughed. "I bought a suit two years ago. And a tie and a shirt and shoes, if you must know. I had to go to a wedding."

"And let me guess. That's the only time you've ever worn it, right?"

"No," he said, shaking his head. "I wore it again."

"Another wedding?" she asked.

"A funeral," he said. "A friend of my mom's."

"That was my second guess," she said, hopping out of bed. She grabbed the throw blanket, wound it around herself, and tucked in the corner like a towel. "I want to see it. Is it in your closet?"

"Hanging on the right..." He pointed, admiring her shape in the makeshift toga.

She opened the closet door and pulled out the hanger, taking a moment to inspect it. "You're right," she said. "It's a nice suit."

"There you go, sounding all surprised again."

Still holding the suit, she looked over at him. "Wouldn't you be?"

In the morning, Sophia returned to campus while Luke rode off to inspect the herd. They'd made plans for him to pick her up the following day. To his surprise, he found her sitting on his porch when he got home later that afternoon.

She was clutching a newspaper, and when she faced him, there was something haunted in her expression.

"What's wrong?" he asked.

"It about Ira," she said. "Ira Levinson."

It took a second for the name to come back to him. "You mean the guy we rescued from his car?"

She held out the newspaper. "Read this."

He took the paper from her and scanned the headline, which described the auction that was to take place the next day.

Luke furrowed his brow, puzzled.

"This is an article about the auction."

"The collection is Ira's," she said.

It was all there in the article. Or a lot of it was, anyway. There were fewer personal details than he would have expected, but he learned a bit about Ira's shop, and the article noted the date of his marriage to Ruth. It mentioned that Ruth had been a school-teacher and that they'd begun to collect modern art together after the end of World War II. They'd never had children.

The remainder of the article concerned the auction and the pieces that were going to be offered, most of which meant nothing to Luke. It concluded, however, with a line that gave him pause, affecting him the same way it had Sophia.

Sophia brought her lips together as he reached the end of the article.

"He never made it out of the hospital," she said, her voice soft. "He died from his injuries the day after we found him."

Luke raised his eyes to the sky, closing them for a moment. There was nothing really to say.

"We were the last people to see him," she said. "It doesn't say that, but I know it's true. His wife was dead, they had no kids, and he'd pretty much become a hermit. He died alone, and the thought of that just breaks my heart. Because..."

When she trailed off, Luke drew her near, thinking about the letter Ira had written to his wife.

"I know why," Luke said. "Because it kind of breaks my heart, too."

32

Sophia

Sophia had just finished putting in her earrings on the day of the auction when she saw Luke's truck come to a stop in front of the house. Though she'd teased Luke earlier about having only a single suit, in truth she owned only two, both with midlength skirts and matching jackets. And she'd purchased those only because she'd needed something classy and professional to wear to interviews. At the time, she'd worried that two wouldn't suffice, what with all the interviews she'd no doubt line up. Which made her think about that old saying...how did it go? People plan, God laughs, or something like that?

As it was, she'd worn each of them once. Knowing that Luke's suit was dark, she'd opted for the lighter of the two. Despite her early enthusiasm, she now felt strangely ambivalent about going to the auction. Discovering that it was Ira's collection made it more personal somehow, and she feared that with every painting, she'd recall how he'd appeared as she'd read his letter in the hospital. Yet to not go seemed disrespectful, since the collection obviously meant so much to him and his wife. Still feeling conflicted, she left her room and went downstairs.

Luke was waiting just inside the foyer.

"Are you ready for this?"

"I guess," she temporized. "It's different now."

"I know. I thought about Ira most of the night."

"Me too."

He forced a smile, though there wasn't a lot of energy behind it. "You look terrific, by the way. You're all grown up."

"You too," she said, meaning it. *But . . .*

"Why do I feel like we're going to a funeral?" she asked him.

"Because," he said, "in a way, we are."

They entered one of the enormous exhibition rooms at the convention center an hour before noon. It was nothing like she'd expected. At the far end of the room was a stage, surrounded by curtains on three sides; on the right were two long tables on elevated daises, each bearing ten telephones; on the other side stood the podium, no doubt for the auctioneer. A large screen formed the backdrop on the stage, and at the very front stood an empty easel. Approximately three hundred chairs faced the stage in stadium formation, allowing the bidders an unobstructed view.

Though the room was crowded, only a few of the seats were taken. Instead, most of the people wandered the room, examining photographs of some of the most valuable art. The photographs stood on easels along the walls, together with information about the artist, prices of the artist's work achieved in other auctions, along with estimated values. Other visitors clustered around the four podiums on either side of the entrance, piled high with catalogs that described the entire collection.

Sophia moved through the room, Luke by her side, feeling slightly stunned. Not just because this was once all Ira's, but because of the collection itself. There were works by Picasso and Warhol, Johns and Pollock, Rauschenberg and de Kooning, exhibited side by side. Some were pieces that she'd never read or even heard about. Nor had the rumors of their value been exaggerated; she gasped at some of the estimates, only to discover that the next set of paintings was worth even more. Through it all, she found herself trying to reconcile those numbers with Ira, the sweet old man who'd written about nothing but the love he still felt for his wife.

Luke's thoughts seemed to mirror her own, for he reached for her hand and murmured, "There was nothing in his letter about this."

"Maybe none of this mattered to him," she said, baffled. "But really, how could it not?" When Luke failed to answer, she squeezed his hand. "I wish we could have helped him more."

"I don't know that there was any more that we could have done."

"Still…"

His blue eyes searched hers. "You read the letter," he said. "That's what he wanted. And I think that's why you and I were meant to find him. Who else would have waited around?"

When the announcement was made for people to take their seats, Luke and Sophia found a couple of empty ones in the back row. From there, it was almost impossible to see the easel, which disappointed Sophia. It would have been great to be able to see some of the paintings up close, but she knew those seats should go to prospective buyers, and the last thing she wanted was for someone to tap her on the shoulder and ask her to move later. A few minutes after that, men and women in suits began to take their seats behind the phones on the elevated tables, and slowly but surely, the overhead lights began to dim as a series of spotlights beamed down to illuminate the stage.

Sophia scanned the crowd, spotting her two art history professors, including her adviser. As the clock approached one, the room slowly grew quieter, the hushed murmur gradually fading out completely when a silver-haired gentleman in an exquisitely tailored suit strolled to the podium. In his hands, he held a folder and he spread it wide before reaching into his breast pocket for his reading glasses. He propped them on his nose, adjusting the pages as he did so.

"Ladies and gentlemen, I'd like to thank all of you for coming to the auction of the extraordinary collection of Ira and Ruth Levinson. As you know, it's unusual for our firm to host such an event in venues other than our own, but in this case, Mr. Levinson didn't leave us much choice. It's also rather unorthodox for the particulars of today's auction to have remained somewhat vague. To begin, I'd like to explain the rules regarding this particular auction. Beneath each of the seats is a numbered paddle, and..."

He went on to describe the bidding process, but with her thoughts drifting to Ira again, Sophia tuned it out. Only vaguely did she hear the list of those who'd chosen to attend the auction—curators from the Whitney and MoMA, the Tate, and countless others from cities overseas. She guessed that most of the people in the room were representatives of either private collectors or galleries, no doubt hoping to acquire something extremely rare.

After the rules were outlined and certain individuals and institutions thanked, the silver-haired gentleman focused the attention of the audience again. "At this time, it is my pleasure to introduce to you Howie Sanders. Mr. Sanders served as Ira Levinson's attorney for many years, and has prepared some remarks he'd like to share with you as well."

Sanders appeared then, a bent, elderly figure whose dark wool suit hung off his bony frame. Slowly, he made his way to the podium. There, he cleared his throat before launching into his speech in a voice that was remarkably vigorous and clear.

"We're gathered here today to participate in an extraordinary event. After all, it is very unusual for a collection of this size and significance to go unnoticed and unremarked upon for so many years. Until six years ago, I suspect that very few in this room even knew of the existence of this collection. The circumstances of its creation—the how, so to speak—were described in a magazine article, and yet I admit that even I, the man who served as Ira Levinson's attorney for the past forty years, have been astounded by the cultural importance and value of this collection."

He paused to look up at the audience before going on. "But that is not why I'm here. I'm here because Ira was explicit in his instructions regarding this auction, and he asked me to say a few words to all of you. I confess that this is something I would rather not have been asked to do. Though I am comfortable in a court-room or in the confines of my office, I am rarely required to face an audience of this nature, where many of you have been charged with the responsibility of securing a specific piece of art for a cli-ent or an institution at a price that even I have difficulty compre-hending. And yet, because my friend Ira asked me to speak, I now find myself in this unenviable position."

A few good-natured chuckles were audible from the audience.

"What can I tell you about Ira? That he was a good man? An honest, conscientious man? That he was a man who adored his wife? Or should I tell you about his business, or the quiet wis-dom he exuded whenever we were together? I asked myself all these questions in an effort to discern what it was that Ira really wanted me to say to all of you. What would he have said if he, not I, had been standing before you? Ira, I think, would have said this to you: 'I want all of you to understand.'"

He let the comment hang, making sure he had their attention.

"There is a wonderful quote I came across," he went on. "It's attributed to Pablo Picasso, and as most of you probably realize, he's the only non-American artist whose work will be featured in today's auction. Years ago, Picasso was quoted as saying, 'We all know that art is not truth. Art is a lie that makes us realize truth, at least the truth that is given us to understand.'"

He faced the audience again, his voice softening.

"Art is a lie that makes us realize truth, at least the truth that is given us to understand," he repeated. "I want you to think about that." He scanned the auditorium, searching the faces of the hushed audience. "I find that statement profound on a number of levels. Obviously, it speaks to the way in which you might view the art that you will examine here today. Upon reflection, however, I began to wonder whether Picasso was speaking simply about art, or whether he wanted us to view our own lives through that prism as well. What was Picasso suggesting? To me, he was saying that our reality is shaped by our perceptions. That something is good or bad only because we—you and I—believe it to be so, based on our own experiences. And yet, Picasso is also saying that it's a lie. *In other words, our opinions and our thoughts and feelings—anything we experience—need not define us forever.* I realize that to some of you, it may seem that I've strayed into a speech about moral relativism, while the rest of you probably think I'm just an old man who's gone completely off the rails here..."

Again, the audience laughed.

"But I'm here to tell you that Ira would have been pleased by my selection of this quote. Ira believed in good and evil, right and wrong, love and hate. He'd grown up in a world, in a time, where destruction and hate were evident on a worldwide scale. And yet, Ira never let it define him or the man he strove daily to be. Today, I want you to view this auction as a memorial of sorts to all that he found important. But most of all, I hope you understand."

🌿

Sophia wasn't quite sure what to make of Sanders's speech, and glancing around, she wasn't sure that anyone else was, either. While he spoke, she'd noticed a number of people texting on their phones while others studied the catalog.

There was a short break then as the silver-haired gentleman conferred with Sanders before the auctioneer returned to the podium. Again he put on his reading glasses and cleared his throat.

"As most of you are aware, the auction has been scheduled in phases, the first of which will be happening today. At this point, we have not determined either the number or timing of the subsequent phases, as those will no doubt be affected by the progress today. And now, I know that many of you have been waiting for the parameters of the auction itself."

Almost as one, the crowd began to lean forward in attention.

"The parameters, again, were set by the client. The auction agreement was quite specific in a number of...unusual details... including the order in which the pieces would be offered today. Per the instructions that all of you received in advance, we will now adjourn for thirty minutes to allow you to discuss the order with your clients. As a reminder, the list of paintings that are definitively being offered today can be found on pages thirty-four through ninety-six of the catalog. They are also represented in the photographs along the walls. In addition, the auction order will be listed on the screen."

People rose from their seats, reaching for phones; others began to confer. Luke leaned over to whisper in Sophia's ear.

"Do you mean that no one here knew the order of the works? What if the one they wanted didn't come up for sale until the end? They could be here for hours."

"For such an extraordinary opportunity, they'd probably wait until the end of time."

He motioned toward the easels lining the wall. "So which one do you want? Because I have a few hundred dollars in my wallet and a numbered paddle beneath my seat here. The Picasso? The Jackson Pollock? One of the Warhols?"

"I wish."

"Do you think that the sale prices will approach the estimates?"

"I have no idea, but I'm pretty sure the auction house has a good handle on that. It'll probably be close."

"A few of those paintings are worth more than twenty of my ranches."

"I know, right?"

"That's crazy."

"Maybe," she admitted.

He swiveled his head, taking in the scene. "I wonder what Ira would think about all this."

She recalled the old man she'd met in the hospital, and the letter, which never mentioned the art at all. "I wonder," she said, "whether he would even care."

❧

When the break was over and everyone was back in their seats, the silver-haired gentleman stepped toward the podium. In that instant, two men gingerly carried a covered painting to the easel on the stage. While Sophia expected a palpable buzz of interest now that the auction was getting under way, she realized when surveying the room that only a few people seemed to care. Again, she saw them tapping away on their phones while the speaker prepared his introduction. She knew that the first major work, one of the de Koonings, was scheduled to go second and that the Jasper Johns was scheduled to go sixth. In between were artists Sophia had a harder time identifying, and this was no doubt one of them.

"First up is a painting that can be found on page thirty-four of the catalog. It is oil on canvas, twenty-four by thirty inches, that Levinson, not the artist, called *Portrait of Ruth*. Ruth, as most of you are aware, was Ira Levinson's wife."

Both Sophia and Luke snapped to attention, focusing on the easel as the painting was unveiled. Behind it, magnified, was the painting projected on-screen. Even with her untrained eye, Sophia could tell it had been painted by a child.

"It was composed by an American, Daniel McCallum, born 1953, died 1986. Exact date of the painting is unknown, though it is estimated to date anywhere from 1965 to 1967. According to Ira Levinson's description of the item, Daniel was a former student of Ruth's, and it had been gifted to Mr. Levinson by McCallum's widow in 2002."

As it was described, Sophia stood to get a better view. Even from a distance, she knew it was the work of an amateur, but after reading the letter, she'd found herself wondering what Ruth had looked like. Despite the crudeness of the rendering, Ruth still appeared to be beautiful, with a tenderness of expression that reminded her of Ira. The speaker went on.

"There is little else known about the artist, and he is not known to have created additional pieces. For those who did not make arrangements to view the piece yesterday, you are allowed at this time to approach the stage to study the painting. Bidding will commence in five minutes."

No one moved, and Sophia knew that no one would. Instead, she could hear the rise of conversation, some people chatting while others quietly suppressed the nerves they were feeling at the next item up for bid. When the real auction would start.

The five minutes passed slowly. The man at the podium showed no surprise. Instead, he thumbed through the papers in front of him, seemingly no more interested than anyone else. Even Luke seemed disengaged, which surprised her, considering that he, too, had heard Ira's letter.

When the time was up, the speaker called for silence. "*Portrait of Ruth* by Daniel McCallum. We will commence the bidding at one thousand dollars," he said. "One thousand. Do I hear one thousand?"

No one in the audience moved. At the podium, the silver-haired man registered no reaction. "Do I hear nine hundred? Please note that this is a chance to own part of one of the greatest private collections ever assembled."

Nothing.

"Do I hear eight hundred?"

Then, after a few beats: "Do I hear seven hundred?..."

"Six hundred?"

With every drop, Sophia felt something slowly begin to give

way inside her. Somehow, it wasn't right. She thought again of the letter Ira had written to Ruth, the letter that told her how much she'd meant to him.

"Do I hear five hundred dollars?..."

"Four hundred?"

And in that instant, from the corner of her eye, she saw Luke raise his paddle. "Four hundred dollars," he called out, and the sound of his voice seemed to ricochet off the walls. Although a few people in the audience turned, they appeared only mildly curious.

"We have four hundred dollars. Four hundred. Do I hear four hundred and fifty?"

Again, the room remained silent. Sophia felt suddenly dizzy.

"Going once, going twice, and sold..."

Luke was approached by an attractive brunette holding a clipboard, who requested his information before explaining that it was also time to settle. She asked for his banking information or the form he had filled out earlier.

"I didn't fill out any forms," Luke demurred.

"How do you wish to settle?"

"Would you take cash?"

The woman smiled. "That will be fine, sir. Please follow me."

Luke walked off with the woman and returned a few minutes later, holding his receipt. He took a seat beside Sophia, a sly grin on his face.

"Why?" she asked.

"I'd be willing to bet that this painting was the one that Ira liked best of all." He shrugged. "It was the first one up for sale. And besides, he loved his wife and it was a portrait of her and it didn't seem right that no one wanted it."

She considered that. "If I didn't know you better, I'd think you were becoming a romantic."

"I think," he said slowly, "that Ira was the romantic. I'm just a washed-up bull rider."

"You're more than that," she said, nudging him. "Where are you going to hang it?"

"I don't know that it really matters, do you? Besides, I don't even know where I'll be living in a few months."

Before she could respond, she heard a gavel come down before the speaker leaned in to the microphone again.

"Ladies and gentlemen—at this time and before we go on, per the parameters of the auction, I'd like to reintroduce Howie Sanders, who wishes to read a letter from Ira Levinson, in Ira's own words, regarding the purchase of this item."

Sanders emerged from behind the curtain, shuffling in his oversize suit, an envelope in his hand. The silver-haired gentleman stepped aside to make room at the microphone.

Sanders used a letter opener to slit open the top before pulling out the letter. He took a deep breath and then slowly unfolded it. He scanned the room and took a sip of water. He turned serious then, like an actor readying himself for a particularly dramatic scene, before finally beginning to read.

"My name is Ira Levinson, and today, you will hear my love story. It isn't the kind you might imagine. It's not a story with heroes and villains, it is not a story of handsome princes or princesses yet to be. Instead, it's a story about a simple man named Ira who met an extraordinary woman named Ruth. We met when we were young and fell in love; in time we married and made a life together. A story like so many others, except Ruth happened to have an eye for art while I had eyes only for her, and somehow this was enough for us to create a collection that became priceless to both of us. For Ruth, the art was about beauty and talent; for me, the art was simply a reflection of Ruth, and in this fashion, we filled our house and lived a long and happy life with each other. And then, all too soon, it was over and I found myself alone in a world that no longer made any sense."

Sanders stopped to wipe his tears, and to Sophia's surprise, she heard his voice begin to crack. He cleared his throat and Sophia leaned forward, suddenly interested in what Sanders was saying.

"This wasn't fair to me. Without Ruth, I had no reason to go on. And then, something miraculous happened. A portrait of my wife arrived, an unexpected gift, and when I hung it on my wall, I had the strange sense that Ruth was watching over me once more. Helping me. Guiding me. And little by little, the memories of my life with her were restored, memories that were tied to every piece in our collection. To me, these memories have always been more valuable than the art. It isn't possible for me to give those away, and yet—if the art was hers and the memories were mine—what was I supposed to do with the collection? I understood this dilemma but the law did not, and for a long time, I didn't know what to do. Without Ruth, after all, I was nothing. I loved her from the moment I met her, and even though I'm gone, you must know that I loved her with the final breath I took. More than anything, I want you to understand this simple truth: Though the art is beautiful and valuable almost beyond measure, I would have traded it all for just one more day with the wife I always adored."

Sanders studied the crowd. In their seats, everyone had gone still.

Something was happening, something out of the ordinary. Sanders seemed to realize this as well, and perhaps in anticipation, he seemed to choke up. He brought a forefinger to his lips before going on.

"*Just one more day,*" Sanders said again, letting the words hang before going on. "But how can I make all of you believe that I would have done such a thing? How can I convince you that I cared nothing about the commercial value of the art? How can I prove to you how special Ruth really was to me? How will you never forget that my love for her was at the heart of every piece we ever purchased?"

Sanders glanced at the vaulted ceiling, before coming back to all of them.

"Will the individual who purchased *Portrait of Ruth* please stand?"

By then, Sophia could barely breathe. Her heart was pounding as Luke rose to his feet. She felt the attention of the entire audience on him.

"The terms of my will—and the auction—are simple: I have decided that whoever bought the *Portrait of Ruth* would receive the art collection in its entirety, effective immediately. And because it is no longer mine to offer, the rest of the auction is hereby canceled."

33

Luke

Luke couldn't move. As he stood in the back row, he sensed a stunned silence in the room. It took several seconds for Ira's words to register, not only for Luke, but for everyone present.

Sanders couldn't have been serious. Or if he had been serious, then Luke had misunderstood him. Because what it sounded like to Luke was that he'd just acquired the entire collection. But that wasn't possible. It couldn't be possible. Could it?

His thoughts seemed mirrored by the audience itself. He saw baffled expressions and frowns of incomprehension, people throwing up their hands, faces showing shock and confusion, maybe even betrayal.

And then, after that: pandemonium. It wasn't the chair-throwing variety of riot witnessed so often at sporting events, but the controlled rage of the entitled and self-important. A man in the third row in the center section stood and threatened to call his attorney; another cried that he'd been brought here under false pretenses and would be calling his attorney as well. Still another insisted that fraud had been committed.

The outrage and anger in the room began to rise, first slowly and then explosively. More people rose to their feet and began shouting at Sanders; another group focused their attention on the silver-haired gentleman. On the far side of the room, one of the easels crashed to the ground, the result of someone storming from the room.

And then, all at once, faces began to turn to Luke. He felt the mob's anger and disappointment and betrayal. But he also sensed in some of them a pointed suspicion. In still others, there glinted the light of opportunity. An attractive blonde in a form-fitting business suit edged closer, and then all at once, seats were pushed aside as throngs of people began to rush toward Luke, everyone calling out at once.

"Excuse me . . ."

"Can we talk?"

"I'd like to schedule a meeting with you . . ."

"What are you going to do with the Warhol?"

"My client is particularly interested in one of the Rauschenbergs . . ."

Instinctively, Luke grabbed Sophia's hand and pushed back his chair, making room for their escape. An instant later, they were dashing toward the door, the audience in pursuit.

He pushed open the doors, only to find six security guards standing behind two women and a man wearing badges of the sponsoring auction house. One of them was the same attractive woman who had taken his information and almost all the cash he'd had in his wallet.

"Mr. Collins?" she asked. "My name is Gabrielle and I work for the auction house. We have a private room for you upstairs. We anticipated that it might get a little hectic, so we made special arrangements for your comfort and security. Would you please follow me?"

"I was thinking of just heading to my truck . . ."

"There's some additional paperwork, as you can probably imagine. Please. If you wouldn't mind?" She gestured toward the hallway.

Luke looked back at the approaching crowd. "Let's go," he decided.

Still clutching Sophia's hand, he turned and followed Gabrielle, flanked by three of the guards. Luke realized that the others had remained behind to keep the audience from following them. He could vaguely hear them shouting at him, bombarding him with questions.

He had the surreal impression that someone was playing a practical joke on him, though to what end, he had no idea. It was crazy. All of this was crazy...

Their group turned the corner and headed through a door leading to the staircase. When Luke turned to peek over his shoulder, he realized that only two of the guards remained with them; the other stayed behind to guard the door.

On the second floor, he and Sophia were led to a set of wood-paneled doors, which Gabrielle opened for them.

"Please," she said, ushering them into a spacious suite of rooms, "make yourselves comfortable. We have refreshments and food inside, along with the catalog. I'm sure you have a thousand questions and I can assure you that they will all be answered."

"What's going on?" Luke asked.

She raised an eyebrow. "I think you already know," she said, without directly answering the question. She turned toward Sophia and offered her hand. "I'm afraid I didn't catch your name."

"Sophia," she said. "Sophia Danko."

Gabrielle tilted her head. "Slovakian, yes? A beautiful country. It's a pleasure to meet you." Then, turning to Luke again: "The guards will be posted outside the room, so you don't have to worry about anyone disturbing you. For now, I'm sure you have a lot to think about and discuss. We'll leave you alone for a few minutes to review your collection. Would that be all right?"

"I guess," Luke said, his mind still spinning. "But—"

"Mr. Lehman and Mr. Sanders will be in shortly."

Luke lifted an eyebrow at Sophia before surveying the well-appointed room. Couches and chairs surrounded a low, round table. On the table stood an assortment of drinks, including a bucket of champagne on ice, a platter of sandwiches, and a sliced fruit and cheese selection on a crystal dish.

Next to the table lay the catalog, opened to a particular page.

Behind them, the door closed and Luke found himself alone with Sophia. She glanced at him, then cautiously approached the table and studied the open catalog page.

"It's Ruth," she said, touching the page. He watched as she ran her finger lightly over the photograph.

"This can't really be happening, can it?"

She continued to stare at the photograph before turning toward him with a dazed and beatific smile. "Yes," she said, "I think it's really happening."

❧

Gabrielle returned with Mr. Sanders and Mr. Lehman, whom Luke recognized as the silver-haired gentleman who'd presided over the auction.

After Sanders introduced himself, he took a seat in the chair and blew his nose in a linen handkerchief. Up close, Luke noticed the wrinkles and bushy white eyebrows; he suspected the man was somewhere in his mid-seventies. Yet a hint of mischief underlay his expression, making him seem younger.

"Before we begin, let me address the first and most obvious question that I'm sure you've been pondering," Sanders began, resting his hands on his knees. "You're probably wondering, Is there a catch? Did you, by purchasing the *Portrait of Ruth*, indeed inherit the entire collection? Am I correct?"

"That's pretty much it," Luke admitted. Ever since the commotion in the auditorium, he'd felt utterly at sea. This setting... these people... nothing could have felt more foreign to him.

"The answer to your question is yes," Sanders said in a kindly voice. "According to the terms of Ira Levinson's will, the purchaser of that particular piece, *Portrait of Ruth*, was to receive the entire collection. That is why it was offered for sale first. In other words, there is no catch. There are no strings attached. The collection is now yours to do with as you wish."

"So I could ask you to just load it up in the back of my truck and I could bring it all back to my house? Right now?"

"Yes," Sanders answered. "Though considering the size of the collection, it would likely take a number of trips. And given the value of some of the artwork, I would recommend a safer mode of transportation."

Luke stared at him, dumbfounded.

"There is, however, an issue which you will have to consider."

Here it comes, Luke thought.

"It concerns estate taxes," Sanders said. "As you may or may not be aware, any bequest in excess of a certain amount is subject to taxation by the United States government, or the IRS. The value of the collection is far in excess of that amount, which means that you now have substantial tax obligations that you will have to meet. Unless you're worth a fortune—and a large fortune at that—with substantial liquid assets to cover these taxes, you will most likely have to sell a portion of the collection to meet them. Perhaps even half of the collection. It depends, of course, on which pieces you choose to sell. Do you understand what I'm saying?"

"I think so. I inherited a lot and I've got to pay taxes on it."

"Exactly. So, before we go any further, I'd like to ask whether you have an estate attorney with whom you prefer to deal. If not, I am happy to make recommendations."

"I don't have anyone."

Sanders nodded. "I suspected you didn't—you're rather young. That's fine, of course." He dug in his pocket for a business card. "If you call my office on Monday morning, I will provide a list. You are not required, of course, to use any of the names I suggest."

Luke inspected the card. "It says here that you're an estate attorney."

"I am. In the past, I served in other areas, but estate work suits me these days."

"Then could I hire you?"

"If you wish," he said. He motioned toward the others in the room. "You've already met Gabrielle. She's a vice president of client relationships at the auction house. I also wanted you to meet David Lehman. He's the president of the auction house."

Luke shook his hand and exchanged pleasantries before Sanders went on.

"As you can probably imagine, arranging the auction in this manner was...challenging in many respects, including a financial one. Mr. Lehman's auction house is the one that Ira Levinson preferred. While you are not obligated to use them in the future, as Ira and I were working out the details, he asked me to request that the purchaser strongly consider his preexisting relationship with them. They are considered one of the top auction houses in the world, which I think your own research will bear out."

Luke searched the faces surrounding them, reality slowly sinking in. "Okay," he said. "But I couldn't make that kind of decision without talking to my attorney."

"I think that's a wise decision," Sanders said. "Though we're here to answer any questions, I would recommend you retain an attorney sooner rather than later. You will benefit from a professional to guide you through what will likely be a rather complicated process, not just concerning the estate, but other areas of your life as well. After all, you are now, even after you pay the taxes, an incredibly wealthy man. So please, ask any questions you wish."

Luke met Sophia's eyes, then turned back to Sanders.

"How long were you Ira's attorney?"

"Over forty years," he answered with a trace of wistfulness.

"And if I hire an attorney, that attorney would represent me to the best of his or her ability?"

"Since you are their client, they would be obligated to."

"So maybe," Luke said, "we should just get that out of the way right now. How do I hire you? In case I want to talk to Mr. Lehman here?"

"You'd need to provide me with a retainer."

"How much would that be?" Luke wrinkled his brow in concern.

"For now," Sanders said, "I think a single dollar would be sufficient."

Luke drew a long breath, finally coming to terms with the enormity of it all. The wealth. The ranch. The life he could create with Sophia.

With that, Luke pulled out his wallet and inspected its contents. There wasn't much left after purchasing the portrait, just enough to buy a couple of gallons of gasoline.

Or maybe less, since he used part of it to retain Howie Sanders.

Epilogue

———— 🍂 ————

In the months that followed the auction, Luke sometimes felt himself to be acting out a part in a fantasy that someone else had scripted for him. On David Lehman's recommendation, another auction had been scheduled for mid-June, this time in New York. Yet another had been scheduled for mid-July, and another in September. The sales would include the majority of the collection, more than enough to cover any taxes that were due.

On that first day, with Gabrielle and David Lehman in the room, Luke also explained the situation with the ranch, watching as Sanders took notes. When Luke asked if there was any way he could access the money he needed to pay off the mortgage, Sanders excused himself from the room, only to return fifteen minutes later, where he calmly explained to Luke that the senior vice president of the bank with whom he had spoken was open to extending the lower payments for another year and perhaps even deferring the interest payments entirely for the time being, if that was Luke's preference. And in light of Luke's newly affluent circumstances, the bank would consider extending a line of credit for any improvements he wanted to make as well.

All Luke could do was choke out a couple of words. "But…how?"

Sanders smiled, that glint of mischief surfacing again in his eyes. "Let's just say that they would like to strengthen their relationship with a loyal customer who has suddenly come into means."

Sanders also introduced him to a number of money managers and other advisers, sitting next to him during the interviews, asking questions that Luke barely understood, much less thought to ask. He helped Luke begin to grasp the complexities that went along with wealth, reassuring him that he would be there to assist him in all that he would need to learn.

Despite how overwhelmed he sometimes felt, Luke was the first to admit there were far worse problems to have.

Initially, his mom didn't believe him, nor would she believe Sophia. First she scoffed, then after he reiterated what had happened, she grew angry. It wasn't until he called their local bank and asked for the senior vice president that she began to accept that he might not be kidding.

He put her on the phone with the bank officer, who reassured her that she needn't worry about the loan for the time being. While she showed little emotion during the call, answering in monosyllables, after she hung up she drew Luke into her arms and wept a little.

When she pulled back, however, the stoic mother he knew was once again in place.

"They're being generous now, but where were they when I really needed them?"

Luke shrugged. "Good question."

"I'm going to take them up on their offer," she announced, wheeling around. "But once that loan is paid back in full? I want you to find another bank."

Sanders helped him with that, too.

Sophia's family came down from New Jersey for her graduation, and Luke sat with them on that warm spring day, cheering as she crossed the stage. Afterward, they went out to dinner, and to his surprise, they asked if they could visit the ranch the following day.

Luke's mom put him to work all morning, both inside and outside the house, tidying up while she made lunch. They ate at the picnic table in the backyard, Sophia's sisters alternately gaping at their surroundings and staring at Sophia, no doubt still trying to figure out how Luke and Sophia had ended up together.

Yet they all seemed remarkably comfortable together, especially Sophia's mom and Linda. They talked and laughed as they toured the ranch, and when Luke turned toward the garden, it warmed his heart to see the straight, neat rows of vegetables that his mom had just planted.

❦

"You could live anywhere, Mom," Luke said to her later that night. "You don't have to stay on the ranch. I'll buy you a penthouse in Manhattan if you want one."

"Why would I want to live in Manhattan?" she asked, making a face.

"It doesn't have to be Manhattan. It could be anywhere."

She stared out the window, at the ranch where she'd been raised.

"There's no place I'd rather live," she said.

"Then how about you let me get things fixed up around here. Not piecemeal, but all at once."

She smiled. "Now that," she said, "sounds like a first-rate idea."

❦

"So, are you ready?" Sophia asked him.

"For what?"

After graduation, Sophia had gone back home to stay with her parents for a week before returning to North Carolina.

"To tell me what happened in South Carolina," she said, fixing him with a determined expression as they walked into the pasture in search of Mudbath. "Did you ride Big Ugly Critter? Or walk away?"

At her words, Luke felt himself flashing back to that wintry day, one of the bleakest points in his life. He remembered walking toward the chute and staring at the bull through the slats; he recalled the current of fear surging through him and the taut bowstrings of his nerves. And yet, somehow, he forced himself to do what he'd come to do. He mounted Big Ugly Critter and adjusted his wrap, trying to ignore the pounding in his chest. *It's just a bull*, he told himself, *a bull like any other*. It wasn't and he knew it, but when the chute gate swung open and the bull exploded out of the gate, Luke stayed centered.

The bull was as violent as ever, bucking and twisting like something possessed, yet Luke felt strangely in control, as if he were observing himself from some distant remove. The world seemed to move in slow motion, making it feel like the longest ride of his life, but he stayed low and balanced, his free arm moving across his body to maintain control. When the horn finally sounded, the crowd surged to its feet, roaring its approval.

He quickly undid the wrap and jumped off, landing on his feet. In a replay of their prior encounter, the bull stopped and turned, nostrils flaring, his chest heaving. Luke knew that Big Ugly Critter was about to charge.

And yet, he didn't. Instead, they simply stared at each other until, incredibly, the bull turned away.

"You're smiling," Sophia said, interrupting his thoughts.

"I guess I am."

"Which means... what?"

"I rode him," Luke said. "And after that, I knew I was ready to walk away."

Sophia nudged his shoulder. "That was dumb."

"Probably," Luke said. "But I won myself a new truck."

"I never saw a new truck," she said, frowning.

"I didn't take it. I took the cash instead."

"For the ranch?"

"No," he said. "For this."

From his pocket he removed a small box, and dropping to one knee, he presented it to Sophia.

He heard her sharp intake of breath. "Is this what I think it is?"

"Open it," he said.

She did, slowly opening the lid and focusing on the ring.

"I'd like to marry you, if you think that would be okay."

She looked down at him, eyes shining. "Yeah," she said, "I think that would be okay."

*

"Where do you want to live?" she asked him later, after they'd told his mom. "Here on the ranch?"

"In the long run? I don't know. But for now, I like it here. The question is, do you?"

"Do you mean, do I want to live here forever?"

"Not necessarily," Luke said. "I was just thinking we might stay until things get settled. But after that? The way I figure it, we could live just about anywhere we want. And I'm thinking now—with a major bequest or gift, let's say—you could probably get a job in the museum of your choice."

"Like in Denver?"

"I've heard there's a lot of ranch land out that way. There's even ranching in New Jersey. I checked."

She cast her gaze upward before coming back to him. "How about we just see where life takes us for a while?"

*

That night, as Sophia lay sleeping, Luke left the bedroom and wandered out to the porch, relishing the lingering warmth from the day. Above him, half the moon was visible, the stars spreading across the sky. A light wind was blowing, carrying with it the sound of crickets calling from the pastures.

He looked upward, staring into the dark reaches of the heavens, thinking about his mom and the ranch. He still had trouble fathoming the path his life had suddenly taken, nor could he reconcile it with the life he once had lived. Everything was different, and he wondered whether he would change. He found himself being drawn frequently to memories of Ira, the man who changed his life, the man he never really knew. To Ira, Ruth meant everything, and in the quiet darkness, Luke pictured Sophia asleep in his bed, her golden hair spread over the pillow.

Sophia, after all, was the real treasure he'd found this year, worth more to him than all the art in the world. With a smile, Luke whispered into the dark, "I understand, Ira." And when a shooting star passed overhead, he had the strange sense that Ira had not only heard him, but was smiling down on him in approval.

Author's Note

The Longest Ride was one of my favorite novels to write, partly because I discovered so many fascinating events and stories in the process of conceiving and researching the book. For instance, I wanted to incorporate an element about modern art into the story line, as I'm interested in twentieth-century art and would someday like to start a collection of my own. But all of my novels are set in North Carolina, and I struggled to find a way to link modern art to my home state...until I stumbled across Black Mountain College while researching North Carolina–based history on the Internet.

Founded in 1933 in Asheville, Black Mountain College was a short-lived academic experiment of sorts that gave birth to many of the greatest modern American artists of the twentieth century. Robert Rauschenberg, Jackson Pollock, Josef Albers, Cy Twombly, Willem and Elaine de Kooning, Franz Kline, and many other seminal figures emerged from a fertile period in the institution's brief life—and to think that this occurred right in my own state of North Carolina! It is a little-known chapter in the history of modern art, and when I learned about it I knew it would end up playing an important role in my novel. You can read more about Black Mountain College and its fascinating history here: www.BlackMountainCollege.org/history.

My next challenge was to conceive of a dramatic conclusion to a story involving parallel love stories and the theme of modern art. The most visually and dramatically satisfying moments in the art world are usually related to creation or sale, and I opted for the moment of sale, because I've always found the theater of art

auctions quite riveting. I started researching art auctions, curious about accounts of particularly interesting or exciting auctions
that might serve as inspiration for my ending. What I discovered
was a sweet, uplifting Christian parable (and popular American
folk tale) about a man whose son has died, and who gives away
his art collection to the buyer of his son's painting. (You can read
a summary of the many forms this folk tale has taken over the
years here: www.snopes.com/glurge/son.asp.) This parable was
not a perfect model for the larger story I wanted to tell, but an
element of it intrigued me, beyond the obvious drama of an auction that hinges on a single painting: What does art truly mean
to a collector? Is the connection to art purely aesthetic, or also
emotional? Particularly given how esoteric the period of Abstract
Expressionism is often perceived to be, I wanted to figure out a
way to demonstrate the powerful connection even a collection
of abstract artwork could have...if it were somehow linked to a
deep and abiding love for a spouse.

Finally, I knew I wanted to include a story line in this book
about bull riding, as I've been enthralled by the sport from the
first moment I saw those crazy cowboys riding two-thousand-
pound enraged bulls on TV! It's also a sport native to North Carolina, so it's a natural and exciting backdrop for one of my novels.
I did quite a lot of research on the sport to get the details right,
but if you were intrigued by Luke's life and my descriptions of his
events and want to learn more, be sure to check out the website
of the Professional Bull Riders Inc. at www.pbr.com.

Trying to craft a gripping and emotionally engaging story that
incorporates bits and pieces of these disparate components was
quite a challenge for me, but I hope the result is a novel with
diverse story lines and emotional content that you'll remember
forever. Thank you for reading *The Longest Ride* and for your
continued support over the years.

Warmly,
Nicholas

Discussion Questions

1. Sofia and Luke come from very different worlds. What do you think draws them to each other? Do you think opposites attract?

2. When Ira has his accident, he is visited by his dead wife, Ruth. Have you ever felt the presence of a departed loved one?

3. After the rodeo, Brian is confrontational with Sofia, and Luke comes to her rescue. How would you react in a similar situation?

4. At first, Ira is very shy around Ruth. How does she draw him out of his shell? What are the major differences between romances in the 1940s and the present?

5. Ira decides to enlist in the air force during World War II, and returns unable to have children. Because of this, he decides to break off his engagement with Ruth. How does this affect Ruth and Ira's relationship? Would you have made the same decision?

6. In the beginning, Marcia believes that Luke is just a rebound relationship for Sofia. Do you think they were moving too fast?

7. The relationship between Luke and his mother, Linda, is very close. How does she react to him putting himself in danger and why? How would you react if someone close to you was taking these kinds of big risks?

8. Ruth and Ira think they've found a surrogate son in Daniel. How would you describe Ruth and Daniel's relationship? Can you understand why Daniel never reconnects with Ruth and Ira?

9. Ira tells the reporter that he and Ruth chose their art based on Ruth's preferences. Why does the art collection hold so much significance for Ira after Ruth dies? Are there any objects that hold special memories for you?

10. Luke claims he needs to keep competing to save the ranch, but Sofia thinks he has other reasons: "You're doing it so that you won't have to feel guilty! You think you're being noble, but you're really being selfish!" (pg. 299) Can you understand both positions?

11. Why do you think Luke needs to go up against Big Ugly Critter one last time before he quits? Have you ever done something dangerous or ill-advised to prove something to yourself?

12. What drives Luke and Sofia to visit Ira in the hospital? Do you see similarities between Ira and Ruth's love story and Luke and Sofia's?

13. Sofia decides to forgive Marcia for dating Brian behind her back: "She made a mistake. She didn't mean to hurt me... And she came through when I needed her. So yes, just like that. I'm over it" (pg. 365). Could you have forgiven Marcia so easily? What does this say about Sofia as a character? Do you think friendships can survive betrayals of this kind?

14. Ira makes the auction of his art collection his final love letter to Ruth. What does his decision say about the importance of sentimental value and monetary value? Did this book make you think differently about your own life and the things you value?